LOVE LIES BENEATH

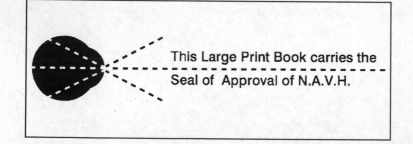
This Large Print Book carries the
Seal of Approval of N.A.V.H.

LOVE LIES BENEATH

ELLEN HOPKINS

THORNDIKE PRESS

A part of Gale, Cengage Learning

GALE
CENGAGE Learning·

Farmington Hills, Mich • San Francisco • New York • Waterville, Maine
Meriden, Conn • Mason, Ohio • Chicago

GALE
CENGAGE Learning®

LIBRARY OF CONGRESS CATALOGING-IN-PUBLICATION DATA

Hopkins, Ellen
    Love lies beneath / by Ellen Hopkins. -- Large print edition.
       pages cm. -- (Thorndike Press large print core)
    ISBN 978-1-4104-8396-6 (hardcover) -- ISBN 1-4104-8396-7 (hardcover)
    1. Large type books. 2. Psychological fiction. I. Title.
PS3608.O647L68 2015
813'.6--dc23   2015025589

Published in 2015 by arrangement with Atria Books an imprint of Simon & Schuster, Inc.

Printed in Mexico
1 2 3 4 5 6 7 19 18 17 16 15

This book is dedicated to everyone who's ever fallen in love with the wrong person, especially those who stayed longer than they should have, trying to make it work.

IT'S SAID

That every soul enters
this world an immaculate slate
awaiting the imprint
of parent and teacher,
the scribbling of providence.

But no truth is absolute.

More often than supposed,
a mind is born defective,
hairline fractures
spidering the native psyche,
flaws invisible to the eye.

Some cracks can't be mortared.

ONE

As gyms go, this one is exceptionally clean. Hardwood gleams beneath the December sun flurrying down through the fog-misted skylight, and the place smells more like floor polish than the afternoon regulars' liberal drips of sweat. Even the Pilates mats manage to shed the odor of perspiration, and that pleases me. I prefer to inhale the scent of exertion only during coition.

Coition. Good word. Appears before "coitus" in the dictionary, and though they mean the same thing, the softer "shun" sounds chicer than the "tus" to my ear. Not that class is requisite to the act itself, but in conversation, tone is everything.

"Tara! Concentrate. Your form is terrible. Straighten your back. Lift your chest."

I do as instructed but complain, "Squats stink. And anyway, I thought you appreciated my form."

Nick slinks closer, bends to lower his face

close to mine, and I wait for his tongue to tease the pulse beneath my ear. Instead, he slaps my behind, hard enough to sting. "You told me your goal is perfection. You're not there yet." His words slap sharper than the gesture. "That's why you need me."

Honestly, most personal trainers could accomplish the task. I've handpicked a half dozen over the years, trying them on for size, so to speak. I've kept Nick the longest because of ability above and beyond, not to mention outside of the gym.

I do enjoy specialized service, and Nick has exceptional talents. Still, he has bruised my ego.

"I don't need you at all, Mr. de la Rosa. In fact, I think we're finished . . ." The look on his face is priceless. I'm an excellent tipper. "With squats and thrusts and weights, at least for today. As for the postworkout workout, give me thirty to shower and I'll meet you out front."

"You are a wicked, wicked woman. Almost scary, in fact."

"Almost? You underestimate me, sir."

Our little exchange did not go unnoticed, and envious eyes follow my retreat toward the women's shower room. That's correct, ladies. He and I are doing the filthy, and you're right to be jealous. What Nick de la

Rosa may lack in discretionary income, he more than makes up for in carnal creativity. Who needs to go out when one can have so much fun staying in, playing doctor?

My locker is well stocked with aromatic soaps and lotions, but before I use those I take a few minutes to douche away feminine fragrance, heightened by the previous ninety minutes of effort. One of my exes called me fastidious. Another claimed I'm obsessively clean. But, as my late, great first husband once told me, "A sweet pussy invites the tongue to tango." I plan on plenty of oral dance in an hour or so.

Meanwhile, I run the water hot, perfume my hair with gardenia-scented shampoo, and soften my skin to silk with this fabulous vanilla-cedar shower gel. My eyes are closed against the final rinse of conditioner when a voice flutters softly within the tiled walls.

"What is that amazing incense smell?"

"It's body wash from Kiehl's."

"Expensive?"

"Not too." I blink away water, and when I identify the person on the far side of the conversation, I hope the showerhead's splash disguises the serrated intake of my breath.

Penelope teaches yoga, and while she's something to see in a tank top and stretch pants, naked she is simply exquisite. In a side-by-side comparison, I can hold my own against pretty much any woman here. But Penelope is one of those rare young things whose obviously natural curves and fawn suede complexion rival anything my pricey plastic surgeon could accomplish. If I had hackles, they'd be bristling.

"You can find the body wash online. Vanilla and cedarwood." I grab a towel, cover my imperfect assets, and try not to stare at Penelope as she and I trade places.

For the next twenty minutes, I work serums and moisturizer into my skin before applying foundation. Not sure why I'm bothering. It will all come dripping off in a little while. Oh well. At least I'll look attractive until then and turn a few heads on my way to the door.

December shrouds San Francisco in gray. I step out into the heavy, wet curtain and am happy I took the time to blow-dry my hair, which is long and thick and would stay damp otherwise. My stylist calls it problematic because it takes extra time to color. But I'm determined to keep it as close to its original fox red as possible. My sister is two years younger, and at not quite thirty-nine her hair has gone completely silver. It's actually striking on her, but the look would be wrong for me.

I stand back against the building beneath a wide awning, watching sidewalk travelers hustle by. Everyone walks quickly here, worried more about what's behind them than the appointments waiting for them up ahead. It's an eclectic stream — high school kids with prominent piercings, street dwellers of various ages and genders, a young black woman in short leather, an older white man in ankle-length mink.

It's quite the show, and I'm enjoying it well enough until it strikes me that I've been loitering here for a very long time. I look in through the big plate-glass window, beyond weight machines and treadmills. Oh, there he is, in loose jeans and a flimsy flannel shirt that doesn't exactly hide all the lovely musculature I've almost memorized.

Nick starts in this direction, but before he can take a dozen steps, Penelope cozies up behind him, pouts against the back of his neck, and lifts on her toes slightly, saying something into his ear. He spins and now his face is hidden. But I can see hers clearly. Her smile is more than flirtatious. It's tinted with affection. And her eyes, locked on his, tell a story I really don't want to know.

I have hackles after all. Rage sizzles, white-hot, and my hands tremor. Unreasonably, it's Penelope my inner bitch wants to maul. It's not her fault Nick wants his steak and his cupcake, too. She must sense the devil's gaze, because her head swivels, side to side. When she glances over Nick's shoulder and notices me glaring through the glass, she gives him a playful shove. Does she realize he's meeting me? Do they have some quirky arrangement?

Nick turns his back on pretty Penelope, heads straight for the door, and when it opens a shock wave of anger hits him square. He looks at me, and I swear he has no idea why I'm pissed. "What's wrong?"

I force my voice low and level. "Why do you think something's wrong?"

"Well, I don't know, Tara. Maybe it's your body language." He reaches for my elbow, tries to steer me clear of curious eyes on the far side of the window.

I yank my arm away and hold my ground. "Do not touch me again unless I say it's okay. Understand?" He nods, dumbstruck, and I continue. "Does she know we're sleeping together?"

"Does who know?"

"Stop playing stupid! God, I hate when men play stupid! Penelope. Does she know? You two obviously have something going on."

Nick starts up the sidewalk, sure I'll follow, or at the very least let him leave me standing here like an idiot. "You don't own me, bitch."

I have no choice but to take the bait. But I'm not going to be gutted without a fight. I catch up to him and strike from behind, jabbing with words. "I'm sorry, Nick. I thought you liked our arrangement, that it was mutually beneficial."

He stops, turns to face me. "I do like it. But there was never any mention of exclusivity."

"You are seeing Penelope, then?"

"Well, yeah. And others. It's not like I'm engaged to any of you. Like I said, you don't own me."

Maggot.

"I believe you said, 'You don't own me, bitch.' "

The smirk slips from his face. "Uh yeah, guess I did, and I'm sor—"

"Shut up." Damage control? I don't think so. "No one talks to me like that, Nick, least of all hired help. And, make no mistake, that's exactly what you are . . . uh, were. I do hope your 'others' are as generous as I have been, because there will be no more under-the-table supplemental income from me. Come to think of it, I might have to

1099 you."

My turn to smirk, and he doesn't like it. "Go ahead and try. You paid me in cash and can't prove a thing."

That makes me laugh. "Do you really think I wouldn't take steps to protect myself, just in case you turned out to be the weasel you are? You know those nanny-cam things? So happens I have a boudoir cam. I don't suppose you ever noticed I always paid you before you got out of bed?"

Not completely true, but close enough. The camera covers the entire room. Anyway, it's not like I'd really 1099 him, but it won't hurt to make him sweat a little. Damn, I am going to miss his sweat. But I could never have sex with him again, knowing he might have just come from someone else's bed. Who wants to sleep with a harem?

"So, we're finished?"

Cheeky little bastard. "You needed confirmation of that?"

"What about the gym?"

"This city is crawling with personal trainers. I'm sure I can find another one as multifaceted as you. Meanwhile, I can handle my own workouts. I really don't need you, or anyone, to tell me how to squat." I start to walk away. Turn back. "You never did say if Penelope knew about me."

He stares at me stupidly for a moment. Then he dares, "I didn't see the need to disclose the dirty details."

My hackles lower and I smile. "I think I should take up yoga. Don't you?"

I turn my back on him, and as I start to walk away he calls, "You say one word to her and you will be very sorry."

In a low, measured voice, I reply, "I hope that's not a threat. This is a game you can't win."

He changes tactics. "You don't understand. I love her."

"Then why have you been fucking me?"

I leave before he can answer. Wounded. Envious. I don't even know what love feels like. It's unfair an asshole like Nick should know. But if it's even remotely like having sex on the side with whomever, all the while claiming your heart is taken, maybe it's just as well that it's outside my realm of experience.

Two

Traffic tonight is the absolute worst. I arrive at the Marriott twenty minutes late, decide to go ahead and pay the exorbitant parking fee, and pull in to valet. A decent-looking young man (very young!) rushes to open the door for me, semidrooling. But whether that's because of my legs or my silver-over-midnight-blue Corvette, I really can't say.

I hand him the keys. "You *will* take very good care of her, won't you? I don't want to smell hot engine." I pause for effect. "Unless it's *yours.*"

He cocks his head sideways, confused. Then it hits him and he laughs, cheeks flushing a furious red. "H-h-here's your claim check," he stutters. "And I'll be careful with your car."

"I know you will." To be certain, I hand him a twenty.

The View Lounge is on the thirty-ninth floor. Cassandra is already here, and she's managed to score us a table by the immense spoked window overlooking downtown, all the way to the water. "You're late."

She is direct, and I like that. The last thing anyone needs is a backstabber in friend's clothing. Speaking of clothing, hers is expensive. Impeccable. We frequent the same stores, preferring the sweet little boutiques on Chestnut or Fillmore to shopping-mall standards.

"Sorry. I got delayed at the gym, and traffic was unusually ugly."

Cassandra sips her drink. "Delayed *at* the gym, or after?"

She and I actually met at that gym, and we chose it for similar reasons.

Cassandra was in the middle of a divorce and looking for no-strings play. When the dissolution was finalized, she moved to Pacific Heights and found a new place to work out, closer to home. The trainers, she tells me, are equally qualified. "Hold that thought. I need one of those." I nod toward her drink and then signal a nearby waiter. "Blood-orange sidecar, please."

As I wait for my drink, I give her the lowdown on Nick, Penelope, and his possible others. I don't inform her that when I got home I called the gym twice. The first time, I canceled my membership, due to inappropriate behavior on the part of my trainer. The second, I asked to talk to the yoga instructor. Our conversation did not include class times.

"Ah well," I finish as the sidecar arrives. "Nick was spectacular in bed, but not exactly husband material."

Cassandra looks at me incredulously. "Surely you're not in the market for another husband?"

"Why not?" I take a long swallow of deliciousness, which burns just enough to remind me my stomach is empty. "Hey, are you hungry? I haven't eaten a thing since breakfast, and then it was only granola and yogurt."

"Go ahead and order something, but don't change the subject."

"What was the question again? Oh, yeah. Husbands. I know 'three' is supposed to be the charm, but it didn't quite work that way for me. Why shouldn't I want another one?"

"Are you kidding me? Your life is perfect: a brilliant home on Russian Hill; a BMW, Corvette, and whatever that big thing is —"

"Escalade. For the snow, you know."

"Right. Your once-a-year ski trip or whatever."

"I try to get up there at least a couple of times a season," I correct. "In fact, I'm leav-

20

ing day after tomorrow for a week. December doesn't reward the Sierra with this much snow very often, so I called Melody and she was free and —"

"Stop avoiding the issue! It's not like you need a husband for a satisfying ski trip, either. God, Tara. Your time is your own. Even your fund-raising stuff happens when you feel like putting in the effort. You have no problem getting laid when you want. And besides, the ink is barely dry on your divorce papers. I take it your attorney prevailed?"

"Well, of course. Finn left *me* for the Barbie doll. I didn't leave *him*. Besides, he'd do just about anything to avoid controversy right now. He founded his company on quote-unquote Christian principles, not that I ever once saw him go to church. It was just a way to tap into loopholes that freed him from certain government intrusions. He's decided to go public. He stands to make a whole other fortune and the settlement was a drop in the proverbial bucket. Plus, now he can show off his token brat, legitimize his heir-to-be. Apparently the girl's pregnant."

Cassandra looks amused. "Well, that's something you weren't ever going to be, right?"

"Certainly not. I made sure of that a long time ago." Allow some alien being to grow inside me, stretch my body into an unrecognizable shape, scarring my skin irreparably with fat silver marks? And as if all that isn't bad enough, nurture that child (and perhaps a sibling or two) into adulthood? Call me selfish. Call me scared.

But being a parent was never a goal.

Since we're talking offspring, I probably should inquire about *her* kid. "How's Taylor doing? School going okay?"

It's a staccato conversation.

New school, the Athenian.

Expensive school but worth the tuition, especially since her ex is paying it.

Boarding school, so she only sees the kid every other weekend and holidays.

Competitive school, and so far he's maintaining a 4.0.

I do my best not to yawn.

Finally, our waiter stops by, inquiring about a second round. "That gentleman over there would like to buy it for you ladies."

He points to a decent-looking man, sitting alone three tables away. When we glance in his direction, he lifts his hand as if saluting. I reward him with a smile and mouth a silent thank-you. He responds with a subtle flick of his tongue.

"I think you've impressed him," says Cassandra.

"The cut of his trousers impresses me."

"Like you can see that from here?"

"Have I never told you about my superpower? Able to discern the size of a penis across a crowded room."

It's not that funny, but Cassandra laughs anyway, almost snorting out the last of her drink. Luckily, the waiter arrives with two more.

"See?" says Cassandra. "Complete strangers buy you drinks. Bet you could sweet-talk him into dinner, too. Why on earth would you consider matrimony again when you can have the fringe benefits without giving up your independence?"

It's a fair question. "Companionship. I really hate living alone. But since a proposal is not on the table, I'll settle for the fringe benefits." My eyes settle on our benefactor, the invitation, I hope, apparent.

"Get out! You're not seriously considering hooking up with that man?"

"Why not? He's good looking, isn't he?" Who needs Nick de la Rosa, anyway?

"Serial killers generally come in attractive packages, you know."

I assess the man carefully. Expensive suit.

23

Silk. Tailored. (Do creepers wear Armani?) Meticulously styled salt-and-pepper hair — he has an excellent barber. Perfect teeth, at least they look that way from here. Predatory eyes, but they meet mine straight on. I don't think he has a whole lot to hide. Besides, I kind of like carnivores. "Don't worry about me. I can take care of myself. Anyway, I hear serial killers give great head."

"Jesus, Tara, you're insane. Oh, lovely. Here he comes." Cassandra turns slightly toward the window.

I, on the other hand, rotate in the direction of the approaching stranger, crossing my legs into the aisle to give him a better look, one he seems to appreciate.

"May I join you ladies?" The rasp in his voice is sexy as hell.

"Well, I don't know. What do you think, Cassandra?"

She glances at her watch, stands. "I think I should go. I've got an early morning and, besides, three's a crowd."

"Aw, don't go," he says. "Sometimes three's just right."

But Cassandra tsks disgust. "Only when the third is an *invited* guest."

She stalks off without saying good-bye and Mr. Uninvited watches her go.

"Too bad." Then he turns back to me.

"Well, then. Are *you* inviting?"

I gesture for him to take Cassandra's vacated seat. "It's the least I can do. Thanks for the drink — er, two drinks, I guess. Can't let a great sidecar go to waste."

The man sits, placing his own drink on the table. From the smell, I'd say it's decent scotch, but on the rocks. Waste of good whiskey, pouring it over ice cubes.

"Sidecar? What's that?" he asks, and when he brings his eyes level with mine I notice they are neither brown nor green, but somewhere in between. Gold. Reptilian.

"Cognac — good cognac, by the way, and I'm afraid your bill will reflect that — Cointreau, and in this case, blood-orange juice in place of lemon."

"May I taste?" He points to Cassandra's glass.

I shrug. "Help yourself. It's your drink, really."

He takes a sip, and I can tell he wants to hate it. But that, of course, is impossible. "Nice." It's a long sigh. He indulges in a deeper swallow, then says, "So, I'm Ben. And you are . . . ?"

I could lie, but why? The truth is easier to remember, and what's to worry about my name? "Tara." My voice is thick with cognac, and I remember I haven't eaten.

Ordering food will slow things down, however. Do I want to linger with Ben, or will inebriated sex do? I glance at my watch. Seven thirty. "Would you mind if I have something to eat?"

He looks vaguely disappointed, which only makes me more determined. "Excuse me? Waiter? Would you please bring an antipasti platter?" I offer Ben a semiapologetic smile. "Happy to share. I'm starving, and this will give us time to chat."

Impatience shimmers, and he's quite obviously assessing his chances. Keep on guessing, Ben. I like confidence in a man, but not when it bloats into conceit. "Of course," he says finally. "Wouldn't want you to pass out on me."

Game on. "Highly doubtful, unless you're concealing roofies somewhere?"

He displays teeth and, indeed, they are artificially perfect. "No need to coerce. I aim only to please. Are you a local, or traveling?"

"Does it matter?"

"Not really. I come from Phoenix."

"As opposed to Mars?"

His laugh is genuine. "As opposed to Lansing, where I was born and raised."

"Is Lansing home to many serial killers?"

He barely twitches, and I think that must

26

be a good sign that he isn't one. "Not that I'm aware of. Why do you ask?"

"Something to do with an earlier observation."

"About me?"

"Who else?"

Bluntness can be the key to reading the stranger across the table. I watch his reaction — a slow rise of humor creasing the corners of his chameleon eyes. "The last thing I purposely killed was a fifth of Glenfiddich 21. Great going down, but I paid for it the next day, and it probably worried my ulcer just a little bigger."

Well spoken. Drinks decent liquor. I see no wedding ring on his finger, no shadow indicating he wears one most of the time. "Anyone waiting for you back in Lansing?"

"Only my mother, and she suffers from dementia, so she's never quite sure who I am, let alone where I am or when I might show up for a visit."

Pretty sure he's serious. "How about in Phoenix? Someone there who might be stressing over what you're up to tonight?"

"Nope. You?"

"Not at all."

The small talk is interrupted by the antipasti's arrival. The waiter inquires about another round. Our glasses are almost empty. Ben has finished his scotch, plus most of Cassandra's sidecar. If he truly has an ulcer, it must be screaming.

I nod. "This one's on me. Scotch or sidecar, Ben?"

"Sidecar, since you appreciate the taste. And thank you."

"The pleasure's all mine."

"Oh, I hope it's not *all* yours." He winks. "Maybe we could make it a contest."

On another day, his certainty of the evening's outcome might very well leave me — and so, him — cold. But this afternoon's disappointment, plus three very good drinks and Ben's overall charm, has chipped away at any resistance. Our bills come and I notice he signs his to his room.

"You're bunking here, then?" The verb, a sliver of a past I've worked very hard to leave far, far behind, makes me cringe.

But Ben grins amusement. " 'Bunking' is apropos. I prefer the Four Seasons, but my company booked the reservation, and since a top-floor pencil pusher approves my expense account, I didn't think I should complain." He gives my legs a long, lustful appraisal. "Looks like it was a fortuitous choice."

The last sentence is more question than statement, and it inches my answer closer to the affirmative column. One-night stands can be fun, but rarely are they fulfilling. So if they're not fun enough, what's the point? "How early do you have to be up in the morning?"

He shrugs. "My meeting's at eleven. That much I planned on my own."

I decide to be direct. "My orgasm ratio requirement is three to one, in my favor. Can you accommodate that?"

"Huh. I wouldn't have pegged you for an underachiever."

I can't help but laugh. "Is that a yes?"

"Better than that. It's a promise."

THREE

Ben's company, at least, booked one of the nicest rooms this particular Marriott has to offer — a smallish suite with a very nice view. Outside the big window, the night-engulfed city has blossomed with lights. An anonymous couple of them belong to my house. My home. One I'd never invite a stranger into.

As unfamiliar men go, Ben seems decent enough. I watch him hang his jacket in the closet, appreciating the care he takes, both with his clothing and with what I can see of his body beneath the loose cling of his shirt. Broad shoulders taper to a trim waist and solid hips. He works out, but not obsessively.

He goes over to the minibar. "Nightcap?"

"No, thanks. I don't want to get sloppy on you."

He laughs warmly. "I thought that was the whole point. Mind if I have one?"

"Be my guest. Just don't forget about my requisite ratio." I slip out of my own silk jacket and lay it gently over the too-prominent office chair. "I'll be right back, okay?"

I take my purse into the bathroom with me, not because I'm worried about Ben inspecting its contents, but because it contains an emergency hygiene kit. Most of it I don't need tonight, but I prefer my breath not carry a hint of salami, so I spend a couple of quality minutes with a toothbrush and mouthwash. Then I free my hair from the confines of the chignon I was wearing, releasing gardenia perfume to fight the masculine scent of Ben's own cologne, hanging heavily in the too-small lavatory.

Lavatory. Good word. Comes right after "laboratory" in the dictionary, and let's face it, most lavatories would make interesting laboratories, at least if you could stomach such experiments.

By the time I've finished, Ben has made himself quite comfortable on the sofa, shoeless and shirtless but for a tight sleeveless undershirt that showcases his beefcakeyness quite nicely. He stands as I come into the room. "Good Lord, look at you. Your hair is amazing."

Unbelievably, my cheeks flush heat. Such

a small compliment, and yet it completely erases any small sense of hesitation. I move straight into his arms, tilt my chin up toward his face. "My father always said flattery deserves a just reward." That's a lie. I never met my father and have no idea where the saying came from. But all that matters now is the reward.

I open my mouth, inviting his whiskey-soaked kiss, and when it comes, it's light-years from gentle. It's tongue and teeth, on my lips, at my neck, and dipping inside the V of my blouse, which opens suddenly, as if by spell. And just as mysteriously, my bra unclasps, spilling the tips of my breasts into the depth of his moan.

Ben lifts me out of my heels, discovers I'm wearing stockings — the classic kind requiring a garter belt, a fact he uncovers when his hand explores the length of my leg, all the way to where thigh meets torso. He draws back, studies me for a second. "Real seamed silk? You are one of a kind, do you know that?"

"Actually, I do."

"I think we'd better work on that three-to-one deal right now."

He drapes me across the couch, facedown, lifts my skirt, exposing satin, lace, and peeks of skin. One hand tangles into my hair, pulls it to one side, and he snarls against my nape. The other hand spreads my legs just enough to reach the narrow satin strip, which he moves to one side. "Look at you, all slick and ready."

Ben plays a masterful game. His thumb slides up inside me and tilts to find the hidden spot just behind my pubic bone, while his forefinger wedges against my clitoris. They move in rough unison, on the border of pain, the pressure exquisite. It doesn't take long to initiate my orgasm, punctuated by a whispered "Yes!"

"Oh, no. That won't do at all." Ben flips me over, brings his face very close to mine. "I don't want you to whisper. I want you to scream."

I issue the challenge. "Make me."

He unzips my skirt, lets it fall to the floor. Then he leads me into the other room, props me against the foot of the bed, reaches behind me, and cups my butt. Lifts. "Lie back and don't move." One by one, Ben unsnaps the garters, gentles the stockings from my legs, licking the sensitive place behind my knees. It's a challenge to stay still, and when I fail to meet it, he reaches up and pinches my nipples. Hard. "You ask my permission before you so much as twitch. Understand?"

Eyes watering, I manage to stutter, "I uh-uh-understand." For the two seconds it takes him to tug my panties down over my hips, a trill of fear makes me wonder if I might have miscalculated the man. But then I remember the pepper spray, stashed in my purse, which isn't far away. Besides, that shimmer of trepidation is rather an aphrodisiac.

And now the persistent tide of his tongue laps the most intimate parts of me, a low sea of pleasure. He has asked not one selfish thing of me yet, and that thought brings renewed confidence. I do my best to lie perfectly still, but that becomes impossible as I build toward a second climax. "Please. May I twitch? I don't think I can come without moving."

"You'd better scream."

I do. And I don't have to fake it at all.

Ben straightens, unzips his trousers. It's time for the big reveal, always an interesting turn in a tale of sex with a stranger. Jockey shorts do nothing to hide what's behind them, alert and at the ready. I am mildly disappointed. I was hoping for at least an eight on the one-to-ten scale. Ben is a six. No less, but definitely no more.

He is, however, skilled, and compensates with enthusiasm what he might lack in size.

He manages to bring me off twice before finally succumbing to my well-rehearsed cock play with an extended shudder. "Jesus, woman, you've drained me dry."

Three cheers for condoms.

Ben is peeling his off when his cell phone rings a definitive tone — *Rhapsody in Blue.* Unbelievably, he answers. "Hello? No, no. It's not too late. I was up anyway. Working." He winks at me, then mouths silently, *My wife.*

His wife! No. He told me . . .

"My flight gets in around eight tomorrow night," he continues.

I bolt out of bed, locate my panties, and tug them on, wrestling with a low creep of temper. Oh, why bother to fight it? The bastard deserves it. "Hey, baby, come back to bed," I say, loud enough for his wife to hear. "I need you to make love to me."

Ben starts to stutter. "I-I-I . . . No, it was the TV. Adult programming. Sorry. It's just, I'm so . . ."

He can't get away with this that easily. This time I yell, "Ben! Please! I'm wet and waiting."

I grab my clothes and run into the bathroom, locking the door behind me. He's going to be pissed. Still, I take a quick minute to wash before getting dressed. I don't want to smell him. When I emerge, he's standing, quite naked, between the way out and me. "What the fuck did you do that for?"

"You told me you weren't married."

"No, I didn't."

"But you said —"

"I said no one would be wondering what I was up to tonight, and she wouldn't have."

"Well, I hope she's doing more than wondering now, you no-good prick."

Rage ignites in his eyes. "What the hell did I do?"

"It's called adultery." Just in case, I reach into my purse. "I enjoy a one-night stand from time to time, but not with a married man. Maggots like you don't deserve someone special, waiting for them to come home. Marriage is more than a promise. It's a contract. It isn't sleeping around on business trips. You're disgusting."

He starts toward me, fists clenching, and I display the pepper spray in my hand. "Go for it. Please, please, give me the excuse to blister your face. How would you explain that to your wife?"

"You wouldn't dare."

"Don't bet on it. Now get out of my way." I start toward the door, but he doesn't move, so I lift the small canister, flip back the lid, and aim the nozzle toward his face. "Did you know you can't wash this stuff off? You just have to wait for it to quit burning." I walk purposely forward. "You have exactly two seconds to move. One . . ."

He reads the commitment in my voice correctly and steps to one side. "You are a crazy fucking bitch."

"No, Ben. As Emilie Autumn says, 'I'm stark, raving sane.'"

FOUR

My Russian Hill home is, indeed, stunning. Its five bedrooms and three baths are much more than I need, but then they were more than Finn and I required, living together. Except for the baby his fiancée is currently expecting, his children are all grown and on the East Coast. Their visits were rare and didn't last long. One of them, his daughter Claire, never appeared at all. Apparently, she didn't approve of his marrying me. And as for other visitors, only my sister ever stayed overnight.

I could downsize, of course, but this property is unique, both in its location and in the way I've made it my own. Finn allowed my interior decorator carte blanche, and together we created something truly beautiful — modern, but a million miles removed from sterile. The walls are neutral, the artwork hanging on them anything but. And the three-story views are breathtaking.

Best of all, though, I could afford the outrageous mortgage on my own if I had to; I don't have to. Finn agreed to cover it until such time as I decide to sell the place, and then the equity is mine. I don't plan to put it on the market anytime soon.

The garage is street level, my bedroom on the uppermost floor, which means taking a lot of stairs as I load the Escalade with ski equipment and suitcases. When I fly, I travel light. But if I'm driving, I tend to take more than I need. And when winter driving in the Sierra, I purposely pack extra clothing, blankets, and windshield-washer fluid. Plus a small shovel, just in case, all-wheel drive or no, the Escalade slips into a snowbank or something.

I'm up early to do it and on the road by nine thirty. It's two hours, traffic willing, to my sister's home near Sacramento. She swears she'll be ready to go when I arrive, but that's rarely the case. Still, even with a layover, we should make it to South Lake Tahoe by late afternoon. Melody prefers the lake's quieter west shore, but I like the nightlife offered on the Nevada side of the border. I also like skiing Heavenly Valley. Lots of great memories there.

I get mired a bit in the tail end of the morning commute, but once I'm over the

Bay Bridge, onto I-80 east, it's clear sailing. With the satellite radio tuned to Lithium, I set the cruise control on seventy-five and get lost in nineties grunge. Lots of memories there, too, not all of them so good. But the music was. Gin Blossoms. Goo Goo Dolls. Counting Crows. Everclear. I still love this stuff.

I pull up in front of Melody's house a little before noon. On the front lawn is an almost-life-size Santa's sleigh, pulled by only six reindeer. Christmas lights drip from the roof and encircle the trees. The houses on either side boast similar displays. This neighborhood must be ridiculous at night.

Mel is not standing curbside, suitcase in hand, so I go ring the bell. Her oldest daughter answers the door, scowling. "Oh, hey, Aunt Tara."

"May I come in? What's wrong? Not happy to see me?"

Kayla steps to one side to let me by. "No, it's not you. Sorry. I just had a fight with my boyfriend. Squeaky little a-hole."

"Just one of many, hon. Just one of many."

"That's what I'm afraid of."

She's a willowy brunette, pretty without working too hard to be that way. She won't have a problem finding another boyfriend if she wants one.

"So why are you home? Shouldn't you be in school?"

She shrugs. "I had a half day. Mom's in the kitchen, by the way."

I believe I've been dismissed. I follow the scent of coffee and yeast past tinseled railings and holiday villages to the big, airy, oven-warmed kitchen. "Oh my God. Don't tell me you baked bread this morning." Three loaves cool on the counter. "That's why they invented bakeries, you know."

Melody stops loading the dishwasher long enough to smile a hello. "If I lived in San Francisco, I'd have that option. Do you know how far I'd have to drive to find a decent bakery here?"

"Seriously, Mel. Who bakes anymore, especially on the day they're taking off on a ski trip?"

"A ski trip the rest of her family won't be enjoying. The least I could do was leave them decent bread."

She can take her cheerful-housewife routine and shove it. "How close are you?"

"I'll be ready as soon as I finish cleaning up."

"Can't Kayla do it? She's pissed, not disabled."

"I could ask her, of course. But it's faster if I just do it than argue with her for twenty

41

minutes. Anyway, I'm done." She starts the wash cycle, rinses her hands.

"Anyone ever tell you your parenting skills are lacking?"

The slender rebuke draws no anger. "Only my husband. And his aren't any better. Just call us Mr. and Mrs. Walkalloverme."

Irritation prickles. I wish she'd rise up to defend herself once in a while. It's bothered me ever since we were kids and Mom would go off on one of her rants. Loudmouthed me always took the brunt of her punishments while soft-spoken Melody receded into the background, barely there.

"Quick potty stop, and we're on our way."

Twenty minutes later we are, turning south to meet Highway 50 east. It's a gorgeous drive, but I'm very happy the weather is good. The curvy two-lane makes for ugly going in a blizzard. Today, it's clear and crisp outside. Korn comes on the radio. Their music is a mile outside my comfort zone, and a deviation for this channel. Still, when Melody reaches over to turn down the volume, I'm even more uncomfortable because it means she's moving into sister-chat mode.

Melody: Blah-blah-blah, your divorce.

Me: Blah-blah-blah, rehearsed answer.

Mel: Blah-blah-blah, plans for the future.

Moi: Blah-blah-blah, one day at a time.

The only way to disengage from small talk about me is to engage in small talk about her. "So, how's Graham?"

Melody's husband is a pediatrician, and quite popular among greater Sacramento soccer moms, due to his all-American good looks and highly cultivated bedside manner. As far as I know, that hasn't negatively affected their marriage. They'll celebrate their twentieth anniversary in a few months.

"He's great. I don't know if I told you this, but he and a couple of his friends have put together a band. Just for fun, you know. Graham plays the drums, and . . ."

I tune out for a short, sweet span. I love my sister, but she does know how to stretch a story. She should have been a novelist instead of a technical writer. Or maybe an epic poet. We are passing Placerville before I notice she's stopped talking, as if waiting for an answer. "I'm sorry. What did you just say?"

"Hmph. I asked if you'd thought any more about Christmas."

They invite me every year, and I usually have a good excuse to say no. This year, there's no husband, no conflicts, no real reason not to agree. I could lie, but untruths become so tiresome. "You know I hate to intrude. Christmas is a family day."

"Um . . . hello? You're family."

"Not Graham's, though."

"Believe it or not, he takes ownership. What's mine is his, et cetera."

Truthfully, I'd rather spend the holidays alone on the moon than pretending good cheer with the Schumacher clan, but I keep that to myself and change the subject. "So what do the girls want for Christmas?"

"Jessica's hot for the latest iPhone. She's barely twelve, but apparently all her friends have one. Suzette wants a new snowboard. She progressed really far last year and is ready for something a little more extreme. By the way, she's royally pissed that she couldn't come on this trip. Maybe next time we could bring her along?"

"I don't see why not. And what about Kayla?"

"All she really wants is a way into the San Francisco Art Institute."

"Art?" Shows how much I know about my nieces. "What kind of art is she into?"

"She's an incredibly talented illustrator, but what really interests her is computer animation and film. Barring a career there, she'd settle for graphic design."

Wow. Who knew? I suppose it wouldn't hurt to show a little interest in the girls. "So why SFAI?"

"It's an exceptional art school, and close enough to feel like familiar ground. But it's so expensive! I don't suppose you have any connections on the scholarship committee?"

"I might know someone who knows someone." The main campus is very near my house, and one of Finn's grown children is an alumnus. Yes, I'm acquainted with people there, or at least people who know people. But that's not really the point. "If tuition is a problem, you can always ask."

"Oh, Tara, that's so sweet of you, but —"

"Don't tell me. Graham would never accept my money. But he wouldn't have to know. He could think it was a scholarship, and it would be, from an anonymous benefactress. Anyway, it's an option."

There. Christmas gifts accomplished. One iPhone, with AppleCare. One upscale snowboard, plus Tahoe ski trip. And one thirty-thousand-dollar, give or take, tuition.

FIVE

The conversation devolves all the way to trite as Melody launches a deep discussion about the relative merits of glucosamine for canine joint problems. Seems her seven-year-old golden retriever can't keep up with the junior black lab, and one vet says "yada yada" while the second says "yada." I think we need to spice up this dialogue.

"Maybe Barney should try yoga," I joke.

"Yoga?" She is seriously consternated.

"Yeah. I'm actually considering it myself."

"I thought you said yoga's for wussies."

"It might be. But I've got an ulterior motive."

"Do tell."

So I do. And, because I don't want to discuss dogs anymore, I go ahead and add the part about Ben. By the time I get to the pepper spray, we have crested Echo Summit and are dropping down the steep, winding road into the Tahoe Basin. Mel sits quietly for a second or two. Finally, she says, "Are you insane? How often do you pick up men in bars?"

"Once in a while," I admit. "But rarely, and never while married. I do have some small sense of morality."

"Morality? Tara, look what happened! And think of what might have happened! It's like the older you get, the more reckless you become. Do you have a death wish or something? Sometimes you remind me of Mom."

"Don't say that. Don't ever say that! I am *nothing* like her!"

Silence mortars the wall that has risen between us. I don't want to talk. Don't want to think, especially not about our mother, who I work very hard to maroon on the outermost fringe of recollection. Twice today she has intruded my present, this time at Melody's invitation. And now that she's here, she will fight to stay.

As the highway straightens, I can let off the brake, and as the Escalade picks up speed I am teleported backward in time and space to the bed of an old Ford pickup. It was the wilds of Idaho, and legal to have passengers in the back. But Mel and I were just kids and pretty much terrified. Not that Mom cared. She wanted our old collie, Liz,

47

sharing the seat with her.

"I'll go slow," she promised. "Don't worry. It'll be fun."

At first, she kept her word, and we bumped along the rutted gravel road, nice and easy. But my mother had this thing. Later we found a term for it — borderline personality disorder. What that meant was one minute she was perfectly sane; the next, something inside her brain clicked and she went off. That meant different things on different days.

Sometimes she turned violent, striking like a rattlesnake, usually without provocation. (And when provoked, she was more like a nest of rattlers.) Other times, her behavior was erratic. Self-destructive. Impulsive. Reckless. Yes, that word, and that day, that's exactly what she was.

Suddenly, she was foot to the floor. That old truck fishtailed and bucked, throwing Mel and me side to side, up and down. I was ten, and she was not quite eight. I did my best to hold her down, keep her safely inside, but I was certain that she'd go flying. I didn't care so much about myself. By then I was pretty sure I wouldn't live to see junior high. But I had made it a point to take care of my little sister as best I could.

I can picture the scene; it's like watching

an old movie — tears streaking the dirt on Melody's cheeks and me pounding the window, screeching, "Please, Mama, please slow down." She never let off the gas when she turned to look at me, grinning. If we'd been devoted churchgoers, the kind who believed in a devil and demons, I'd have sworn she was possessed. But all I knew was what I saw. My mother was crazy.

Devil or no, we probably would have ended up in hell that afternoon, except a big old elk chose that moment to cut across the road in front of the truck. Instinct insisted Mom hit the brakes and when she swerved to miss the massive animal, Liz fell off the seat, onto the floorboard. The collie yelped, and Mom went berserk.

I will never, ever forget the way she jerked the Ford into park. The smell of oil, dripping onto the overheated engine, mixed with the cloying lift of dust. The driver's-side door slammed open. "Look what you made me do!" Mom directed her roar straight at me.

"What, Mama?" I pushed Mel against the cab, positioned myself in front of her.

"Poor Lizzie is hurt. And it's your fault. Come here, you little monster."

I had no choice but to comply. It would hurt worse if I made her climb over the

49

tailgate and come after me, plus she might get hold of Melody, too. Her fury tended to melt after a fist fall or ten. And since they'd all be aimed at me, I figured I might as well try to plead my case.

"But I didn't do anything. And Liz is A-OK." The collie in question had hopped back up onto the seat. She sat there, nose against the window and panting gently, watching the drama rising to a pinnacle.

"Don't you dare tell me what's what! You get over here right now, or else."

I knew enough not to argue anymore, and crawled across the pickup bed to the tailgate, which my mother let drop, threatening both the hinges and me. I lowered my head into my chest, let the blows fall against my back, my arms. Better than my face, experience told me. Better than my face.

I don't remember exactly what that beating felt like. Bare-fisted, Mom's whoopings were pretty much alike. I can, however, recall the sounds: Liz's whining; Mel's hiccupping; the *tick-tick* of the truck's engine, still running; the circling cry of a hawk on the hunt. And the odors, yes, those are fresh as yesterday: Pabst and Camels, burnt Quaker State, damp rabbitbrush, the stink of rage-fueled perspiration. The last I often smell in my sleep, at the edge of every dream, and I can smell it now, lodged in memories I can't quite push away.

"Earth to Tara." Melody yanks me back into the present. "You might want to check how fast you're going. There's a highway patrol car just up ahead."

I glance down at the speedometer. Twelve over. "Thanks for the warning. Hope he's got something else on his mind."

Luckily, a sweet little BMW goes tearing by in the other direction. The cop hangs a quick U-turn, and the ticket belongs to the other guy. Love when that happens.

"Where were you, anyway?" asks Mel, referring to my masochistic reverie.

"Idaho."

"Ah. Idaho. Never a good place to go."

"Speaking of that, have you heard anything from her lately?" Our mother doesn't dare talk to me. I cut her off completely when I turned eighteen, and she seems happy enough to accept this as the status quo. Any communication comes through Melody, who is more forgiving than I. Then again, she has less to pardon.

"Mom e-mailed a few weeks ago. She's still in Rialto, shacking up with a trucker. This one, she says, is full of good lovin'."

Prostitution is legal in the rural counties of Nevada, and most truck drivers would rather pay for more upscale tail than take what our mother happily gave away in exchange for room and board. Vegas proved a less-than-fertile hunting ground, so she moved to Southern California, where the prowling for truckers full of good lovin' was easier.

"Rialto, huh? Didn't I read something about a string of recent kitten hangings there?" Mom always hated cats.

"Not funny."

"I wasn't going for humor there, Mel."

Six

We check in to a two-bedroom villa at the Timber Lodge, right in Heavenly Village. I've been skiing this resort since well before the redevelopment that brought the gondola all the way down into the town of South Lake Tahoe. Even Melody has to agree that this is convenient, at least as far as accessing the mountain. It's a short walk across the street and over the state line into Nevada for nightlife, and the sensational restaurants the casinos use to lure tourists.

One of my favorites is the Sage Room, inside Harvey's, and that's where we have a reservation tonight. The sidewalks and streets are clear and mostly dry, so I chance wearing a dress and footwear that would be iffy in a snowstorm. Melody, of course, dresses much more conservatively, but she still manages to pull off "chic" in nice jeans and a sapphire-blue angora sweater. Okay, the UGGs knock off a couple of style points. I'll remind her to keep her feet under the table.

We order "for two" spinach salad and chateaubriand, plus a fabulous bottle of Napa Valley cabernet. "Pretty sure the waiter thinks we're dating," says Mel. "He gave us a funny look."

"Hey, if you weren't my sister, and if I happened to swing that way, I'd date you. You're gorgeous."

She huffs. "Whatever. I need to lose thirty pounds, and my hair makes me look sixty."

"They do have this stuff called dye, if that bothers you. But I think the silver is beautiful."

"You going au naturel, then?" Her smile means she doesn't expect an answer.

I give her one, anyway. "Beautiful, on *you.*"

"So . . . what are you after?"

"What do you mean?"

She sighs. "It's just, you don't give me compliments very often."

"Really? Well, you *are* beautiful. For looking sixty, I mean."

We laugh together, but uneasily, so I'm glad when our first course arrives, diverting our attention. As Roberto tosses spinach and sweet dressing tableside, I try to remember a recent compliment I paid my

54

sister. Last ski trip, I told her she'd definitely improved. Does that count? No, probably not. The last time I said something nice about the way she looked was . . . I can't remember.

Mel sips her wine. "This is brilliant. When did you develop a taste for cab? As I recall, you used to be more the chardonnay sort."

"Finn loved the Napa Valley, and we toured the wineries several times. We took a class with an oenologist . . ." Puzzlement crinkles Mel's eyes, so I explain, "A master vintner, if you prefer. The science guy behind the barrels? Anyway, once you learn about tannins and soil and palette and such, you feel more like experimenting. After a while I came to prefer big reds. The bolder, the better."

Oenology. Good word. Silent *O*. Comes after "odoriferous," which interestingly means both unsavory (offensive) and savory (sweet smelling). Sort of like Finn, in fact.

"One good thing that came out of your marriage, I guess."

"Yes, and along with it, an entire cellar of great wines, not to mention the house where the cellar's located."

"So you're planning to stay in the city, then? You weren't sure last time I talked to you."

55

I swallow the last bite of my salad before answering. "For now. There's nowhere I'd rather be, and it's a good place to host parties conducive to generous giving by the San Francisco elite."

"Elite, or elitists?"

"They're pretty much synonymous."

She shakes her head. "And yet they're donating to a cause that helps homeless people. Seems oxymoronic, no?"

"They don't care about the cause, Mel, only that other people see them whipping out their checkbooks."

"Huh. And what about you? Are you truly concerned about San Francisco's downtrodden?"

Is this a test? Do I mind if I flunk it? "I'd like to see fewer of them on the streets."

"That's not what I mean. Do you enjoy your work?"

"I love it."

"Why?"

"It's creative, challenging. And no one's making me do it." I leave out the part about the challenge being to convince some stone-hearted douche bag to cut loose with a little (most likely inherited) cash, and when I accomplish the task, it's a win. The bigger the check, the bigger the win.

The steak is every bit as good as I expected

it to be. I usually like my meat a little less done, but Melody can't stand to eat it bloody, so we compromise with medium rare. Even this firm, it's delicious. We take our time, savor each bite and each sip of wine. I am almost finished when I realize the only conversation I'm hearing is at the next table. Have we run out of things to say already?

We skip dessert, wander through the casino on our way to the late-night cabaret show, which starts in about an hour. "Hope you don't mind I chose sexy over silly," I tell Melody. "But I wasn't sure we could make the earlier show."

"I'm a big girl. I think I can handle boobs and G-strings."

"Good to hear." But, then, why has her face blushed so red? "I'm more interested in the vocals, by the way. And maybe the dance, though that's open for debate. Voice is hard to fake. Sort of like boobs."

The cheer of a winning roll draws my attention to a nearby roulette table. Anticipation prickles the back of my neck. Normally I'm more of a poker girl, but only if I'm on my own, with several hours to kill. "We've got a little time. Let's play for a few."

"You know how I feel about gambling." Mel's voice is stern. Having spent our teen years in Las Vegas, we witnessed the gaming dependency from many angles. Mom had a problem, and so did a number of her revolving-door boyfriends. Sometimes that resulted in hungry days.

"Yeah, but we're playing with my money, so no worries. In my experience, betting someone else's chips stimulates the good-luck fairy."

Reluctantly, she follows me to the crowded table. A couple of guys in uniforms make room, and when I plunk down a wad of cash, ask for hundred-dollar chips, one of them whistles. "Did y'all just hit the lottery, ma'am?"

I laugh. "Oh, I hit it a while ago. I hit it three times, in fact."

The cute young marine looks really confused until Melody clarifies, "She's talking about her husbands."

"Ex-husbands, and yes, I am."

I don't play systems or try to outsmart a game that was invented to keep the house well afloat. Winning at roulette is all about luck, which is either with you or not on any given day.

When I try to give Mel a stack of chips, she shakes her head. "You play. I'll watch."

"Okay, then, give me two numbers between one and thirty-six."

"Twelve and fifteen." Two of her kids' ages.

I put a hundred-dollar chip on each, plus one on the zero and another on my personal favorite, thirty-three. Then I ask the marine, who is playing dollar chips on red or black, for one more number. "If it hits, I'll share," I promise, placing one last hundred-dollar bet on his preferred twenty-one.

The dealer spins the wheel, rolls the ball. Round and round it goes, drops into the sixteen. Ugh. It's a collective groan. Everyone loves to watch high-roller bets, share the giant rush of adrenaline attached to having five hundred dollars at stake. So I give it to them again. I play the same numbers, with a similar result. Again. And again.

A cocktail waitress comes by and asks about drinks. Everyone orders a freebie. Everyone except Mel and me. Alcohol would take the edge off my rush.

Melody, I'm pretty sure, thinks she needs to babysit me, a fact that's confirmed when she hisses in my ear, "What are you doing? Five hundred dollars a spin? You're down six grand!"

"You have to play big to win big." To prove it, I put two chips on each number. What the hell?

My sister's acidic glare could melt skin.

"That's half of Kayla's tuition right there."

The dealer spins the wheel. Rolls the ball.

"Probably more like a quarter, and I told you, I've got that covered. Anyway, what good is having more money than you can spend in a lifetime if you can't take a chance with a little every now and then?"

Round and round. Slowing down. The ball drops into the four, and Melody grunts. No, wait. It takes a fortuitous bounce, straight into the twenty-one! The table cheers, and the marine clamps his arm around my shoulder, tugs me into him and kisses me, hard. "Maybe I'll catch a little of that luck," he says. "I hope it's contagious."

The dealer pushes a tray of chips — seventy of them — across the table. I hand one back as a tip and give two to the Marine. "Merry almost Christmas, sweetheart."

One thing I do know is when to call it a night. Melody accompanies me to the cashier, "pissed" etched on her face. "What's wrong? I won, didn't I?"

"No. You broke even, minus the three hundred you gave away. You could have lost the whole thing! Who does that? Who takes that kind of risk?"

She is seriously clueless. "It's only money,

Mel. Some people risk much, much more, and those people wager lives."

SEVEN

We have great seats in the cabaret — a dead-center booth at the back of the first riser. The show is called *The D-Factor* (*d* for "diva") and is presented something like the *X Factor* television show. Eight women cover today's hottest pop songs, and for the most part they're pretty good, though I doubt they'd get paid nearly as much as they do if they sang fully clothed. *X Factor* (as in X-rated) would be a more fitting name, but they'd probably get sued for using it.

Two "judges" and an emcee, all male, ask the girls inane questions, then make requests, like "show me your best Miley Cyrus." As I suspected, the vocals are better than the twerking, though the men in the audience would probably disagree. It's interesting to watch their reactions, especially the older gents right down in front, who are getting way more than an eyeful.

The members of the audience are supposed to clap approval after each performance. A higher noise level adds points to the girls' scores, which are kept tallied on a lighted board. Melody has been anything but raucous with her applause, and now she actually yawns.

"Not impressed, I take it?"

She sips her drink — we've both moved to sidecars — before answering. "The show is entertaining enough, I guess. A couple of them seem like they could have more mainstream careers."

Onstage, a dark-skinned girl (okay, they could have been a little less obvious) attempts a Beyoncé number, "Irreplaceable." The young woman is pretty enough, but physically, she's no match for Ms. Knowles, and so her dance suffers. "You've got to have legs like a Thoroughbred to pull off this number," I tell Mel.

"Back in the day, you could have done it."

Back in the day, I could have. And, had my life not taken a hard right turn, I might be up on that stage today. At twenty, I was a dancer in a Vegas strip club. I started at eighteen, right out of high school. In some demented corner of my brain, I figured the money I earned — and it was decent money, especially for someone that young — would pay my way through UNLV.

I wasn't sure what I wanted to be, but I thought a college degree was the key to success, especially since my mother didn't believe it. I would have done anything not to be like her, and if she wasn't going to support my dream of higher education, well, amen. I'd find a way to handle it myself.

There are a couple of problems with stripping, the main one being that most customers are absolutely positive you do more than take off your clothes for pay. Had I stayed in the business longer, perhaps I would have, but there was still enough Idaho innocence left in me to be disgusted by the thought. Giving a stranger a peek wasn't so bad, but I didn't want the guy's hands on me, let alone his other body parts. Imagine where the nasty things might have recently been poking.

Even though I avoided that, the work was demanding. But I made bank, more than some of the other girls. Probably because word got around among the pedophile underbelly that there was a kid dancing at the Jellybean Club. I always did look young for my age. And making that easy cash — upward of five hundred dollars a night on weekends — made it harder and harder to commit to earning my BA.

One night this moderately attractive middle-aged man came into the club. He sat in the front row, and as far as I could tell, his eyes never left me, though other girls offered a lot more to look at. He returned the following evening, and the one after that, and his tips got bigger and bigger. I asked around about him.

"His name's Raul Medina," my favorite bouncer, Scotty, told me. "He owns a chain of pawnshops. Seems like a decent guy."

"Yeah, except he hangs out in strip clubs," I joked.

"Doesn't mean he's not a decent guy."

One of the other girls had been eavesdropping. "Raul's wife got killed in a car wreck a few years ago. Drunk driver took 'er out. Their little kid, too."

"How do you know?" I asked.

"I spent a little time with the guy. He was lonely. Paid me to fuck, but he wanted to talk first."

Raul was, indeed, lonely. The next time he came in, he waited for me to go on break, then sent a note back with Scotty. *You've caught my eye. Would like to spend some time with you. No strings. Nothing kinky. Just want to talk. Cordially, Raul.* He didn't say he'd compensate me for my company, but it was implied. I could have declined, but something about the man had piqued my interest. Besides, I liked the word "cordially."

I agreed to a cup of coffee, and we met up at a little diner off the strip. Strangely, I felt shy. I mean, he'd seen just about every inch of my flesh, but exposing my personality was something else altogether. Good thing he was easy to talk to.

He told me his story first — how his grandfather, a Peruvian immigrant, started collecting stuff from yard sales. Whatever he could find, repair, and resell to make ends meet for his growing family. How Raul's father was the only child of six to see the value in that and continue the tradition, building storage sheds in back of his rented property to house excess items. How when he passed, too young, of cancer, he left everything to sixteen-year-old Raul.

"He made me promise to take care of my mother and sisters," Raul said. "I was just a kid, but I made that vow. I worked hard in school. Learned about business. Saving. Investing. I got my college degree, but even before I did, I opened my first store. The biggest lesson I ever learned was to be fair with my customers, even though they weren't being fair to themselves."

"What do you mean?" I asked.

"Gambling is a sickness, like any addiction. I've never yet met a gambler who didn't know he was sick, yet they rarely ask for help, or walk away. If you have a fever, you take aspirin, right? A pawnshop is the opposite of aspirin. It won't fix you; it only enables your illness. So I made sure never to cheat my customers, take advantage of the weak. I thought it was the least I could do.

"Somehow, I always made a profit. Then, I invested that profit, invested again. One store became six, and they all flourished. They're still healthy. The economy may fluctuate, but good or bad, there will always be a demand for ready cash, especially in a city like Las Vegas."

As he talked, I studied him. For a guy in his late forties, he was decent looking — caramel skin; gold-flecked brown eyes; black hair, salted with gray. He had a gorgeous smile, with perfect teeth, not a single filling or need for one. He told me that was the one thing he made sure to do for himself. I liked that about him. That, and he always smelled clean. Not perfumed. Just straight soap-and-water clean.

"Now you know all about me," he finished. "Tell me about you. What's your story?"

I gave him the basics. Crazy mother. No father, at least not one I could identify. Grew up in Idaho. Mom chased a loser boyfriend to Vegas five years before, when I was fifteen, then pretty much left me and my younger sister to fend for ourselves. I managed to graduate high school, was working my way through college.

"One tip at a time?" he asked.

"That's right. Slow going, but I'm determined."

"You have a man?"

"Lots," I joked. But when I saw he was serious, I amended, "If you mean do I have someone special in my life, the answer is no."

"Why not? Pretty girl like you."

"I guess dancing sort of puts things in perspective, you know? All those men, worshipping my body, with no concern about who I am or what I want or what would make me happy. If I let them, they'd have sex with me, and then they'd discard me."

"But sex is only part of a relationship. What about love?"

I laughed. "What about it? I've never seen it, at least not up close."

"That is sad. Twenty years old and you never —"

"Hey, now. I'm not a virgin."

"You didn't let me finish. Twenty years old and you've never been in love? That needs to change, and very soon."

I wouldn't say I married Raul for love, but he never knew that, and over the next few weeks, he definitely fell in love with me. He was kind and caring, and that was not something I'd ever experienced, either. He took me out of the club, whisked me away from that life and into his lovely home, but only after our nuptials at a quirky Elvis-themed wedding chapel. "I don't want you to be my lover," he told me. "I want you to be my wife."

Raul valued education. In fact, I credit him with feeding my fascination with language. I've always had a love for words, one of the few traits I share with my sister. As kids, when things got rough at home, we'd escape into music, listening to our favorite songs over and over, until we'd committed the lyrics to memory. R.E.M. Genesis. The Cure. Duran Duran. And later, Nirvana. Green Day. Pearl Jam. Hole. There were times I would have sworn Patty Smyth was singing straight to me.

But Raul taught me the importance of cultivating a good vocabulary. "To earn the respect of the world, you must learn to speak eloquently," he said, "and you must understand the meaning of your words. There isn't much worse than a person who assumes knowledge he doesn't possess."

He put me through school, allowed me to earn my degree at my own pace. He taught me business. Investment strategies. How to manipulate a better deal. To appreciate quality over quantity. How to drive a stick shift — in a really fast car.

And, yes, he showed me how good sex can be when your partner wants to please you. I wasn't a virgin when we got married, but Raul Medina was most definitely responsible for my first orgasm.

Raul also taught me to ski, or at least provided me with the ability to learn, putting me in private lessons at Mammoth, Kirkwood, Diamond Peak, Squaw Valley, and Alpine Meadows. Each mountain had its challenges, and each instructor, strengths. By the time I first skied Heavenly, I didn't need lessons anymore. Raul continued to take them because, he said, he wanted to keep up with me. Though he tried very hard to do just that, he couldn't. And, as it turned out, he shouldn't have tried.

I was twenty-three and a widow. It was my first funeral and the last time I let myself cry. Tears are a sign of weakness. The wolves gathered quickly.

WATER NEVER DISAPPEARS

it only reinvents itself,
liquid, solid
liquid
gas, liquid,
forever
in random echo.

Every drop
encapsulates
the beginning,
its undulating
glass a window,
opening
into Genesis.

You wake to platinum
beads of dew,
the very first
morning
breaking within
the clutch
of dawn
dampened grass,

consider
that we are essentially
water and wonder
how many eons

we squander,
every time
we allow
ourselves to cry.

EIGHT

The day dawns a splendid, sharp blue, as if I ordered it up especially for Mel and me. The snow on the mountain fell early and furiously this year. Coverage is supposed to be exceptional, between Mother Nature's generosity and Heavenly Valley snowmaking, which is legendary. December's deep chill has kept the mountain pristine, and I'm eager to track it up.

"Ready?" I call.

Melody comes tromping out in what look like brand-new ski boots and a tangerine-colored powder suit, which must have cost a pretty penny. But the excessive padding does nothing for her figure, and the color is not the best against her pale, freckled skin. Then again, with her helmet and goggles on, you can't see much of her face.

"What do you think? Graham picked everything out and gave it to me for an early Christmas present."

Oh . . . it looks really comfortable, and I definitely won't lose you on the mountain. I just hope you don't get *too* hot."

"I just hope you don't freeze your tushie off."

She's referring to the form-fitting black wool ski pants and violet turtleneck sweater I'm wearing. "No worries. My parka is killer warm. My tushie's in no danger." I slide into said jacket, slip on my favorite pair of Oakley sunglasses. "Let's do it."

"I don't suppose you've got a helmet stashed in your pocket somewhere?"

"You're kidding, right? And ruin my perfect hair?"

The joke does not amuse her. "After what happened with Raul, I'd think you'd be a little more cautious."

"When you hit a tree going that fast, a helmet won't save you. It wouldn't have changed a thing."

Wisely, she drops it. We collect our skis and head on up the gondola. Heavenly is a big mountain, with a lot of wide, well-groomed intermediate runs. We spend most of the morning maneuvering those. It's Wednesday, pre–winter break, so the crowd isn't too bad. Another week and this place will be a nightmare.

Those people don't know what they're

missing today. The snow is crisp, the breeze delicate, and the air temp cold, but not uncomfortably so. You couldn't get a better day, unless you're a spring skiing aficionado. I dislike slush, so I prefer to schedule my trips earlier in the season.

Melody would be content to ski the big boulevards all day long, but I'm starting to hunger for steeper fare. At the top of the Sky Express, I signal for her to stop. "Why don't you take the Ridge Run down? I'll take Ellie's and meet you at the bottom."

We're standing at the lip of the black diamond run. She peeks over the edge and shudders. "I suppose I should be grateful you're not heading over to Mott Canyon."

Heavenly's two Nevada-side canyons, Mott and Killebrew, are notoriously difficult — precipitous, skier-tracked, obstacle-lined thoroughfares, for serious double-black-diamond skiers only. I've tried them a couple of times, but never with really great snow. "I was thinking about heading over there after lunch. For now, I'll just go this way. See you at the chair."

I don't wait for further discussion, just point my skis downhill and away I go, taking long, sweeping S-turns, in total control. My pulse quickens and my legs remind me this run is more difficult than the last, but the challenge is exhilarating, and so is the speed, nothing between the rush and me except air. This is why I love this sport.

About halfway down, I hear shouting above me. "Watch out! Oh shit! Oh shit!"

I don't dare turn to look, but it sounds ugly, and the "oh shit"s are getting closer, and suddenly I am hit from behind. I cartwheel to one side, legs splitting awkwardly. One ski brakes in a pile of powder, while my downhill speed carries me forward. *Whop!* Holy mother of God, I think I just lost my right knee.

The good news is I finally stop, unlike the bastard who ran into me and is still tumbling toward the bottom of the run. The bad news is, when I try to stand I fail the knee test. Strangely, it doesn't hurt much. But no way can I take a turn. The knee wobbles and pops too easily sideways, its center loose. Ligament tear, for sure.

I drop onto my butt in the tattered snow. Two boarders stop to check on me. "You okay?"

"Could you contact ski patrol, please? I'll need a sled."

One guy takes off. His buddy stays with me. "Whoa, that was gnarly, dude."

"Tell me about it."

"You cold? You're shaking."

"Not cold. Pissed." There goes my season, first day out.

"Don't blame you. That guy sucked. If you're warm enough, I'd pack that knee in snow, try to keep it from swelling."

"How did you know it's my knee?"

"We could see it go from up there, man. But as bad as it is, check that out." He points to a still figure near the bottom of the slope. Ski patrol is already gathered around him. "That dude took a radical fall, man. It'll be Care Flight taking him out of here, all the way down to Reno. All you get is a sled and maybe an ambulance to Barton Memorial. Unless you've got a ride."

"I do, actually, although it's valet-parked down in the village. My sister can drive me from there, though. Hey, if you happen to see a lady in a ridiculous orange powder suit, would you let her know she can probably find me in first aid later? Tell her to bring me a drink."

"Like, coffee or what?"

"Like whiskey. Neat."

He laughs, then reaches into an inner pocket of his jacket. "If you don't mind risking germs, I've got this." He extracts a metal flask. "Not whiskey. Jäger."

The kid doesn't look too germy. Why not? "You sure?"

"Hell yeah. Oh, look. Here comes your chariot."

I take a big slug of the licorice-flavored liqueur, just as my own personal pair of ski patrolmen arrive. The young one is tall and stocky, the fortyish one built like a miniature mule. It is the ass who gives me an appraising once-over and says, "Been drinking today, have we?"

I bring my eyes square level with his. "Did you ask the guy who took me out from behind if he'd been drinking today?"

"It's hard to question someone who's unconscious."

"Yeah, well, my sitting here with a destroyed knee had nothing to do with me drinking. I never touched a drop before this one, and I kind of feel like I deserve a good belt, considering an out-of-control jerk — who was totally conscious at the time — just annihilated both me and my entire season. Now, you want to do your job, or what?"

I start to hand over the flask to my boarder buddy, reconsider. "Do you mind?"

He shrugs. "Help yourself."

After a long, slow swallow, I return the flask to its owner. "Many thanks, and thanks for hanging out with me until the inquisition arrived."

"Hey, now," says Tall and Stocky. "I haven't said a word."

"That's why I like you. Well, that and you're sort of cute."

The guy blushes and starts to ready the sled as the boarder takes off, calling back over his shoulder, "I'll be on the lookout for orange."

NINE

My ride off the mountain is quite a production. The ski patrolmen — tall and stocky Trevor, and miniature-mule Will — forgive my Jägermeister indulgence when they observe the state of my knee. Despite their packing it with snow so quickly, it is ballooning. This, plus its purpling mottle, is all too obvious when Will slices the leg of my ski pants most of the way to my groin.

He whistles. "I've seen some ugly knees in my time. That one is up near the top of my list. Does it hurt?"

"Oddly, not really."

"It's going to." He wraps it in cold packs, pulls the remains of my pants leg down over the swollen lump.

Trevor lifts me easily, lays me flat on the bed of the sled, and secures a blanket over me with a couple of wide tie-downs. "I've never been tied up before," I joke. "Promise this will be fun?"

Will actually chuckles. "Oh, yeah. The best time you'll ever have, and all you have to do is lie there. We, on the other hand, have our work cut out for us."

They do. Will moves around to the front, where he'll have to pull once we reach flat terrain. Meanwhile, he steers while Trevor takes the cheater strap at the rear, acting as the brake. Both men snowplow down the steep face, denying their skis — and so, the sled — momentum.

It still feels fast to me. Air movement stings my eyes. Despite their watering, I'm aware of the stares of those we pass, especially when we reach the landing where lines form for the Sky Express chair. It's embarrassing, but I understand they can't help it. It's like passing a car accident.

Nothing much to see here, people. The blanket isn't pulled up over my face. I'm alive and kicking, at least with my left leg. Not sure about the guy who hit me, though. We go past his quiet form at a distance. Ski patrol is keeping everyone back, making room for Care Flight to land so they can load the man into its belly. I can hear the snarl of the helicopter's approach. The snowboarder was right. I'm glad I'm not leaving the mountain that way.

Across the flats, we slow significantly, then

83

it's a short drop to a gentle beginner's roundabout. It takes almost a half hour to arrive at the first aid station at the top of the gondola. "Don't weight your right leg," instructs Will as he and Trevor help me stand. "We'll get you inside."

One arm around each of their necks, I hobble, one-legged, to the door, where a note informs us: *Back soon.* We push on through, anyway. The stark room is dingy white beneath dim fluorescent lights. "Wow. This place could use a face-lift."

"Hey, now," corrects Trevor. "This here is a state-of-the-art first aid station."

The men help me onto a gurney, adjust the back so I can sit up. "I'll go deal with the sled," says Will, starting for the door. "Nice skiing with you, ma'am."

Ha-ha. Very funny. "You *will* get the name of the man who ran into me, right?"

Will stops, turns back toward me. "So you can send him a get-well card?"

"In case my insurance company needs to get hold of him," I correct.

"Standard operating procedure. If they — or you — have any questions, you can always contact the resort's legal department directly. Which reminds me . . ." He locates a clipboard and pen. "Please fill out this report and give it to the on-duty when he gets back. He's probably helping out up on the mountain."

He exits as Trevor elevates my right leg and places a fresh ice pack on my knee. "How's that feel?"

"Useless."

"That's right, and I expect you to keep it that way until someone smarter than me tells you otherwise. Now, is there someone who should be informed about your accident?" He's just so earnest, I kind of want to kiss him, if only for the shock value.

"You mean, like my lawyer?"

"I kind of thought you *were* a lawyer." He grins. "But, I meant like your husband. Or a relative."

"I'm not married. And the only relative who might care is my sister, who's here somewhere. I'd call her, but she never takes her cell out on the mountain. Says she wants to disconnect from the real world when she's skiing."

Now he loses his smile. "Did you tell her she'd be a lot safer carrying her phone with her?"

"It wouldn't do any good. Melody maintains a serious list of rules to live by. Besides, her *phone* is much safer *not* going out on the mountain with her."

Which elicits a nervous laugh. "I hope she

skis cautiously, then."

"No worries. Mel's definitely not the out-of-bounds kind of skier. And it would be a cold day in hell before you'd find her limping her way down a Killebrew run."

"That's very good to hear. Now, do you need anything before I go?"

I glance around the room, which is naked except for a miniature desk, two more gurneys (because a first aid station can never have too many), and a door, which probably leads to a bathroom. "Go? As in, you're leaving me here all alone?"

"Sorry, ma'am, but my job is on the mountain."

"But . . . what am I supposed to *do*?"

"What am *I* supposed to do? Stay here and entertain you?"

I really want to act pissy, but that will definitely get me nowhere, so I'll attempt "helpless" instead. "No, no. Sorry. I didn't mean it like that. But could you . . . I mean would you mind . . . I, um, need to use the restroom. Could you possibly help me? Just to the door, I mean. I think I can take it from there."

Trevor's cheeks flush cranberry. "Oh, of course. Why didn't you just say so to start with?" He whisks me off the gurney as if I am weightless, sets me down just across the bathroom threshold. "Be super careful not to twist that leg sideways, and try not to bend that knee."

He shuts the door, and I take my time. He's given me the excuse, but even if he hadn't, accomplishing the task is tricky. I manage to keep my right leg mostly extended, but when I sit it does slant toward the floor, flooding the knee with fluid. Suddenly, it hurts, and it hurts a lot. I manage to quell the rising scream, which escapes as a very loud "Jesus!"

Trevor knocks on the door. "Everything okay in there?"

Other than the sledgehammer pounding my patella, and the hot drain of blood from my face, everything is just peachy. "F-f-fine," I manage, flushing the toilet. "Be right there." I have to talk myself into standing, however.

By the time I finally manage to zip my pants and wash my hands, I've regained a little composure, at least until I turn away from the sink, forgetting my knee just long enough to twist my weighted right leg sideways. The ensuing *pop!* forces that scream from my mouth after all.

Trevor flings open the door. "Holy shit! You're white as an albino's ghost." Fascinating colloquialism.

"Yeah. This thing decided to hurt after all." I avoid the details. Only an idiot could have forgotten that injury in the space of three minutes. "Could you get me a couple of ibuprofen?"

He decides to isolate the knee, and by the time he's finished applying an elastic bandage, the on-duty attendant, Sierra, arrives. She assesses his work, gives an approving nod. "Good job, T. I'll take it from here."

Trevor pats me on the shoulder. "As soon as your sister catches up with you, go straight to the ER, okay?" His newfound concern borders on comical.

"Cross my heart." He starts to leave, but I stop him. "Hey, Trevor? Thanks for the expertise. Not to mention the entertainment."

It's after two by the time Melody finally stumbles in, tired from the unaccustomed exercise. I'm sipping hot tea and reading an old *Ski* magazine, fairly comfortable, or at least as comfortable as I could convince Sierra to make me, with an extra pillow and one of her personal Vicodins.

"Are you okay?" Mel demands.

"Most of me. Except my right knee. That is most definitely *not* okay."

"Do you know how scared I was when

that guy — who was stoned out of his head, by the way — snowboarded up to tell me you were here?" She storms over to the gurney. "How did he know I was your sister?"

I tip my hands like a spokesmodel might. "This lovely powder suit is the approximate color of orange marmalade, and designed to conceal every flattering curve so stoned snowboarders won't be tempted to ravish you."

"You. Are. Hilarious." Mel yanks off her helmet and shakes her head, trying to loosen the sweat-plastered mess beneath it. "Now, don't you wish you'd been wearing one of these?"

"One: I don't think they make helmets for your knees. Two: my head is just fine. And, three: if my hair looked like that, ski patrol wouldn't have stopped for me."

She doesn't find the joke funny. "Why are you so stubborn? Think of what might have happened. It could have been worse!"

"Could have been better, too."

"Okay, so now what?"

"I'm told I must go straight to Barton Memorial for a learned opinion."

The Tahoe area offers a wide range of outdoor recreations — skiing, biking, hiking, boating, Jet-Skiing, rafting, and even more unusual activities like paragliding and skydiving. So it makes sense that South Lake Tahoe's small hospital has one of the best orthopedic centers in the country, staffed by doctors well versed in sports medicine. That information came via Sierra, who tells Mel now, "We'll bring her down the gondola via gurney."

I've had some time to think about the logistics. "Why don't you go on ahead, stow your stuff, and have valet bring the Escalade around? The ticket is in my purse. Unless you want to take a couple of more runs first."

She gives a "yeah, right" eye roll. "Looks like you just cut our vacation short."

"Hey. I prepaid the hotel and bought lift tickets for four days. No matter what's happened to me, you can still ski. In fact, I expect you to."

"We'll see." Her voice remains terse, but her expression softens, going all sisterly concerned. "Okay. Catch up to me in valet."

As she reaches the door, I call out to her, "Hey, Mel? At least I didn't hit a tree!"

TEN

We pull into Emergency late afternoon. I will say this about Barton Memorial: it's a beautiful facility, with a rock and pale wood facade that melts into its surroundings. Mel goes inside to request a wheelchair and I sit looking at the forest, which serves as a buffer, both for noise and also for less impressive housing tract views. South Lake Tahoe has taken a lot of time to create its woodsy design, especially with its later redevelopment. It must be nice to live up here, at least in the off-season.

The ER must not be too busy today because after the initial paperwork I don't have to wait very long for an exam. A nurse takes my vitals, then hands me over to the on-call doctor, who looks to be around sixteen years old. "I know what you're thinking," he says when I eye him suspiciously. "No worries, though. I am an actual certified physician. But even if I wasn't, I'd say we'd better take X-rays, as well as an MRI."

The nurse returns, hands me a hospital gown. "Do you need help putting this on?"

"I think I can handle it. Should I leave something on under?"

"Panties only, unless they have anything metal. No metal. No jewelry." She glances at the five-carat pink diamond engagement ring, now worn on my right hand. "I'll leave that with your sister if you want."

"Please. And since this is going to take a while, would you ask her to go get some other clothes? These pants are trashworthy."

"Will do." She takes my ring, plus a pair of sapphire studs, admiring them noticeably as she leaves. I hope they make it to Melody, but if not, they're insured.

I manage to shed what's left of my clothing in favor of a fashionable pink tent, which sort of ties closed in back. I'm still working on the second bow when someone knocks on the door. "You decent?"

"Loaded question, one I plead the fifth on. But you can come in."

The tech, whose name is Timothy — not Tim — helps me into a wheelchair and escorts me to X-ray. When they finish irradiating me, it's off to the magnetic resonance imaging machine. I'm glad it's not my brain they want to look at, as I'd be claustrophobic with my head immobilized inside this behemoth. Instead, Timothy faces me toward it, feet first.

"Lie back and try to relax," he says, clamping the top piece of what's called a knee coil in place. Then hands me a set of earphones. "The machine is loud. What kind of music do you like?"

"Anything louder than the machine?"

"Death metal?"

"Not that loud. Something with a decent beat and lyrics I can decipher."

Timothy smiles. "You got it."

I'm sort of surprised when it's country he chooses (he looks more preppie than cowboy), but not totally disappointed. It docs fulfill my general request, and I can listen to almost anything for a half hour, which is about how long the procedure takes. When it's over, Timothy wheels me back to the examination room.

"Someone will be in to discuss the results in a little while," he says.

"Any chance at some pain medication in the meantime?" The Vicodin has vacated my premises.

"I'll see what I can do."

"If my sister's here, can she keep me company?"

"I'll see what I can do about that, too. Meanwhile, here's something to read."

I spend fifteen minutes with a very old *People* magazine before Melody comes traipsing in, carrying a shopping bag. "I tried to find something loose over the legs, but nothing in your wardrobe fits that description. So I brought a pair of my lounging pants. They might be big in the waist, but we can pin them." She sits on a wheeled stool, amuses herself, rolling it forward and back. "How are you? Any news?"

"Nope. Waiting on results. And painkillers."

Moments later, Dr. Babyface comes in to address the latter. "I'll give you a prescription for an opiate, but want you to wean off it and straight onto eight-hundred-milligram ibuprofen as soon as possible. Your file says you drink alcohol daily?"

I nod. "Pretty much. Unless I don't feel like it."

"I ask, because many pain medications contain acetaminophen, which can cause serious complications in combination with alcohol . . ."

He goes on about *what* complications, and what he'll prescribe instead, et cetera, et cetera. I don't know exactly what he says because I tune out almost immediately. All I really want is a pill right now. Finally, not quite as if reading my mind, he goes over to a cabinet and finds a sample of something or other, hands it to me with a paper cup of water.

"That should kick in fairly quickly."

"What is it again?"

"Vicoprofen. Hydrocodone and ibuprofen. Be sure to eat plenty of fruits and vegetables because one of its side effects is constipation . . ." He lists more, but I quit listening at "nausea and vomiting." I'll simply refuse them.

"How long until we hear something about the tests?" asks Mel when he finishes.

"Anytime now, actually. You were lucky today . . ." He realizes the irony of what he just said and grins like a goon. "Okay, you could have been luckier. But one of our best orthopedic surgeons happens to be here. This is Dr. Lattimore's designated surgery day, and he had just finished up some paperwork when you came in. He decided to stick around and is assessing the films right now."

Just about the time my head goes light and my knee quits aching, the door opens, and in walks a most amazing man. He's maybe forty, tall and sinewy beneath careless expensive clothes. His hair is the deep golden color of lager, well barbered, but uncombed and slightly askew. Generally, I'm not big on the casual look, but it works perfectly for this guy.

"Good afternoon . . . er, I guess technically, it's evening. I'm Dr. Lattimore. I specialize in sports injuries. And you, Ms. Cannon, have a doozy."

"Doozy? Is that official doctor language?"

He laughs, and it's honey rich. Inviting. "Yes, actually. It's Latin for 'one destroyed knee.' You've torn both your anterior cruciate ligament and your medial collateral ligament. In addition, your meniscus looks like it went through a meat grinder. You must have been moving!"

"Yes, and I was cruising along just fine until I got rear-ended."

"So, what does that mean?" demands Melody.

"And you are . . . ?" The good doctor turns in her direction.

"Melody's my sister. And my mom. All rolled up in one."

"I see. Well, what that means is reconstructive surgery. A single ligament tear can often be rehabbed successfully without it, but not two, and the cartilage complicates things further." He moves toward me, assessing.

96

"You look like an athlete. I'm sure you'll want to heal as quickly as possible, and this is the best option."

He reaches the side of the gurney, pulls back the sheet to examine my knee. His fingers are long tapers, manicured and suede skinned, and when he touches my leg, tiny ripples of energy radiate upward, clear to my thigh. Whoa. What was that?

Whatever it was, I'm pretty sure he felt it, too. Our eyes meet, and I see that his are the green-gray of the ocean beneath rain. "Phew," he says, palpating my knee very gently. "You're going to be swollen for a while, and we can't do surgery until the swelling subsides, or we'd risk scar tissue." He pauses, fingertips still exciting my nerves. "Don't know why I'm saying 'we.' Once you can bend and straighten without a problem, you can have the surgery done at the hospital of your choice."

When his hand withdraws, I notice no wedding ring, nor any white shadow indicating one is worn outside of the workplace. "So, does that mean I'm bedridden, or what?"

"Not at all. You should stay off that leg for at least two weeks, but I'll give you some exercises to do. You'll want to regain strength and range of motion as soon as possible. But don't stand for long periods or walk too far without the crutches I'll send home with you. We'll brace it for now, too."

"Can she drive?" asks Mel.

"Not for a while. You can chauffeur, right?"

Melody smiles. "Looks like it's Christmas at my house, after all."

God help me.

The nurse comes in with a sheaf of papers, gives them to the doctor, who in turn hands them over to me. "As promised, the pre-op exercises. Plus one of my business cards, in case you decide you want to do the surgery at Barton. Dr. Rice will finish up in here, and you'll be on your way. Sorry about the circumstances, but it's been a pleasure meeting you."

He reaches out to shake my hand. I am subtle but direct when I don't let go immediately. I want him to feel the electric rush when I lock his eyes with mine and lower my voice. "Would it be out of line to ask for your cell number? In case something comes up in the middle of the night?"

"Highly unusual request," he says. But he grins, retrieves his business card, and scribbles on the back: *Cavin, 530-777-8992.*

ELEVEN

I'm not surprised Dr. Cavin Lattimore gave me his number. But Melody is stunned, not only by the gesture but also by my boldness in requesting it. We are back in the room, and I'm on the sofa, leg pillow-propped on the coffee table, in front of a gas fire in the faux fireplace.

"Cavin," I sigh. "Great name, huh? I've never met a Cavin before."

"Have you no sense of shame?" Mel asks.

"Shame? I'm not familiar with the word. Does it hurt?"

"Your sense of humor leaves much to be desired. I mean it, Tara."

"Look. The attraction was mutual, obviously. And life is too short for games." Except when they bring you pleasure or accomplish a goal.

"Are you really going to call him?"

I pick up my phone and dial, expecting it to go straight to voice mail.

Instead, he answers. "Cavin here."

"Oh, hello," I purr. "This is Tara Cannon."

"Tara? Oh, yes. ACL, MCL, and meniscus. Everything okay?"

"Well, I wouldn't exactly say that, but I'm as comfortable as can be expected."

"Heat for the pain. Ice for the swelling. Keep alternating the two."

"I'll remember that, thanks. But, actually, why I called was more personal. This happened to be day one of a five-day ski vacation. I'm sure my sister would love to get in a few more runs, and it's going to be awfully lonely all by myself in this hotel room. Since you're not officially my doctor — yet — would you let me buy you dinner one night? As a thank-you, I mean."

He doesn't point out the fact that I'll still be alone during the day, or that I'd be leaving Melody to eat dinner solo. I know he can say no, and probably should. But he agrees. "I have to work late tomorrow. How about Friday night? I'll make the reservation at my favorite Italian bistro. Assuming you like Italian?"

"I love all things food and wine, as long as they're divine. It will be my treat, though."

"Tell you what. Since there's no challenge in a footrace, I'll arm wrestle you for the bill. I've got your number now, so let me get back to you with a time tomorrow, okay?"

"Absolutely. Talk to you then."

As soon as I end the call, Melody pounces. "You are unbelievable."

"Oh, come on. You should believe me by now. Hey. Would you mind opening a bottle of cab?"

She goes to the little kitchen, digs for a corkscrew. "Doesn't it ever worry you — going out with strangers?"

"We're having dinner, Mel. Italian. In public. Anyway, don't worry. As a rule, serial killers don't have medical degrees."

Melody pours two tall glasses of wine and as she hands me one, there's a knock on the door. Our pizza has arrived. It isn't dry-aged Kobe, but as pizzas go, it's gourmet, loaded with white garlic sauce, extra cheese, and lots of veggies.

"Good thing I burned a lot of calories today," Mel says around a healthy mouthful.

"I wish I would have burned a lot more. I'll have to be careful about what I eat for a while, or I'll end up a regular porker. Pizza today, celery and carrot sticks tomorrow."

"Are you sure you want me to ski without you? How will you entertain yourself?"

I shrug. "Movies. Junk TV. I've got books

on my iPad. And, if I get really bored, I'll hobble down to the lobby to people watch, or use the computer in the business center. I'll be fine. Just don't forget to bring back something not fattening for dinner." There's no room service at this hotel.

"What if you get hungry during the day?"

"I'll pay someone to run over to the market or something. Please stop worrying. I really don't need you to mother me."

"I'm not sure about that. I kind of think someone has to." Mel helps herself to another slice, offers a second to me. "Go ahead. You won't get fat tonight."

What the hell? I allow the self-indulgence. Mel turns on the TV, finds an old chick flick — *When Harry Met Sally.* We eat pizza, drink wine, and watch Billy Crystal and Meg Ryan cycle through relationships while ignoring a mutual magnetic pull in favor of trying to maintain a sex-free friendship. That, of course, is impossible.

I sigh. "The problem with corny movies is love always wins the day."

"That's why I like 'em." Mel's voice is thick with satiation plus inebriation. "Besides, what's wrong with love winning the day?"

"It's fiction."

"You don't believe it can happen?"

"Pretty sure not. I've never experienced it. In fact, I've never even seen it."

"Wait a minute. What about Graham and me?"

I've got a spectacular buzz going on, too, thanks to Vicoprofen and three glasses of cabernet. It makes me not care what I say. "You got married because you were pregnant, Mel."

Her body stiffens, though her voice remains watery. "Doesn't mean we didn't love each other. We did . . . do."

"Which explains why you're still together, I guess. But you didn't marry for love. You married because you thought it was the right course of action."

Mel is quiet for a minute. Then she says, "There would have been a wedding eventually, Tara. But I was not only determined that my baby would have a father, but that the whole relationship would be legal. I was not about to let my child be raised the way you and I were."

Watching our train wreck of a mother drink herself crazier and crazier. Offer up her body for money or booze or simply a night of companionship. Subject us to her parade of bottom-feeder boyfriends — their leers, lewd comments, and sometimes their hands. There was no love in our house or trailer or weekly hotel room, except for sisterly affection. So, I understand what she's saying.

Still, now as then, I question her motives. From where I sat, it looked as if not only her marriage but also the pregnancy itself were Melody's means of escape, something I recognized from personal experience. Whatever love went along with that was just the maraschino atop the hot fudge.

Maraschino. Nasty fruit. But cool word.

TWELVE

By the time Friday evening rolls around, I'm just about bonkers. I've exhausted every recreation — cinema, soap opera, reading, voyeurism — not to mention the ears of the bellmen I monetarily convinced to bring me food and drink from the nearby grocery store. It's weird, because I live alone, and am happy that way. But at home I've got regular haunts where I can satisfy my slender desire for human companionship.

Melody has cut short both her ski days, leaving later and returning earlier than she would if I were in charge. She claims she's doing it for me and up to a point that's probably true, but I think she's happy her legs aren't as sore as they'd otherwise be. I should feel guilty, deserting her tonight. But dinner with Dr. Lattimore is an enticing proposition.

"You okay in there?" she calls through the cracked bathroom door.

"Sort of. But there's nothing you can do to help."

Getting ready for the evening is proving problematic. As I shower, I keep forgetting about my knee, which has been freed from the brace for the soap-and-water routine. Weighting it gently is fine. But once or twice I move it sideways, and the lateral motion reminds me of the injury. Painfully.

It's nice to immerse myself in familiar perfumes, however. Two days without and, despite spending most of that time sans exertion, I was ripe. Moping makes me perspire, and since it's unearned sweat, it stinks more.

Putting on clothes is also more challenging. Even slipping into panties takes twice as long as it should, since the knee isn't bending much. It's still awfully swollen, despite alternating heat and ice packs and popping Vicoprofen for pain and inflammation, plus straight ibuprofen for the analgesic affect. Rather than try to look sexy — hard to do in this condition — I'm going for a romantic look tonight. Luckily, Melody brought a couple of long, flowing skirts. Definitely more her style than mine, but I'll make it work.

She lays them on the foot of my bed. "Which one do you like?"

"The solid is okay, but I prefer the paisley. I can wear it with my green sweater." That, at least, is sexy — soft angora, cut just low enough to allow a long peek of cleavage without giving away the entire view.

"What about shoes? You can't wear heels."

Damn. "I can't wear UGGs, either."

"Hold on." She goes into the other room, returns with a shoe box. "See if these will work. I saw them in one of the shops today and thought of you."

Inside the box is a soft gold pouch, and inside of that, a pair of ballet flats in matching material. "Thanks, Mel. These are perfect."

I manage makeup and hair without a problem, though I have to sit for the blow-dry. My leg does begin to ache whenever gravity forces too much fluid into the knee. I just pop another pill and keep on. It's only been two days. I can't be hooked yet, can I? It's not that I need one, it's that I want one.

Cavin is picking me up at six forty-five for our seven o'clock reservation. I start to limp down to the lobby, supported by the crutches I can almost maneuver. "What about a jacket?" asks Mel, holding the door.

"It's not that cold out, is it? A jacket will spoil the look."

"I'm sure you'll survive without one, unless your doctor runs his car off into a snowbank and you two are lost for days."

"Don't worry. We'll find a way to stay warm."

She grins. "I'm not worried about that at all. But here, take this just in case." She wraps a pretty crocheted shawl around my shoulders. "It's not real warm, but it will help some. And it doesn't spoil the look. Have an amazing time."

"You sure you're okay here alone?"

"It's only one night. No problem. And, by the way? I kind of like the softer, more feminine you."

"Thanks. But I'll take sexy, with two functional legs, in full open view. Don't wait up for me, Mom."

My date (and how long has it been since I've had an actual date, anyway?) awaits me near the front door. He watches my awkward gait across the lobby, and as I get close, he holds out his hand. "Allow me to help you, madam?"

Wrong, wrong, wrong. It should be miss, or ms. And I shouldn't need help. I feel ridiculous, not that I'd betray a hint of that. "Thank you, kind sir. I think I need a little crutch practice."

"I told you you can find instructional videos on YouTube. Preferable, however, is getting you off those things ASAP. But for tonight, I am happy to assist. My car is right outside."

He steers me to a spotless Audi Quattro, pewter over impeccable white leather still wearing new-car scent, and not the kind the car wash tucks under the seat. I whistle. "Nice ride, Dr. Lattimore."

"Cavin, please. And thank you. It's only a couple of weeks old, so I'm still getting used to it. Hold on." He coaxes the passenger seat all the way back, to better accommodate my unbendable leg. Good thing it's my right one. I'd never manage to get it under the steering wheel.

"Now I see why you said I can't drive for a while. Not going to happen all trussed up like this, that's for sure."

"Hey, I didn't go to medical school for nothing, you know." He leans the crutches against the car, guides me into the plush seat, and helps me swing my legs inside. "We're off. Hold on tight."

"Just don't end up in a snowbank, okay? I didn't bring my coat."

It's a short drive to the restaurant, so conversation en route is minimal and revolves around Cavin being a personal acquaintance of the head chef, whose torn rotator cuff he repaired. "He's always happy to show off a little, so be prepared for something outside of the box."

Turns out, Chef Christopher has a very special prix fixe menu in mind. The maître d' seats us at an intimate table in front of the very real fireplace, burning actual apple wood logs. It is out of the way of foot traffic, so I know Cavin informed them he'd be bringing a disabled date. I am thankful for that, however, as I can stretch my leg straight without bothering anyone except, perhaps, our waiter, who is more than accommodating. "We can push another chair up under the table if you want to elevate that knee," Paolo says.

"Is everyone in the Tahoe service industry familiar with the treatment of orthopedic injuries?" I ask.

"Everyone I know," answers Cavin, grinning.

Paolo hands us our personalized four-course menus. "If there's anything on here you don't like, Chef is happy to substitute."

Eggplant crepes with smoked salmon. Caesar salad. Veal saltimbocca or fresh sea bass, sautéed with garlic, lime, and cilantro. Chocolate chip bread pudding with amaretto cream sauce.

I order the fish; Cavin chooses the veal. Paolo inquires about drinks.

"Do you like champagne?" asks Cavin.

"Only if it's excellent champagne. Are we celebrating something?"

"I think we are," he says. "Cristal?"

"Perfect."

Paolo brings the bottle, pops the cork, and when we raise our flutes, Cavin offers a toast: "To chance meetings."

And I add, "To possibilities."

The Cristal is fabulous, the atmosphere romantic, and if the fragrance can be trusted, the food promises to be sublime. But the company trumps it all. Cavin is charming. Funny. Straightforward. I like that in a man. Cat-and-mouse is such a tiresome game.

"Where are you from originally?" I ask.

"Southern California born and raised, that's me."

"LA?"

"San Diego, but I graduated from UCLA, and that's where I went to med school. How about you?"

I skip over Idaho. No need to sour the lovely atmosphere. "I went to UNLV."

"Vegas? Don't think I've ever met someone who was actually from Las Vegas. It's one of those places you visit, but don't stay."

"I would have left sooner, except I married a man with deep roots there."

"Do tell."

Over delectable eggplant crepes, Cavin hears the story of Raul, minus the strip-club part — omission, which does not strictly qualify as deception.

"I take it that didn't work out?"

"In a manner of speaking. He died in a skiing accident at Heavenly. I was a widow at twenty-three."

"Wow. Sorry. That must have been tough."

"Emotionally, yes. But I was young. Resilient."

Paolo interrupts, refilling our glasses and clearing the first-course plates. It seems like a good time to change the subject, or at least redirect it.

"What about you?" I ask. "Have you ever been married? Oh, wait. It probably seems like a ridiculous question, but . . . you're not married now, right?"

"Would we be here if I was?"

"You never know. Some men find fidel-ity . . . Oh, what's the word I'm looking for? Impossible. Yes, that's it."

Cavin laughs. "Not me. And I've been divorced for eight years."

"Kids?"

"My son, Eli, is seventeen."

"Seventeen? You married young, too, then."

"Way too young. I was twenty, still an undergrad. And I was a father at twenty-two. It was ludicrous, really, maneuvering med school and residencies while trying to keep a wife and child happy."

Quick calculations net Cavin's approximate age. Thirty-nine. Good number. "Does Eli live with you?"

"No. When Melissa and I split up, she returned to LA, and he went with her. Then she met her new husband, who moved them to Sacramento. Eli goes to a boarding school in the Bay Area while she and Russell circle the globe."

"Sounds like fun. Is Russell a pilot?"

"No, a politician. A diplomat."

"Oh. Poor Melissa."

"What makes you say that?"

I sip my champagne, deciding how much to confess. "My second husband was a politician. When Raul died, he left me secure financially, but I had no clue what to do with myself. I was a business major, but not cut out for the day-to-day oversight of six pawnshops. I decided to hire interns to deal with the nitty-gritty and focus on the S corp management and investment strategies. That left me a lot of free time.

"It happened to be an election year, so I volunteered to campaign for a Republican legislator from southern Nevada. Don't ask me why. I'd never given a thought to politics before. In fact, I'd never registered to vote before. But Jordan and I happened to have mutual friends. One night I went to a fund-raiser. We met, hit it off, and by the time election night rolled around, I stood by his side at his acceptance speech, not as a campaign worker, but rather as his new bride."

"Love at first stump?"

The silly joke draws my wry smile. "I guess I thought so then. I'm not sure I had a clue what love was. To tell you the truth, I'm still not sure I know."

Why did I say that? Pain pills, champagne, or the combination, that was a very big admission. Too big for a first date. Maybe any date. Cavin could be put off completely. Instead, he prods gently, "Surely you don't mean that."

I shrug. "Maybe not. But attraction and love are two different things, and hindsight, I've heard told, is twenty-twenty."

Paolo delivers our second course, and I'm glad to veer away from frank discussions of love — or the lack of it. As dinner progresses, we continue to share very personal information. By the time the bread pudding arrives, he knows my second marriage lasted eleven years, during which I learned more than I ever wanted to about deep pockets, corporate influence, and backroom negotiations. When Jordan decided to run for the US Senate, I issued an ultimatum. He chose DC.

The split was amicable — so amicable that I suspected infidelity. That proved accurate, and not with one woman but several. The settlement was overly generous. In exchange, I promised to keep his dubious morality, personal and professional, our little secret. Eight months later I met Finley Cannon at a Vegas trade show. He steered me straight into the fast lane and moved me to San Francisco.

"What about children?" Cavin asks.

"Nothing about my life has been conducive to parenting. But I never really craved the experience, or regretted my decision not to have children." And if I ever needed a reminder, all I had to do was visit Melody for a couple of days. Other than the raging-hormones thing, her kids aren't so bad now. But when they were younger? Insanity. "Do you enjoy being a father?"

He looks away, stares at the fire for a silent few seconds. "I was so busy when Eli was little, I don't remember much of his child-hood. I taught him to ride a bike, and to snowboard, and those days are pleasant memories. Now I don't see him very often. School holidays, sometimes, and over the summer break. He's grown into a stranger, really. I know he's smart — genius-level IQ — but his grades don't always reflect that. And he's manipulative."

He doesn't elaborate, and though my curiosity is screaming for more, it probably isn't wise to ask for details. "I have a niece who's that age. I think all teenagers are manipulative, up to a point. Always looking for detours around the rules. It comes with the 'I'm grown-up, you can't tell me what to do' thing. I had the same attitude. In fact, I still don't much care for rules."

"Ah, see, but medicine is all about rules. Which is why I feel the desperate need to escape every now and then."

Chef Christopher emerges from the kitchen and comes over to the table, seeking praise. When I reward him with a healthy dose, he offers a nightcap, which Cavin and I are happy to accept. By the time Paolo brings the bill, I'm just a bit blurry around the edges, and that is a rare delight.

Cavin tries to hand Paolo his credit card,

but I'm clear enough to stop him. "My treat, remember?"

"But I wouldn't have ordered the Cristal."

"That's okay. I would have."

Cavin surrenders reluctantly.

"Have you never had a woman buy you dinner before?"

"Actually, no."

"I think you need to set your sights higher."

He smiles. "I think I just have."

THIRTEEN

It's still relatively early when Cavin drops me back at the hotel. He pulls up as close as he can get to the door, comes around to help me out, waving away the bellman. "How do you feel about kissing in public?"

"With the right man, I'd do more than kiss in public, though maybe not in full view of a hotel lobby."

He laughs gently, pulls me into his arms. "We shall remain circumspect. For the moment."

His amaretto-laced kiss is respectful. That in itself is unusual enough, but what's ridiculous is how much it's turning me on. Maybe it's the float of Black Orchid cologne over the cling of Italian food. Maybe it's the soft pillow of his lips, or the way our tongues seem like old friends, just saying hello. Whatever it is, I want more.

Apparently, so does Cavin. When he pulls back, maintaining circumspectness, his face doesn't retreat very far. "I'm surgery-free tomorrow. May I play tour guide, and perhaps cook dinner for you?"

"You can repair broken bodies and manage a kitchen, too?"

"I am a man of many talents, milady."

"That, I believe. And I'd love to."

He brushes his lips against mine, a promise in the gesture. "I'll pick you up around one, if that works for you."

"Absolutely."

I can feel his eyes on my back, watching my lurching gait. "We'll spend a little time practicing that," he calls. "I'll even teach you how to do stairs."

Tonight I avoid stairs and take the elevator up to the room. Mel is still awake. "Waiting up for me?" I ask.

"Well, of course. Do you think I could sleep? How did it go?"

"Okay."

"Okay? Just okay?"

"Okay, it was better than okay. I prefer not to jinx myself." I give her a run-down, from the antipasti to the dolce. "We really connected. No sex of course . . ." I gesture to my leg. "Jeez. I wonder how long it will be before that's a viable possibility."

"When was the last time you had dinner with a man — not work related — that

119

didn't result in sex?"

Valid question. "Considering I've been married most of my adult life, albeit to three different men, my dinner dates not related to work have been rarer than you might assume. And, believe it or not, they haven't all led to sex. I do have standards."

"Good to know. Does that include the men you pick up in bars?"

Ouch. "So you know, that isn't something I do very often, either. But, yes. And my first rule, always, is that they're not married. Casual sex is one thing. Adultery is something else altogether."

"Why don't you just masturbate? It would be safer."

"Yeah, but a whole lot less fun. Anyway, I was almost thirty before I masturbated. It took marriage to make that happen. Singlehood is the very time to audition a partner or two."

"Audition. So you're in the market for a serious relationship?"

"I'm not exactly shopping, but should one present itself, of course." And now, because I don't want to discuss my sex life, let alone my probably obtuse sense of morality, I inform her, "By the way, Cavin is picking me up tomorrow afternoon. He wants to show me some of his favorite places, and then cook dinner for me."

Mel huffs. "You want me to spend another evening alone?"

"Normally, I'd never ask it of you. You know that. But I think whatever is happening between Cavin and me could be something really special."

I do, and that is strange. I'm generally not a believer in the hazy notion of fate. I'm far more of the "take charge and make things happen" kind of girl. But this feels different. It feels out of my control.

"I guess I can't argue with that," says Mel, though it comes out a thin whine. "Especially since you'll be spending the holidays with us. I already told Graham to make sure the downstairs guest room is made up for you."

"I'm sure he's *super* excited, too."

"Oh, come on. Why is it you think Graham doesn't like you?"

Dirty looks. Disparaging remarks. The way he tunes out completely anytime I'm talking. What Mel will never know is that when they first started dating, good ol' Graham tried to put the moves on me. I told him if I ever found out he'd cheated on my sister, I'd kick his spindly ass. That was back in the day when I used such colloquialisms. I've cultivated my language over the years.

Once in a while, I still think rural Idaho trash talk, but it's rare for me to utter it out loud.

"I'm afraid Graham is under the impression you and I have way too much fun on these trips. Your husband, dear sister, considers me a bad influence." That part is no doubt true.

Mel laughs. "Well, we can't get into too much trouble wrapping Christmas presents and such. Anyway, he didn't complain when I told him you were staying with us for a while."

He probably got a good chuckle over the reason. He came skiing with us exactly once and spent most of his time riding my wake. Some men get pissy about stuff like that.

"Hey," Mel says. "Wouldn't it be interesting if we both end up married to doctors?"

"Whoa, Speed Racer, slow down, would you? I wouldn't mind getting married again someday, but that day is a long way off. Besides, Cavin and I have just barely kissed. I'd definitely need to take him for a test drive, if you know what I mean. And that won't happen tomorrow."

"Good. Maybe it's you who needs to slow down, and this was God's way of showing you that."

"God? You think God sent that guy

careening into me so I couldn't have sex with strangers?"

"God can do wondrous things. This one would be a rather mundane task for him, I imagine."

I study her face, her body language. She isn't kidding. "Just when did you discover God?"

She shrugs. "I've been going to church for a while."

That's news to me. "Really? How long?"

"Five or six years."

"Why haven't you ever mentioned it?"

"I figured it would probably annoy you."

You are correct about that, little sister.

Our mother took us to church on those rare Sunday mornings when she wasn't fighting a hangover. Insisted we believe in a holy trinity that nothing about her represented. I suppose when I was very, very young I had some small morsel of belief. But that crumbled as soon as I realized the Jesus she claimed to worship expected things she never even tried to deliver. Specifically, things like loving others more than herself.

Especially her children.

"Does your family go to church with you?"

"The girls do. Well, usually. Kayla makes excuses sometimes."

"And Graham?"

"Graham sleeps in on Sundays. He says if I have a problem with that, I should take it up with God."

"Why? Because God expects women to be subservient?"

She smiles. "No, dear. Because God made Sunday a day of rest."

"Oh. Right."

As our mother herself might say, I forgot more Bible than I ever knew.

Thank God.

FOURTEEN

Cavin picks me up at one o'clock on the dot. I like promptness in a man. Better to make him wait a few minutes if necessary than to sit, anticipating his arrival. I, too, am right on time this afternoon, however. And when I exit the hotel, I'm glad I brought my jacket. The wind has fangs today.

"It's supposed to storm this afternoon," Cavin explains as I finesse my way into the Audi. "The road around Emerald Bay can get hairy. In fact, they often close it in winter. Right now, it's clear, so we've got a good chance of outracing the weather. The view, especially if you've never seen it, is worth the risk, in my humble opinion. But it's up to you."

"I'm always up for an adventure."

"As I suspected."

He drives cautiously enough as we motor south through town and turn west onto

Highway 89, through a beautiful tract of old-growth forest. "I thought they clear-cut the lake in the eighteen hundreds," I say, showing off my rudimentary knowledge of local history.

"They pretty much did. Virginia City needed the timber to shore up its silver mines. But the family who owned this particular property happened to be early environmentalists who wanted to preserve the forest. Hold on." He turns off the highway and onto a street marked Valhalla. "This is the Tallac Historic Site. Once upon a time, the wealthy partied here. Now you can rent the historic mansion for weddings, et cetera."

"So, the wealthy still party here?"

"I guess that's an accurate statement. I'd park and show you around. The buildings really are quite lovely. But it's more work than that leg needs right now. And besides, it's starting to flurry."

Tiny feathers of snow drift down, melting as soon as they hit the warm windshield. "Think it's okay to keep going?"

"Yeah. It will be hours before this becomes anything real."

Cavin steers the Audi back onto the highway, and now he picks up speed. The road soon becomes a curvy climb, and I enjoy watching him put the car through its motions, downshifting instead of braking whenever possible. Finally we crest the pass, and here the highway becomes extremely narrow. Tahoe comes into sight, far below, and we reach a spot where we can also see Cascade Lake, to the south. "Wow. You were right. The view is amazing."

"Just wait."

A few minutes later, he pulls into a turnout, well off the highway. He comes around to help me out of the car and walk me to the brink of a several-hundred-foot vertical drop. A waterfall careens down over the granite, disappearing into the rock face, then reappearing again in a series of fountains. Emerald Bay glistens, green beneath bursts of sunlight fighting the flurries, as fists of wind pummel our backs, urging us toward a precarious plunge.

Cavin steps behind me, encircles me with his muscular arms, and for a millisecond I get a flash of menace. That fraction of a thought should bring me discomfort. Instead, it's thrilling somehow. Wonder what it would be like to step over.

With my feet firmly planted, Cavin lifts my snow-frosted hair, kisses my neck. "Beautiful, isn't it?"

"Breathtaking."

"You're not afraid of heights?"

"I'm not afraid of anything."

Cavin tugs me gently backward, steps between the cliff's edge and me, looks down into my eyes. "I love fearlessness in a woman. Can't stand the helpless-female ploy."

I smile. "My sister says I'm reckless."

"Are you?"

"Not at all. I'm a calculated risk taker."

"That makes two of us."

He kisses me, boldly this time, no one to observe but the birds fast on the wing toward cover, as it starts to snow more heavily. I return his kiss with every ounce of passion I can muster, more sure with each passing second that this connection is very real. Eventually, however, the need for air, plus the threat of a blizzard, pulls us apart.

"Maybe we'd better go before we get stranded," I suggest.

"I suppose you're right. We still have quite a little drive ahead of us."

A thin white veneer slicks the asphalt, and I'm comforted by the Audi's solid German engineering as we cruise down past the Rubicon bluffs and around the meadows of Meeks Bay, through Tahoma and into Tahoe City. It is snowing earnestly now, and we creep along behind a line of overcautious drivers. By the time we reach Incline Village, it's late afternoon, the solstice daylight failing.

"I had planned to cook dinner for you, but my kid showed up last night, sulky as ever. I thought he was spending winter break with his mom, but turns out she and Russell decided to go to Hawaii, sans adolescent attitude."

"I see."

"Actually, you'd have to meet Eli to really understand. He's a difficult kid. I'd go ahead and introduce you, but I'm afraid you'd run the other way without looking back."

"I told you, I don't scare easily. Anyway, I doubt I'll be doing much running for quite a while."

Cavin laughs. "Guess I should choose my words more carefully. Tell you what. I know this great hamburger joint. Why don't we grab a bite now, then we'll swing by the house for dessert and you can meet Kid-zilla? That way we have a fair-to-middling chance of getting you back to your hotel before they break out the plows."

"I am hugely disappointed that I will not be able to observe your culinary expertise, but I do understand."

The burgers, at least, don't disappoint,

and the fries are worth every fat-soaked bite. Good thing I didn't eat earlier. He's driving much more carefully now; it's another half hour around to the east shore and Cavin's Glenbrook home, which is perched on a forested hill across the highway from the lake. Up the road climbs, flanked by tall Douglas fir and sugar pine trees.

We pull into what must be a heated driveway, for the snow melts in thin tracks, and park beside a late-model Hummer. "Eli's car?"

Cavin nods. "A birthday gift from his stepfather."

"Wow."

"Indeed."

He comes around to open the passenger door and finesse me to my feet. When I stand, my eyes have a hard time processing what they see. Even from the driveway, the view over and through the trees to the water is drop-jaw gorgeous.

"I never thought a view could rival my own, but I guess I was wrong."

"Most people think lakefront property is preferable, but I like being up here, away from the traffic. I can always find a beach if I want one. The main problem is maneuvering this hill when the weather turns crazy."

"Have you ever gotten snowed in?"

"Absolutely, on many occasions. Come on. I'll help you inside."

Cavin slides an arm beneath my shoulder blades and lifts slightly, relieving the weight on my ridiculously loose knee. He guides me along the snow-slicked walkway to the front door. The main entry opens straight into a great room, with big glass windows framing the travel-poster vista. No partitions separate the kitchen, dining area, and living room, which boasts a massive stone fireplace on the far wall. There is little in the way of artwork, and no carpets cover the hardwood floor. Compared to the modern gleam above white carpeting that is my house, this one defines Tahoe-rustic, and yet it's completely inviting.

"Home, sweet home," says Cavin, directing me to a chair. "Make yourself comfortable. Wine?"

I consider. "Don't suppose you could approximate a sidecar?"

"Approximate? I believe I can accommodate." He goes over to the wet bar, tucked away in a corner of the great room, and busies himself with cognac, triple sec, and a squeeze of fresh lemon.

I observe appreciatively. "You are a doctor of many talents."

"Thank you. But to be fair, you haven't

seen anything yet." He pours club soda for himself, brings the sidecar to me.

"Trying to quit?"

He shakes his head and points toward the window. Just beyond, snowflakes the size of half-dollars tumble from the sky and collect into decent slush on the big deck. "I think a sober driver is in order this evening. I've got crème brûlée in the fridge. Eli must be downstairs in his room. Should I ask him to join us?"

"Of course."

"I'd yell for him, but he'd never hear me. His current method of tuning out the world is Viking metal through headphones. Be right back."

Cavin picks up a remote sitting on the black granite countertop, presses a button to turn on some music. Gin Blossoms.

He isn't gone very long. The tick of his footsteps, light against wooden stairs, precedes him. And once he reappears, the noise follows him into the kitchen, where he extracts three bowls of crème brûlée from the stainless steel refrigerator. I assume that means Eli will make an appearance soon, and he does.

His approach sounds much heavier than Cavin's, and I expect a hulk of a kid. Instead, the boy who comes through the door has the look of a distance runner — tall, like his father, but not particularly bulky. And, despite his overly long wheat-colored hair, which could really use a stylish cut, he carries Cavin's charmed good looks, including those storm-cloud eyes. Exceptional genetics.

"Hello, Eli. I'm Tara."

He doesn't respond immediately, at least not verbally. But he lowers his eyes to meet mine, and the connection is discomfiting, like a static electric shock. "Hi."

"Sorry if I don't get up, but —"

"It's okay," he interrupts. "I can see what your problem is."

I can't quite interpret the connotation. Literal? Sarcastic? Accusing? I choose to play ignorant. "Yeah, well, it was not my best day skiing, and it trashed my vacation."

"That's too bad. My mom trashed my vacation."

Cavin seems to be trying too hard not to sound hurt. "Hey, now. Your vacation has just begun. There's some fine snow up on that mountain."

"Which would be great," Eli responds, "except for all the tourists tracking it up, not to mention face-planting."

The intent of his statement is clear. Game on. "Don't worry. It's not the tracks that will get you. It's the guy who decides he's equal to a run that's way over his head. That's a clear and present danger." I wink at him, and he actually smiles.

Cavin brings a tray over, allows me to choose my bowl, and then sets the rest on the coffee table. "Hope you like. It's a specialty of the house."

It's amazing, and that's what I tell him. Then I turn to Eli, who's picking the brown sugar crust off the custard. "Your father says you go to school in the Bay Area."

"Yeah. The Athenian. Lucky me. My mom figured I needed better grooming if I wanted half a chance at Stanford."

"I see. Stanford's tough, all right. It's very ambitious of you."

"Uh, Stanford is her idea. Not mine."

"Oh. Well, I happen to be acquainted with the Athenian."

"Really?"

"In a roundabout way. I have a friend whose son goes there. Do you, by any chance, know Taylor Andaman?"

"Everyone knows everyone at the Athenian." Which doesn't exactly answer my question. "So, are all your friends rich?"

"Eli . . ." warns Cavin.

"That's okay," I soothe. "Actually, most of the people I know are well-off, yes."

"Including you?"

"Why? Is that important?"

He heaves his shoulders. "Nope. Not to me. But it's a prerequisite if you want to date Dad."

"Eli!" Cavin shifts his weight as if to rise.

I put a hand on his knee to stop him and lock eyes with the brat. "Nothing wrong with having high standards, is there?"

Eli smiles, revealing teeth that must be the product of excellent orthodontia. "Personally, I prefer slumming. Rich women are boring."

"Not nearly as boring as privileged kids."

His grin dissolves. "You just might have a point. Well, if you'll excuse me, pudding has a laxative effect on me."

Nice. He leaves his bowl, brown sugar shards crusting the sides, on the coffee table, starts toward the door. "Great meeting you, Eli." And he's gone. I turn to Cavin and smile. "That went well, don't you think?"

He grimaces. "At least you didn't run. Finish your drink while I load the dishwasher. Then I'd better get you back to your hotel."

By the time we're on our way, maybe three inches of snow have accumulated on the roads. It's slow going, and I'm grateful that

Cavin chose to play designated driver. One small lapse of judgment could lead to serious consequences. Unlike most of the other men in my life, this one is cautious, and while that might once have bothered me, tonight I appreciate his prudence.

"Thank you for a great day." I don't want to distract him, but I need him to know I'm interested in pursuing something more, so I rest my hand on his leg, just above his knee.

"No. Thank *you.*" He lifts my hand to his lips and then replaces it, a bit closer to his inner thigh. "Meeting you was quite unexpected, and absolutely my pleasure."

"Would that I could pleasure you more. But this is definitely a case of wrong time, wrong place."

"No apology necessary. I'm happy to accept your IOU. Tomorrow's your last day here, yes?"

"That's right. We'll probably just kick back. Melody's done a lot more skiing than she's used to. And I . . . Well, I don't really have much of a choice. Just so you know, Doc Lattimore, this injury really stinks."

"It's a bad one. If you have any questions about presurgical rehab, don't hesitate to call. You've got my number."

"Can I call even if I don't have any questions?"

"If you don't call me, I'll call you."

He pulls up in front of the hotel and parks. I'm reluctant to say good-bye. "If you ever decide to give up doctoring, you could become a tour guide. Thanks for the private excursion."

"Anytime. And the encore will be even better."

His kiss good-bye is filled with promise.

ENIGMA

You are roused into the dark
soup of morning, crawl your way out
of a green dream of summer.
One foot explores the far side
of the quilts, withdraws again, stung
by subzero tentacles that have infiltrated
the weather stripping.

You want to slip back
into the ignorance of slumber,
but a jolt of frustration has jump-started
your brain, and once the words
have coalesced, they repeat themselves,
a stutter: *It's a long, long way to June.*
There is no detour except to rise.

But this day brings a singular
reward, for in the frozen
night, a fog has lifted, crowning
barren branches with tiaras of ice.
Against an azure mantle, they shimmer
in soft December sunlight, dazzle
cynical eyes, then melt like memories.

Upon the hoarfrost, you spy a flutter
of rust and fix your gaze on
the feathered enigma — a robin, huddled

in the cold white snare. Framed by the
  tangle,
he is a picture of despair and you wonder
why a creature capable of flight
would choose to stay and weather winter.

FIFTEEN

I expect to find Mel sitting in front of the fake fire, comfortably reading or watching TV. Instead, she's pacing. "Oh, thank God," she says when I totter through the door. "You're back early. I didn't want to call and bother you if you were having a good time, but . . . Wait. What happened? Why are you back early? It didn't involve pepper spray, did it?"

"Not even. It involved snow. You do realize it's dumping outside, right?"

"It is? I mean it flurried a little up on the mountain, but when I got the text I came back down to try and manage a little damage control. Is it supposed to quit?"

"I don't know. Why? And what text? Mel, I have no idea what you're talking about." There are, like, five conversations going on at once, and they're all coming out of Melody's mouth.

She flops on the sofa, crestfallen. "It's

Kayla. She's having an episode."

"Episode?"

"Sometimes she goes a little off the deep end. She's threatening suicide."

"Because of her boyfriend?"

"He's not her boyfriend anymore. But no, he's not the reason. Apparently, she's getting a B minus in American History, despite massive extra-credit work, and she's certain her GPA will condemn her to community college."

This is keeping my sister away from the latest HBO miniseries? "But she'd never do something so extreme over something so not extreme. Right?"

"I don't know," she admits. "Sometimes I worry she inherited the family *gene.*"

"You mean Mom's BPD."

She nods. "It often manifests in late adolescence, and she seems to demonstrate some of the symptoms, including over-the-top reactions to relatively insignificant things. Not to mention relationship problems. I feel sorry for Jeff."

"Jeff?"

"Her last boyfriend. They were together almost a year."

"The 'squeaky little a-hole'?"

"Is that what she called him? He's such a nice young man. She just kept seeing things that weren't there."

"You mean, like ghosts?"

Mel rolls her eyes. "No. Like disrespect or inattentiveness."

That does sound like our mother, who demanded respect and attention. "Has she seen a therapist?"

"Yes, but don't tell Graham. He insists she has no problems beyond the usual female kind. BPD is difficult to diagnose correctly, and is often confused with other things. Not only that, but medications are hard to get right, especially in teenagers. Antidepressants can actually exacerbate suicidal thoughts in young people. Anyway, if it's okay with you and we can travel safely tomorrow, I'd like to cut our vacation short a day. What do you think?"

Oh, great. Extra time at the Schumacher abode, while their oldest daughter flips out and has a giant meltdown over a B minus grade, and her father just nods and says whatever. I seriously must rehab the knee while I'm there so I can get myself home ASAP. "If that's what you need to do. Not like I'll miss a whole lot if I don't hang around here."

I call down to the desk and ask for a local weather report. "Clearing by midmorning" is the answer. Assuming that's close to cor-

143

rect, we should make it no problem, especially once the roads have been plowed. The Escalade is all-wheel drive and would make it anyway, but I'm not always comfortable driving in a blizzard. No way would I trust Melody to get us over that mountain in a whiteout.

Regardless, looks like we'll be able to leave, so we decide to go ahead and pack up. Before I start, I spend a few minutes online, ordering rush delivery gifts. Christmas is on Friday. We can pick up the iPhone at an Apple Store near where Mel lives on the way home. The Sports Authority gift card should arrive no later than Thursday. The Art Institute is trickier, so for now I'll just give Kayla cash and a promise to make some inquiries. Maybe that will make her relax about her report card.

This trip was my gift to Mel, but I should probably get something for Graham. Let's see. What's a good gift for a self-centered prick who refuses to acknowledge the possibility that his daughter might be a little unstable? Maybe a copy of *Mental Illness for Dummies*? Okay, probably not.

As I'm thinking about it, it occurs to me that I should probably let Cavin know we're departing tomorrow. I call, expecting to leave a voice mail. Instead, he picks up. "Oh, hello. Sorry to bother you. I didn't think you'd answer."

"No bother. Just sitting here, watching it snow. What's up?"

"I wanted to tell you that we're cutting out of here a day early. One of Mel's kids is having some health issues." Not exactly a lie.

"Oh. Sorry to hear that."

"She'll be okay. Just needs her mother. Hey, while I've got you, you're a good person to ask. I'm trying to figure out what to get Mel's husband for Christmas. What's a good present for a pediatrician with a bad attitude?"

He laughs. "When in doubt, gift liquor. It's every off-duty doctor's best friend, and a surefire mood enhancer."

"Alcohol. Of course. A nice añejo should do. Many thanks for the suggestion."

"Anytime, fair lady. Safe travel over the pass. Oh, by the way. I'll be coming through San Francisco next month."

"Really? Business or pleasure?"

"Both, I guess. The headmaster at Eli's school wants me to stop by for a 'discussion.' He wouldn't elaborate over the phone."

"Sounds ominous."

"There's a lot about my son that sounds

ominous. He seems relatively mellow at the moment, however. But anyway, after my visit to the principal's office, I'm planning a short vacation. I keep a house in Carmel so I can escape the mountains in favor of the ocean a couple of times a year. I'm still a San Diego boy at heart, I guess. If you'll be around, I'd like to stop by and see how that knee's coming."

"I'm not going anywhere. Give me a heads-up and maybe I'll cook for you."

"I accept your generous invitation. And I'll bring the Cristal."

One thing's been pestering me, so I unshrink my inner violet and blurt, "Will you be spending Christmas with anyone special? I mean . . . I'm sorry to be blunt, but are you seeing anyone else? I dislike unpleasant surprises."

"I'd rather you be blunt than coy. And I'll answer your question the same way. I go out from time to time, and once or twice I thought I might get serious about someone, but I currently maintain no love interest. And truthfully, I haven't enjoyed a recent date anywhere near as much as I've enjoyed being with you. As for Christmas, Eli and I will probably ski and get takeout. Afterward, I'll ply myself with heavily spiked eggnog and watch *It's a Wonderful Life* alone, while he hangs out in his room, playing World of Warcraft or something. Sounds kind of pathetic, huh?"

"Actually, it sounds better than Christmas at Mel's, though you might want to skip pudding for dessert. And thanks for your honesty."

"Dishonesty is the surest way I know to ruin a relationship. I have nothing to hide."

That I doubt. Everyone has something to hide.

SIXTEEN

The drive back to Sacramento was a tedious slog, plenty of time to consider the ins and outs of this budding relationship. Logistically, there are plenty of problems. Distance. Schedules. Deep snow over the mountain passes. All those are conquerable, however, if we discover a true desire to be together.

I've been at Mel's for four days now, enough time to dampen the initial attraction, but all it's done is make me want to see Cavin again, and soon. It's strange, because I've never felt exactly this way about a man, especially not one I know so little. I can't call the feeling love, but it could be its predecessor. Maybe? I'm not certain.

With way too much time on my hands, and scant entertainment, I've been dissecting my life. Other than total financial stability, there's not a whole lot to like about it. My mother and her string of miserable men made the first eighteen years unbearable. And while there were decent periods during my marriages, the bad outweighed the good in the end. I married all three men for stability. There might have been romance, but nothing I felt for any of them approached love. At least I don't think so.

The absolute truth is, people like me aren't meant to fall in love. I'm completely in the dark about that experience, so how will I know if that's what this thing with Cavin will become? Pathetic. I sound like a twelve-year-old girl.

I know that for a fact because I've been listening to a twelve-year-old girl argue with her fifteen-year-old sister ever since I got here. And when she's not doing that, she's on the phone with her friends, discussing the facets of upper-middle-class preteen existence. Basically, this means that though they have not one valid thing to whine about, they complain about everything. It's alternately fascinating and maddening.

Right now, in fact, I hear Jessica say, "I want to open presents tonight. *Everyone* opens presents on Christmas Eve except *my* family."

Pause for a response.

"I don't know. Dad says if we open them tonight, tomorrow won't be as much fun."

Pause for a response.

"I'm pretty sure I got an iPhone. It better be the new one."

It is. One hundred twenty-eight gigs, too. That phone can do everything but pay for itself, but she'll probably complain that it's not the right color. In a way, I understand that Mel wants to spoil her daughters, and not just with stuff. She showers them with compliments and encouragement, even when they don't deserve it, over-compensating for her own sterile childhood.

My cell rings and I grab for it, sure it must be Cavin. But no. It's Finn. "Merry Christmas," he says, and I can hear Pregnant Barbie chattering in the background.

I choke back my distaste. After all, I did ask for a favor. "You, too. What's up?"

"That thing you wanted? Handled." Finn is a man of few words.

"Already?"

"I happened to run into the right person at a party last night. He said it shouldn't be a problem. I'll give you details later, but figured you'd like to know."

"Thank you, Finn. I suppose I owe you one."

"No, but this makes us closer to even. Have a great evening."

150

The power of connections. I've learned to never, ever underestimate it. Even in matters of divorce, burning bridges is generally counterproductive to forward movement. Not that revenge is a bad thing, as long as it remains anonymous. But what if something you need lies buried on the far side of the river behind you?

Mel's planning a big Christmas dinner tomorrow — turkey or ham or whatever — so tonight it's pizza, ordered in from a great little local pizzeria. Suz comes to get me, knocking on the open guest room door.

"Aunt Tara? We're ready to eat. Can I help you?" Of the three kids, she's the only one who cares to understand the extent of my knee injury, mostly because she participates in the kinds of sports that could net her a similar catastrophe.

"I think I've got it, thanks."

I've found if I'm very careful about any sort of sideways movement, I can manage to limp around the house sans crutches. The hallways are narrow, the distance between rooms relatively short. I make my way to the kitchen, where we're eating tonight instead of the formal dining room, which is already set for tomorrow's celebration.

Pizza fragrance hits my nose immediately, all yeast and garlic. "Oh my God, that smells heavenly. But two pizzas in as many weeks? Before the one I shared with Mel at Tahoe, I don't think I've touched pizza in over a year."

"Why not?" asks Jessica, who's at the counter, helping herself to a slice.

"Should be obvious," comments Graham, coming up behind me. "She's afraid it will go straight to her butt."

"Graham!" Mel spins, turning her back on the apples she's slicing for tomorrow's pie. "That was rude."

"Was it? Sorry." Okay, he's obviously halfway to inebriated, but still.

"That's okay. He's right. When you hit forty, you have to be careful with carbs, no matter how hard you work out. Once in a while, however, you should just go ahead and indulge, and that's what I plan to do."

"Suz, would you please go call Kayla to dinner?" asks Mel.

"Kayla! Dinner!" Suzette's shout reverberates off the carnation-pink walls.

"That's not what I meant. I could have done that."

"Don't worry about her," says Graham. "She'll eat if and when she gets hungry."

He carries his plate to the dinette, slides across the alcove bench, making room for Jessica. I sit on a chair at the end of the

152

table, where I can stretch out my legs.

"Why are you so sullen tonight?" Mel directs the question toward her husband.

Graham shrugs. "Extended-family pizza night. Always a good time."

Kayla sweeps into the kitchen. "Pizza. Yum."

"Hey," says Graham. "Bring me a beer."

Just what he needs. Man, he's always a little cool, but rarely does he get outright pissy. "What's wrong, Graham? In need of a snotty-nosed-kid fix or what?"

The girls all laugh, and their father flushes a fabulous cranberry shade. But before he can respond, Mel loudly pops a Heineken, hands him the bottle. "Well, we're very happy to have you all to ourselves for a few days."

Not a single soccer mom in sight. Maybe that's what he's missing. I search for conversation. "So, Mel says you're in a band, Graham."

He actually smiles. "That's right. We're even booking gigs."

"What kind of music do you play?"

"Old music," says Suzette.

"Lame music," adds Kayla.

"What, no hip-hop?" I ask.

"Grunge," explains Graham.

"Ah," I say. "A return to your glory days."

His smile dissolves and we retreat into wordless reverie, finish our pizza that way. Every now and then, I glance around the table. No one looks happy to be here, despite the deliciousness on our plates. Food can't fix this family. Strangely, I didn't realize it was so broken. It took total immersion to see it.

I clear my throat. "Normally, I'd be happy to wait until tomorrow morning to open presents, as per Schumacher family tradition. But I think everyone could use a little holiday cheer tonight. Shall we adjourn to the living room?"

Graham shoots me one nasty look, but the girls whoop and clear the table. I leave the room to let him argue it out with Mel, commenting as I go, "I've got something for you, too, Graham. Maybe it will make you feel better."

In my experience, tequila only makes one meaner, but perhaps the exceptional quality of this particular bottle will have a different effect on him. Or maybe he'll skip the experience altogether and wander off to bed. I go to my room, gather the gifts I haven't bothered to wrap. Hmm. The liquor and crystal shot glasses are still in their plastic bag. That will do. I tuck everything else in there, too. What the hell?

The family, including Graham and two tail-thumping dogs, is in the living room, where Melody has turned on the Christmas tree lights and some soft holiday music. "Sorry I didn't get around to making these pretty, but it's what's inside the paper that counts anyway, right?"

I reach into the bag. First up, "This one's for you, Suz." I hand her the Sports Authority gift card, value: $750. "I checked out some boards online. This should cover one shredding Burton, plus some hard-core bindings. Oh, and next ski trip, you're invited along."

Suzette's face lights up. "Thanks, Aunt Tara! Hey, can we try Kirkwood? All my friends say it rocks."

"I don't see why not." It's a long way from any casino action, but that wouldn't be a concern, anyway, with a teenager along.

"Okay, for Jessica. I hope it's the right color." I offer her the small white box.

"One hundred twenty-eight gigs? Who cares what color it is? Look, Mom!" She dances across the room to show off her new iPhone, then twirls back to give me a hug. "Thank you! How did you know this is what I wanted?"

"It's what every girl wants, isn't it? I can help set it up if you want. I have one just like it, except mine is black. Oh . . ." I reach back into the bag. "Here's a case, the kind with a battery. I have a feeling you'll use it."

Now I hold out the bag. "Hope you'll enjoy this, Graham. A friend of mine says doctors need to let their hair down when they take a few days off." Obviously, he could use more than a few, but I tuck that away.

He reaches into the bag, reluctantly, as if expecting a gag gift. Or a spider. Instead, he extracts the glasses first, and then the tequila. When he reads the label, he gives a low whistle. "Single barrel, aged eleven years? This must have cost a pretty penny."

"Enough so you don't want to add mixers. That's sipping tequila right there. Have a taste. And, if you don't mind, pour me one, too. Please and thank you."

What can he do but comply? As he busies himself, I turn to Kayla, who is looking at me expectantly. "As for you, I hear you've got a dream college in mind."

She nods. "But I don't think I can get in there."

"I think you can. Finn is acquainted with someone on the board. I asked him to put in a good word for you. He called earlier. Said it's all taken care of."

"Really?" she squeals, like a kid coming

down a very tall slide. "You mean it?"

"Hold on just a minute," interrupts Graham, handing me a glass. He takes a sip out of his, tilts his head approvingly. But then he remembers his objection. "Even if they'll let you in, we can't afford it, Kayla. Not unless you get a scholarship, and you know your grades aren't good enough."

"But, Dad —"

"I'll take care of it, Graham. That's my Christmas present to Kayla." I lift the glass up under my nose, inhaling the sharp scent before tasting.

"I won't hear of it."

"Why not?" Kayla screeches.

Graham tries to remain calm. "It's too much money. I'd be in her debt forever."

"No, you wouldn't," I say. "This has nothing to do with you."

"It has everything to do with me! If I can't do this for my daughter, no one will." He downs his drink, slams the glass on the coffee table with enough force that I'm sure it will shatter. Somehow, it survives.

Kayla dissolves into tears. "Daddy, please . . ." Daddy. Nice touch.

"This is not up for discussion." He exits in a huff, goes upstairs to his bedroom, leaving the tequila on the table, still open.

I think that's an invitation. I pour myself

another, offer, "How about you, Mel? A little fortitude before you try to placate your husband?"

"Better not." She trails after him, followed by the dog duo.

The two younger girls excuse themselves — Jessica to go fiddle with her new phone, and Suz to peruse the Sports Authority website. Kayla stays put. "Why is he such an asswipe?" she asks.

"Most men are asswipes."

"Why?"

"Beats me. Some leftover Neanderthal tic that makes them believe they're the superior sex."

"Maybe I'll just become a lesbian."

I laugh. "I don't think that's something you become, but I know what you mean. On the other hand, the thing about men is they're utterly predictable. Women, not so much."

"You mean you could have predicted that my dad would be a jerk about the Art Institute?"

"Actually, I did foretell this very reaction. Your father never really liked me much, and he resents the fact that I can take care of the tuition when he can't."

"That doesn't mean he has to be rude." She watches me sip the smooth amber tequila. "Do you think he'll change his mind?"

"I don't know," I admit, "but I hope so. I shouldn't have said anything. That was my original plan. To make him think it was a regular scholarship."

"It's ridiculous!" she says, anger rising. "Why can't he understand how much this means to me? I hope he chokes on his pride."

"That would be nice, kiddo. That would be nice."

Two beats to consider, and she lowers her voice again. "Do you ever think about revenge?"

"Only when it's useful. And then I do more than just think about it."

SEVENTEEN

Christmas morning. I let myself sleep late. When I finally wake, prodded by stabs of sunlight through the blinds, I stay in bed, basking in the warmth beneath the big quilt. No use hurrying into the stress of the day. No use fighting the wake of last night's trouble before I must.

Mel, no doubt, is busy in the kitchen. Graham? Who cares? Probably sleeping off his foul mood. The girls? I don't know. Not much noise on the far side of the door, which seems unusual. Have they already opened all the presents that were stacked so neatly beneath the tree? Surely they're not waiting for me.

I reach for my cell to check the time, find a new-message notification. Cavin. *Just wanted to wish you a very merry Christmas. Hope it's filled with love and laughter.* From anyone else, I'd think *How Hallmark.* From him, I'm thinking *How sweet.* I never think

How sweet. Something is definitely wrong with me.

The clock informs me it's after eleven. I should haul my behind out into the light of day and go make sure there aren't three breathless kids awaiting my appearance. Before I do, I text Cavin back. *Ho-ho-ho. That's probably the extent of today's laughter. Thanks for thawing the chill a little. Talk to you soon.*

I manage to wiggle into a velour warm-up suit without popping my knee out of place once. Practice makes perfect. The swelling is down quite a bit, but every sideways mistake is painful. Right now it doesn't hurt at all. I pop a Vicoprofen anyway. Not all pain is physical.

The bedroom door opens into silence. "Hello? Merry Christmas?"

The living room is empty of people, the tree devoid of presents. Guess they opened them without me after all. The paper and bows and boxes are all neatly disposed of but for bits awaiting the vacuum. The tequila bottle still sits, opened, on the coffee table, but the glasses are nowhere in sight.

Dinner is in the oven, as evidenced by the smell of roasting turkey, drifting this way from the kitchen. I follow it but find no sign of the chef, who has left a trio of pies cool-

161

ing on the counter. There's coffee, still hot, in the carafe and when I pour myself a cup, I notice Melody's note: *The girls and I went to church. Back by 12:30. Help yourself to whatever. Except pie. We'll have dinner around three, so keep it light.*

I grab a yogurt out of the fridge, and when I start toward the dinette, I notice both ovens are on. Turkey *and* ham. Damn, that's a lot of food for six people. I foresee a lot of leftovers in the coming week. Maybe I should just hire a car service to drive me home before we get down to ham bone and beans or fowl carcass soup.

The newspaper is on the table, so I catch up on what's happening in the world on this Christmas Day. I'm almost to the sports section when Graham comes in from outside, dripping sweat.

"Did you go for a run?" Stupid question.

He pounces on it. "No. I perspire naturally in forty-degree weather. Just have to step outside."

"Sarcasm does not become you, my dear. Anyway, I don't see a need for hostility. Can't we remain cordial, at the very least? After all, it *is* Christmas."

He braces himself up against the kitchen counter. Obviously, this seconds-long exchange with me has been too much for him, and he's trying to choose his words carefully (for once). "I'm tired of you interfering in my life."

I might feel slapped, except I have no idea what he's talking about. "Excuse me? How, exactly, do I interfere in your life? I only see you a couple of times a year." And that's only if I'm unlucky.

"Right. And every time you manage to make me feel inferior." There it is. That tic. "Pricey ski trips. Expensive gifts. Out-of-sight tuitions."

"Graham, I'm only trying to help."

"We don't need your help. I don't want your money. Just keep it, okay?" He storms off, hopefully to shower. The kitchen's lovely scent has been tainted.

It's interesting, really. His obvious contempt for me borders on hatred. It can't be because I shunned his moves over twenty years ago, can it? Not that it really matters, except for his digging in now will negatively affect his daughter. I know he cares about her. Maybe he doesn't want her to leave home. Whatever his rationale, he is definitely being, as Kayla would say, an asswipe.

About the time I finish my second cup of coffee and the classifieds, Mel and the kids get home. The girls peel off, head in separate directions. Melody goes directly to the oven to check on dinner's progress and baste the turkey. "Thanks for keeping an eye on things."

Is that what I was doing? "I was mostly keeping an eye on the newspaper, but you're welcome."

"Did you see Graham?"

"I did, yes, coming in from a run. He's still pissed at me."

"Oh."

"Any idea why?"

She closes the oven door, goes to pour a mug of coffee. "I think he's more petulant than pissed. He's a proud man, Tara. That's all."

"You might remind him of that proverb: pride goes before destruction." It was one of our mother's favorites, usually uttered right before she decided to try to beat the conceit out of me.

Mutually, silently, we let it drop.

"So, what's up with all the food? Are you expecting more people than the six of us? Like, maybe the entire block?"

She laughs. "The girls love turkey, but Graham claims it gives him indigestion. His family always had ham, and that's what he wants, so I do both. There will be lots of leftovers, but ham keeps well."

It's two hours until we're gathered at the

table, plates filled and grace said. Dinner is delicious, which is good. It gives everyone the excuse to keep conversation to a minimum. If Kayla bothers to look up from her turkey, it is to glare at Graham, who pretends not to notice. From time to time, Jessica and Suzette trade jabs about who's stuffing herself with the most stuffing, and how anytime now they'll totally resemble plump plucked fowl.

Melody and I sip a lovely full-bodied Syrah. Graham kind of gulps his, emptying his glass at twice the speed we do. After we finish eating and the plates are cleared, the kids disappear while we adults adjourn to the living room. Graham turns on a football game and dives straight into the tequila.

"Want some?" he asks, noticing me watching him slurp.

"No thanks. Think I'd better stick to wine."

"Suit yourself." He turns his attention back to the game.

So do I. I'm not a football fanatic, but I do understand the play and find it interesting to watch from time to time. Besides, what else is there to do? Suddenly, Graham bolts from his recliner, face white. "Shit!" He sprints to the hall bathroom, slams the door.

"Oh!" Melody's voice holds concern. "Is he sick?"

"Sure looked that way to me."

Mel goes to check on him, returns momentarily. "Man. It's coming out of both ends, and rapidly. That bathroom is a war zone. Hope you don't have to pee anytime soon."

"There's always the backyard."

"That sure did come on fast. He didn't eat any turkey, did he?"

"Not that I saw." My eyes settle on the tequila. "Maybe it was that." I gesture toward the bottle.

"How much did he drink?"

I shrug. "Not that much."

A question oozes out of yesterday. *Do you ever think about revenge?*

Turkey, flu, or tainted tequila, Graham is sick for a couple of days. Finally, he materializes from isolation like a time-confused vampire — shaky, drained, with skin the approximate color of unbaked piecrust. His mood was foul prior to this; it's time for me to vacate the guest room.

Melody is in the backyard, feeding her mutts. I step outside the back door. "I think I need to go home."

"Sick of our company already?"

"I think somebody around here's sick of mine."

"Can you drive safely? And what about all those stairs? How will you get around?"

"I've been mulling that over. Kayla has another week off school, right? Maybe she could drive me home and help me unpack. Maybe run to the store for groceries and such. Then I can hire a car to bring her back. What do you think?"

She watches the dogs push their emptied bowls around the patio. "Makes sense, I guess. Have you asked her about it?"

"Not yet. I wanted to talk to you first. What about Graham? Will he get upset?"

"Considering the way Kayla's been moping around the house, I doubt it. But what about once you're home? You'll need some help, at least for a while. Why don't you consider hiring someone to do errands and steer you up and down all those steps?"

"Great idea. I'll look into it."

I'm too old for a nanny, and I cherish my privacy. But come to think of it, there are a lot of college students looking for part-time jobs. And some of them are men.

EIGHTEEN

Turns out, Kayla's happy enough to escape, and surprisingly, Graham is agreeable to the plan. Maybe he figures spending a couple of days in my company will make her hate me enough to refuse any offer of money. I've been thinking about that, too, and might have come up with a workable solution.

The one thing Kayla isn't so happy about is my insisting we leave first thing Monday morning, meaning no later than nine o'clock. Teens and their sleeping in! But I've never actually ridden in a car she was driving before. I'd hate to see us stuck in anything like traffic, especially when she settles behind the wheel of the Escalade and says, "Whoa. This vehicle is huge. Does it actually fit in one lane?"

My jaw unhinges a little. "I do hope you're kidding."

She laughs. "Uh, yeah, Aunt Tara. I've got

this. No worries."

Kayla drives almost overcautiously, like most young drivers, at least when they have an adult supervisor riding passenger. Once we reach the freeway, this becomes too obvious. "It's okay to drive a little over the limit," I tell her. "Especially out here. Go sixty-five, you're liable to get run off the road."

"I just didn't want to scare you."

"That isn't easy to do. I decided a long time ago to swiftly and completely excise scary people from my life."

"You mean people like your mother." It's a statement.

What has Melody told her? "Exactly."

"I wish Mom was brave enough to do that."

"What do you mean?"

"June calls sometimes — she insists we call her June, says she can't stand the name Grandma or even Grandmother — and I swear, Mom turns into a mewling little kid."

"Really." It's news to me. "I don't suppose *June* asks for money."

"What else? Doesn't she ever ask you?"

"She wouldn't dare. Anyway, I doubt she even knows my current last name, let alone how to get in touch with me. And that's the way I want to keep it. You haven't said anything, have you?"

She shakes her head. "Not me. What *is* your current last name, anyway?"

"Very funny." But we both laugh.

We are driving through Fairfield when I finally venture, "On the Art Institute thing, something your mom said the other day sparked an idea. What if I hired you as a kind of a girl Friday? Part-time, of course, with a highly inflated salary. Graham can't say no if you're working for your tuition, do you think?"

"Work?" It's a whine. "What would I have to do?"

My first thought is to dismiss both the invitation and the offer of money. But then I remember she's still a kid, and a privileged one at that. "Run errands. Help me plan parties. Nothing that might ruin a manicure."

"Sorry. I didn't mean it like that."

I appreciate instant contrition. "Apology accepted. Should we give it a try?"

"Why not? I'd do practically anything to get out of that house and into this school. Maybe even mess up my nail polish."

We manage to make it home, fingernails intact. I instruct Kayla to pull into the garage, and when I open the door, she whistles. "Three cars? Are you kidding?

170

Hey, can I drive the Corvette?"

I smile. "Not today."

"Tomorrow?"

"I'll think about it. Right now, will you please carry my suitcase upstairs? My bedroom is on the third level — it's the big one, with the fireplace. You can choose any of the guest rooms. I'm parking myself on the second floor for now. It's going to take me a few to get up the stairs. Make yourself comfortable."

It takes six or seven minutes to crow-hop up two long flights of stairs, and when I finally reach the living room, it feels as if my left leg took the brunt of the climb. Mostly because it did. Mel was right. I'll need to find some temporary help. Kayla's only staying two days.

I wiggle out of my jacket, hang it next to the door, and am immediately sorry. It's cool in the house, so I hobble over to the thermostat, dial up the heat, and turn on the gas fireplace, if only to fool my psyche into believing it's warm.

I wander room to room, making sure everything's in order, and it seems to be. The effort is taxing. Time to quit feeling sorry for myself and take charge of my recovery. Rehabbing the knee is going to suck. But it's necessary.

By the time I flop onto the sofa, Kayla bustles into the room. "God, this place is beautiful! How come you've never invited me for a visit before?"

"I don't know. Guess I never thought you'd be interested in hanging out with your old aunt."

"Can I see what there is to eat?"

"Of course, but there won't be much in the fridge. We'll have to order in. You like Chinese? There's a great little place right around the corner."

"Chinese is amazing, as long as it's spicy. Do they do Szechuan?"

"Of course. Bring me my phone, please? It's in my jacket pocket."

I order the food — Szechuan chicken for Kayla, double-hot twice-cooked pork for me — give her directions to Kung Pow Jack's, send her on her way. She's a bit reticent about walking in the city after dark. "Don't worry," I tell her, "this neighborhood is totally safe."

"If you're sure . . ."

"I am. Listen. I might chance the shower while you're gone. Be sure to lock the side door behind you. Grab a garage-door opener from one of the cars and come in that way."

"Okay." Off she goes.

I take a few minutes to go through voice mails and text messages.

From Melody: *You home yet? Call and let me know you arrived safely.*

Also from Melody: *Kayla forgot her meds. You don't happen to have any Abilify, do you? I'll have her doctor contact a pharmacy near you. Which one do you use?*

Wonderful. Mental note: Call Melody back right away.

From Cassandra: *Uh, Tara? Where are you? That guy didn't kill you and toss you into the bay, did he?*

From Barton Memorial Hospital, an automated *We want to know how we did. Please visit us online and fill out a short survey.*

From someone named Larry Alexander: *Finn gave me your number regarding your niece's admission to the San Francisco Art Institute. Please call me at your earliest convenience to discuss.*

Finally, a text message from Private: *You shouldn't have fucked with me. Expect an unpleasant surprise.*

I take a deep breath. If somebody really wanted to hurt me, he wouldn't have issued a warning, which means he just wanted to scare me. And that is something not easily accomplished. My only real concern is I'm still not very mobile, which makes me question the timing. Only a few people know about my knee. Does the person behind the text? Why am I assuming it came from a man?

As for guessing who he might be, there's a decent list of suspects, none of whom seem capable of overt violence. Regardless, I keep culling the roll, and three possibilities remain near the top: Ben, who doubtless had some explaining to do when he went home to his wife; Nick, the disgusting little sidewinder who I poked with a very long stick; and Graham.

I'm pretty sure Ben is clueless about how to reach me. I keep revisiting that night. Did I tell him my name? Tara, yes, that much I remember confiding. But Tara isn't an uncommon name. Tracking me down wouldn't be impossible, but would it be worth the effort? Doubtful.

Nick is more likely, but why would he go to the trouble of making his number private? He's not that smart, anyway, and if he was pissed enough to threaten me, he wouldn't think to do it in such a covert manner. Besides, for all his vociferous bravado, that man is a coward at heart.

Which leaves Graham. But I can't think

of one good reason why he'd attack me like this. I've been plotting a backdoor approach to the tuition, but he isn't privy to that information, and even if he was, that wouldn't rate an "unpleasant surprise." Unless he blames me for his diarrhea?

There is a fourth possibility, actually — wrong number. My voice mail greeting is an all-purpose "I can't take your call, please leave a message," spoken by a generic female. The logical side of me says this is a reasonable explanation. My instinct, however, insists on caution.

Said prudence makes me a bit overprotective of Kayla, and that worry, combined with her missing medication, prompts me to send her home early. The last thing I need to deal with right now is a major depressive episode.

Kayla is not especially happy about leaving when I break it to her the following morning. "But I didn't get to drive the Corvette."

"Next time."

"What about shopping? Your cupboards are pretty much bare."

Good point. I could probably get myself to the store, but no way could I carry up bags. "Okay, fine. We'll go to Trader Joe's together. But after we get back, you're out of here. What I will do for you, however, is set up a time to go tour the Art Institute, maybe over your spring break. I got a call from one of their directors. I'm pretty sure you're in."

"No way! You're amazing!"

"I take care of my tribe." No one else really matters.

Descending stairs is even harder than climbing them. This is ridiculous. Kayla waits for me at the bottom, looking up anxiously. "Can we take the 'Vette? Please?"

There's room in the backseat for shopping bags, but it's a lot harder to load them in and out. Still, why not? "I guess. As long as you don't mind the grunt work in addition to chauffeuring."

As she backs carefully out of the driveway, I notice a strange car parked across the street — a well-used sedan, dark gray with obvious patches of primer, that's out of place in this neighborhood. Normally that wouldn't bother me much, but I'm a little suspicious right now, especially because there's a pudgy man sitting in the driver's seat. He seems to be writing. Maybe he's a Realtor and my neighbors are listing their house. Maybe he's an assessor, or canvassing. Maybe he just parked there randomly. Whoever he is, a sharp whisper of paranoia tells me something about him is off. We are four blocks away before it hits me: he never even glanced in our direction. Who doesn't look at two attractive women driving in a Corvette?

The grocery run takes forever. Even with the cart to lean on, my knee starts to feel loose around ten minutes in. At twenty, it throbs from the effort of trying to hold together while moving in a forward direction. I know I'm supposed to walk, but that's easier said than done. I'm glad I have a stationary bike as well as a treadmill at home. Weight-bearing exercise will be problematic. I definitely want to schedule that surgery as soon as possible.

We stock up on things that can go into the freezer. Fresh fruit and vegetables will be hard to keep, so I choose resilient produce like apples and carrots over quick-to-overripen things like bananas and broccoli. "Ice cream?" asks Kayla.

"Better not. That will go to my butt faster than pizza."

"Yeah, but how else will you celebrate New Year's Eve?"

"I almost forgot about that. Thanks for reminding me. Let's go find the champagne."

Eight bags and $346 later, I watch Kayla

stuff the backseat. "The limo isn't coming for you until two. That gives us almost two hours. Do you want to hit the freeway for a little spin? Surface streets aren't really a fair test of a sports car."

"Hell yeah! But what about the groceries?"

"They'll be okay for twenty minutes, especially since I vetoed the ice cream."

It's the perfect time of day to put the 'Vette through its paces without much interference from traffic. I don't let her go very far, but she's pedal-to-the-metal long enough to get a feel for the big engine's power. The weather is beautiful, cold steel blue, and by the time we head back into my neighborhood, I'm starting to dread cooping myself back up inside.

The beater sedan is gone from across the street, and there's no FOR SALE sign up in the yard. Not sure why that nagged at me so much. It wasn't Ben, or Nick, and certainly not Graham. Nor was it anyone I've slept with or blown off. All must be copacetic. I do my best to shrug off the lingering worry.

By the time the car service arrives for Kayla, the pantry and freezer are well stocked, the reusable shopping bags neatly folded and put away. "I won't walk you downstairs," I tell her. "My knee's finished for today. Would you please lock the side door behind you?"

"Of course. Thanks for everything, Aunt Tara."

"You're most welcome. I'll be in touch about that school visit. Keep your grades up. I'm in your corner, but we want everything leaning your way."

I walk her to the head of the stairs, and as she descends I remind her again to lock the door. Then I watch out the window as the driver helps her into the backseat, as a good chauffeur should. He goes around the Lincoln, slides in behind the wheel, closes the door, signals his desire to pull away from the curb.

He has to wait for the automobile cruising slowly past, too slowly for someone focused on going to or from home. It's the same sedan that was parked across the street earlier, at least I think it is. Same color. Same general model and age. I can't see the driver, but a tremor of nerves brings sweat to my upper lip.

Both limo and sedan are now nothing more than blurry rear ends, heading away from my home. I can't believe a stupid wrong number has put me so ridiculously on edge. I make my way into my office, a windowed nook tucked behind the kitchen. Normally the 180-degree vistas, coupled with one of my favorite paintings hanging on the glass-free wall, uplifts me. Not today.

Today I go over to a small bank of monitors, flip the switch that turns on the security camera system. I haven't used it since Finn left. He was paranoid, not me. But, hey, it's here, and offers some small sense of safety, even though what I really want is invincibility.

Finally, I call a locksmith to install a remote entry system so I can control who comes and goes through the downstairs door from the relative security upstairs. The whole time he's working, I keep my eyes on the monitors and the pepper spray within easy reach.

NINETEEN

For the next couple of days I plunge myself into busywork, most of it centered around a spring fund-raiser — a black and white ball at the Fairmont. There are lots of nitpicky details to fuss over. Appetizer menus. Liquor selections. Centerpieces. Finalizing the jazz band's contract. Invitations.

Most of that time is spent sitting, so I invest thirty minutes, three times a day, alternating treadmill, stationary bike, and gentle stretches, plus hefting five-pound dumbbells to keep the breasts in proper place and ward off arm flab. Despite what should be a maintenance routine, every time I happen past a mirror, I see a fat girl looking back at me. And despite every effort to the contrary, that zips me straight back to Idaho.

Mom's boyfriend at the time was a mechanic, and one mean SOB, even if he was pretty great at keeping the old Ford tuned up. His relationship with Mom was volatile, but that was nothing new. What I hated most about him was how he always referred to me as Chunk.

Yeah, I was a chubby kid, but what can you expect when you're fed a diet of Kraft macaroni, Spam, and Frosted Flakes? I was heavier than my sister, mostly because I always cleaned her plate of whatever she didn't finish. She was a nervous eater.

Lester never missed an opportunity to remind me of my size. "Hey, Chunk, how's it going today?" "Hey, Chunk, bring me a beer." "Hey, Chunk, you're looking mighty fine. I like your hair that way."

His attention escalated, not that Mom seemed to notice. One day I came home from school and he was there alone, watching TV and guzzling a Schlitz. "Where's Mom?"

"She had to go pick up your sister. The bus broke down." Mel was still in elementary school, and I'd moved up to junior high.

I went into the kitchen to do my homework.

"Hey, Chunk, bring me a beer." Nothing new. What was new was that when I offered the can to Lester, he grabbed my hand and pulled so my face came very close to his. "I bet I never told you how much I like fat girls, did I?"

Something in his eyes told me this was bad. Very bad. But I knew better than to challenge him. I looked away. "No, you never did."

"Come here and let me show you. Want some beer?"

I shook my head. "No thanks."

"Sure you do." He tipped the can into my mouth until the beer ran down the front of me. "Aw, what did you do that for? I think you need a spanking."

He yanked hard, and I went over his knees and before he gave me a single swat, I could feel his dick grow hard against my belly. "Please no!"

"Don't worry. It won't hurt much. What's a fat butt for?"

Down came his hand. Once. Twice. Three times. Four. The pain was awful, but the embarrassment was worse. I started to cry. Sob. "Please."

"There now, see, you're begging me for it. Just like the fat, little whore you are. And that ain't right." He paddled me until my ass throbbed and he came, soaking his underwear and the belly of my shirt. Then he pushed me roughly to the floor. "Go clean up before your mother gets home. Say one word and I'll give you the rest next time."

I knew better than to tell Mom anyway. She wouldn't believe me, or she'd blame me. But I made damn sure there would not be a next time. And that very afternoon, I mostly quit eating, nibbling only enough to keep me from passing out and filling up the rest of the way on water. Another mother might have noticed. Not mine. Not until I'd lost twenty pounds and needed pants that wouldn't fall down.

I've kept control of my weight since, although I've learned to do it with exercise, only resorting to a highly regulated diet when necessary. Like now, since I can't fight intake with output. I'll eat less and do my best to work out more.

I wean myself from the harder meds, managing the pain with ibuprofen. By day three, I can even handle the stairs, though not at a sprint. Still, every now and then, I make a mistake and my knee reacts in a most horribly unpredictable way.

I despise how that makes me feel. Like my right leg has wrested control of itself. Like my body isn't always listening to my brain.

I'm still not completely mobile, so I spend several hours searching online for my guy Friday. I mean, I guess I'll take a girl, if her résumé and hourly rate merit. But if I can find an attractive young man who'll fetch my groceries and mail, and maybe massage the stress from my shoulders, hey, why not? I'll interview a half dozen — five men, one woman — on Monday.

This is New Year's Eve, and while a large cross section of America will be out partying somewhere, I'll be alone at my computer, drinking champagne. Good champagne, but drinking it solo always makes me a little lonely. I consider calling Cassandra but change my mind. She always goes out on New Year's Eve. I went with her last year, and while we had fun, the logistics were a nightmare. Parking is always trouble in San Francisco, but tonight it will be impossible, and I can't possibly walk any distance. Nope. No partying for me. God, I hope this isn't a glimpse of my near future.

I cycle through e-mails, and then click over to my favorite news source. Might as well keep tabs on what's happening in the world. But it isn't international headlines that catch my eye. No, it's one much closer to home: SENATOR JORDAN LONDON UNDER INVESTIGATION. Jordan London. My ex-husband, the politician with very deep pockets.

There's a short video clip, with Jordan

standing beside a gorgeous Porsche and an even more gorgeous young blond. Jordan looks composed, but I can detect a subtle nervousness in his voice when he speaks into the reporter's microphone. "I don't get too worked up over information leaked from anonymous sources. If and when this person chooses to step forward, I'm happy to respond to her — or him — directly. Until then, I've got nothing to say."

I research a little deeper and find that a nameless tipster alerted the press to some rather large gifts that Jordan failed to disclose. Over the years, according to this supposed close acquaintance, those alleged bribes have amounted to several hundred thousand dollars.

That, I believe. One of the reasons I wanted to distance myself from Jordan was that I'd witnessed things that could have easily sent him to prison, and I wasn't about to go down with him. I'm surprised, really, that he's gotten away with it for this long.

Now his words sink in. "I'm happy to respond to her — or him . . ." As if he believes a woman turned him in. Does he think it was me?

You shouldn't have fucked with me.

Could that have been Jordan?

No, it wouldn't have been him.

186

But maybe somebody he hired?

Like some creepy little man in a beat-up sedan?

I halt that internal conversation. This is ridiculous. I haven't gotten another threatening text, nor seen the car in question cruising the neighborhood again.

Suddenly, my cell, which apparently I left on vibrate, dances on my desk. My hand jerks forward instinctively, but I pull it back until I can see the caller ID. Oh. It's Cavin. "H-hello?"

"Everything okay?" His voice is melted cheddar.

"Much better now." Which somehow sounds like an admission, rather than the compliment I meant it to be.

"I was just sitting here watching it snow, and thought I'd wish you a Happy New Year. You doing anything fun?"

"Drinking a little champagne . . ." Trying to drown my paranoia.

"All by yourself?"

"All by myself. I'm not a huge fan of public New Year's Eve revelry, but even if I were, I wouldn't be going out dancing. Not this year."

"I understand. How's the knee?"

"I've been working it. My range of motion is improving, and it doesn't hurt as much.

It's definitely not right, of course."

"Even surgery might not make it one hundred percent."

"I'll settle for ninety-nine point five."

He snickers. "We'll do our best. Anyway, I wanted to let you know I'll definitely be coming through the city next week. Still want me to stop by?"

Delicious little shivers prickle the back of my neck. I want to see what this man is made of. "Absolutely."

"No plans I might be disturbing?"

"None at all. But even if there were, I'd invite the disturbance."

Now he laughs outright. "That's very good to hear. I'll probably be there early afternoon on Wednesday. Does that work?"

"Perfectly."

"Should I bring dinner?"

"I believe I said I'd cook for you, didn't I?" A quick mental inventory of the freezer's contents makes me wonder if it's possible. Hopefully by Wednesday, I'll have hired someone to buy fresh ingredients, however. "Tell you what. You can bring dessert."

"Wine?"

"I'll let you choose a bottle or two from my cellar. No worries about driving after. I've got a guest room. Three, in fact."

He lets that sink in, and then he dares,

"What if I prefer the master?"

I let *that* sink in. "Then I guess you'll just have to be persuasive."

After we say good-bye, I open my laptop and e-mail Mel: *Guess who just called to wish me a Happy New Year. Did you guess Dr. Gorgeous? There's something special about this guy, and I'm not just talking an incredible bedside manner. He's coming to dinner next week. Wonder if I can get a leg transplant by then. This one is damn ugly.*

Her reply comes sometime later: *Don't be impetuous. You can always keep your clothes on! Let me know how it goes with Dr. Gorgeous.*

Impetuous? Me? I've got days to plan. As for my clothes, I suppose I could keep them on, sister dearest. But where's the fun in that?

TWENTY

The first Monday in the New Year dawns a particularly dreary gray, great fists of fog smothering any sense of view. Claustrophobia threatens, despite the interior spaciousness, and I find myself longing for a long walk beneath vibrant blue sky. Even if the mist burned off and my knee was willing to cooperate, however, it couldn't happen today.

I scheduled the personal-assistant interviews at sixty-minute intervals. All six candidates were students, so none of their résumés suggested particularly outstanding job performance. Still, the position I'm hiring for requires neither a degree, nor even high-level intellect. I did request references, and despite the holiday weekend managed to contact most of them. Not that you can always count on the recommendations of friends and family members, if that was, indeed, who they were.

I also did quick background checks through an Internet service, however reliable that might be. One of the guys had an overabundance of traffic violations. No way I could let someone like that drive one of my vehicles, and since his might very well get impounded, I crossed him off my list. He wasn't particularly happy when I let him know not to come, and why. "Fucking tickets?" he stormed. "You call that a good reason?"

"Maybe not. But your reaction is a pretty good indicator that you are not what I'm looking for." Had he calmly offered a rational explanation, I might have changed my mind.

And then there were five.

The first arrives at ten o'clock sharp. I made it clear that punctuality is a requisite, so he draws no demerits there. I sit at my desk, eyes behind the video screen, watching him approach the door. He wears casual dress-to-impress, and his stride is confident. When he reaches for the intercom button, he looks up, and when he notices the security device in place, he smiles for the camera. It's a nice smile, on a very nice face — boyishly handsome is the phrase that comes to mind.

The buzzer rattles.

"Good morning. Your name?"

"Charlie Bent."

It matches the one at the top of my list. Still, I request the password I gave him in a semi-inebriated fit of caution.

"Misbehave."

Good word, as long as I'm the one doing the misbehaving. "Thank you. I'll let you in. Please come straight up the stairs to the second floor."

I punch in the code to unlock the door and bolt it behind him once it closes, and by the time he crests the top step, I've made my way through the kitchen to greet him. Like most people do the first time they take in my living room, Charlie stops dead in his tracks to assess what he sees. "Wow. Amazing place. Your neighbors must be very jealous." Bonus points.

We sit and talk for a half hour. I ask a long list of questions, all of which he answers quite reasonably. But I'm as interested in his body language and diction as in what he has to say. He's a business major at UC San Francisco, and his schedule can accommodate the ten hours per week I'm asking for. He enjoys shopping, is familiar with some interesting bakeries and butcher shops, and often frequents the city's varied farmer's markets.

"I'm a native San Franciscan," he finishes. "I'll never leave, even though it's hard to afford a place of my own."

"You have roommates?"

He nods. "Teddy and Ron. But they're not really roommates. More like my landlords. They're an older couple with plenty of money. It makes them happy to help out poor, starving students, so my rent is more than reasonable. It's pretty much subsidized."

Huh. Small world. "Sounds like a fortuitous relationship." Hmm. Wonder if he's gay, too. If so, it isn't noticeable on first meeting, not that it really matters.

"Any other questions for me?"

"Yes. How are you at massage?"

Charlie grins. "I give a mean shoulder rub. Feet, too."

He had me at shoulders.

"Would you be able to start tomorrow? As you can see, I'm unable to get around very well."

"Of course. We're still on semester break."

"I'm offering twenty dollars an hour. Does that work for you?"

"Plus mileage?"

Ballsy, but I don't mind that, and gas is expensive in the city. "I'm interviewing several others. I'll let you know by the end of the day."

Concern surfaces in his eyes. He's afraid he went too far. Still, he doesn't back down, and I like that, too. "I'll be waiting for your call."

It's a long day, my predictable questions netting mostly predictable answers. None of the other four candidates asks for mileage on top of the per-hour pay. But I weed them out, one by one, each for a different reason.

Bryan, though thoroughly qualified, arrives fifteen minutes late. His excuse is traffic, something he really should have factored in, if, indeed, that was the reason.

Paul, who is striking, nevertheless is relatively new to San Francisco, and I prefer someone familiar with its haunts. And his fulltime school schedule, plus another part-time job, might make accommodating my needs difficult.

The one woman I interview pretty much defines "ditz." Who knows? At some point, I might want an actual conversation with whomever I hire. Cinda would bore me to tears.

Finally, there's Bernard. No doubt about his gender identity. He practically preens as we chat. And when I ask about his ability to relieve stress through massage, he huffs something about sexual harassment. Which totally makes me laugh. "The last thing I'm looking for in a bed partner," I tell him, "is a guy who looks better in an apron than I do."

Once I lock the door behind Bernard, I call Charlie. "Looks like you're hired. Can you stop by tomorrow and pick up a grocery list?"

"Around eleven?"

"Sounds good."

"How will I pay for everything?"

"Cash."

Two beats. "You trust me with your money?"

"I don't trust you at all. How much I trust you in the future totally depends on what you do with what I give you. Anyway, I know where you live."

"Really? How?"

"Uh, it's on your job application?" I don't mention his landlords and I happen to be well acquainted. Messing with me wouldn't be a good plan, at least not if he wants to hang on to his subsidized living arrangement. Keeping my temper in check is something I practice, in no small part because my mother never could manage it and the last thing I want to do is resemble her. But I do have triggers, and once in a while revenge just feels good. "See you at

195

eleven sharp."

Charlie passes his first test with an A-minus grade. He shows up right on time. We discuss the items on my list to make sure we're on the same page regarding fresh versus dried herbs, possible substitutions, the exact cut of meat I want, and so on. Charlie, it turns out, isn't familiar with osso bucco.

He manages to secure everything I want, except for leeks, which he substitutes scallions for. Thus the A minus, even if his claim that every leek he saw looked a bit suspect is true. You never know. I give him the benefit of the doubt, or he'd have scored a B plus instead. Then again, he does get extra credit for the shoulder rub.

The change seems correct, considering the higher-end markets he shopped at, and the ten — yes, ten! — shopping bags full of stuff he had to schlep up the stairs.

And he seems overjoyed at the generous tip I gave him on top of his hourly, under-the-table pay. So, overall, I'm cautiously optimistic that Charlie will work out just fine. Besides, I maintain my wild card, hold it close to my chest.

TWENTY-ONE

On Wednesday afternoon, I'm maneuvering dinner preparations, working on the polenta to go under the osso bucco. Veal shanks simmer gently in a spicy, oniony sauce. The kitchen smells heavenly, and this time I am responsible, not my homebody sister. I may not cook like this very often, but it doesn't mean I'm hopeless in the kitchen.

January dreariness tries to weigh me down, but I refuse to sink beneath it. At least until my cell phone, which has been snoozing on the counter, buzzes. Guess I left the ringer off. Disappointment stabs at me. Cavin isn't coming, or he's mired in freeway quicksand. By the time I wash the cornmeal from my hands and dry them with a dish towel, the phone has stopped ringing. The voice mail message is from Unknown. Two words: *Almost there.*

Trepidation shimmers, a coppery aura. I lower the heat beneath the polenta, leave it barely simmering while I go into my office and rotate the camera toward the street. Nothing seems out of the ordinary. A car goes by, too fast to be worrisome, except to a pedestrian, midcrossing. Here comes another, a dark pewter sedan, cruising slowly, as if looking for an address. It pulls up against the curb in front of my house, and I think about calling 911.

But now I recognize the car. It's an Audi Quattro, one I've ridden passenger in. Cavin exits the driver's-side door and circles to extract a couple of bags from the trunk. A heady brew of relief, consternation, and sudden desire splashes over me. He's even more attractive than I remember, and though tall and powerfully built, he moves with the grace of a savannah cat. I watch him press the intercom button.

"What's the password?"

He glances up at the camera and winks. "Cristal."

Good enough. I greet him at the top of the stairs. He sets down the bags, reaches into one, and conjures a dozen autumn-colored roses, which he presents with a flourish. "For you, fair lady."

When was the last time a man came courting with flowers? Years. Decades, even. Pretty sure Raul was the last. I accept the bouquet, moving in very close. Cavin takes the hint, tilting my chin so our eyes meet, and when I part my lips in clear invitation, there is no hesitation. This kiss is downpour on fallow ground. Satisfying. Liberating. Necessary. Longing threads my body, bold in its intensity, challenges all sense of caution. And that scares me. Fear wins out for the moment and I pull away, offer a gentle smile. "Wow."

"Understatement."

"I'd better go put these in water. Have a look around if you'd like, and then meet me in the kitchen." I can feel him watching my uneven gait as I turn and walk away. Appreciating the sway of my hips, or assessing the state of my knee, I'm not sure. Maybe both.

I locate a vase and dig through a utility drawer to find a sharp pair of shears. Cavin finds me trimming the ends of the stems and arranging the roses to satisfy my sense of balance. "Stunning place, Tara. Did you do the decorating yourself?"

"Just me and a high-price designer. My ideas. His execution."

"Excellent teamwork." Cavin sniffs the steamy air. "Is that osso bucco?"

"It is. You're not opposed to veal, are you?"

"Only when I see pictures of it on the

hoof." He places his bags on the counter, empties them. "I know you said you've got a great cellar, but I wasn't sure if it includes Cristal, so I brought a couple of bottles, just in case. I think we need to toast the fledgling year. And, as promised, I also brought dessert. Hope you like cheesecake."

It looks to be New York–style chocolate swirl. What's not to like? "I adore cheesecake." I finish the flowers, put them to one side, and go back to work on the polenta. "This will just take a few. Why don't you chill the champagne and open that bottle of cab for now?" As he works the corkscrew, a question surfaces, and it's one I need an answer to or I'll be uncomfortable all evening. "Did you call and leave a voice mail right before you got here?"

"I did. Why?"

"The message popped up as from an unknown number."

"Oh, right. I apologize. I'd been getting an inordinate number of spammy calls. I'd decided to change providers, anyway, so I went ahead and got a new number, and kept it unlisted. I'll make sure you have the new one."

"Do you have to inform your entire address book of the change? Sounds like a lot of work."

He laughs. "My 'entire address book' isn't that extensive, at least not when it comes to my private phone number. Hey, I don't go giving it out to everyone, you know."

"You gave it to me."

I turn to face him and he hands me a glass of wine. "True. And that is rare."

"Why, then? Why me?"

"You mean, besides the fact that you're drop-dead beautiful, not to mention smart and witty?"

"You couldn't have known all that when you gave me your card."

Cavin shrugs. "Something told me I wouldn't be sorry. So far, I'm anything but." He lifts his glass. "Here's to that little voice inside my head."

We seal the toast with another kiss, even sexier than the last. I think I'm in trouble tonight. My favorite kind of trouble.

Dinner turns out perfectly — the polenta is fluffy, the meat tender, the veggies finished just right. And then, there's the cheesecake, which Cavin picked up from one of my favorite bakeries. Cristal is an excellent accompaniment, its crisp bubbles the ideal foil for the weight of the dense dessert.

The only thing better is the conversation, which segues from talk of pastry chefs to art galleries to higher education. I mention Kayla's aspirations, my ability to help.

"You wouldn't happen to have any pull at the Athenian, would you?"

"You talked to the headmaster."

"I did. He's decidedly unhappy with my son, and it's not just because of his dismal report card, or even his lack of ambition, which is truly mind-boggling. No, apparently someone hacked the school computers and changed a lot of grades. They can't prove it was Eli, but there are rumors to that effect."

"But he didn't change his own grades?"

"No."

"Then why bother?"

"Good question."

"Even if it was him, it sounds like a harmless prank."

"Prank, yes, and you or I might find it vaguely amusing. But the teachers who had to go back and re-create a semester's worth of grades for fifty-some students didn't think it was very funny."

Good point. "I don't suppose Eli has admitted responsibility?"

"Uh, no. And he didn't look the slightest bit guilty when he denied knowing a thing about it. Of course, my son is a well-practiced liar."

I think I'll leave that one alone.

Cavin insists on doing the dishes. "You cooked. I'll clean up. I want you to stay off that leg so you'll be in good shape for the post-dessert dessert."

"I think I like the sound of that."

Cavin is quick to finish in the kitchen. By the time I visit the bathroom, making sure my feminine hygiene will support what I hope is coming very soon, return to the living room to light the fire, and settle on the big sectional, he has not only loaded the dishwasher but also opened the second bottle of champagne.

He saunters into the living room, sets an ice bucket on the coffee table, then pours two tall flutes and offers one to me. "Happy New Year, beautiful lady."

We clink glasses and he sits very close beside me, clothes, hair, and skin steeped in Italian zest. It's a bigger turn-on than the champagne, honestly, something I don't mention. I mean, eau d'osso bucco? Hardly an aphrodisiac to most, I'm sure. But personally, I want to lick him, forehead to foreskin. Hmm. Does he have a foreskin? Damn, now I'm wondering.

But I'll allow him the first move. In some weird, recessed nook of my brain, this small gesture is an invitation to intimacy, and it's been a very long time since I've welcomed that. A sliver of me is terrified. All the rest keeps whispering that if things don't work out as expected, I've still got an extensive collection of vibrators. Orgasm for the sake of orgasm, however, becomes less and less a goal, and so does conquering a man simply for the sake of victory.

Does that mean I'm getting old?

FORGED BY FIRE

Tempered by age, youth's constant fire
burns down into quiet embers,
awaiting a sudden gust of desire,

longing only the heart remembers.
For the brazen heat of skin and flesh
burns down into quiet embers

'til circumstance and need enmesh,
one kiss and two hungry bodies cry out
for the brazen heat of skin and flesh,

no second thoughts, no hint of doubt,
desperate for the exquisite rain,
one kiss and two hungry bodies cry out.

Inferno ignites within passion's refrain,
burns itself out and smolders, cinders,
desperate for the exquisite rain,

downpour only the cresting hinders.
Tempered by age, youth's constant fire
burns itself out and smolders, cinders,
awaiting a sudden gust of desire.

TWENTY-TWO

We sip champagne and watch the fire, and I am hyperaware of the growing heat of his body through silk trousers and wool cardigan. As if to verify, he asks, "Mind if I take off my sweater? I'm getting a little warm."

"Only a little?"

He stands, slips the sweater up over his head, and I marvel at the cut of his physique — not so much "built" but sensibly athletic. He skis, of course, and probably runs. But I don't think he spends every off-hour working out in a gym, which pleases me. I've kind of lost my taste for gyms.

Cavin notices me staring. "What?"

"Nothing. Just admiring."

"I see. May I be direct?"

"Always."

"I never want to assume, but I'm hoping you'll want to share that master bedroom with me tonight. Is that a possibility?"

"No. It's a probability, although I will need some help up the stairs."

He nods. "I think I can arrange that. But first, I have to run down to my car. I packed a toothbrush, just in case."

"Of course. The light switch is right there by the door. Please be sure to lock up behind you when you come back in."

I watch him go and can't help but notice the slow, sultry creep between my legs. The idea strikes that what one-night stands are missing is the tarried bloom of desire, no need to hurry toward a pleasure-soaked moment or two, and then hurry faster away. Cavin and I have all the time in the world.

He returns with a leather overnight bag, and that makes me smile. "Must be a very big toothbrush."

"Not so big, really. But you should see the tube of toothpaste. Let me take the bag upstairs, and then I'll come back for you. That is, if you're ready."

I'm more than ready. I just hope we can accomplish the ultimate goal with a limited number of positions. It's pretty much the missionary. "Take your time. The master is at the far end of the hall."

"What about the Cristal?"

"No need to let it go flat."

"Copacetic."

Copacetic. Excellent word.

He disappears through the bedroom stairs portal. I turn off the gas to the fireplace, ascertain that the sliding glass door is locked. I've never had an unwanted visitor come in this way, but it isn't impossible. And lately the neighbor's dog, who's usually so quiet, has been barking at night. I'm probably just feeding my suspicion, but why take a chance?

My knee throbs insistently, doubtless from this morning's workout, followed by a lot of time standing in the kitchen. I lift the hem of my plum knit skirt. The swelling has definitely increased. I've avoided the pharmaceuticals for several days, but this seems like the right time to ingest something heavier than ibuprofen. I pop one from a bottle stashed in a kitchen cupboard, chase it with Cristal. Bubbly and poppy, one crazy cocktail, and it's starting to kick in right around the time Cavin returns, dressed down in flannel pants and a snug T-shirt. His hair is wet and smells like my favorite shampoo, even from here. So much for eau d'osso bucco.

"I took a quick shower. Hope you don't mind. Between freeway driving and headmaster stress, I was smelling a bit too . . . masculine."

"I thought you were going to say 'Italian,' which is the only thing I noticed. But you are always welcome to my hot water and soap."

"Ready to go upstairs?"

"As ready as this knee will permit."

"Never fear, fair lady!" He crosses the room in three long strides, scoops me up into his arms. "Prepare to conquer the stairs."

"You're not really considering carrying me, are you?"

"I think it's the most efficient use of our time. Hold on tight."

I wrap my arms around his neck, lay my head against his shoulder, hope for the best. He doesn't falter as we ascend, and I'm reminded of a scene from a movie. "Just call me Scarlett O'Hara. You are a strong man, Rhett Butler."

" 'Twas nothing, my dear. And here we are."

The room is dark, except for two lit candles, one on each of the end tables flanking the fainting couch. Cavin sits me gently there, beneath the big window. Outside, the winter moon finesses her light through the thin veneer of fog, casting an interesting sheen. It filters in through the plate glass, settles around me like a halo.

Cavin gives a low whistle. "Wow. I wish you could see how incredible you look right now. I'd take a picture, but I'd be afraid someone else might see it, and I want you all to myself." He leans down, brings his mouth an inch away from mine, and looks into my eyes. "Champagne now, or after?"

"I'm not thirsty."

"Good. Unbutton your blouse."

His voice is husky, sexy as hell, and I like that he has taken charge. I comply with his request, one button at a time. He watches without moving until the deed is accomplished. Now he kneels in front of me, eyes even with my breasts, which he coaxes from the lacy confines of my bra. His fingers encircle my nipples, bring them taut against his lips and the tip of his tongue, just beyond.

He takes his time.

This is not what men do.

This is not what I do.

They hurry.

I hurry.

And then it's over.

I realize, as he pulls away, stands, and begins a slow striptease, that my usual impatience for orgasm has not always served me well. My imagination did not sculpt him nearly well enough. He is lean but strong, and even in this mellow light, I can see his muscles work as he takes off his shirt, lays it over the back of the couch.

Cavin lifts me, carries me to the bed, and the kiss we share is filled with need, but also something else. My head spins with the word — promise. He perches me on the edge of the mattress, helps me out of my blouse and bra, pushes me onto my back to take off my skirt. Suddenly, I feel anxious about my imperfect body.

"Try not to look at my knee."

"I've seen worse. Anyway, looking at it isn't the issue. Not injuring it more critically is the challenge." I hear his trousers unzip, wait as he puts them with his shirt. The floor creaks beneath his return, and now my panties slip down, drop to the floor. "Open your legs. I want to see what's in between them."

Can he tell how wet I am?

Cavin slides a hand up my left thigh, and now he can have no doubt how wet I am. "Holy hell, woman." One finger. Two. Three, inside me. He thrusts and pulls.

Slowly.

Gently.

Faster.

Harder.

A moan escapes as I start to tense. But he

211

stops, makes me wait. "Oh, no. Not yet. I'm not letting you off that easy."

"You mean, getting me off?"

"That, either."

He leans up over me, kisses me hard, then his mouth travels the length of my body, stopping to kiss less usual places — along my collarbone and inside the bend of my elbows. His tongue circles my nipples, traces the curve of my breasts, draws a thin line down my torso and over my belly button. Now he lowers his face.

Licks my right leg, from knee to thigh.

Licks my left leg, from knee to thigh.

By the time he arrives at the sweet spot in between, I'm shaking.

He pauses. "Are you cold?"

"Not even close."

His tongue begins a relaxed upward roll, exploring the landscape of my womanhood. The pace of this lovemaking is completely unfamiliar, and it's driving me toward total lust-fueled insanity. "Lie still," he commands. "Don't you dare come yet."

"I'll try." It's a throaty whisper. "But I'm more than ready for the rest."

"I know. I just don't want to hurt you."

I think he's talking about my knee, especially when he slides a pillow beneath it. But now he strips off his Jockeys. On that one-to-ten scale, he's a definite nine, and fully erect. Length times girth equals what promises to be an unparalleled ride. It makes me want to be reckless.

"Can I ask you a personal question?"

He looks down at himself, then back at me. "At this point, I don't see why not."

"Are you STD-free?"

"I-I brought condoms."

"That isn't what I asked. I've never had an STD, and I can't get pregnant. If you're clean, and I'll take your word for it, I'd rather you not use a condom."

"I'm clean."

"I thought so. Come here."

It's a very good thing I'm this turned on. There's a brilliant little bolt of pain.

Cavin stretches me to the max as he pushes inside, driving all the way against my G-spot, filling me completely. This is something I've never experienced.

"Are you okay?" he asks, and waits for me to say yes. The rocking begins.

He takes his time.

This is not what men do.

This is not what I do.

Except tonight.

TWENTY-THREE

It's been a long time since I've shared my bed with a man overnight. I'm buzzed on pills and champagne, exhausted by two rounds of spectacular sex. But, unlike Cavin, who dozed off immediately, I can't get to sleep right away. I lie here, cooling semen trickling down my thigh, listening to the deep, even breathing beside me. How reckless was I?

A doctor could have an STD and lie about it. But it doesn't seem likely, at least not *this* doctor. I didn't lie about being clean. However, I'm not positive about the pregnancy thing. I quit taking the pill years ago, when marital sex became infrequent, and those rare occasions never resulted in a baby. I've relied on condoms for intermittent liaisons, and remained herpes- and fetus-free. Should I worry now? At my age, is what's left of my egg stash even viable?

Oh well, if things go wrong, there's always

abortion.

I slip out of bed, tiptoe to the bathroom, and douche away whatever seminal fluid is left inside me. Then I run a hot bath, soak for a while to relieve stress and stiffness. Good thing I took the heavier meds. Despite Cavin's careful cushioning, my knee is definitely more swollen than it was before our marathon. By the time I dry off, I'm actually sleepy.

I go back to bed, finesse my way under the covers, naked skin still hot and scented vanilla-cedar. I turn on my side, face toward the window, and am slipping toward slumber when Cavin rolls over to spoon. I'm not sure if he's half-awake or totally dreaming when he whispers, "Mm. You smell good." It's comforting.

I wake to sunlight throbbing in through the window. It disorients me. What time is it? Why does my head feel split open? Why am I naked and why . . . I reach behind me and my hand hits an empty pillow. "Cavin?"

But I'm alone.

I sit up, too quickly. The room wants to spin. I close my eyes, pull in long, shallow breaths. He wouldn't leave without saying good-bye, would he? When I open my eyes again, I turn to ascertain the fact that the far side of the bed is, indeed, unoccupied, and I find a note. *Let you sleep in. Give a shout when you're ready to come downstairs. By the way, you smell good.*

Maybe, but I'm sure I look awful. I test my knee on the short hike to the bathroom. It's sore, but not as bad as expected. The first thing I do is swallow two ibuprofen, chasing them with a big bottle of smart-water. Then I take a chance on the mirror. Yeesh! It's never a good thing to go to bed with my hair wet. Better take a shower so I can shampoo this mess back into proper condition. Lots of lotion and antiwrinkle potions to fight fine lines, followed by barely there makeup, enough to keep Cavin interested.

The jackhammer has quieted in my head and my knee seems cooperative, so I take the stairs on my own and manage the downhill route relatively problem-free. Cavin is sitting cross-legged on the sofa, reading a book. He's wearing faded jeans and a black T-shirt, and I think he's even better looking all dressed down.

"Morning."

He looks up from his reading and smiles. "Afternoon, actually. But just a little after."

"What are you reading?"

"Stephen King's new book."

"You like horror?"

216

"It's a guilty pleasure, I'm afraid." He puts the book on the coffee table, gets up, and comes over to kiss me good morning. It's a very nice hello. "Hey. You were supposed to give a yell. I would have arranged down-the-stairs transportation."

"You keep rescuing damsels in distress in that fashion, you'll need back surgery."

"Just one damsel, and she's no threat to my spine. You hungry? Hope you don't mind, but I threw together a quiche for brunch. There's coffee ready, too."

Where did this guy come from? He "threw together" a quiche? "I'm starving. Let's see what you're made of, Wolfgang."

He takes my hand, leads me into the kitchen, which is warm from the oven. A beautiful quiche sits cooling on the counter, whispering hints of garlic and rosemary. "Sit, and I'll get you some coffee. Unless . . . You do like coffee, don't you? I figured you did, because you buy beans in bulk, but I shouldn't assume. You have a great pantry, by the way."

"I adore coffee, and thank you. I'm a bit of an eccentric when it comes to my larder."

"Not at all. It's in exceptional order. Cream and sugar?"

"Black will do."

Cavin delivers two slices of quiche and

two steaming mugs of coffee to the table, sits on the far side, and waits for me to take a bite. The crust is flaky, the savory custard baked to perfection. I give him a thumbs-up, and he grins. "So, I was thinking. I've got five days in Carmel planned, with nothing to do but read. I'd very much like for you to come along. I know it's short notice, but . . ." He looks at me hopefully.

I swallow the bite, chase with a sip of strong coffee. "Would we have to spend the whole time reading?"

He brings those seafoam eyes level with mine. "You know better than that. Last night was incredible."

"Just wait till I can fully participate, Doctor."

"I'm patient by nature. Meanwhile, I want to spend time with you. Learn what makes you tick."

His forthrightness is alternately refreshing and unnerving. No one knows what makes me tick. Maybe not even me.

So, my choices are: Sit around here alone, fussing over a fund-raiser I had in place a month ago, and working out to keep from going insane (not to mention flabby); or take a long ride down the California coastline to one of the most beautiful little towns in the world, indulge in seafood and excellent vintages, walk on the beach (if my knee will deal with sand), and enjoy brilliant sex a couple of times a day.

I'd say that's a no-brainer.

"Let me make a few calls."

I go into my office to do exactly that. I call Melody to let her know where I'm going, just in case. I call Charlie to have him check on the place a couple of times while I'm gone. And I call Cassandra to rub it in. When I return to the living room, Cavin is on his own phone. I go ahead and eavesdrop.

"Look, I don't care what it takes. Bribe him. Threaten him. Hell, go ahead and kill him. My patient load has almost doubled this winter. I need OR time. I'll be back in a week. Work something out." He hangs up.

"Who was that? Your hit man?"

He smiles. "Not exactly. That was Rebecca, my receptionist. I'm having a hell of a time securing operating room hours. It's financially expedient to do surgeries back to back on the same day. Taking a week off means I'll have patients piled up, waiting."

"Sounds uncomfortable for them and frustrating for you."

"It is. But I'm overdue for a little time off, and now that I'll be spending it with you, I can't wait to put all that behind me."

"If you'll help me put a few things into a suitcase, I'll be ready to go."

"Can I help choose your outfits?"

He does.

TWENTY-FOUR

From start to finish, it's a great five days. The weather is perfect. The setting is perfect. My companion/host/tour guide is perfect, or at least as close to it as a man can come. If I were the type to scare easily, I'd probably run, because instinct hisses that there must be a defect there somewhere. Cavin Lattimore defines the cliché "too good to be true."

His Carmel vacation house perches on a cliff off Highway 1. Because of the curve of the hill, and genius engineering, it overlooks the ocean on three sides. It isn't huge — only two bedrooms and maybe three thousand square feet — but every room is spacious and open, with lots of sunlight through banks of windows and skylights. You almost feel like you're outside, inside.

We walk nearby beaches and stroll through old-town Carmel-by-the-Sea, with its courtyards and hidden paths and eccentric architecture. Cavin's patient with my injured pace, steadies me over uneven stone sidewalks, or carries me across deep pillows of sand, to the firmer damp footing closer to the sea.

"Keep this up, you're going to get a hernia," I joke.

"It's all about proper form, my dear. And your form is better than proper."

We hold hands and kiss publicly, like high school kids making out, no worry of censure. Every now and again, someone will wink, or I'll notice the odd look of displeasure. But for the most part, there is just Cavin and me, insulated by our peculiar bubble of happiness. I haven't laughed this much in a very long time.

On day three, we drive to Monterey and go whale watching. It's relatively early in the annual gray-whale migration from Alaska south to Baja, but apparently they're anxious this year and we're treated to regular sightings. As per regulations, the boat stops at a required distance when whales are spotted. Closer viewing is up to the whales. We get lucky there, too, when a juvenile becomes curious and approaches playfully, spouting very close to the side of the ship where we happen to be standing. He rolls to one side, looking up out of the water as he glides by.

"This is very unusual," announces the on-board naturalist. "And, oh look. Here comes his mama."

Cavin, who is behind me, lifts my hair. Kisses my neck. Mumbles into my ear, "Did you wear your Come Hither Leviathan perfume? I've done a half dozen of these trips before and never seen anything like this."

"Didn't you know? I'm the Whale Whisperer."

We laugh at the ridiculousness of the conversation. I feel almost as juvenile as the young whale. There's a freedom in that, one I've never really allowed myself to experience before. Even as a kid I had to be the adult. This is a rare gift. I turn to Cavin, reach up, and lock my arms around his neck. "Thank you."

"For what?"

"Everything."

The kiss we share is anything but adolescent.

We spend the afternoon at the aquarium and exploring Cannery Row, with Cavin offering narrative insights into John Steinbeck, who not only wrote about this area but was also born and raised here. "He loved this land, and he worked it, too. That's why he became so interested in the plight of migrant workers. Oh, and he was a tour guide at Tahoe for a while. That's where he met his first wife."

Turns out, Cavin is an avid reader and amateur historian, something he demonstrates again on day four. "Having a clear understanding of the past is vital to a healthy future." We are driving past the Henry Miller Memorial Library, on our way back to Carmel from Big Sur. He points to the small building, a converted old house guarded by giant redwood trees. "What do you know about Henry Miller?"

"Um . . . he was married to Marilyn Monroe?"

"No. That was Arthur Miller, the playwright. Henry Miller was a novelist. Have you read his *Tropic of Cancer*?"

"I've heard of it. It was early erotica or something, right?"

"It had quite a bit more substance than most erotica, but it was raw, and at the time France first published it in 1934, it was banned in the United States. It published here in 1961, and led to a series of obscenity trials that tested American laws on pornography. The case went all the way to the US Supreme Court, which ultimately declared the book a work of literature."

"Is it worth reading?"

"Do you like Kerouac or Ginsberg?"

I reach into memory for a favorite quote from *On the Road*. " 'We turned at a dozen paces, for love is a duel, and looked at each other for the last time.' "

"Ah. A fan, I see. Well, many credit Henry Miller with inspiring the Beat Generation. Certainly, Miller qualified as a bohemian, and his books paved the way for theirs. I've got *Tropic of Cancer* and *Tropic of Capricorn* at home. I'll lend them to you."

"And what about you? Do you qualify as a bohemian?"

He laughs. "Hardly. Although, you do encourage my inner hedonist."

"Is that so? Too bad you haven't gotten a glimpse of mine yet."

"I wouldn't say that. Just because she hasn't been able to come out and play yet doesn't mean I haven't caught sight of her."

Despite being largely confined to the missionary position, the sex we've shared has been great. I do, however, harbor a growing desire to experience straddling his exceptional cock, not to mention taking him from behind. When it comes to a healthy sex life, variety isn't just *any* spice. It's the salt and pepper.

By day five my knee has ballooned.

"You've worked it a lot," observes Cavin. "Let's forgo the sightseeing and chill here at home. I'll run to the store for dinner provisions and you can read this." He hands me a copy of *Tropic of Cancer.*

Before he leaves, he settles me on the patio in the pale sun, with my knee packed in ice. Then he tucks a blanket over my legs. "Warm enough?"

I nod. "Did anyone ever tell you you'd make a good doctor?"

"Only my mom. My teachers said I should try farming."

"Really?"

"I'll leave you with that image and see you in a bit."

He kisses me good-bye and I introduce myself to Henry Miller. I immerse myself in his stream-of-consciousness rant and must get sucked all the way under because at some point Cavin returns with groceries and I find I've read close to half the book.

He puts away the perishables, comes outside, and gestures toward the slim volume. "So, what do you think?"

"I think he was a brilliant writer, and a terribly disturbed man."

"Self-absorbed, certainly, even narcissistic. Disturbed? I guess that depends on your definition."

"Oh, I wasn't complaining. Most of my favorite authors fit my definition of disturbed. Painters, too. Something about the artistic temperament. In fact, I recently read a fascinating article about the correlation between creativity and depression. There's a part of the brain that refuses to turn off for artists, so they're always thinking. That, and they have an overwhelming need to control both their fictional characters, and the 'characters' who populate their real lives."

Sounds like me. Wonder if I've got a book somewhere inside.

"Anyway, that intrinsic darkness only serves to make their work more interesting." I throw back the blanket.

"I happen to agree. I take it you're ready to come inside?"

"Either that or grow roots right here."

I excuse myself for a bathroom break and when I return to the kitchen, Cavin is slicing fruit for a salad. The berries and bananas are already in a pretty crystal bowl and he's just started on the mango.

"Oh. No mango for me."

"You don't like mangoes?"

"I do, but they don't like me. I'm highly allergic."

"Really?" He puts down the knife.

227

"Really. It's funny because there are two kinds of allergies to mango. One is topical. Some people can't touch them. Apparently, they're related to poison oak, which doesn't bother me at all, and I can peel mangoes all day long. But I've got a food allergy, which is enzyme related. One bite, my tongue swells up and my throat wants to close."

"I hope you carry an EpiPen."

"I do, but even a hard-core antihistamine will do in a pinch."

"Have you had more than one reaction?"

"Three, each worse than the last. Sometimes mango sneaks into things like 'tropical cobblers' or fruit trays. Even juice cross-contamination will nail me."

He picks up the mango, drops it into the trash.

"Why did you do that? You can eat it."

He shakes his head. "Wouldn't want to cross-contaminate you when I do this." He pulls me into him, kisses me sweetly. "Now, how about a mango-free mimosa?"

It's the beginning of the end of an excellent day.

TWENTY-FIVE

It's the beginning of the end of an excellent vacation. Cavin drops me off at home, helps me up the stairs, stays only long enough for an extended good-bye. He's got a surgery at Tahoe in the morning, and a decent drive ahead of him.

"What about my knee?" I ask before he goes. "When should I schedule surgery?"

"It's getting close, but I'd give it a little more time. Do you want a referral to someone here in the Bay Area?"

"Oh, no. I'd rather you operate."

He clucks his tongue. "A week ago, I probably would have agreed, but now I'm afraid it would straddle the ethics line."

"No one would have to know."

"I would know."

I slide my arms up around his neck. "Aw, but I trust *you.*"

He kisses the tip of my nose. "The problem is, I've become awfully attached to

229

you over the last few days, and my feelings just might cloud my judgment."

"Sounds serious."

"It is. But listen. Barton does have one of the best orthopedic teams in the country. If you want to schedule there, I can refer you to one of my partners."

"Well . . ."

"I'll sweeten the pot. You can recuperate at my house. That way I can keep an eye on your recovery."

"Is that the only thing you want to keep an eye on?"

"I think you know better than that."

He kisses me, and it's full-throttle, and I realize how much I've enjoyed not only his company but also the regular sex. My lips still touching his, I mumble into his mouth, "I'm going to miss you. Have time for a quickie?"

Cavin takes my hand, tugs me over to the couch, pushes me down on the cream suede cushions. Then he lifts my hips, pulls until he can prop them up on the sofa's broad arm, where he kneels. Up goes my skirt, and my legs gently part and his face dives between them.

The lap of his tongue.

The plunge of his fingers.

The draw of his lips against my clitoris.

I want to protest. Ask to reciprocate. But I want more to ride this surf to completion, and that's what I do. Cavin kisses one thigh, then the next, then the first again, back and forth as he withdraws. "I hope that wasn't too quick."

A sigh escapes me as I close my legs, straighten my skirt. It was much too quick, but I say, "It was just right, but I'm afraid I owe you now."

"No worries. I'll make sure you pay that debt. Now I'd better take my leave before you convince me to stay."

He isn't gone an hour before this great swoop of loneliness settles over me. Weird. I'm used to being alone, but right now I feel emptied. I wander the house, which the housekeeper has cleaned as per my orders. Today it seems sterile. I go into my office, flip on the security camera, which shows a street devoid of traffic. I turn on my computer, scour my e-mail. Nothing important, just a couple of fund-raiser RSVPs and credit card bill payment receipts. The only phone message is from Melody, wanting to know details about my "romantic rendezvous." I'll call her back later. Right now I want to keep every one of them locked up inside.

Instead, I call Charlie, ask if he can go

shopping tomorrow. He's agreeable, so I give him a list. Fruit. Vegetables. Quinoa. Eggs. Raw almonds and pistachios. No complex carbs. No dairy. I've vowed to eat healthy for a couple of weeks to make up for the calories I consumed in Carmel. I'd go ahead and work out, but my knee is complaining as it is.

I try to read but am too distracted, especially when the next-door dog starts yapping. Annoying, but does it mean anything? I check the windows and camera but spy nothing out of the ordinary. Still the mutt keeps barking. It must be as bored as I am. Rather than go one hundred percent stir-crazy, I call Cassandra and arrange to meet her at Robberbaron, a favorite nearby wine bar.

It's a long slog down the steep stairs to the street, where I meet the cab I called, still not trusting that my leg can work the gas and brake pedals correctly. For once, I arrive ahead of my friend. The place is relatively uncrowded, so I choose a table near the front door, where Cassandra can spot me easily, and I don't have to walk farther than necessary. The down-the-stairs hike left me with a decent limp.

Apparently, the bartender notices, because he hustles over with a menu. "Hello again."

Apparently, he has noticed *me* before.

I look at him — not too young, handlebar mustache, curly hair, too long over the ears. Yes, I've noticed him before, too, though I couldn't manage to call him by name without reading the badge on his chest. "How's it going, Jasper? I'm meeting a friend, but she shares my taste in wine. Bring a bottle of the Syrah/Grenache. And we'll have a bar picnic — salamis, prosciutto, the chevre, and whatever your cheese of the day is."

I'll start the no-dairy-no-bad-for-you-meats diet tomorrow. By the time Cassandra arrives, so has the wine. The food joins us soon after. She's anxious for information but waits politely while Jasper delivers the tray, which is liberally stocked with crackers, nuts, meats, and cheeses. As soon as he returns to the bar, she pounces. "Okay, give."

Give? What am I, fifteen? "What *are* you talking about, Cassandra, darling?"

"Come on, Tara, I'm dying here. What's this big development? I mean, really. Where have you *been* for the past month?"

Where do I start? With skiing, I guess, since that's where Cassandra and I last left off. The complete story, including Christmas at Mel's, the weirdness with Graham, and hiring Charlie, takes a good twenty minutes. I omit any mention of creepy phone calls and shady sedans. I've decided to bottle that paranoia.

My friend absorbs every word. When I finish, she says, "I'm concerned."

"Why?"

"We've been sitting here for a half hour, and there are a couple of great-looking guys over there who keep trying to catch your attention. You haven't so much as blinked in their direction."

"Really?" I turn to look. They're cute, but I don't return their come-on smiles. "I never even noticed."

"That's why I'm worried. I've known you for a long time, and you are always hyper-aware of every man in the room. You take inventory."

Her directness makes me smile. "Usually, I'm shopping, or at least window shopping."

"Exactly, but not tonight. This doctor of yours must be one very special man."

"He is."

"Oh, speaking of your men, you know that personal trainer you used to boink?"

"Nick?"

"That's the one. He's working at my gym now."

"Is that so?"

"He says a former client got him fired. Well, actually, a heartless, horny bitch of a former client. For some reason, I thought of you. Was that you?"

"What if it was?"

"I guess my question would be why?"

I construct my answer carefully. "Nick is not a careful man. He throws threats around without thinking. Some people prefer not to be threatened. Some people fight threats with action."

I'm not sure what her reaction will be, so I'm happy when she lifts her glass. "Cheers." I accept the toast, but then she asks, "What about people who fight action with action?"

Twenty-Six

The question irritates both my daily routine and vain attempts to sleep at night. And there's another one, too, inspired by my friend Cassandra's counsel: am I really ready to tie myself down, commit to another full-time monogamous relationship, no matter how perfect Cavin Lattimore appears to be? The answer I keep coming back to is, I want to find out.

My surgery is scheduled for crack of dawn Monday morning. I'm not looking forward to the procedure and post-op rehab, but I'm definitely anticipating walking without a limp again, not to mention the freedom of driving, which I still worry about attempting. The entire core of my knee is mush. I'm fearless about some things. Dying in an auto accident because I can't hit the brakes in time isn't one of them.

Charlie has helped me pack enough clothes for an extended stay at Cavin's.

"You sure you're not just moving in?" he jokes, after he returns from his third trip down to the Escalade.

"That offer has not, as yet, been put on the table."

"Good. I'd hate to lose my job already. In fact, I've been brushing up on my shoulder-rubbing skills. Want me to demonstrate?"

"A tempting offer, but another time. I want to get to my sister's before that god-awful Sacramento rush begins."

Charlie is driving me as far as Mel's, then my sister will chauffeur the rest of the way. Both will return via car service so I'll have the Escalade available postsurgery rehab. Which means another two nights in Mel's guest room, something Graham will just have to deal with.

"Okay, if you're sure, let's plan on a rain check. You ready?"

I've locked the doors. Left the security system on. Visited the bathroom. "Let's go."

Charlie is careful behind the wheel, at least with me in the passenger seat. Aggressive California drivers bother him not at all. He stays in the middle lane, drives five miles over the limit. Normally this might aggravate me, but it's a nice day and I've been cooped up, and I'll be sequestered in the days to come, so I appreciate having this time to enjoy the scenery, such as it is. The winter hills have yet to green, and there's a lot of concrete between home and Mel's.

Turns out, there's a fair amount of cement between Charlie's ears, too. You'd think someone born and raised in San Francisco would have a little more cognizance of world affairs, but when it comes to big-picture ideas, he's pretty dense. I resign myself to his stories of university antics. He's enjoying playing a rather diverse field — male, female, undecided — and at this point, he hasn't declared himself, either. Actually, some of those anecdotes are rather amusing.

Finally, he says, "Oh, I almost forgot. When I told Teddy I was working for you, he said you two are well acquainted."

"That is true. He's on the board of an LGBT teen center. I helped him do some fund-raising."

"Why didn't you mention it? Did you know that's who I was referring to when I told you who my landlords were?"

"I figured it was probably them, but I rarely give everything away to someone on first meeting. Haven't you ever heard that it's good to hold your trump cards close to your chest?"

"Did you think you'd need a trump card?"

"You always need a trump card."

Apparently, Graham has played his trump card and gone golfing with buddies until Sunday afternoon, when Melody and I are scheduled to leave. Mel's house is half-empty when Charlie and I arrive. Not only is Graham away, but so are two of the girls. Suzette and her new snowboard went to Tahoe along with a group of her friends. Kayla and her new boyfriend are currently AWOL, a fact that is not discussed until after Charlie's on his way back to the city.

Mel and I are settled in the living room, sipping early glasses of wine while Jessica and one of her friends play Xbox in the den. "This guy — Cliff — is a real piece of work," Mel says. "Twenty years old, supposedly going to University of the Pacific, but I don't think he spends much time at school."

"Kayla met him after she got back from San Francisco?"

She nods. "He's a barista at a Starbucks she happened into. According to Kayla, 'He smiled at me, and I smiled back, and we just knew we were meant to be.' I mean, gag me."

"You don't like him much, I take it?"

"He couldn't look any more like a loser if he had a capital *L* stamped on his forehead."

"But Kayla will see through that. She's a

smart girl."

"Maybe eventually, but right now she's mired in that hormonal lust-confused-with-love stage. Which today means she waited for her father to leave before calling Cliff to come pick her up. Not one word to me until she texted that she planned to spend the night with a friend. Said friend, when I checked, had no idea Kayla was going to stay overnight. But she had heard about a big party somewhere and as far as she knew, Kayla and Cliff were on their way there. When I tried to call Kayla, her phone went to voice mail. I texted her, of course, and, of course, she hasn't responded. So, what do I do? Call the cops?"

"And say what? That your daughter and her irresponsible boyfriend are going to a party without your permission? Even without that information, law enforcement wouldn't bother to look for her until she's been missing for twenty-four hours."

"That's what I mean."

For about the millionth time, I'm glad I've managed to avoid pregnancy. And, apparently I'm still blessed. Despite plenty of passionate Carmel sex, my period started right on schedule.

"Guess you'll have to deal with it when she gets home and try not to worry in the meantime."

"Deal with it, how? I seriously doubt grounding her will work."

"Maybe you'll just have to trust that you've raised her with enough of a moral sense that she'll keep herself out of trouble. Alternately, you could always hire a hit man to take Cliff out."

Mel takes a sip of wine. "Don't suppose you know any, do you?"

As it turns out, the hit man is unnecessary, at least for the time being. Kayla arrives home midmorning. I happen to be near a window when Cliff pulls his belching Kia against the curb. From here I can see them kiss good-bye, and there's nothing sweet about the gesture. The boy is brave, I'll give him that. He walks Kayla right up to the front door, and that is where I confront them, before Mel can.

"What do you think you're doing?"

Kayla wears the remnants of last night's party — smeared makeup, dead booze breath, clothes that smell of sex. And the black pupils of her eyes tell me she did more than drink, though I think I won't confide that to my sister. Sometimes keeping secrets is the best move.

Kayla sputters at the direct question, but Cliff is prepared. "Just bringing my baby home, safe and sound."

I keep my voice steady. "Kayla, come inside. Your mom is beside herself with worry. As for you . . ." I step between the two of them, drawing a petulant protest from Kayla, one I ignore completely. "If you ever disrespect either my niece or my sister like this again, you will be very, very sorry."

Cliff attempts to inflate himself to big-man status, fails completely. Still, he dares, "Yeah? Whatcha going to do about it?"

The smile I give him is one I reserve for moments exactly like this one. "You know what, Cliff? The world is full of impotent jackals like you, and I've made it a personal goal to dispose of as many as possible. Just how is something you will find out, if you don't pay proper respect to this family. You will start by apologizing to Kayla's mother . . ."

"Aunt Tara!"

I turn toward my niece. "What? Did I embarrass you? But you're not embarrassed to lie to your mom, get high and fuck all night, then come home looking like a common streetwalker? Get inside!"

At this point, Melody arrives on the scene to investigate the commotion. "Oh my God, Kayla, just look at you." She says nothing to Cliff, who tries to walk away.

"Stop." The menace in my voice is enough to halt him. "If you are, in fact, interested in maintaining a relationship with your 'baby,' I suggest you locate some small sense of decency and offer a sincere apology to my sister."

I am more than a little surprised when he actually turns around, looks at Mel, and mutters, "Sorry."

Kayla freaks out. "You don't have to apologize!" she yells at Cliff, before turning her anger in my direction. "And you don't need to rescue me! I'm an adult. I can take care of myself."

Mel steps into her mom role. "You may be beyond the age of consent, but you're hardly an adult, as your recent actions demonstrate. And if you'd like to keep living here, this will be the last time you pull a stunt like this. As for you, young man, please understand that this household cannot function without simple rules, one of the most important being that we know where our children are at all times. Bending rules with deceit will not be tolerated. Do you understand?"

"Yeah. Whatever. But just so you know, she told me it was okay with you."

I'm not sure who looks more shocked, Melody or Kayla. The two stand there staring like they've never seen each other before. Down the block, a very large truck downshifts, turning onto the street with a loud chuff. Cliff uses the distraction as an opportunity to make his escape. He takes off and Kayla yells after him, "Hey, everything's cool. Text me, okay?"

He responds with a shrug and an almost obscure flick of his hand. I shut the door between his retreat and us, as Kayla bursts into tears. I am not impressed.

"No one loves me but Cliff."

"Oh, blah, blah, blah. Poor little unloved Kayla. Lose the melodrama, would you? If that boy cared about you at all, he would have dropped you off at a reasonable hour last night."

"The least you could have done was answer my text," interrupts Melody.

"Why? So you could tell me to come home?"

"So we would have known you were all right. And then so I could tell you to come home."

Kayla changes tactics, softening. "Look, by the time I got your text, we were too wasted to drive. I figured you'd rather have me safe than out on the road in that condition."

Mel's face flushes consternation. "Wasted?

244

Wasted on what?"

Kayla rolls her eyes. "It was a *party*, Mom." Way to avoid a definitive answer.

"Yes, well, there will be no more parties for quite a while. And, while I appreciate your not allowing your *wasted* boyfriend to drive you home, there are plenty of taxis in this city. Or I would have come to pick you up."

She snorts. "Right. Call my mommy."

"If you're going to act like a stupid kid, yes."

"I'm not a kid. I'll be eighteen in April."

"And I'll still be your mommy."

Kayla storms off to her bedroom. Melody trails, dragging a stern lecture along. I watch them go, thinking about the strong need for independence I had at that age. The difference was, I possessed the skills to pull it off, and a mother who didn't care anyway.

TWENTY-SEVEN

I start toward the kitchen, where a strong cup of coffee is waiting. I'm almost there when the doorbell rings, and I turn around. Cliff? What could he possibly want? I fling open the door. "Did you forget —"

I haven't seen her in decades. And while I'd like to say those years have not been kind to her, it would be a lie. She has gone slender, and there is pride in her carriage, perhaps even conceit. Her hair is cut stylishly short, and colored a pale titian. The only real evidence of her age is the whittled web etching her face. Could insanity be the fountain of youth? Or maybe it's just all the "good lovin'." Beyond her, I notice the out-of-place semi loitering curbside.

She stares at me for a long minute, finally nods recognition. "Tara. What a surprise."

My mother walks past me, smelling vaguely of diesel and sincerely of tobacco, yanking her bulky male companion over the threshold as if to avert having the door slammed in their faces. Excellent instincts, as ever.

"What are you doing here?"

"What? No hug?" She opens her arms. "It's been a real long time."

I back away.

Something ugly surfaces in her eyes. "Where's your sister?"

"Dealing with a problem child."

"Melody Ann!" she yells. "Where the hell are you?"

Melody Ann. Two names, the second used as punctuation. And suddenly, there's the venomous mom of my nightmares. I knew she'd slither out from the woodpile sooner or later.

The man, at least, seems to have the wherewithal to be discomfited by the outburst. "Now, June . . ."

Her head rotates slowly in his direction. "What?" she snaps.

"Nothing."

Mel comes rustling down the stairs. "Mom? What are —"

"Not you, too! What am I doing here? Jesus H. Christ on a crutch! Can't a woman drop by to see her daughter when she happens to be driving past the neighborhood?"

Mel and I exchange confounded looks. I'd

better let her do the talking. "No. It's just . . . I mean . . ."

I can't help myself. "She means it's not like you drop by every week or so, or even every year or so. Or, in my case, not even every decade or so. So what do you want?"

Rather than answer, she moves past us into the living room, where she makes a slow, assessing circuit. We have little choice but to follow. She stops in front of a framed family portrait hanging on the wall. "Beautiful kids. Too bad I don't know them." She turns toward Mel. "You've done all right for yourself."

Ah, here it comes. The shakedown. "You want money."

"You always were a blunt bitch, Tara. But no, believe it or not, I'm not asking for a handout. Will over there earns a decent paycheck, and he's happy enough sharing it with me."

"So what *do* you want, then?"

She takes a deep breath. Exhales, initiating a crusty cough. She really ought to give up smoking. "Connection."

"What the fuck do you mean, connection?" Goddamn it, Idaho pops up on the doorstep and the classless Tara I've worked so hard to dispose of claws her way out of the crypt.

Mom throws back her shoulders, lifts her chin. "Look. Will's on a long haul, and I'm riding shotgun. We were passing by, so I thought we'd stop in. I'm not getting younger, you know. I'd like a little time with my family before I die. Is that too much to ask for?"

I toss a glance at Will. "Did you have something to do with this?"

He has been staring, slack-jawed, but now his gaze falls toward the floor. "Well . . . uh . . . why would you think so?"

"Because my mother never gave a shit about us, not even when we were little. She hasn't said one word to me in thirty years. Why would she care about *connection* now, unless someone else suggested it might be important?"

"You know something, Tara Lynn? Communication is a two-way street. You could have picked up the phone and called me any damn time."

Anger crawls up the back of my neck, seethes into my cheeks. I fight to keep my temper in check. "You know what? You're absolutely right. I don't suppose we really have much to say to each other." Obviously the bonding she wants doesn't include me, and that thought makes me change tack.

"Did you know I was going to be here today?"

She looks me straight in the eye, shakes her head. "It was an unpleasant co-incidence."

The woman always could stun me silent. She circles the room again, trailing haughti-ness like perfume. Attack seems fruitless, so instead I withdraw to the kitchen and pour wine in favor of coffee. The rich purple cab reminds me of blood, its full-bodied taste gone bitter. I fucking hate my mother.

In the other room, Melody calls for the girls to come say hello to their grandmother. I have no clear idea how much they know about her, or if she's ever visited before. This could be interesting. I gulp down the wine into my empty belly, pour another glass, feeling marginally mellower with the slow ascension of an alcohol buzz. This could be *really* interesting.

Mom and Will have perched on opposite ends of the sofa. Melody sits on the raised hearth, ready to officiate if necessary. Jessica is on the love seat with her overnight guest, Laura. Kayla has yet to appear. I stand in the doorway, ignoring the throb in my knee, sipping cabernet for breakfast, something Mom doesn't fail to notice.

"You celebrating something?" she asks.

"Hell yeah." I lift my glass. "Here's to unexpected reunions. Should I pour you a glass?"

Her expression tells me she's tempted, but she says, "Kind of early, isn't it?"

"Not today."

Kayla finally stomps into the room, still pissed and scowling.

"Glad you could join us," says Melody, nerves finally showing.

"I was trying to manage some damage control, and considering it's *your* fault, I don't see why you're mad at me."

"My . . . ?" Mel wants to say what I'm thinking, but this isn't the time, and she knows it, so she shifts direction. "You remember your grandmother, don't you? Can you please say hello?"

It finally dawns on the girl that there are a couple of strangers on the sofa. She turns on the dubious charm. "Oh. Sure. Hi, June. It's been a while, and I don't think you were with . . ." She redirects her question toward Will. "Have we met, um . . . ?"

Even beneath the chin and cheek stubble, the man's blush is obvious. "The name's William, but you can call me Will. Everyone does. And no, we haven't met before today."

Mom pats the cushion between her and

William. "I'd like you to come sit here next to me."

I'm surprised at how easily Kayla complies, but she does, and sitting so close beside my mother, the resemblance is spooky. It's almost as if Graham wasn't involved in the genetics at all. When they talk, their speech patterns are similar, and driven by some tic of the psyche to begin almost every sentence with "I." I want. I need. I'm going to. I wish. I will. I hate. It doesn't take long for it to become tiresome.

Jessica and her friend must agree. They both hold their phones in their laps and it's obvious they're texting each other. Every now and again their fingers move, their eyes drop, and suddenly they're smiling. Stifling giggles. That might be annoying, too, except it's so apropos.

Will looks bored, but he pays them the attention Mom would absolutely demand. My semi-inebriated brain clicks into snapshot mode.

Wonder how long he's been Mom's lay-o'-the-day.

Wonder if he realizes how many there were before him.

Wonder how long until she moves on to yet another.

Wonder if he wonders, too.

Melody seems content enough to listen to the exchange for a while. Then she must notice Jessica's distraction, because she tries to insert her into the lopsided conversation. "Jessica will be a freshman next year. She's trying out for the cheerleading squad."

Mom downshifts. "Good move. Cheerleaders get all the cute guys."

Jessica's and Laura's heads swivel toward each other, and they exchange eye rolls. Then Jessica turns back to Mom, and in complete seriousness says, "I'm not working my butt off to make the squad so I can get dates."

"Really?" responds Mom. "So why, then?"

"It's my sport, and I'm really good at it. Maybe even good enough to get a college scholarship. Anyway, boys are overrated."

Mom reaches across Kayla, pats Will's knee. "Oh, I don't know. I think they're kind of useful, if you know what I mean."

"Jesus, Mother! Could you be any less appropriate?" My small outburst releases a big knot of tension.

"What? You think girls this age don't know what sex is?"

"I'm sure none of us cares that you still engage in it."

"What do you mean, still? You're never too old to have a little fun. Right, Will?"

The younger girls burst out laughing, and their texting fingers fly. Will and Melody fidget, and Kayla wears an aura of amusement. Personally, I've had enough. "If you'll excuse me, I've been standing on this knee too long. I'm going to lie down for a while. It was, um . . . interesting to see you again, Mother, and nice to meet you, Will."

As I retreat to the guest room, I hear her say, "She really shouldn't drink this early in the day. Makes her mean."

Behind me, the "connection" continues. I can't disconnect fast enough, and by the time I reach the bedroom my head is, in fact, whirling from the wine and surprise encounter. I set the glass on the dresser, toss myself down on the bed. Around and around I go. But before long, the spinning slows and I can comfortably close my eyes.

You're never too old to have a little fun.

I spiral backward to an afternoon in Las Vegas. I was sixteen, and I arrived home from school on a half-day release. Apparently Mom didn't get the message because when I walked through the door, the first thing I noticed was that the place reeked of booze. The second thing I noticed was my mother, having a little fun on the sofa with some anonymous man. I don't remember his face, but I'll never forget seeing his cock,

254

which was long and thin and curved to one side. When he noticed me watching, wide-eyed, he plunged it between my mom's open legs like a dagger.

I put my hands over my eyes but couldn't stop myself from saying, "Disgusting. I'll never sit on that couch again. Can't you do your screwing in your bedroom?"

From anyone but my mother, I would have expected embarrassment. I was not particularly surprised that she wasn't bothered in the least. "It's hot in there," she said. "This is nice, in front of the swamp cooler."

It was more than hot. It was sweltering, and I was wearing shorts and a tank top. Old Crooked Dick took a good, long look. "You've got a great ass," he remarked, as if I'd find it a compliment. And then he dared ask, "Hey, June. You ever had a three-way with your daughter? Might be kinda kinky."

I gritted my teeth, knowing what Mom's reaction would be. Of course, it wouldn't come until after Mr. Kinked Cock hit the road. All she said right then was, "What are you, some kind of perv? Tara there doesn't even have sex yet. Do you, girl?" She kept it light, but I could tell she was boiling.

"This is the closest to sex I've come, and if this is what it looks like, I don't think I'll

255

be trying it anytime soon."

I turned to go to my room and was almost there when the disgusting dude called, "You could do a whole lot worse for your first than this right here. This thing is one of a kind!"

The truth was, I'd already had sex, and found it mildly pleasurable, if ultimately dissatisfying, in the way most teen sex is. But that was not information to share with my mother, whose expected punishment came swiftly after the man left but before she showered. The door slammed open, and the odor of recent rutting preceded her into the room.

She had on only an oversize T-shirt, one some man had left behind. Her hair was an untamed nest, and her eyes betrayed her insanity. "What the fuck do you think you're doing, wearing clothes like that out in public?"

"It's a hundred degrees outside. Everyone's wearing shorts."

"Not shorts like that. You look like a streetwalker."

I wanted to toss back the cliché "Takes one to know one." Instead, I tried a halfhearted "Sorry," knowing it wouldn't be good enough.

"Sorry? I'll make you sorry, bitch."

She charged me full-bore, her anger not at my clothing but at the idea of my drawing the man's attention away from her. Her fists were moving before she reached me, and for once, I refused to let them connect meaningfully, raising my arms to cover my face. That only enraged her more.

But this time, something wild reared up inside me, and it fed on years of past abuse. I turned on her and freed the beast. Physically, we were evenly matched. Psychologically, she stood zero chance. I allowed myself no choice but to win, and exact some small measure of revenge for too many years beaten down.

She never hit me again.

TWENTY-EIGHT

I claw my way up out of an Idaho nightmare, wake in a house fallen silent. Idaho. Mom. Oh yeah, she was really here, not a nightmare at all. But where did everyone go? I sit up, too fast. I feel as if someone split my skull with an ax. Wine for breakfast. Right. And now, headache or no, I'm starving.

The living room is empty, and a glance out the window confirms that Mom, Will, and semi have deserted the neighborhood. In the kitchen, I find a sandwich and note from Mel: *Jess and I took Laura home. Check in on Kayla, please. We'll be back before dinner.*

A half dozen bites and the sandwich has vanished. It was tuna, not my favorite, but this afternoon I'm not picky. I chase it with water and three ibuprofens — one for my knee, two for my head. Guess I'd better go see what Kayla's up to. Normally, I wouldn't bother, but Mel did ask me to, and besides, I've nothing better to do.

As I put my plate in the dishwasher, I notice the wine bottle sitting on the counter is empty. I definitely didn't kill it. Maybe Mom had a glass or two after all. I start toward the staircase, but as I exit the kitchen, I hear noise out on the back patio and divert to investigate.

When I open the sliding glass door, the scent of skunk nearly knocks me over. Kayla turns at the sound. In one hand, she's holding a tumbler of what appears to be what was left of the wine; in the other, there's a smoking pipe. "Oh, hey, Aunt Tara. Wanna hit?" She slurs her words, and she can barely keep her bloodshot eyes open.

"What are you doing, Kayla?"

"I think it's called self-medicating."

"I think it's called underage drinking. And I don't suppose you have a prescription for that marijuana, do you?"

She finds that hysterically funny. "It's just a little weed. Bet you've tried it before, and don't tell me you didn't drink when you were my age."

"Actually, I tried pot exactly once in high school, and hated how out of control it made me feel, especially since the guy who supplied it immediately attempted to take advantage of me. As for alcohol, I didn't start drinking until after my first husband died. I was in my midtwenties. Regardless, do you really think this is wise?"

"Sometimes you want to escape, you know? Give your brain a little vacation." She takes a final hit off the pipe, taps the burnt contents into the winter-browned grass, rubs them in with her foot. Then she mostly empties the glass in one long pull.

"That's a waste of good grapes. Wine like that should be sipped, not gulped. It isn't Gallo."

"Whatever. As long as it does the trick."

Kayla puts the glass down on the wooden picnic table and tucks the pipe into a pocket. Then she sits on the slider, tilting her face up into the pallid February sunlight, closing her eyes. I settle into the adjacent wooden chair, watching her rock slowly back and forth. I know it's a ridiculous question, but I ask it anyway. "Does this have something to do with my mother dropping by?"

That, too, makes her laugh. "Are you kidding? Why would that bother me?"

"She has a way of making people nervous."

"I didn't notice. Like, how?"

I shrug. "I don't know. Maybe it's just me.

She and I have never exactly been close."

"How can you not be close to your mother?" She opens her eyes and fixes them on me, truly curious.

"That's a very long story, one your own mom should probably share with you. But since you asked the question, it must mean you feel close to Melody. So why the meltdown?"

"I want her to let me grow up."

"Then you'll have to act like a grown-up. Drinking and smoking dope don't qualify as adult behaviors, by the way. And what you did last night was inconceivably selfish and rude. How long have you known Cliff?"

"Two weeks."

"So in what universe can you possibly believe that you two are in love? Love requires careful cultivation. It's not something you can screw your way into." Like I have a clue about the cultivation part. The screwing-your-way-into element, however, I know something about. "He's cute and all, but he's a loser, Kayla. And, to be totally frank, right now you're looking a lot like a loser, too. I thought you had big dreams."

"I do." It's a whisper.

"Then don't give them up for a boy." I purposely don't use the word "man." "And most definitely do not drown them in a bottle of booze or let them go up in a trail of smoke. Look. I've gone out on a limb for you. It isn't often I ask favors of an ex-husband, and this one was major. I expect you to excel at the Art Institute — keep up your grades, and no disappearing acts with scummy guys who are only out for themselves. Your future is on the line here, Kayla, and 'self-medicating' with alcohol or illegal drugs, or even taking a chance on some nasty virus, is only going to damage it. I don't know what you're hiding from, but if it's something big, tell me right now. If it's not, this is just plain stupid."

She thinks quietly for a minute or two and finally admits, "Sometimes I wonder if I'm crazy."

"Everyone wonders that sometimes."

"No. I mean really, certifiably insane. Like, possessing some sort of distorted personality trait, one that makes me reckless, and also makes me believe, no matter how hard I try not to, I will drive every important person from my life. So I spend hours figuring out ways to test them."

How much should I tell her? "Look, Kayla, if you're really worried about that, let your mother know, and tell your therapist. There is a syndrome called borderline personality disorder, and one of its symptoms is thinking everyone in your life will desert you. Only a professional can help you figure out if what you're feeling is rooted there, or just a manifestation of teen angst."

"Did you feel this way when you were my age?"

"Not exactly."

I felt alienated.

Friendless.

Family-less.

Resentful.

Pissed.

Belittled.

Abused.

But I also felt in charge. Of my present. My future. I wasn't, but that was my youth talking, and it wasn't long before I found my ticket to complete control of my life.

"Were you popular in high school?"

"No. I've never had a lot of friends. High school was especially tough because we moved to Las Vegas from Idaho, and not even 'big-city' Idaho, if you can call any of the cities there big. Beyond the radical lifestyle change, which took a whole lot of getting used to, our home was unhappy. Unstable. I would never have brought someone else into it. It's hard to build friendships that work in one direction."

"That's sad."

"It didn't feel that way at the time, but looking back, I guess it was."

We sit quietly for a few minutes. I push away the recently resurrected snapshots of my mother having sex on the sofa. Bring a friend home? I choke back a laugh.

Finally, she says, "This house used to be happier. I don't invite people over anymore."

"Why not?"

"Seems like Dad is always pissed at something. Usually me."

"All kids feel that way, don't they?"

"Maybe. But this is different. We used to be pretty close. But now it seems like he keeps pushing himself farther and farther away. Not just from me, but from the whole family. I think it started with his band."

"You mean, like, maybe he's experiencing a midlife crisis?"

"Something like that."

"Also not that unusual for someone his age."

But I swear if I find out he's been sleeping around, or if his behavior in any way hurts my sister, the next bottle of tequila will do more than give him the runs.

The wind has picked up, pushing a few

264

high clouds in front of the sun. Kayla shivers. "Guess we should go inside." She stands, reaches for the tumbler, which slips out of her hand, shattering against the patio cement. Wine-painted glass sprays everywhere. "Fuck."

Oh well. At least it will give her something to do instead of feel sorry for herself.

I leave her busy with the cleanup, return to the relative warmth of the house — the heat tempered slightly by the chill of recent revelations. Silence drapes the rooms heavily. Some music might lighten the mood, as long as it's music I love, and there's plenty of that on my phone. I retrieve it from my purse, notice I've got a new message.

From "Private."

You should have listened. Better watch your back, bitch. I've got eyes on you.

Fear begins a low throb inside my head. I limp quickly into the front room, stand to one side of the window to scan the street. Two cars, neither the beater sedan, cruise slowly, in opposite directions. Despite their tarried speed, I don't get negative vibes from either of them. This is a neighborhood where children ride bikes in the street, so cautious driving is called for. Four houses down, on the far side, a van is parked at the curb. Is there someone inside?

265

Can't tell.

Should I call law enforcement? And say what? Nothing came of the last message. Why should this one be any different? And what could they do, anyway? This isn't even an overt threat. Whoever "Private" is, he seems to know just how far to go.

I'm still pondering as Mel's car motors past the van, pulling into the driveway to park in the garage. I hear her come in the back door, yacking at Jessica, who howls laughter. "Anyone home?" calls Mel.

"In here."

I take one last look out the window, where nothing seems amiss, and there's still no sign of a human presence in the van. Mel bustles into the room. "You should have seen . . ." Her voice trails away when she sees my face. "What's wrong? Your face is white. Are you sick?"

She doesn't need to be privy to my worry, which is probably pointless anyway. "Just a little headache. What should I have seen?"

Mel launches a lengthy story. I don't hear a word.

SHED OF SKIN

Freed within her exile, the serpent
slithers boldly, strikes
without compassion,
splendor in the death dance.

Ah, patient is my sister.

No hurry now but to sup
before the meal grows cold,
she enfolds her victim tenderly,
awaits the egress.

Therein lies the victory.

Could Eve have denied her,
so beautiful in patterned scales, cool
in calculated treachery, sensuality
defined in the flick of her tongue?

Temptation is her legacy.

Enhanced by evolution,
perfected by time's passing,
she expels the weight of Eden
in gushes of sweet venom.

To grow, she must leave herself behind.

Subtle stretch. Elastic. Pinpricks
of sensation. Inner fabric gives
way in painless liberation.
Sister emerges, new.

Sin such as this commands envy.

TWENTY-NINE

Graham arrives home on Sunday, almost on time, after an early-morning round of golf with his friends. Melody greets him with a lukewarm (aka married) kiss and, for not the first time, I wonder what's left between them. Considering he has been gone for two days, and she is about ready to escort me out the door, the answer isn't hard to discern. Marriage equals ho-hum, at least after a couple of decades. For me personally, it didn't take nearly that long.

We hit the road around two. It's a clear winter day, no hint of snow in the forecast, so the trip should be a piece of cake. The plan is for both of us to stay overnight at Cavin's, leave the Escalade there in the morning, and he'll drive us to the hospital. Mel will stay long enough to make sure I come up out of the anesthesia, safe and hopefully sounder than before I go under.

We've opted to take Interstate 80, and

then drop over the mountain past the Northstar ski resort. The route is more direct to Cavin's place, and Mel is still a little uncomfortable with the big SUV, which can almost drive itself on the freeway. Once she's got it comfortably pointed in the right direction, I ask the question I avoided last night.

"So, how often do you see Mom?"

"I've been wondering when you would ask me that. The answer is, not often. The last time she stopped by was probably three years ago. She was with a different guy, and they stayed for lunch. Then I didn't even hear from her for several months. She e-mails from time to time. Calls once in a while."

"Did this time seem any different? I mean, like, do you think she's dying or something?"

Mel snorts. "She looks awfully healthy, don't you think?"

Too healthy. It's irritating. "And she never asks for money?"

"She always asks for money. Including yesterday. I gave her everything I had on hand. Which reminds me, we need to stop at an ATM."

"Why?"

"Uh . . . because I need some cash?"

"No. I mean, why did you give her any money?"

She infuses her reply with a massive sigh. "Look. Handing her a few bucks is the quickest way to get rid of her. All that stuff about connecting with the kids is crap, but then you already knew that."

"She put on a pretty good act."

"Mom always was the queen of melodrama. Too much time absorbing soap operas or something. Anyway, most of that was for your benefit."

"I know." This song comes on the radio — a reggae-sounding "Smoke Two Joints" by a band called the Toyes. That, of course, reminds me of my niece. I attempt subtlety first. "Did you talk to Graham about Kayla?"

"You mean about her staying out all night? No."

"Why not?"

Another protracted sigh. "Because if I would have, there would've been a huge blowup and it wouldn't have changed a thing. Not to mention, you and I would not be here right now. We'd be back at the house, and I'd be scrambling to make everything okay."

"Everything isn't okay with Kayla."

"What do you mean?"

I relate the circumstances of yesterday afternoon's encounter. "Did you know she smokes marijuana?"

Mel is slow to respond but finally admits, "Yes. I've smelled it on her before but have tried to ignore it. I'm sure it's just a phase and besides, to tell you the truth, she's easier to get along with when she's a little buzzed."

"Are you serious?" I most definitely did not expect this. Melody has always been the Mother of the Year type.

"In all honesty, I think pot helps her more than her meds do. I've done some research, in fact, and there is a good deal of anecdotal evidence that THC can battle anxiety and maybe even depression. It's natural, and not physically addictive, like the prescription drug she takes. I wish they'd just go ahead and legalize it everywhere. Of course, the pharmaceutical companies will fight that tooth and nail."

My sister is full of surprises.

"You don't think smoking dope might impair her judgment a little? Like maybe enough to make her believe it's okay to stay out all night with her boyfriend?"

"I think she would have chosen to do that with or without marijuana."

"I assume, with or without marijuana, she

has enough sense to use birth control?"

"She's been on Depo-Provera for almost two years now. One shot. Twelve weeks of protection."

"Except from STDs."

"Well, there is that. Hopefully, between her health classes and my harping, the message to use condoms, too, will have sunk in."

"Does Graham know about the pot? Or the birth control, for that matter?"

"Are you kidding me? He'd totally over-react."

Whoa. Not only has she gone hippie, but she also keeps secrets from her husband. What else don't I know about Mel?

"How about you? Have you smoked weed?"

She laughs. "Would you let me drive your car if I told you I have?"

"Not with me in it."

At Truckee, we turn off the interstate, onto Highway 267 toward Tahoe. A steady stream of cars pours from the Northstar portal — skiers, going home after a fabulous weekend. I'm jealous. Luckily, most of them travel the opposite direction, back toward the cities. Those we do have to follow are probably locals, because they maneuver the pass in a competent, most untouristy manner.

The whole time we climb, I contemplate how many things I never suspected about Melody. I believed I knew her inside out, and it's worrisome in a way, although it is a good reminder to never assume nor take things for granted. That a person is married to a doctor and goes to church doesn't mean she's a perfect, law-abiding soccer mom. And even if she's your sister, one who has always confided in you, that doesn't mean she has confessed everything. God knows there's information about me that Mel isn't privy to. Pretty sure she'd prefer it that way.

The evenly sawed five-foot berms along the roadways inform me winter has made a regular appearance at Tahoe this year. And as we ascend the hill to Cavin's, the snow stacks are even taller. Someone has cleared a place for the Escalade in the driveway, however.

We are still sitting in the Cadillac when the front door opens, and out comes Cavin, dressed in Sunday-casual clothes that highlight his physique — slim, long-sleeved T-shirt, butt-hugging jeans. "Wow. I forgot how handsome he is," says Mel.

"You should see him naked."

She doesn't respond, and I wonder what she's thinking — *How inappropriate,* or *Yeah, that might be interesting*? Either way, her face colors slightly.

Cavin comes to unload my gigantic suitcases. But first, he circles and opens the passenger door, poking his face inside. "Hello, beautiful lady." It's been a month since Carmel, and his kiss makes me realize how much I've missed being with him. It is sweet and lingering, despite our one-woman audience. When it's over, he grins. "You nervous?"

"Nah. I've kissed a guy before. In fact, I've kissed *you* before."

He rolls his eyes, looks toward Melody, as if asking her to translate.

"Oh! You mean, am I nervous about the surgery? Should I be?"

"Nope. You're in good hands, and I'll be keeping an eye on those hands."

"Good, then I'm still not nervous."

"Good, then I hope you're hungry. You probably won't feel like eating much post-op tomorrow, so I went all-out tonight. Let me help you down, and I'll get your bags."

Mel and I follow him inside. It's warm and neat and smells divine. "Roast chicken?" I ask.

"Cornish game hens, wild rice, and artichokes. No mangoes. I'll stow your luggage, then we'll open some wine."

Once he's out of the room, Melody comments, "A doctor who can cook? That's a killer combination. If I were you, I'd hang on to this one."

One day at a time, darling sister. One day at a time.

THIRTY

For not being nervous, I'm pretty damn anxious about going under. Sometimes they do arthroscopies using local anesthesia, or a spinal block. But my knee is in need of total reconstruction, and that will put me on the table for several hours. As the nurse inserts the IV, I'm actually shaking.

"Hey," she soothes. "This doesn't hurt that much. Do needles bother you?"

"Not usually. I just don't care for the idea of being knocked out."

"You've never had surgery before?"

"Only for my wisdom teeth, and when I woke up afterward, the way the dentist leered at me gave me the creeps. I hate feeling helpless."

"No worries." She tapes the needle to the hollow of my inner arm, leans close conspiratorially. "I hear you've got a very special watchdog observing. But even if he wasn't, Dr. Stanley isn't the leering type."

"How do you know about my watchdog?"

She gestures toward the door, where Cavin just happens to be standing, facing the other direction, talking to Melody. "I've got eyes." Now she lowers her voice. "Barton isn't all that big. Word gets around. Congratulations. He's a keeper."

Two people in less than twenty-four hours. Not that I necessarily disagree, but it's almost enough to make me take a harder look. Everyone's got flaws. Some you can live with, some not so much.

"I'll go let them know you're ready for the anesthesiologist. Your sister wants to come in first. Is that okay?"

"Of course."

I watch the nurse go, fresh and trim, even in her paisley scrubs, and wonder if she has a thing for Cavin, or if they've ever hooked up. Probably not, considering his desire not to manipulate the boundaries of ethics. Still, when she passes him, he can't help but look, and jealousy jabs, straight-razor thin and just as sharp.

Mel shuffles across the room, sits in the wheeled chair bedside. "You good?"

"Yeah, except I think that nurse has a crush on my doctor."

"I wouldn't worry if I were you. That man is crazy about you."

A Band-Aid for my wound.

"We'll see. How are things at home?"

"Want to trade places?"

"That good, huh?"

"Let's just say if I could, I'd stay up here a few extra days."

"So, do."

"Can't. I've got a big project due."

"A writer's job is portable."

"True. But a mother's job isn't. Especially the mother of teenagers."

We leave it there and Dr. Stanley comes marching in, clipboard in hand, to deliver some pre-op cheer and post-op instructions. "You won't be in the mood to listen later," he says, before rattling off a very long list of dos and don'ts.

"You expect me to remember all that?"

"I'm sure Dr. Lattimore will remind you, if memory fails. The main thing is, don't push too hard for the first week or so and stay off your feet completely, except to use the bathroom, for the first three days. And ice. Lots of ice."

"You sure the knee will be better after it heals?"

"Good as new."

"Really? Can you do the rest of me, too?"

He chuckles. "The rest of you appears fine to me. Wouldn't you agree?"

The last sentence was addressed to Cavin, who has come to escort me to the OR. "Better than fine," he answers. "Ready?"

"Give me one second? I need to tell Melody something." The two doctors step away from the bed and I wiggle my finger, inviting Mel closer. "If anything should happen — not that it will, this is routine and all — but if there's some weird complication or something, all my affairs are in order. I've established a trust, named you executor. I e-mailed my attorney's name and number last night. Just in case."

She pulls back, surprised. "Me? I . . ."

"What?"

"I've never even considered what might happen if you . . ."

"Died? It's bound to happen sooner or later, hopefully the latter. There's a lot at stake, Mel. I wouldn't want Mom to get her filthy hands on any of it. No way she will, the way I've structured the trust. If you want to be overly generous with your own funds, fine. But, please, never give her a cent of mine."

"Whatever you want."

"No. Promise me."

"I promise."

Mel gives me a hug.

Cavin wheels me into the OR.

The anesthesiologist does his thing.

Defying professionalism, Cavin kisses my forehead before he goes to wash up and don surgical scrubs.

As I wait to slip into oblivion, I think about the lovemaking we shared last night. Though still limited by my range of movement, we made sure it was the very best yet because it will be several days at least before we can indulge again. Can't wait to see what it's like once I'm good as new.

I'm aware of movement and know that Dr. Stanley and his crew are arranging the instruments he'll need — the scope he'll insert in the small incisions they'll carve. The camera attached to the scope, which will transmit images onto a screen. Surgical drills, saws, biters, shavers, scissors, and so on. Saline solution. Sutures. Oh yes, I've done my homework.

They'll remove torn cartilage.

Trim torn structures.

Graft tendon to repair torn ligaments.

They'll . . .

I float up out of darkness into muted light. It's heavy, or the air is. It's hard to take a breath. I wheeze in one. Another. Three. And now it's a little easier. Except my head throbs. And I think I want to vomit. But it hurts to move, so if I puke, it will be all over myself. Where am I?

"Oh, good. You're awake."

"Cavin?"

He takes my hand. "Yes, it's me. How are you feeling?"

"Awful."

"Define awful."

"Headache. Nausea. General discomfort."

"Sounds about right. Any pain in your knee?"

"Oh, man. Not until you mentioned it."

"I'll get you some promethazine for the nausea. Once that's not a problem, you can have pain meds. I think we'll keep you here overnight. I've got a surgery in the morning. By the time I'm finished, you should be good to go. Meanwhile, get some rest."

Despite my being asleep for however many hours, rest sounds good. Wait. "What time is it? Did Mel leave yet?"

"Not yet. It's a little after two and the car is coming at three."

"Can I see her?"

"Of course. You're in Recovery. We'll need to move you to a regular room. Then she can have a short visit, as long as you're still awake. If you doze off, we won't bother you, however. Can I pass on a message in case that happens?"

"Yes. Tell her not to worry about calling my lawyer."

THIRTY-ONE

It's a good thing Cavin is overseeing my recovery, for a couple of reasons, the main one being he insisted from the day he brought me home that I push through the pain and work on extension. It hurts like hell, but I've had plenty of time to read up on postsurgery recovery, and without encouraging my knee to straighten, I could lose range of motion permanently.

He also has access to the latest gadgets, including this cool machine that combines cryotherapy with intermittent pneumatic compression. It's more effective than ice, continuously cycling cold fluid through a knee wrap. And the IPC stimulates tissue healing, at least theoretically.

The first three days are frustrating because, other than the stationary stretching exercises, I can't do very much. Despite the lack of activity, I'm tired and in a fair amount of pain because I'm trying to wean myself off the oxycodone as quickly as possible. I have to keep my knee elevated and hooked to the machine. I can feel my butt growing fatter by the hour.

Cavin alternately cheerleads and scolds. The truth is, I need both, and he seems to instinctively know which way to push, and when. At the moment, he's examining the incisions, something I'm glad I don't have to do on my own. For someone who prides herself on total independence, I'm a wuss when it comes to wounds.

"Looks good," he says. "No sign of infection. And the swelling is subsiding."

"It itches like crazy."

"That's not uncommon, though I'm sure it must be annoying."

"Not nearly as annoying as all this time on the couch."

"No worries. You'll be up and running in no time at all. Well, no actual running for a while."

"Stationary bike?"

He manipulates my knee gently, assesses the size of my grimace. "In a day or two, but only for fifteen or twenty minutes at first. If you push too hard, it could be counterproductive. You can add time as the extension improves."

"Don't suppose you have one lying around

somewhere, do you?"

"So happens I do, and other equipment, too. But I want you to leave the treadmill and elliptical alone for a while. Nothing weight bearing for several weeks, please, or until I say it's okay."

"Ooh. I love when a man takes charge."

That elicits an honest laugh. "I'll keep that in mind, though I've got a feeling that would be quite the challenge."

"Very true. But you're not the type to back away from a dare, are you?"

"Some things are worth fighting for." He smoothes the bandage back over the stitched incisions, turns to give me a passion-peppered kiss. "Hungry?"

"Starving." I trace the outline of his lips with my tongue, and the implication is clear.

He gifts me with his perfect smile. "That should probably wait a few days, too."

"Fine." I pout theatrically. "Then I guess I'll have to drown my disappointment in a glass of wine."

"When was the last time you took your meds?"

"No worries, Doctor. I'm managing my pain completely with ibuprofen today."

"Excellent. Very good to hear, in fact, and in that case, I'll join you."

As he swivels toward the kitchen, I call,

"Mind if I turn on the evening news?"

"Help yourself."

The remote is within easy reach, and images float up on the big flat screen above the fireplace. I've been largely relegated to television as entertainment for three days, so I know the channels by heart. My preferred evening news is straight-on CBS. The fringe channels can be interesting, but I question the veracity of their journalism from time to time. Mainstream network news, at least, competes among the Big Three for viewers. Which doesn't always make the stories accurate, but at least they're more fact than opinion.

The broadcast is ten minutes old, so I've missed the threats of war and world terrorism segments. Those are of little interest anyway, because there's not too damn much I can do about the global quest for power. I catch a story about novel applications for drones, and just as Cavin returns with refreshments the newscast turns to "the Nation." Up first, this headline: GRAND JURY INDICTS US SENATOR JORDAN LONDON ON BRIBERY AND CONSPIRACY CHARGES. As the story goes, the anonymous tipster whispered into the ear of the FBI, turning them on to information about mining interests funneling beaucoup bucks into Jordan's offshore accounts in exchange for favorable swing votes. A sting operation netted more than enough information to convince the grand jury of an ongoing, complex system of influence peddling.

"Phew" is my initial reaction.

"What?" Cavin hands me a glass of Syrah.

"Remember I told you about my ex-husband, the politician? Well, that's him."

Cavin turns toward the television, where an obviously upset Jordan London tells the microphones thrust in his face, "No comment." Now he ushers a stunning young woman, different from the last, into the same spectacular Porsche.

"Sounds like he's in trouble."

"Yes, it does. Although he has friends in many places, including federal benches."

"Wonder who blew the whistle."

"I kind of think he thinks it was me."

"Why?"

I relate how I first heard the story a month or so ago, and though I debate whether or not to mention the "Private" caller, in the end I go ahead and share that, too.

"Why didn't you tell me?"

"I didn't know you quite as well then, and didn't want to scare you away. I mean, who wants to date a girl who comes with her own personal stalker? Besides, I decided it must have been a wrong number. Nothing else has happened since. I'll admit I was a bit paranoid for a while, though." Okay, that was a lie. I still don't want to chase Cavin away, and as soon as I know for sure who "Private" is, I'll take care of the problem myself.

"But what about London? Do you really believe he thinks you're the whistleblower?"

"Maybe."

"That makes no sense. Why do it now? And what would be in it for you?"

"Revenge." The word slices, bayonet-edged. I blunt it some. "Served up ice cold, and a little moldy?"

His eyes register confusion, perhaps even a hint of suspicion. I could backpedal completely, cry joke, but that would sound like a pathetic excuse. Luckily, he decides it was funny without prompting. "Ha. Well, I promise to never do you wrong. Moldy revenge sounds utterly intimidating."

I tilt my glass against his, the fine crystal chiming a toast. "I'll drink to that."

After Caesar salad plus grilled prawns, we spend the evening drinking wine and watching a made-for-HBO show that's all the rage, though I can't figure out why. The storyline has to do with a tired detective. Nothing new in the history of television, except for the overt violence, full-frontal nudity, and nicely simulated lovemaking. During the boring parts, we make out like kids closing in on "all the way" without actual penetration.

Talk about hot.

THIRTY-TWO

Friday morning, Cavin is on call, and our breakfast is interrupted by the telephone, informing him of an emergency surgery. Apparently, some hotshot snowboarder was messing around and fell from the lift, first chair up the mountain. Bummer, dude.

"Sounds like I'll be three or four hours at least," he says, slipping into his jacket. "Then I'll probably stop by the store. Anything you need?"

"A shower."

He laughs. "It should be okay today. But wait until I get home, okay?"

"Afraid I might slip?"

"No. I want to see you naked."

His good-bye kiss makes me believe that.

The thought of more hours sprawled on the sofa makes me crazy. Think I'll see if I can find that stationary bike. I hope it's not downstairs, but I fear it is. On this level is the great room — kitchen, living, dining.

Eli's bedroom is downstairs. I remember that from when I was here before Christmas. Near as I can tell, having not been down there as yet, it's a daylight basement situation, carved into the hill. I assume there are other rooms on that level, too, and it makes sense that's where a workout room would be.

Still, this floor demands exploration, even on crutches. First, I open the door to the master suite, which shares the great room's evergreen filtered view of the lake. It's tastefully done, or likely redone, in masculine shades of teal and brown. The room is spotless. Not a single sock litters the beige wool carpeting. The king bed is made, its geometric patterned quilt tucked neatly with even hospital corners. After three nights on a futon, albeit a comfortable futon, the thought of crawling between these sheets, inhaling the scent of Cavin's slumber, makes me antsy, though the idea of an accidental dream-fueled kick makes me understand his insistence that I sleep alone for several nights.

The furnishings are simple mahogany, and beautiful, if spare. There's a highboy, maybe six feet tall, on one wall, with a matching long dresser adjacent.

Above it hangs a huge painting of Tahoe

at sunset. I wander over to look at the series
of framed photographs. One is vintage —
the cars tell me circa the mid-1950s, so if
the people propped against the hood are
relatives, they must be Cavin's grand-
parents. There are a couple of photos of who
I think must be his parents — one a little
dated and one more recent. In the second,
the man is alone. Did they divorce? I suppose I should ask. He knows more about
my background than I do about his, and
he's been privy to only the most basic
information.

There are several pictures of Eli. Cavin
shares most of them, mementos of special
days — on the mountain, at the ocean,
camping somewhere wooded. One draws
my eye more than the rest. It's Eli as a small
child, holding a pretty woman's hand and
looking up at her with such adoration that I
know it must be his mom. She is petite and
wears her pale hair long, with no bangs or
layers or embellishment. And she is here on
Cavin's dresser still. The thought gives me
pause. Divorce for me meant divorcing
myself from framed memories. I don't even
keep them in boxes. Of course, I never had
children to remember my exes by.

From soap fragrance to accoutrement, the
sprawling bathroom carries no hint of

woman. There's a jetted tub and an immense shower with endless glass in place of doors. I'm dying to situate myself beneath the brass shower head, turn the water hot-hot-hot, and let Cavin watch me soap myself head to foot, inch by inch, with the exception of one knee. That, I'll still have to keep dry somehow.

Master-suite circuit complete, I wander across the hall. The room beyond the carved oak door is Cavin's study. As offices go, it's expansive, with more than enough space to accommodate the massive teak desk and chocolate suede massage chair. A pair of tall, narrow windows look toward the road. Cavin keeps them shuttered, but a skylight allows a cascade of illumination. Bookcases cover two walls, floor to ceiling, and there is little space left for new editions. Two cubbies, however, hold nothing but photographs. I move closer to see who might occupy such obvious places of honor.

The woman is no more than thirty, and stunning, her sharp features (Italian? Greek?) accentuated by spiked black hair, tipped platinum. She prefers form-hugging clothing that shows off her slender figure — short skirts, leggings, leather jackets. Not someone I'd picture as Cavin's type.

Too hip.

Too BDSM.

Too young.

But she must have been (is?) his type, because he's in three of the six featured photos, and their intertwined poses leave no doubt they were (are?) crazy about each other. I'm confused as to tense. These pictures can't be very old, because Cavin hasn't aged since they were taken — several months, maybe? There are no other signs of her here. He swore he maintains no allegiance to other women. Surely, he wouldn't have invited me to stay if she were still deeply ingrained in his life. So, why house these on his bookshelves, where she can watch over him as he works? A sobering thought rises like smoke. Maybe she died?

Uneasiness begins a slow churn in my gut. Half of me wants to dig through Cavin's personal stuff, seek out clues. The other half wants to escape, go home, shed myself of lies. But I can't leave on my own, and even if I could, I don't want to exit his life without knowing what the truth is. Don't want to vacate his life at all, because I really have no idea what love feels like. But this, I believe, is the closest I've come, and I deserve the experience.

I take one last glimpse of the photographs, imprint them in my brain to try to make sense of later. My knee pulses pain from the morning's effort, and I opt for pharmaceutical relief, the kind ibuprofen can't bring. Before it kicks in, I decide to make some hot tea. Not sure why. It's generally not my thing. I've yet to actually use the kitchen, so it's work to locate the simple things I need — kettle, mug, honey, Earl Grey. Luckily, Cavin is the well-organized type. I put water on to boil, and when I finally find the stash of teas, all requiring a strainer, it occurs to me that I've never seen Cavin drink any caffeinated beverage but coffee. So whom does the tea belong to?

Jealousy strikes, sinks its fangs. I want to believe I'm the only woman in Cavin's life, but logic claims that's a ridiculous notion. Monogamous men tend to fall into a couple of categories — overtly religious, or clearly unsuitable for sex, period. Neither guarantees complete faithfulness. That's why they invented Internet porn.

Tea brewed and pill kicking in, I settle back onto the sofa, pull out my laptop, and try to work. Not easy, floating on opiates. Not easy, with pictures of a spiky-haired woman flickering into and out of internal view. Not easy, as morning creeps beyond twelve o'clock and on toward deep afternoon.

Where the hell is he?

The thought is tumbling when my phone rings. Caller ID informs me it's Melody. I debate inviting her drama until the third ring. Ultimately I decide it's better than the internal conflict. "Hey, Mel. What's wrong?"

"How did you know something's wrong? Did she call you?"

"Who?"

"Kayla. She and Graham got into it this morning. I think . . . I think she ran away."

"What makes you say that?"

"Apparently, when I took Suz to the orthodontist, Kayla packed some clothes and left. I assume, with that Cliff person."

"I haven't heard a word from her. But I wouldn't worry too much. Where would they go? She'll cool off and come home."

"I hope so." She sounds unconvinced. "Kayla's been heading in the wrong direction for a while now. I'm afraid she's lost all sense of reason."

I've heard marijuana can do that to a person, and what if it's become a gateway to harder stuff? I should probably leave that alone. "What were she and Graham fighting about?"

A long, soundless pause. "You."

Maybe it's the pill, or maybe I just need a good laugh, because that's what I do. "Me?

What about me?"

Another bloated second or two of silence. "Graham's trying to plan our summer vacation. At breakfast, he took a vote — Hawaii or Disney World. Kayla said she didn't care, as she'd be spending her summer with you, working as your personal assistant. Did you tell her you'd hire her?"

It takes a minute to remember the conversation I had with Kayla. "Yes, I guess I kind of did. I told her she could work for me as a way of repaying her tuition. But I never said anything about summer."

"Well, apparently she thinks she's moving in with you right after graduation. Graham, however, does not agree."

How did I become this embroiled in my sister's family? I've avoided it forever, and now suddenly, I'm at the root of most of their problems. Not really, of course, but I'm sure that's how Graham sees it, and maybe my sister, too.

"Look, Mel, I was just trying to help out. If your husband can't conquer his pettiness, there's no one to blame but himself. But I've got enough problems of my own without creating a whole new subset involving Kayla. Tell me what to do and I'll try. And why are you mad at *me,* anyway?"

On the far end of the line, there's a massive sigh. "Sorry. It's not your fault. It's just that Graham has been impossible to get along with lately. It almost feels like he's purposely picking fights so he has an excuse to leave."

"You mean, leave for good?"

"I'm not sure. All I know is, the band's gigs seem to push later and later into the night, and once or twice he's called to let me know he wouldn't be home until the next morning."

Like father, like daughter? "Have you confronted him?"

"What for? It wouldn't change anything."

Her passivity annoys me no end. If there's one thing I've learned it's that a woman's intuition about such situations is rarely wrong. Once suspicion surfaces, an aggressive response is required.

Besides, sometimes aggression just feels good.

THIRTY-THREE

I'm dozing when Cavin finally comes in, carrying pizza (pizza again?), wine, and a bouquet of flowers the approximate size of a small tree. I glance at my phone, which tells me it's a little past four. Two dozen amber-colored roses can't change that.

"Where have you been?"

It's a harsh stutter, and he stops, tries to measure my mood. Finally, he puts his stuff on the kitchen counter, comes over to the couch, bends to give me a kiss. "Sorry. I should have called to let you know I'd be later than expected. I'm afraid I'm out of practice."

His own words are gentle and threaten to melt the ice wall I've built this afternoon. But then I remember the photos. I gesture toward the pizza box. "Thought you were going to the store."

"Ran out of time. The first surgery was complicated, and then another emergency came in. Some days are like that. But, hey, that pizza is the best in town. Hungry?"

Cavin returns to the kitchen, reaches into a low cupboard for a vase. I watch him arrange the flowers with skillful, almost dainty hands. "You're good at that."

He smiles. "I'm good at many things, milady. How was your day?"

"Boring."

"Did you do your exercises?"

"Of course."

I did. Sort of. Actually, I flaked on most of them. They're becoming tedious.

"Do you want to eat in here tonight?" Cavin carries the roses to the table, where they become a beautiful centerpiece. The man does everything right.

Everything right.

Too good to be true.

He's a great catch.

Better hang on to this one.

The knee feels rested when I rise, make my way to the table, one slow step at a time, determined to leave the crutches behind.

"Hey. You're not weighting that leg, are you?"

"Not much."

"Seriously, sweetheart —"

"I'm okay!"

Too sharp. He studies me inquisitively,

seems to consider saying something, then to change his mind, and goes to the kitchen to open the wine. He brings two crystal glasses to the table, returns to the kitchen for silverware, napkins, and plates of pizza. I remain silent during the entire exercise.

When he finally sits, he looks me straight in the eye. "What's wrong?"

I've got two choices: Deny there's a problem and continue to stew. Or come right out and tell him what's bothering me. Candor (exceptional word) is my middle name. "I thought there was no one else important in your life."

"Tara, there isn't."

"Who's the woman in the photographs in your study? She looks pretty damn important to me."

His cheeks flush color, but he doesn't deny or even sidestep. "Okay, look. The truth is, Sophia and I were serious, or at least I thought so then. But we went our separate ways over a year ago. I haven't gotten around to putting away the pictures. In fact, I don't use that room very much, and forgot they were even there. If I had something to hide, I would have stashed them, don't you think?"

Okay, he's got me. Anger segues to curiosity. "But she's still alive?"

"Why wouldn't she be?"

I shrug. "Just a weird feeling I had."

"As far as I know, she's very much alive, and taking Broadway by storm. But we haven't spoken in months."

"Broadway?"

"She's a producer. She was working in Reno and we bumped into each other skiing."

"How long were you together?"

"Almost two years."

"So, what happened?"

His turn to shrug. "She wasn't the person I thought she was."

His tone informs me he's finished with the story. I'll leave it alone for now, but one day I'll worm the rest out of him.

The pizza is almost as delicious as the truth.

Even more delectable is the shower I take after dinner. It's hard to appreciate something like cleanliness unless it's denied you for several days. Cavin's bandage waterproofing is primitive — trash bag and duct tape — but it does the trick. I run the water to steaming, which fogs the endless glass.

"Hold on just a minute," calls Cavin. "I thought the point was for me to see you naked."

303

"There's plenty of room in here," I invite. "And I can't reach my back."

I'm conditioning my hair when he joins me. "Give me the soap."

He starts just below my jaw and works his way down, kissing a trail in the suds he creates on my skin. Water streams from his hair, and it's sexy as hell, but not nearly as sexy as the things he does to my nipples with his lips and teeth and tongue.

"You're going to get soap in your mouth."

Cavin drops cautiously to kneel on the slippery tile. "I'm going to get more than that in my mouth."

Careful of my trash-bagged knee, he lathers the skin between my thighs, slips soapy fingers inside me.

Out.

In.

His tongue circles my clit, and his fingers move.

In.

Out.

He is the most skilled lover I've ever had, and I'm moaning. Rocking.

Forward.

Back.

"Stop. Or I'll come."

He doesn't stop.

"My turn."

I can't bend or kneel, so oral is impossible, but stimulating him with conditioner-slicked hands is quite the turn-on.

For him.

For me.

It takes both hands to fully encircle his girth, and in long, quickening strokes, I bring him off. When he orgasms, so do I.

THIRTY-FOUR

Over the weekend, Cavin gets a friend to help him move the stationary bike upstairs. At my request, they place it in front of the big window, adjacent to the sliding glass door, where I can at least pretend I'm cycling outside, especially if I can crack the slider and inhale the scent of cedars and pines.

Jon doesn't stick around very long after they're finished. "Did I scare him away? I know I've looked better, but . . ."

"I don't think that's the problem, sweetheart." Cavin explains that Jon is a surgeon, but not the orthopedic kind, and they often compete for OR time, which sometimes puts them at odds. "He and I don't hang out all that often, and when we do it's usually just to catch a couple of beers and maybe watch a game."

"Game? You do sports?"

"Baseball and football. Very little in

306

between, though sometimes I'll pay attention to March Madness or the World Cup. How about you? You into sports?"

"Only the ones worth betting on," I joke.

He smiles. "My kind of woman. You ready to try the bike now?"

Cavin helps me onto the seat, which he adjusted so that pedaling will bring my knees to full extension. My first real exercise in over a week feels great. Except it hurts.

"Give it twenty minutes, tops," Cavin instructs, "and add a little time every day." He turns and starts to leave.

"Where are you going?"

"To tidy my study."

By the time my twenty minutes are up, Sophia has vanished, at least from view. If there's one thing I'm sure of about men, they lie when it suits their needs. That might hold true for women, too. Who knows? I've never been intimately involved with a woman, so I've never had to put one to the test.

Week two of my recuperation, I'm diligent about exercise. I add time to the bike every day. Seek more difficult stretches for my legs. Do rep upon rep with a pair of dumbbells borrowed from Cavin's workout room. He warns me not to push too hard. But nothing is gained from slacking off. Right now, I'm all about the gain.

Cavin is conscientious about communication this week. On Thursday, he calls to let me know he'll be a little late. When I ask why, he tells me it's a surprise. I'm fresh out of a postworkout shower, running a comb through dripping hair, when he breezes through the bedroom door, hands behind his back. His goofy grin belongs to a little boy. He whips out the gift with a flourish. "Happy Valentine's Day."

"Val—"

"Well, technically, it's Saturday, but I couldn't wait."

The last time anyone remembered me on Valentine's Day was . . . I seriously can't recall.

"Hang on." I dry my hands with the towel that's lying across my lap. The box is wrapped in what looks like old-fashioned wallpaper, raised red paisley atop gold foil. It's elegant and unique, and I open it with care.

Inside is a smaller one, jewelry-box size, on top of tissue-protected lingerie — a plum satin teddy and matching robe. "Can't wait to see you in it," he says. "Now, open the little one."

The heart-shaped ruby earrings are of exceptional quality. After all that time around pawnshops, I know jewelry, and he did not skimp. These were quite expensive. "Oh, Cavin. They're perfect."

"You really like them?" That little boy again.

"I adore them. Here, I'll put them on."

"And the teddy later?"

"It will probably look better on me in a month or two."

"Nonsense." He drops the robe I'm wearing from my shoulders, and his hands travel the contours of my body. "All things considered, I can't imagine you — or anyone — ever looking much better than this."

Way to clarify, Doctor. "Actually, I was referring to my knee. Wounds and provocativeness are oxymoronic, no?"

"Provocativeness? That's a lot of syllables to say hotness, yeah?"

"What's a syllable or two among friends?"

We laugh together, and it's a genuine bond. He likes words, too, and I like that. "Anyway, let's take a peek at those incisions. I don't think they actually qualify as wounds."

They are healing quickly, at least I think they are. They don't itch like they used to, and don't require much in the way of gauze over the Steri-Strips that keep the newly forming skin from stretching to the point of damage.

Cavin confirms this. "How would you like to move off the futon and into my bed?"

"Let me think." I rest two fingers against my chin. "Um . . . I'm not sure. Can you sweeten the offer?"

He tugs me to my feet, folds me into him, kisses my forehead. "I think that can be arranged. Now I've got a question for you. Feel like dinner out on Saturday evening? Chef Christopher has something very special planned, and Paolo has reserved the best table in the house."

Except for a single postsurgery follow-up with Dr. Stanley, I haven't been away from this place in almost two weeks. I'd kill for a few romantic hours out. "You bet, but only if I'm pay—"

"No way. You paid last time."

"But I don't have a Valentine's Day present for you."

He picks up the teddy from the dressing table where I laid it, rubs the smooth satin against his cheek in an extremely suggestive way. "Oh, you most assuredly do, and this is the only gift wrap required."

For the thousandth time, I think how alike we are.

Smart.

Sexual.

Subtle.

The rest of the evening is lovely. So lovely, in fact, I think there must be a storm approaching — the metaphorical kind, not the blizzard they're calling for next week. But tonight is steeped in romance, punctuated with sex. That's still not up to par, but it is improving, and as the old idiom goes, half a loaf is better than none. Or, to paraphrase, getting a little is preferable to celibacy.

We are lying in bed, mostly satiated, when the proverbial tornado hits. "Oh, I forgot to tell you something."

I don't like the way that sounds. "What?"

"Eli is coming up for President's Day weekend. He'll be here tomorrow afternoon and leave Monday. You don't mind, do you?"

Even if I did, what could I say? "Not at all. He and I should get to know each other, anyway."

"Yes, you definitely should. Just don't let his posturing bother you, and take everything he says with a grain of salt. He isn't always completely forthright."

Hmm. I think Cavin just called his son a liar.

THIRTY-FIVE

Cavin is still at the hospital when Eli arrives, earlier than expected. I don't like surprises. I'm just out of the shower, still unclothed, with the bedroom door open when the front door whacks the wall and footsteps slap the entry tile. I yank on the short robe lying across the chair, hobble into the other room to make sure I'm not being accosted by a burglar or something. The plum satin Valentine's Day gift doesn't cover a whole lot.

Eli whistles appreciatively. "Whoa. Nice. Got anything else you want to show me?"

How old is this kid again? "No. I was double-checking to see if you were a criminal. Since you're not, I'll go put some clothes on."

"Who says I'm not? Oh, and hey, don't get dressed on my account."

I do, anyway. I crow-hop back into the bedroom, close the door, and put on a

velour warm-up suit, zipping the top well above cleavage. Then I moisturize, apply a thin layer of makeup, and take the time to blow-dry my hair. By the time I finish, as expected, Eli has gone to his room.

I'm in the kitchen, deciding what to make for dinner, when he reappears and seats himself on a tall stool at the island, watching curiously. I withdraw my head from the refrigerator. "I'm thinking chili tonight. Does that work?"

"Whatever. I'm omnivorous."

"Good. Makes things easy." I go to work, cubing chuck roast.

He doesn't offer to help. "So, are you living here or what?"

"For now, until I can get myself around better. The knee damage was pretty extensive."

"Dad doesn't usually move his patients in."

I believe the kid is baiting me. Game on. "Actually, I'm not his patient. Dr. Stanley did the surgery. I wanted your dad to do it, but he thought it was unethical."

"Because you were fucking him."

"That's correct." I wash meat from my hands, reach into the cupboard for spices to season it. "You don't have a problem with your dad getting laid, do you?"

He smiles, and when he does, I see Cavin there. "Not at all. I just find it interesting, which women he picks. You're different from the last one."

I reach for an onion. "In what way?"

"She was younger." Straight for the ovaries. But then he amends, "But you're prettier. And you know how to cook."

I turn up the heat under the Dutch oven. "You met Sophia, then?"

"Oh, we absolutely met. She's hot."

It feels like there's a subtext. That piques my interest. "Cavin says she's in New York, producing a play off Broadway."

"Huh. For some reason, I thought she was still around. I ran into her at Heavenly not too long ago. But then, she does love to ski, and the East Coast hills pretty much suck."

He seems to know an awful lot about Sophia, whom I don't want to talk about anymore. Fragrance blossoms as I sauté the onion and garlic, add the chili and cumin-spiced meat to brown. "Tell me about your mother."

"What about her?"

"I don't know. Do you get along?"

"Guess so, at least when she's around. I don't see her all that much."

"Cavin says she travels a lot with her

husband. Do they ever invite you to join them?"

"No." His tone says end of conversation.

I go into the pantry to look for ingredients. Kidney beans. White beans. Both within reach. But the canned tomatoes are on a shelf above my head, and I can't chance a step stool. "Eli, can you please help me for a second?"

I hear the bar stool scrape tile, his heavy-footed approach, and when he comes into the pantry behind me, I become fully aware of his height. "What do you need?"

"Tomatoes."

He is opportunistic, maneuvering his body very close to mine. When he reaches around me, his arm brushes my cheek and I can feel the muscle, not sculpted but sinewy. I wonder if the contact was on purpose.

"These?"

"No. Those. The ones that say Mexican style."

He brings down two cans, gives them to me, and as he backs away, his hand brushes my hip. Okay, *that* was not accidental. But there is nothing more, and I ignore the gesture, pretend it was harmless.

Eli returns to his stool and I go back to my chili, feeling the heat of his gaze as I open the tomatoes, add them to the Dutch oven along with beef bouillon and a can of beer. He observes for a while and finally says, "I asked Taylor Andaman about you."

"Really. And what did he say?"

"He said his mom wishes she were you and his dad thinks you're a cunt, but he thinks you're fine. He said you live on Russian Hill, and he's been to your house, and it's fucking awesome." He pauses, gauging my reaction.

I cover the chili, lower the heat, and leave the pot to slow simmer. Then I turn toward Eli, stare him down. "I'd say that's an accurate assessment. But why did you ask him about me?"

"When my dad came to school to bail me out of trouble he mentioned he was going to see you before he went to Carmel. He was kind of salivating."

"Did you know he planned to invite me to Carmel?"

"I kind of figured."

"So you weren't surprised to find me here, then."

"Not really."

"Does it bother you?"

"Why should it? It's his house. Anyway . . ." He eyes me like a cat toying with a rodent. "There are perks."

Before I can respond, the front door opens

and in comes Cavin. "Hey. Something smells amazing. Is that chili?" He heads straight for the kitchen to give me a kiss.

"I felt like doing something creative. Hope you didn't have other plans for that chuck."

"Pot roast, but no worries. This is better. You two getting acquainted?"

I nod. "Eli helped with dinner, in fact."

Cavin looks bemused. "Really?"

"Yep," says Eli. "I fetched cans."

"He's an extremely talented can fetcher," I add.

"Well, thanks for the help, son." Cavin slides an arm around my shoulder, tugs me close. "And what do you think of my lady?"

Eli smiles. "I think you've got your hands full."

Dinner is vaguely uncomfortable. I catch Eli staring from time to time and wish I could interpret his expression. Cavin doesn't seem to notice. Conversation centers around the two boarding together on Sunday, the state of the mountain, and whether or not Motts and Killebrew will offer enough un-tracked terrain by then to make them interesting.

Cavin does detect a hint of consternation. "You don't mind if I desert you on Sunday, do you?"

"It's not that you're going," I answer, "or

even that you're planning on testing the canyons. I'm just jealous that I can't go, too."

"I'm sorry. But there's always next year."

"I know, but that seems like a long way away."

Patience isn't my best thing.

LOW RISE OF MORNING

Postblizzard, elongated fingers
of light poke through the sugar
pine fringe, stretching shadows
across the ermine meadow.

They reach long, and as the sun
lifts, draw back again, scratching
the pristine white, luring
my attention to the fresh fallen

facade. Untracked. Unspotted.
Untouched, but by the scattered
radiance. I am coaxed from
the warmth behind the window

glass, out into the snap of winter
day, tempted by an irresistible
desire to smash footprints into
the diamond crust. Mark territory.

THIRTY-SIX

I don't see Eli on Saturday morning. He doesn't bother with breakfast but heads to the mountain fueled by grab-and-go snacks — protein bars, bananas, and Red Bull — claiming he's good till midday and lunch. Ah, youth! He plans to snowboard all day, pop leftover chili in the microwave for dinner, and eat it solo. Glad I made a big pot.

None of that changes our Valentine's Day plans. Cavin sneaks out of bed early. When I wake to cooling sheets, I think he must have gone to say good-bye to his son and allow myself to doze off. The scent of strong coffee nudges me and I stretch awake again.

"Morning. Happy Valentine's Day. Here, hold this."

Cavin has brought a tray of French roast and scones. He places it across my lap, props pillows behind my back, then climbs into bed beside me. We slather butter and jam on the hot bread, sip coffee, and watch the morning news, which informs us there's a rose shortage this year, explaining the high prices.

"That's the excuse every year," I say. "They should get creative. Like a rogue group of anthophobes loosed armies of spider mites into greenhouses across the country. Much more dramatic, don't you think?"

"Much. But what's an anthophobe?"

"Anthophobia, the fear of flowers. Not to be confused with anthrophobia, the fear of human relationships."

"Thanks for the clarification. I never knew I was an anthrophobe."

"You're afraid of human relationships?"

"Not anymore. Give me the tray."

He moves it to the nightstand and spends thirty minutes proving he's very much into our relationship.

Afterward, he asks what I'd like to do postshower, predinner. The answer is easy. "Escape."

"To where?"

"Anywhere. I just need to see the world beyond your front door."

"Okay. I've got an idea. Let me make a call."

I never realized how important it is to one's mental health to step out into the sunshine on a regular basis. The Sierra air is frosty but so clean it seems newborn, as if nothing but the uppermost reach of the forest has touched it. I do love the ocean, but I could be convinced to live up here the majority of the time.

What might unconvince me is tourist traffic. Three-day holiday weekends coax sports lovers, winter and summer. It's bumper-to-bumper into town. Cavin turns off the highway onto a side street before we reach the Stateline casinos. He pulls into a parking area. On the chain-link fence is a sign: SLEIGH RIDES. There is a small sleigh and one very big horse waiting. In the distance, another larger sleigh, pulled by *two* very big horses, circles the snow-covered meadow.

"Hold on," Cavin instructs, getting out of the car to go talk to a burly guy in a red powder suit. I see him slip money to the man before he comes to help me out of the car. "It's slick out here. Let me help you."

"Are we really taking a sleigh ride?"

"A *private* sleigh ride," he corrects. "We shall go where no men — okay, a few men, but not *that* many men — have ventured before."

He slides one arm around me, half lifts me across the short stretch to where Sam (our guide) and Samantha (the blond

Belgian draft horse named after our guide) await. Cavin lifts me up into the seat, climbs in beside me, and tucks a thick blanket over our legs. "Ready?"

I don't much care for the word "giddy," but it suits the way I feel, my face tilted against this amazing man's chest and our holding hands beneath a down blanket. Samantha pulls the sleigh with a steady gait and Sam repeats area history as we take the elongated track across the meadow and up into the forest. Even with the earthy smell of horse sweat, it's a delightful experience.

"All the times you've been to Tahoe and you've never done this before?" asks Cavin.

I shake my head. "It always seemed like such a passive experience."

"Passive? Guess you never considered this."

Neither Sam nor Samantha seems to mind when we make out like ridiculous kids. Give the horse a carrot and the man a nice tip.

It's a lovely, romantic afternoon, capped off with our Valentine's dinner, an epicurean masterpiece à la Chef Christopher. We are middessert when I notice Cavin's eyes stray toward a curvy young woman Paolo is seating. She notices and flashes an interested smile over her companion's shoulder. It's a short distraction, and when Cavin refocuses in the proper direction, he owns up to the faux pas and apologizes. "Sorry," he says. "Force of habit."

"Old habits die hard."

"Really? Does that include your own?"

I consider the question, and how to answer. "Sexual conquest was never a habit for me, just a game I enjoyed from time to time."

"You're a serious player, though."

"As my mother used to say, anything worth doing is worth doing right."

"I thought you didn't listen to your mother."

"As a general rule, I don't."

"Okay, let me ask you this, then. What about me? Was I a sexual conquest?"

"Oh, good Lord, no." I reach across the table, cover his hand with mine. "I may be serious about you, but this is not a game, at least not for me. And I hope it's more than that for you, too. Anyway, I have no desire to emasculate you. Loyalty can't be coerced."

The statement is semiaccurate. It can't, however, assuage the recent sting. Still, it's not enough to ruin an otherwise wonderful day. One little blemish is all. I make a mental note not to test him, at least for a while. What's the point?

There is only one way to coerce loyalty. And blackmail should always be a last resort.

THIRTY-SEVEN

As fabulous as Chef Christopher's Valentine's Day dinner was, I find myself looking forward to the plebeian cheesesteaks and sweet potato fries we're scheduled to enjoy Sunday, postskiing. I don't ski, of course, but I do ride the gondola to the top of Heavenly and sit in the lodge midmountain, enjoying the fire and a book. It's a hassle getting there, but worth the effort to enjoy a day of people watching. The isolation has grown tiresome.

One great thing about loitering here with a knee brace and crutches is the sympathetic glances that keep passing by. There but for the grace of God, and all. Sometimes they come courtesy of quite attractive gentlemen, not that I'm interested in playing the sexual conquest game. It's just good to know that I could if I wanted to, and that I'd likely win.

Toward the afternoon's end, I'm sipping a

hot toddy when Eli comes stomping into the lodge, kicking snow from his boots. He flops onto the chair adjacent to mine, face red from exertion, or cold, or both. "Why does he have to be such an asshole?"

"Who?"

He shoots me a *What are you, brain dead?* look. "Who else? My dad."

I'm afraid we're headed toward a conversation that should not involve me. So why do I engage him? "What happened?"

"Nothing much." Anger frosts his voice. "Except Dad told me that he doesn't plan to pay for my college."

"I don't understand. Surely he can afford —"

"It's not about finances! It's about me."

Suddenly, the passersby stares tossed in our direction are more concerned than come-on. "Take it easy, Eli. What, exactly, did he say?"

"He said he wouldn't piss away his money on a motherfucking loser."

I'm speechless. I've never witnessed a hint of ill temper in Cavin, let alone that kind of language. "What did you do?"

He slumps forward. "Nothing."

Which, I guess, in teen speak means, *I don't want to talk about it.* So be it. Whatever the problem is, it's between Cavin and Eli, anyway. "Look, I have no idea what this is about, but your father is a reasonable man and —"

"How do you know?"

"How do I know what?"

"That he's a reasonable man." He straightens again, brings his eyes level with mine. "How well do you know him, really?"

Fair question, and it strands me mid-thought. I'm considering my answer when my cell buzzes a text-message warning.

From Cavin: *Have you seen Eli?*

My reply: *He's with me.*

Back again: *Be right there.*

Eli has watched the exchange. "I take it that was Dad?"

"Yes. He said he's on his way."

"Great. I'm going to board down Gun-barrel. I'll meet you at the car."

Off he slinks, determined to leave before his father arrives. I watch him go, physically mature but mostly kid within. It's been a long while since I've tried to relate to a masculine someone his age. The last time had to have been high school, and even then I didn't try to maintain prolonged relation-ships with my male classmates. I dated a few, but not in a serious way, unless you consider having sex serious. I certainly didn't.

The struggle to cast off the vestiges of childhood isn't gender-specific, of course. Kayla is going through a similar phase, and she's no easier to deal with. Certainly, at seventeen, I had wrested complete control of my young life from my mother's grasp, not that she tried very hard to hold on. But had I come from a home with parents who cared, and who gifted me with affection and possessions, would I have acted out in the same way that Eli and Kayla are? Who knows?

Now it's Cavin whose heavy boots thud across the floor. He plops down beside me, offers a kiss before he asks, "Where's Eli?"

"He decided to take Gunbarrel down. He said he'd meet us at the car."

"Oh." His voice is impassive, his expression unreadable.

"Do you want to tell me what happened?"

"What's Eli's take?"

"He said you've decided not to pay for his college and that you said, and I quote, you wouldn't 'piss away' your money on 'a motherfucking loser.' "

Now he looks confused. "Tara, that's not even close. We were on a lift, and to make conversation, I asked about his grades. He admitted they probably don't look very good. So then I asked if he knew what he wanted to do, going forward — had he decided on a career path? He told me he wasn't sure. So then I asked if he'd considered a community college for his core classes, since Stanford isn't exactly looking for kids without clear goals, not to mention outstanding GPAs, and perhaps it would be a wiser investment of his time and college fund. And then he went off on me. Demanded to know how much money is in said college fund, and if I had other plans for it."

"Like what?"

"That was my question, and he had no concrete answer. We were in the unloading zone by then and he just took off. I swear I have no idea why he got so angry."

Calm. Reasonable. Every molecule the Cavin I anticipate. Perhaps Eli's overreaction was nothing more than a surge of testosterone. I don't pretend to understand male physiology. Psychology, I thought I had a handle on, but now I'm not so sure. Strange creatures.

"So, are we still on for cheesesteaks? My mouth has been watering for one all day."

"Personally, I'm starving. Eli can join us or not. You ready?"

He tugs me gently to my feet, sees me safely beyond the door, where he collects his skis. The gondola line is long, but most people are willing to let me hobble to the front and take the handicapped bench. The exception is a pair of twentysomething pretty boys, whose belligerent protests smell like beer.

Jerk One plants himself squarely in front of me. "Who the fuck do you think you are? The Queen of England?"

"Absolutely not. The Queen may be old, but she isn't crippled."

Now Jerk Two joins in. "Yeah, and neither are you, I bet."

Unbelievably, the guy grabs one of my crutches and tries to yank it away. Cavin is immediately in the dude's face, stepping between him and me. "I'd let go of that if I were you."

"Or what?"

The younger man probably outweighs Cavin, but he's flabby, not to mention intoxicated. Cavin is taller. Buffer. When he chest bumps Jerk Two, the guy stumbles backward, lands on his butt, hitting himself in the forehead with the crutch. Someone has called for Security, and I can see a burly uniform headed this way. But there's plenty of time for Jerk One to step up to the plate. He starts to, and I swear all it takes is one look from Cavin to make him back away again. There's something new in Cavin's eyes. Cold. Hard. Fury.

The situation defuses as the rent-a-cop arrives. The Pretty Boy Jerks sputter excuses and express concern for their personal well-being. Burly Uniform takes one look at Number Two (ooh, apt name), still clutching my crutch, a large knot forming on his forehead. The pseudo-cop extricates the crutch from his grasp, hands it to me. "Sorry some people feel the need to be ass-holes."

I take the handicapped bench. Cavin stands beside me, and as the gondola descends I look up into his eyes, where fury has melted into satisfaction. Eli's words rise up inside me. *How well do you know him, really?*

THIRTY-EIGHT

The week starts out on an even keel. Cavin and Eli buried the hatchet long enough to make it through Sunday dinner. It was uncomfortable — bloated by silence — but they didn't argue or even discuss their earlier issue, and it wasn't mentioned again before Eli headed back to school on Monday morning. Hopefully he'll find the ambition to lift his grades up out of the gutter.

Speaking of ambition, the weather gods seem to have discovered theirs. It started to snow a couple of hours after Eli left, and it's been coming down enthusiastically ever since. We're on an El Niño storm track, according to local meteorologists, and as of Thursday, it's a doozy, the snowdrifts outside growing five or six feet high.

Which means no real chance of venturing outside. Last thing I need is to slip and go down. Forward, backward, or doing the splits, it would set back my rehab by months. I keep exercising, probably too much. But I push through the pain and feel myself getting stronger. Strength is what I'm after. I never cared much about being a size zero. Size four and buff is beautiful.

Cavin has several surgeries scheduled this week, so I spend lots of time alone. I am working on a fall fund-raiser when my phone rings. I reach for it absentmindedly, thinking it must be Cavin. "Hey, gorgeous," I purr.

"Um, hello? Ms. Cannon? It's not 'Gorgeous.' It's Charlie. Sorry to bother you, but . . . oh, how are you doing?"

"Getting stronger every day, thanks. Is there a problem?"

I had left Charlie a door code and asked him to keep an eye on the place, water plants, et cetera. I never expected a call, however.

"I'm not sure. It's just . . . well, it appears someone has been in your house."

"Why do you say that? Does it look like there's anything missing?" Anxiety shimmers. Except for the artwork and wine cellar, my valuables are locked in a wall safe, and my valuable valuables kept in a safe deposit box at my bank. A TV or computer I can replace.

"I don't think so. I'm not sure. I mean the

art is still here and all. But there's stuff on the counter and coffee table. Glasses and bottles. Like someone has been helping himself, and maybe a friend or two, to your liquor."

The place was spotless when I left. "Anything else?"

"Well, why it seems weird is because there's no sign of a break-in, like whoever it was knew how to get in."

"Was the alarm on when you got there?"

"No, and that's the thing, I'm sure I activated it before I left last time. Should I call the police?"

"Have you been through the whole house?"

"Yes."

"And nothing seems to bc missing except alcohol?"

"Not as far as I can tell."

"Don't worry about it, then."

"Are you sure?"

I am, because suddenly it comes to me that Kayla went missing a couple of weekends ago, and she knew I'd be here with Cavin. She has since returned home, but I'll bet she and Cliff spent those days in my house, smoking it up and helping themselves to my pantry and liquor. I hate to consider what they might have done in my bed.

But how would they have gotten in? Wait . . .

"Do me a favor and go look in the 'Vette and BMW for garage-door openers." I'm sure there's one in the Escalade because I used it to shut the garage door when I embarked on this adventure.

Charlie isn't gone long. "I found one in the Beamer, but not in the Corvette. Does that mean something?"

Obviously Kayla didn't return it to its proper place, but whether that was purposeful or simple neglect, I don't know. "Yes, I have an idea who it was. I'll change the access from here and let you know how to get in later."

"Okay. Hey, are you coming home soon?"

"Not for a couple of weeks at least."

"Oh." The disappointment is obvious in his voice. "You're still going to need some help, right? That extra money sure comes in handy."

I promise his position is safe, and it is, at least for now. I had planned on turning it over to Kayla, but now I'm not so sure. I don't trust easily and, relative or not, once you chew a hole in that thin veneer, I will write you off completely. Punch one, I'm liable to retaliate.

But dirty dishes and bottles are more like a nibble, so I'll recode the system remotely and let this one go for now. "Do me a favor and tidy up? The last thing I need when I get back are ants. And please check on the place every day until further notice. If you see anything else out of the ordinary, let me know ASAP. I'll text you the new codes later."

He agrees, and I promise to send him a check for his trouble. I try to return to my busywork, but this is bothering me, so I put in a call to Melody. We spend a few minutes on chitchat — knee rehab, kids, blizzard, and dogs — before I finally ask, "Did you ever find out where Kayla disappeared to?" I know she was gone three days without permission, and Graham had threatened to have her locked up.

"Not exactly. She told me they were over at Cliff's, but later I found out he'd been evicted from his apartment. I'm not really sure where they landed, and she hasn't exactly come clean. Why?"

I mention the call from Charlie.

"Oh, I don't think she'd do that, Tara. She respects you a lot, and I know she's counting on your support to get into school next fall. I sincerely doubt she'd jeopardize that."

"Perhaps the marijuana clouded her judgment?" Not to mention trying to impress her loser boyfriend, especially if they had nowhere else to go to catch a buzz and engage in sexual activities.

"I suppose it's possible," she admits. "I'll have a talk with her as soon as she gets home, okay?"

"You're not allowing her to see Cliff anymore, are you?"

She is quiet for a moment. "I'm pretty pragmatic about it, Tara. You tell a kid no, they'll be that much more determined to keep right on doing whatever it is you don't want them to do. That's especially true when it comes to dating. Of course, Graham doesn't feel the same way. He put his foot down, demanded they stop seeing each other."

Oh my God. He and I actually agree on something? "And how's that working out?"

"About like you'd expect."

"What about Kayla's grades?"

I can hear her shrug in the silence.

"A couple of months ago, she was worried about a single B," I pursue. "Have you checked in with her teachers lately?"

White noise swells like an angry beehive, becomes almost deafening. Finally, she says, "What's the use?"

The comment reminds me of our mother.

What's the use, indeed? "I think it's called parenting."

"Really?" The retort is quick, and white-hot. "And how would *you* know anything about parenting? Oh, that's right. You wouldn't. And you never will."

Touché, Mel, touché.

THIRTY-NINE

By week four post-op, I'm starting to feel on the mend. According to my doctors, the bones holding my new ACL and MCL in place are mostly healed. It's the surrounding muscles that must be strengthened to protect the ligaments, and that will take much longer.

I've learned a cool word, too. Proprioceptors. These are receptors located in muscles, tendons, ligaments, and joints that supply information about the position of a limb in space. In other words, your foot realizes where it is in relationship to the floor, your other foot, or the gas and brake pedals. Your tissues have memories. Unfortunately, when you rip a ligament, it loses recollection, so you have to retrain it. And that can take up to a year.

They say professional athletes who push hard during rehab tend to heal more quickly because their muscles regain proprioceptive ability faster. I'm not looking to play football or run a marathon anytime soon, but I want to get around on my own. I've been training with dedication and feel confident I'll be able to drive safely in another week or two. Kayla's spring break begins at the end of March, and I want to be home by then.

When I called her to ask about the garage-door opener, she admitted she still had it but claimed she forgot to put it back, and she sure didn't admit to "borrowing" my house for a few days. In fact, she acted offended that I'd even suggest such a thing. I have no proof, and so I let it drop, though I continue to suspect it was her. Who else could have done it? Still, I promised her a tour of the Art Institute, and so it shall be, not only because I gave her my word, but also because I'd look ridiculous otherwise. You can't go pulling strings only to fray them immediately.

Postworkout, I drain the last bottle of my favorite juice-infused vitamin water. I've been going through it like crazy. I call Cavin to ask if he'll pick up another case, but his cell goes straight to voice mail, so I phone his office instead. His receptionist answers.

"Hi, Rebecca. Is Cavin available?"

"Uh, no, actually. He got a call at lunch and left early."

"I see. Well, thanks, anyway."

Suspicion sizzles. A similar call last week took Cavin away from work prematurely. When he finally arrived home, it was with a good excuse firmly in place. "My dad was passing through, so we went out for a couple of beers."

We've only discussed his family a couple of times. I know his father is a retired medical researcher, and his mom died when he was in high school. He's got a younger brother in the air force, and their "baby" sister is a high-level corporate attorney.

While I wouldn't in a million years introduce Cavin to my mother, I was disappointed. "Why didn't you bring him home? I would have enjoyed meeting him."

"He was actually in Reno, and just for the day, or I would have."

Which explained why he was so late, but not why he didn't let me know until after the fact.

He did apologize for that. "Sorry I didn't call. I have no real excuse, other than it slipped my mind." Then he kissed me very sweetly. "I'm still getting used to having someone around who cares where I am."

All was forgiven, and I haven't given it a second thought until now. Is his dad just passing through town again? And even in that highly unlikely event, would he have forgotten to call again? Which makes me wonder if that's what happened last week. I have no reason not to trust Cavin except, as Eli would say, how well do I really know him?

I expect him to be late, and he is a little, but not inordinately so. He breezes through the door with a multihued bouquet, piquing a fresh round of misgiving. "Flowers? What did I do?"

"Do? You don't have to do anything special to rate a few posies. You just have to be you." He comes over for a kiss, and then glances toward the kitchen, where I am obviously not cooking. "Any thoughts about dinner?"

I shake my head. "I tried to call to ask you to stop by the store, but couldn't get hold of you. Your phone's off, and when I called your office, Rebecca said you left early." I work very hard to keep accusation out of my voice.

Still, he blushes and looks away. Not a good sign. "Yes, I guess I did."

"Your dad again?"

"Of course not." He pulls away, goes into the kitchen, reaches for wine and two glasses.

Uh-oh.

"Should I be worried?"

"Not at all. But I do have something to confess." He returns to the living room and hands me a glass before he continues. "I had lunch with Sophia. She's here visiting a friend and called to say hello."

"I see." I sip my wine, seethe, wait for him to offer some lame explanation.

"Look. We met for lunch, but that was all. The truth is, she was interested in more, but I was very clear that I'm no longer available for 'more.' "

Three hours is a pretty long time. Must have been horrible service. I roll the information over in my mind.

Don't like what he did.

Appreciate the honesty.

How honest was he?

He didn't have to admit that's where he was.

He could have called and let me know.

Really? You would have preferred that?

I would have preferred he didn't see Sophia.

I consider my words carefully. "Cavin, on one hand, yes, I'm uncomfortable with you spending a few hours with an old girlfriend, especially one you were so close to. On the other hand, despite two incredible months together, and the fact that I've lived with you here for several weeks, whatever commitment we have to each other is completely informal. I suppose I've assumed something more, but —"

"Wait."

He sets his glass on the end table, takes mine and rests it beside his. Then he lifts me into his lap, so I'm sitting across his legs. He places one hand on each of my cheeks, rotates my face so I have no choice but to look into his eyes. Gray.

Almost black in this failing light.

"I don't want you to have to assume, but do you really not know? I love you, Tara."

This kiss is not a simple hello, and it holds no apology. It is filled with longing, lust, and, yes, love. Startling. I return it with abandon, then stop so I can lift my sweater over my head, invite his mouth lower. His lips explore the length of my neck, down to the cleft between my breasts, where his tongue takes over. As I sit here, in his lap, his sudden erection pushes against the exact right spot, as if asking to enter. Won't happen with two pairs of pants between us, but the prospect makes me hungry.

But first I relocate myself. I still can't kneel, but because I'm sitting here on this big, fluffy cushion, my face is almost exactly the right height. "Stand up and take off your jeans."

Cavin complies, and I reach for his brilliant cock, invite it against my lips, and circle the knob with my tongue, slowly at first, then in quickening rotations. Then I unhinge my jaw, which is what it takes for my mouth to accept the whole thing, and I teach him the meaning of head, Tara-style, pausing only to slow him down, and once to tell him, "I will make you forget Sophia."

He rocks forward. "Who?"

And now I let him come.

FORTY

Once seeds of suspicion sprout, they take root very quickly. It takes sheer strength of will not to call Cavin's office daily. His declaration of love was at once comforting and disquieting. Comforting, because that's what I wanted. Disquieting, because I can't quite believe it. Perhaps something to do with the timing?

My guess is Sophia is still around, and even if Cavin did tell her he's hooked up with someone else, that doesn't mean she's going to quit trying. I can't stand sitting around here, doing nothing to reassure myself. Mel would tell me I'm being ridiculous, that if Cavin were cheating, he wouldn't proactively admit to lunch and conversation with an ex. The truth is, I've done exactly that before, and it didn't mean I wanted to have sex with that person.

Conversely, however, when I had an idea my ex was messing around on me, I took charge of the situation and hired a private investigator. I can only find two in the immediate area. I choose the one with the most interesting name.

He answers his own phone. "Dirk Caldwell here. How can I help you?"

His voice is high and forced through his nose, and I imagine a beady-eyed rat in a trench coat, whiskers twitching.

"I'm looking for someone to follow my, uh, partner for a few days."

"Partner as in business partner, or love interest?"

"The latter."

"Well, you've come to the right place. I take it there might be another woman somewhere?"

"It's possible."

"No problem."

"When could you get started?"

"So happens my schedule's pretty open right now." Hope that's not a bad sign. "Let's take care of the business end first. With this type of investigation I charge fifty an hour, and I'll need a thousand-dollar retainer up front."

"You expect it to take that long?"

"Probably not, but you never know. I mean, you and he aren't married, right? So this isn't about needing proof to take the dude to the cleaners. You just want to be certain for your own peace of mind."

"That's correct."

"Is the money a problem?"

"Not at all. I'm just not very mobile at the moment." I explain briefly about my injury.

"I can come to you. What's the address?"

When I tell him, there's a long silence on the far end.

"That sounds familiar. Is that your house?"

"No, it's my boyfriend's."

"What's his name?"

"Cavin Lattimore. He's an orthopedic surgeon."

The rat whistles. "Oh, um. I'm sorry, but I recently did some work for Dr. Lattimore. I'm afraid it would be a conflict of interest. I do have a colleague I can recommend, however."

He rattles off a name and phone number, but I quit listening after "conflict of interest." What would Cavin need a PI for? There must be a file around here somewhere, and his study seems like the logical place. It doesn't take long to find it.

I sit at his desk and inspect the drawers. The two large ones on the bottom contain alphabetized filing folders, and in the Cs is one labeled *Cannon.* I pull it, place it on the desk, and open it, revealing a large manila envelope with a business card paper-clipped to the flap. It belongs to "Dirk Caldwell, Private Investigator," and features a grainy photo of a dumpy middle-aged man who I'm pretty sure drives a beat-up sedan. It kind of looks like him.

And there I am, inside the envelope. It's an extensive report. Birth record. Marriages. Divorces. Properties. Businesses. Fund-raising activities. Information about Melody's family. News stories about Jordan and Finn. Raul's death notice. There's even stuff about Mom.

This must have cost a whole lot more than a grand.

The only thing that seems to be missing is my employment history: exactly one job, stripping at the Jellybean Club. Would I be embarrassed if that were included here? Would it make me any more pissed than I already am at having my privacy invaded in such a fashion?

I carry the folder to the kitchen, leave it open on the island counter, and fix myself a drink. Bourbon, straight up. Something to burn going down. Something hotter than the anger simmering inside. When Cavin comes in, I've had three stiff shots of John J.

Bowman Single Barrel. It has raised a decent buzz — almost decent enough to mellow me out. Almost.

Cavin takes in the bourbon bottle, plus the fact that I'm pouring a fourth, adds the pinched look on my face, sums up the situation correctly. "What's wrong?"

I wave at the offending paperwork. "That."

He studies the open folder. "Ah. That. I don't doubt you're aggravated. But might I ask how you came across it? Do you regularly dig through my things?"

"Actually, no."

"Then, how?"

The straightest path to truth is through truth, and I happen to be buzzed enough to confess. "Coincidence, really. I was looking for a PI, and happened to choose good ol' Dirk. He mentioned a conflict of interest, because he'd recently done some work for you."

"You wanted to investigate me?"

"Yes."

I expect consternation. Irritation. Out-and-out in-your-face accusation. Instead, he laughs. "This *is* a small town, isn't it? Pour me one of those?" As I reach for a glass, he sidles up behind me, wraps his arms around my waist. "I understand you wanting to be sure about me. Just like I hope you

351

understand that I needed to be sure about the woman I want to spend the rest of my life with."

I almost drop the glass. "What does that mean?"

He circles around, insinuates himself between me and the counter, gentles the drink away, and sets it down behind him. Then he takes both of my hands in his. "I know this seems fast, but I want to marry you, Tara. Would you consider being my wife?"

"I . . . uh . . . what?"

"I'll get down on one knee if you'd like."

"No!" I reach up, lock my hands behind his neck, search his eyes. "I just never thought . . ."

He kisses my forehead.

Kisses my right eye closed.

Kisses my left eye closed.

"Don't think. Just say yes."

"Yes." The word swims out of some thick, boozy sea, only to become mired in doubt. "But hold on. When did you make this decision? After Carmel? A report like that took some time to assemble."

"Go sit, okay? I'll bring your glass."

Cavin pours himself a matching drink, carries both into the living room, and we nest on the couch before he continues.

"Remember I told you I was serious about Sophia . . ."

How could I forget?

"Look. I thought I knew her, but we were two years into the relationship when I discovered some unsavory things about her."

"Like what?"

"Like she wasn't above sleeping with people to obtain financing for her shows."

"Even while she was with you?"

"Absolutely. There's more. Apparently, she was always short on cash because she maintained a sizable cocaine habit. I couldn't believe I didn't recognize it. Had we actually cohabitated, I probably would have. But she lived in Reno and I lived here. We saw each other a lot, but she had plenty of opportunities to party without me, and took every advantage of that."

Okay, I'm feeling marginally better about Sophia. Whiskey and revelation, a winning combination! "After that, I was gun-shy," Cavin admits. "But then you materialized, like some mythical temptress, and my attraction was so immediate I had to second-guess it, although I also desperately needed to feed it. Cavin the optimist was totally hooked. Cavin the pragmatist insisted he didn't want any surprises if he was to invest time and energy — not to mention love —

in you."

I have to smile at his earnestness. "Well, since I wasn't able to secure Dirk Caldwell, is there any information I should be privy to? Something maybe requiring a prenup?"

"Tara, first of all, I really have no problem with you doing a background check on me. There are other private investigators. Second, I absolutely insist you request a prenup. I don't want your possessions or your money. I only want you. I might, however, ask for a little investment advice. You're one hell of a businesswoman."

I am, in fact, a savvy businesswoman. But think I prefer "mythical temptress."

I take a few minutes after dinner to e-mail my sister: *I've got some news. Cavin asked me to marry him. Believe it or not, I said yes! I know it's kind of quick and all, but the thing is, and I can't believe I'm saying this, I'm pretty sure I'm in love him. Don't tell anyone, okay? I haven't even told him yet.*

Her reply: *Oh, Tara, I'm happy for you. Just please be sure this time.*

See, that's the problem.

FORTY-ONE

Cavin and I decide on a June wedding. Corny, I know, but it happens to be one of the most beautiful months at Tahoe, plus Eli and Melody's kids will be out of school. We'll have the ceremony at some outdoor view venue. Sugar Pine Point maybe, or Camp Richardson. No Elvis (Raul). No rented mansion (Jordan). No yacht (Finn). No Methodist church (Melissa/Cavin).

Chef Christopher will host the reception. We don't expect too many guests — family and a few close friends. Maybe thirty total. We'll invite Cavin's dad, but not my mom. Definitely not Sophia. Still considering Graham. Anyway, now I've got something to plan besides the next fund-raiser.

Meanwhile, I'm going home to San Francisco for a couple of weeks, and I'm driving myself there. My proprioceptors seem to be on full alert, my right foot comprehending where the brake is in relationship to its place in space. Or whatever. Basically, if my brain says stop, my foot can handle the command. I think.

I wait until the weather is clear and the forecast calls for more of the same. The day before I'm scheduled to go, I take my knee for a test drive, with Cavin riding shotgun. I back carefully onto the street, drive down the hill, turn onto the highway, completely without incident. "Hey, it's working."

"That was the plan."

"Next thing you know, I'll be doing jumping jacks."

"I'd avoid those for a while, or any jumping for that matter. And you still don't want to run, or engage in any joint-jarring activities. You can, however, start to walk or swim. Just don't overdo. We don't want you limping down the aisle."

"Whatever you say, Doc Lattimore."

"I like it when you call me that — so Wild West. Hey, maybe I should grow a handlebar mustache. Wax it up. Curl the ends."

"I have no aversion to facial hair. Go for it." Actually, I prefer clean-shaven men, but he's just joking anyway. "Maybe you could get Eli to grow one, too, so you'll match in the wedding pictures."

"The only way I could get Eli to grow a

mustache would be to order him not to do it."

The roads are free of ice, but I drive over-cautiously anyway. This is so not me, but I've got to start somewhere. Today, a drive to the gas station to fill up for my trip. Next week, road racing! Or not.

"So, have you informed Eli about our upcoming event?"

He was hesitant to make the call, though I'm not exactly sure why. I called Melody right away. She thinks I'm crazy to marry a man I barely know but conceded he seems like a pretty good catch. Her overall message was, "If he makes you happy, I'm happy for you."

Cavin sighs. "Yes, I talked to him. He was less than enthusiastic, but then again, that's how he is about almost anything me-related. He wasn't out-and-out hostile, at least. Pretty sure that means he likes you."

"I'm not so positive. Eli's hard to read."

"A well-practiced trait."

We are almost home — I've started to think of it as "home," and soon Carmel will feel that way, too. With San Francisco, we'll have three houses. Seems like a lot for just two people, but they're all so unique, it would be hard to give one up. I suppose it's a conversation worth having. We'll need a good tax attorney in addition to our personal lawyers, who will handle the prenup separately. So much to consider there, too. What do we throw into the communal pot? What should remain separate?

Mortgages.

Investments.

Bank accounts.

Incomes.

Expenses.

All these tedious details could threaten the romance, but without settling them, one or both of us could get screwed. I don't want to approach marriage in terms of possible dissolution. But in my experience, which is relatively broad, forever has no meaning with respect to romantic relationships.

At least there is only one "child" complicating things, unless you count my nieces, who can really lay no legitimate claim to any sort of inheritance. Eli, on the other hand, might consider me a threat to his. I steer the Escalade onto the steep road up through the woods. "You did tell Eli that we've agreed on a prenup, yes?"

"Actually, no. It's none of his business."

"Maybe not. But if he can't be happy about our union, I'd like him, at least, not to be paranoid about it. I want him to feel secure about his birthright."

"I appreciate that, Tara. But I'd prefer he not feel secure about it. I want him to find his own way in the world, to make something of himself, not sit around waiting for me to die so he can inherit his future."

Wow. He means it. Guess I made the right choice, forgoing motherhood. I'd suck at it. I pull off the street, into the driveway, brake perfectly. "That's good to know. Tell you what. I'll leave all major decisions regarding Eli up to you. I'll offer advice if you want it, but truthfully parenting is not on my bucket list, so I'm just as happy to stay out of your way. Deal?"

"No." He turns in his seat to face me. "I want us to be partners in every sense of the word. There will be challenges, of course. We've still got a lot to learn about each other. But communication is the key. I haven't talked a lot about Eli, mostly because there's so much about him I don't know myself. I can tell you he's resentful, to the point of bitterness. But I'm not one hundred percent sure why, or even who he blames for his self-imposed exile. Lots of kids have parents who get divorced."

"I don't think divorce is the benchmark. Melody and Graham are still solidly together, and they're having issues with Kayla. Of course, speaking as an outsider, I find Kayla relatively tolerable, as teenagers go."

When Cavin smiles, tension visibly vacates his shoulders and neck. " 'Relatively' being the operative word. I want to believe this is just a phase for Eli, and normal for a kid his age. But it would have to be a generational thing, I think. At seventeen, I was hot to take on the world, set my own course, and steer full-speed in that direction. Right after I found a way to get laid, of course."

Ooh. Love when little bits of information like that slip out. Virgin at seventeen, married at twenty. One day I'll find out what went on in between, not that it matters except to assuage my ambition to know everything about him. That, I've decided, is the only way to really love someone. To learn everything about him so you can become that person's ideal partner. I've got a distance to go, but I'm willing to work very hard to get there.

Meanwhile, we have a few hours to satisfy more carnal desires. "Ready to come inside?"

"That, my dear, is a loaded question."

The man was reading my mind.

FORTY-TWO

I have to admit I've missed San Francisco, and the house I've made so very much my own. The Tahoe place is nice enough in an upscale rustic way, but there's something about sleek modern architecture that I find extremely appealing. Plus, and some people would probably think I'm crazy, despite the relative proximity of other houses on this street, I feel less claustrophobic here, without trees closing in on every side. My view to the ocean isn't filtered, except by the too-present fog.

The drive isn't a problem. It's Friday, so most of the traffic is moving in the other direction, toward the mountain and spring skiing. The flow into the city will slow toward evening, when suburbanites motor in for weekend entertainments, but I'm too early to be bothered by that. I pull into my garage a little after one, call Cavin to tell him I've arrived safely and miss him already.

I didn't bother to pack much. Most of my clothes are here, and I had Charlie stock up the kitchen and resupply the bathrooms with my favored soaps and lotions. I've rehabbed my knee enough that the stair climb isn't so bad. I'll even sleep on the third level in my own big bed tonight. The sheets will be lonely.

Charlie has been good about clearing away the evidence of my uninvited visitor. I wander room to room, assessing, but find no other hints of a break-in. Everything is in its place, which only underscores my belief that whoever was here was someone I'm acquainted with. I changed the door codes remotely from Cavin's. I change them again now, just in case. Funny how paranoia comes creeping back as soon as I'm on my own again.

Melody and Kayla will be here tomorrow. I've arranged the Art Institute visit for Monday. Larry Alexander was quite accommodating and made it clear that, providing Kayla's tuition is paid, there will be no problem with admission. Strings capably pulled. Meanwhile, we'll take in the de Young Museum and an off-Broadway something Kayla's dying to see. The play poses little problem. The museum, however, means some time on my feet. We'll see how far I've come.

After four hours in the car, my body feels stiff, and my knee is complaining. Rather than take a pill, I opt for thirty slow walking minutes on the treadmill. This is the most actual weight-bearing exercise I've accomplished in many weeks, and it hurts. But it also makes me proud and fills me with the certainty that I'm well on the highway to full recovery.

As the sky darkens and the city illuminates window by window, I consider a solo dinner. I almost call Cavin to reassure myself that he, too, is dining alone. No. I refuse to go there. Building trust is a tedious process.

Instead, I content myself with a Trader Joe's frozen sukiyaki and a big glass of fruit-forward pinot noir. I'm almost finished with both when the intercom buzzes. I go into my office and turn on the light so the camera can inform me who's there. His face is turned away from the lens, but I can tell by his build, not to mention his hair, who it is. "Eli?"

Now he faces the camera. "Yeah. Hi. Uh, can I come in?"

I have to check what I'm wearing. Baggie sweatpants below, baggier sweatshirt above. Everything completely covered. "Of course. Up the steps to the second level."

"Yeah, I kn— Sure."

He knows? He must have noticed the lights. And speaking of lights, I flip the switch that will guide his way upstairs, unlock the deadbolt, and wait for his recognizable clomp. When I'm sure he's reached the landing, I open the door to invite him in. He doesn't wait for formalities, but bolts straight past me without pausing for a greeting. He stops when I close the door and throw the lock. "What? Afraid I'll escape?"

Seriously?

"You are welcome here, Eli, but I'm a little surprised by your visit."

"Why?"

"Well, for one thing, I've only been home a few hours. Did you know I'd be here?"

"Duh. Dad told me."

Duh. Such eloquence. "Shouldn't you be at school?"

"Ever hear of spring break? Started this afternoon." He circles the coffee table. "Mind if I sit down?"

I shrug. "Help yourself. I was just finishing dinner. Are you hungry?"

"Nah. Had a burger."

Eloquence, squared. "Then can I get you something to drink?"

"Got a beer?" He plops down on the sofa.

"I don't serve liquor to minors."

"Beer isn't liquor. Besides, I promise not to tell."

"Sorry."

"Dad lets me drink at home."

Somehow I doubt it. "That's between you and your father." I go into the kitchen to put my plate in the dishwasher, freshen my wine, and look for something nonalcoholic. "Unfortunately, there's not a lot I can offer you. Sparkling water, with or without juice. Vitamin water. Tap water."

"Yeah, I remember."

What does that mean? "Remember what?"

"That you're a health nut. No soda. No junk food."

He picked that up from one weekend at Tahoe? Whatever. I return to the living room, sit in the curved chair I bought for looks, not comfort. I'd be less comfortable sitting next to Eli. "If you get thirsty, you know where the fridge is. So, are you spending your vacation at the lake?"

"I wanted to make it up for some spring boarding, but Mom's home, and she'll only be there for ten days before they take off again. So I'm afraid I'll be stuck in Sacramento. It's a dick hole of a town."

I'm relatively certain his less-than-savory language is meant to test, not outright of-fend, so I do my best not to react to obnoxious terms like "dick hole." "I agree it's not my favorite city. Ugly in all kinds of ways." I glance at the clock. "You've still got a little drive ahead of you. When does your mom expect you?"

"Tomorrow. I was kind of hoping you'd let me crash here tonight."

"Here?"

"Yeah. We can get to know each other better."

The words sink like lead weights, and I'm not certain I like their intent. Better chill it on the wine so I don't say too much. "I guess it's okay if you stay over. But before I say yes, does anyone know you're here?"

"You mean like my parental units?"

"Exactly. Where does your mother think you're spending the night?"

"With a friend. You *are* my friend, aren't you?" His voice is soaked with sarcasm.

"I'm sure you don't need me for a friend. You must have plenty."

"Only a couple, actually. But then, you only need one or two really good ones, right?"

I think about myself. "Right."

"So you can use one more, and so can I."

"I'm not sure it's a parent's job to be a friend, Eli. As for stepparents, pretty sure 'foil' is in the job description."

"You're not my stepmother yet. And even if and when you are, it might be the better course of action for us to be friends."

If? "Was that a threat?"

The corners of his mouth twitch into a grin. "No, no, not at all. Why would I want to threaten you? I just meant I'd rather we feel at ease with each other. Let's start with, would you prefer I call you Mom, or Tara?"

A sharp little laugh escapes me. "Eli, I've worked very hard to make sure no one would ever have the right to call me 'Mom.' Tara will do."

"I figured. Okay, now you ask me a question."

Twenty questions? Is that the game? I consider for about fifteen seconds. Might as well come at him head-on. "How do you feel about your dad and me getting married?"

"I think you're crazy."

"How so?"

"Well, for one thing, what's the rush? There's a reason why people wait — you know, like date — a while before signing up for forever, not that a watery concept like a vow means much to most people."

"It means something to me. Unfortunately, my exes didn't see things the same way." Oops. Too much information, perhaps?

"Exes, plural?"

Rein it in. "Yes, plural. I'll spare you the ugly details, however."

His eyes shimmer amusement. "That's okay. I've seen your file." The snot-nosed snoop expects confusion, shock, maybe even anger.

Counterattack. "So have I, actually, and Dirk Caldwell was relatively thorough. Did you learn anything surprising?"

"Only that you don't seem to care that my dad put a PI on you."

"He really didn't have to do that. I have very little to hide and I'd already confessed most of it. But I understand his caution, especially after what happened with Sophia."

Eli has been sitting slightly hunched forward. At the name, he straightens. "You know about Sophia?"

"Well, of course."

But his demeanor says I might not know everything.

HUSH

Don't speak
to me as the sun
does, vowing in honey
silk voice unswerving
devotion to soil, seed
and bloom, pledges forgotten
with winter flirtation.

Don't promise, like the sun.

Don't shout
at me as the rain
does, hurling coal
throated insults
and sharp punctuation
at earth, already saturated,
and river, risen to flood.

Don't curse, like the rain.

No, whisper
to me as the snow
does, feathering harsh
realities with a sift of white
lies, miniature deceptions,
each unique facade
a fairy tale adrift.

Tell stories, like the snow.

FORTY-THREE

Before I can query him, my cell interrupts our conversation. It's Cavin, and I feel like I should let him know who's currently sitting in my living room, pumping me for information. I probably won't mention that I plan some serious reverse pumping as soon as I say good-bye.

It's your dad, I whisper to Eli, before moving into my office. "Hey there," I coo into the phone. "Guess who dropped by for a visit."

Cavin is floored. "What does he want?"

"A place to crash for the night, and a chance for us to get to know each other, at least that's what he said."

On the far end of the line, the pause is more than pregnant. It's three weeks overdue. "Be very, very careful, Tara. Eli can be . . ."

"Manipulative? Less than forthright? Yes, I understand. You've mentioned it before, and I have to agree. But seriously, don't worry, Cavin. I've got it covered."

Except maybe I don't, because when we hang up and I exit my office, Eli is in the kitchen, helping himself to a glass of fruit-forward pinot noir. He smiles at the consternation I don't try to conceal. "No worries. You didn't serve it to me, so you're off the hook, right? Besides, I'm not going anywhere tonight. No one will ever know."

"Do you like pinot?"

"Actually, I prefer something a little bolder. But as pinots go, this one is very nice."

This boy is wise beyond his years. "Who taught you about wine?"

"My mom bought into the European philosophy that labeling anything taboo only makes a kid want to try it. There was never an alcohol prohibition in my home, as long as it was at the dinner table, under adult supervision."

"So, your mother educated your wine palate?"

"Not exactly, but that's a long story, and one I'm not sure you'll want to hear. May I freshen your glass?"

It's already on the counter, snugged against his own. There's a sip or two left, and that makes my instinct sing. I can't see

371

any unusual sediment or discoloration. Still, the well-schooled woman in me says, "Let me rinse it first. I don't usually backwash, but you never know, and wine is much better without a sukiyaki float."

"That's what I've heard."

Eli returns to the living room. I follow through, rinse my glass, refill it once I'm sure there are no additives. But why would I consider that to start with? And am I really going to share a bottle of pricey pinot with my underage almost-stepson? Apparently, that's an affirmative, because I find myself doing exactly that. He appreciates it like a true connoisseur, one slow sip at a time.

"How often do you drink?" I ask pointedly.

"Whenever I can, though rarely to excess. I don't mind getting buzzed, but I hate hangovers. Worse, I don't like acting stupid."

Can't argue with that, I suppose. Still. "I'd caution against drinking too often, especially at your age. It's bad for brain development."

He snorts. "Too late."

No use lecturing. Besides, I'm a poor example. So I'll change the subject. "Do you have a girlfriend?"

His smile falters and he studies me closely. "Not at the moment. Why?"

"Just wondering."

"You interested?"

"Don't be ridiculous. I'm old enough to b—"

"I love older women," he interrupts. "I love their poise. Their experience. Their ability to carry on a conversation that does not involve boy bands or menstruation."

"Really. And how many older women have you been with?"

He sips his glass empty. "I have admired many. I've had a sexual relationship with one. But then, I thought you knew about her."

"Who?"

"Sophia."

It takes every ounce of self-control I possess not to spit out my wine. Instead, I swallow it so quickly that it rasps my throat. "So-Sophia?"

"Yes. You said you knew about her."

"I think we're having two different conversations. I said I knew about her, meaning her cocaine habit, and her rather dubious sense of morality. I did not, however, have any idea that her sleeping around on your father included sleeping with you. Does Cavin know?"

"Well, yeah. He found us together."

Oh my God. I should probably cut this conversation short, but I really want the details. "How? Where?"

"It was good ol' Dirk who busted us first. Dad suspected Sophia was cheating on him, so he put Caldwell to work. Neither of them expected to find her fucking me, especially not in Dad's house. We should have been more careful, but caution wasn't something I particularly worried about, and when that bitch was soaring on coke, whoa. She would have screwed any dude with a boner."

I look at Eli, more boy than man in my estimation, and even younger when this happened. "But you had to have been, what? Fifteen?"

"Sixteen. She waited until I passed the magic age of consent. In fact, the first time was a slightly belated birthday gift. She said she wanted me to learn from the best. That woman was one hell of a teacher, too, let me tell you. The only problem is, she spoiled sex for me. Vanilla will no longer suffice, and I haven't found a girl closer to my age willing to do the things Sophia did. Thus, no girlfriend."

"Did your dad catch you in the actual act?"

"Uh, yeah, he did."

"What did he do?"

"I think he watched for a couple of minutes. Making sure his eyes weren't lying. Then he turned and walked away. Slammed the door so we'd know he was there. I was banging her from behind. She tried to get up and go after Dad, but I held her until I finished. She was pissed. He was pissed. And I was pissed because I figured it would be our last time."

"Was it?"

"Yep. Right up until I bumped into her on the mountain over winter break. We had a quickie in the woods, for old time's sake."

Bet that's something that didn't come up when Cavin had lunch with her. But this explains a lot. Why he broke up with her. Why he distrusts his son. Why he's nervous about Eli spending the night here. But the kid wouldn't dare try to put the moves on me, would he? And Cavin couldn't possibly believe I'd go for it, could he?

"What did you say to your father afterward?"

"I asked what he would have done if a woman like Sophia had put the moves on him when he was sixteen."

"And how did he respond?"

"He called me morally bankrupt. I told him I was obviously a chip off the old block." The boy, who is a font of clichés, stands. "If you'll excuse me, I've got to take a leak."

"The bathroom is —"

"I know."

He slithers down the hallway, straight to the correct room. Strange. When he comes back, wiping his wet hands on his jeans, I ask, "How did you know where the bathroom is?"

"I noticed it when I came in."

Which makes perfect sense. Except I think the door was closed.

FORTY-FOUR

That's going to bother me all night. It's almost as if he's been here before. But that's impossible. I'd straight up interrogate anyone else. But I don't think that's the best way to approach Eli Lattimore. The closer I study him, the more thought provoking he becomes.

He's smart, no doubt about that. He's got a great vocabulary, and uses it. Doesn't always fall back on teen talk, although when he does it's crude. But he uses that language without apology, and purposefully. He thinks things through before opening his mouth, formulates his sentences to achieve maximum effect. So maybe, if you disregard his looks, he is in reality more man than boy. Which makes the game more interesting, as long as I remember appearances can be deceiving. Oh, and now *I'm* the wellspring of clichés.

Don't judge a book by its cover.

Boys will be boys.

The acorn doesn't fall far from the tree.

The last might be concerning, in the case of Cavin and Eli. However, considering how far this acorn rolled away from her mother tree, I have to feel confident that a child doesn't always reflect his or her parentage.

"What are you thinking?" Eli interrupts my reverie.

"About clichés," I say without hesitation, taking the easiest route.

"Like what about them?"

"Like how they don't always represent the truth, despite how often people rely on them to do exactly that."

"Give me an example."

I don't want to talk about acorns, so I offer this one. "Okay, how about 'honesty is the best policy'?"

"Are you saying it's better to lie?"

"Not always, but in some situations, avoiding the truth might be the best course of action."

"You mean, like if someone asks if you think they look fat."

"If it's someone whose feelings you care about, yes. But I was thinking more like if confiding information might put someone else in danger. Or even if a confession is likely to be detrimental to a relationship.

For instance, I'm wondering why your dad didn't mention your dalliance with Sophia. The only reason I can come up with is that he didn't want to damage the fledgling connection between you and me."

"Has it been damaged?"

"I'm not sure yet. I do know I'll never think about you in exactly the same way."

"Is that good or bad?"

"Remains to be seen."

"So . . . are you a liar?"

Generally, I like the direct approach, but sometimes it can be intimidating. "I'd rather rely on the truth. And when it comes to people I care about, I'm almost always completely honest even if that means telling someone they've put on a few pounds. Why lie about that? They know what the mirror reveals."

"Yeah, well, I bullshit regularly. It's only bad when you get caught middeception . . . Why are you shaking your head?"

"I don't know. You seem to enjoy shock value. The truth is much more conducive to that, in my humble opinion."

"If you're talking about the truth as revelation, then yes, I agree. It's like dessert at the end of a satisfying meal of deceit."

I think I'm glad Eli won't be living with Cavin and me full-time. I could never let my guard down. "Right up until that last remark, I was going to suggest you become a politician. But they refuse that kind of dessert."

"Tell me about it. My mom married one, and diplomats aren't a whole lot better than your everyday congressman. Anyway, politics isn't a lucrative career, unless you're taking bribes. And that doesn't always end well, does it?" He winks at me.

The file.

My file.

Dirk Caldwell's discoveries file.

The file Cavin paid for.

File.

The word prickles.

"I don't think a decision's been made in Jordan's case yet. In fact, I don't think a trial date has been set."

"But he's guilty, right?"

"Do you really think I should comment?"

"Hey, maybe they'll subpoena you. Then would you comment?"

"Then I guess I'd have to, wouldn't I?" The verbal swordplay has grown tiresome. "Would you like another glass of wine? I can open a cabernet if you'd prefer it."

"Something bold from your cellar?"

"How did you know I have a cellar?" That information, I'm sure, was not in my file.

Eli shrugs. "You mentioned it before."

I try to remember our past conversations, but the two glasses of wine I've already had have retarded my recollection. Still, I'm pretty sure I never mentioned the cellar to him. Why would I? Suddenly, I remember Charlie's words, half whispered into the phone: *Glasses and bottles. Like someone has been helping himself . . .*

"Why don't you go choose a bottle? From the top three shelves, please."

He regards me closely, pivots on one foot. "Downstairs, I imagine?"

It's a logical choice, considering the definition of the word "cellar." I nod agreement. "Dug into the hill, through a door in the back of the garage. The switch —"

"I'll find it."

Eli vanishes into the darkness. "Flip on the light!" I yell after him.

Last thing I need is for him to go tumbling and break his neck. I hear no noise to confirm such a dreadful happenstance, however. He is gone long enough that he either got lost or is making a careful selection. Finally, he reappears with a decent bottle of Caymus.

"I'll open it," he says, stopping to collect our glasses before carrying the wine into the kitchen. "The corkscrew is . . ." He opens the correct drawer on the first try.

"Do you have ESP?"

"No, why?"

"You just seem to know your way around my house pretty well. And considering you've never been here before . . . You *haven't* been here before, right?"

The cork exits the bottle with an audible pop. He waits to answer until after he has brimmed our glasses with rich, scarlet liquid. Then he looks me straight in the eye. "Why would you suspect otherwise?"

I could drop the whole thing, but then I'd never know. "Apparently while I was staying at your dad's, someone spent some time here without my permission."

"You mean, like a break-in?"

"Not exactly. My doors are all locked with keypads. Somebody seems to have hacked the codes, along with the security system code."

Eli crosses the living room floor in three long strides, hands me a glass, bends to look into my eyes. "And why would you think that was me?"

"Because it makes more sense than ESP?"

He smiles.

But makes no further comment.

FORTY-FIVE

I drag myself into Saturday morning, groggy and reluctant to throw back the covers. My covers. My bed. I allow myself the luxury of floating here, cushioned by the familiar, blanketed by an overwhelming sense of everything being right, despite a rather tense moment or two last night.

Eli and I managed to finish the cabernet on top of the pinot, and stayed up watching some HBO show he claims he's addicted to. Something about a drug-running vampire, and nothing I'd ever choose to watch. Afterward, I rocked unsteadily to my feet. "My bed is calling to me, I'm afraid. It's been quite a long day."

"Where should I sleep?"

Even as buzzed as I was, the question felt tainted with obscure connotation. I thought for a minute. "My sister and niece are coming tomorrow, and I'm not sure I want to change guest-room sheets. How about the sofa?"

"Aw, come on. What if I change the sheets for you?"

A vague unease descended around me, but I agreed. "I guess we've got a deal. You can take the room closest to the stairs."

I teetered across the expanse of the living room, fighting the whirl of my head and beaten up by the exercise I'd done earlier in the day. I'd just reached the foot of the staircase when I felt Eli's hand at my elbow. "Can I help you? You look a little shaky."

Thoughts volleyed inside my head.

Had I watched my wine the entire time?

I did, and besides, he wouldn't dare.

So why was I so messed up?

Two bottles of wine and not much food.

Anyway, why would he slip me a roofie?

Come on. You know.

Did I need help up the stairs?

Remember the last time you needed help up the stairs?

Cavin swept me into his arms, and . . .

"As long as you don't attempt to carry me."

"Carry you? Who would try such a stupid thing?"

I didn't feel the need to share that memory. Eli guided me with gentle hands, and my focus was drawn to the elegance of his long fingers. "You should play the piano," I suggested, tapping into that well of clichés again.

He surprised me. "I do. And the guitar, too. I'll show you sometime if you want."

His voice was a warm zephyr at the back of my neck, and heat radiated between us, and for just one moment my inner nymph might have been persuaded to invite him into my bed. But that thought dissolved instantly, along with any perceived attraction, within a sudden cataract of unfamiliar emotion.

I love Cavin.

And yes, the word materialized from the ether. Lying here now, I try to decipher what that means. I don't rush the contemplation, but rather open myself up to possibilities. So this is what love feels like. Powerful. Elemental. And it's so new that I'm watery about what to do with it. But I refuse to let it go. I don't dare destroy it, and certainly, veering away from fidelity would crush this devotion like chalk into dust. I've mastered impulse control, but this isn't about proving something to myself or anyone else. This is about accepting a deep human need that I've relentlessly closed myself off from. I'm not positive I can manage it, but I'm damn sure going to try.

I haul myself out of bed and by the time I exit the shower, dripping vanilla-cedar-scented water, I can hear movement beyond the bedroom door. Eli must be up, too. I slip into a springlike floral print dress, hope the day matches my outfit once the morning mist lifts. I actually find myself humming as I head off on my quest for coffee.

Humming.

Love makes a person hum.

Eli has already stripped the bed and is looking for a clean set of sheets in the hall linen closet. "Morning," he says when he sees me.

"Morning. How did you sleep?"

"Great, thanks. That's an awesome bed. Conducive to dreaming."

"Good dreams, I hope."

"Excellent. In fact, you starred in one or two."

The boy is an expert at making me blush. "You can skip the details. When you finish, would you mind taking the dirty sheets down to the laundry room?"

"Not at all. But they're not really dirty. No sweat. No semen."

I can't help but smile. "Wait. You dreamed about me, but you didn't sweat?" I purposely avoid the other s-word, but the insinuation is clear.

"I thought you didn't want details."

Touché, brat.

"I'm going to make coffee. Want some?"

"Please. Strong and black."

"A man after my own heart."

"Maybe. Too bad your heart seems to be taken."

He turns away, pulls a set of sheets out of the closet, goes to make the bed while I finesse my way down the stairs to the kitchen, wondering about the intent of his words. "Seems to be," meaning maybe my heart's *not* taken? Meaning maybe I'm faking it? Or was it simply an overt reference to wanting my affection? Eli is difficult to decipher, and that concerns me. I'm glad his father is easier.

I measure dark roast beans into the grinder, pour water into the receptacle, turn on the machine, and while the coffee perks I call Cavin. It's a weekend, so he should be home unless he went skiing or snowshoeing, or is otherwise recreating. He picks up right away.

We indulge in small talk for several minutes. My knee. His plans for the day. Watching vampire crime lords last night. I want to ask why he omitted the information about Sophia and Eli, but I choose to reserve the query for a time when the young man in question isn't around. It doesn't really matter, except to satisfy my curiosity. When I hear clunking footsteps on the stairs, I decide it's time to sign off. "I miss you."

"It's only been two days," Cavin says.

"I know. Guess I got used to having you around." Can I test this new ground?

"Call me later?"

"Of course. Cavin?"

"What?"

Come on. You can do it. "I love you."

Dead silence on the other end.

"Hello?"

"I'm still here," he replies. "It's just, you do realize that's the first time you've said that to me, right?"

"It's the first time I've said it to anyone."

And now that I've uttered the words out loud, I can't take them back. That feels like complete commitment, which bothers me only a little. Three loveless marriages all ended unhappily. Can love connect two people indefinitely?

Eli returns from the laundry room and I pour two mugs of strong black coffee. "Breakfast?"

"Like what?"

"Omelets? I've got scallions and mushrooms."

"Sounds good. Can I help?"

"You know how to cook?" I hand him a carton of eggs, assign myself the task of chopping the vegetables.

"Sure. Been doing it for years. When you're left on your own, you learn or go hungry. Mom always was too busy to bother with menial tasks like cooking."

More Melissa insights.

"Your dad likes to cook, though."

Eli cracks four shells carefully, empties their contents into a bowl. "Yeah, but he wasn't around. In fact, even when he was still married to my mom he didn't hang out at home very often."

I spoon butter into a skillet to melt, add the veggies to sauté. "He regrets not spending more time with you when you were little."

"Yeah, well, you know what they say about regrets . . ." He pours the whipped eggs into the skillet. "They're like butt holes. Everybody has them. Besides, it's a little late to worry about that now, isn't it? Anyway, talk is cheap, Tara. When it comes to Dad, you might want to remember that."

Fair warning. But what does he mean by it?

389

FORTY-SIX

Eli is just putting on his shoes when Melody and Kayla arrive, each lugging a suitcase. I was hoping he'd be gone. It's ridiculous, of course, considering our families will be joined in just a few months, but somehow I don't feel quite ready for the larger merge.

I offer a quick introduction, observing the way Eli's eyes crawl all over Kayla, who is dressed in a short skirt and tight scoop-neck tee, revealing plenty of skin from the thigh down and cleavage up. She notices his attention and smiles approval. Mel misses the entire exchange.

"So, you're Cavin's son," she says. "You and Kayla must be around the same age."

"Close," I agree. "Except Kayla turns eighteen next month. Eli's birthday is in the fall."

Eli winks at Kayla. "It's all good. I have a thing for older women."

Kayla and Melody laugh, but his so-called

joke lands with a thud at my feet. He's watching for my reaction, but I won't reward him. "You should probably go, don't you think? Your mom will worry."

"Okay," he says, "I can take a hint. Will I see you ladies at the wedding?"

"Wouldn't miss it," exhales Kayla, and when Eli bends to tie his laces, she mouths, *Especially now.*

Where does that leave poor ol' Cliff?

When Eli stands, he takes notice of the oversize luggage. "Can I help you ladies with your suitcases?" He doesn't wait for an answer, but instead goes straight to work playing bellman, which is so not his style. Who's he trying to impress?

The gesture is not lost on Melody. "What a polite young man. Excellent manners."

He impressed her, anyway.

"Gosh, he's so strong!"

And Kayla, too.

He tromps back downstairs. "I put yours in the lavender guest room . . ." He nods toward Melody, then addresses Kayla. "And yours in the blue. I slept in there last night, but don't worry . . ."

Oh my God. He's not going to say anything about sweat and semen, is he?

"I changed the sheets," he finishes. "I'd better hit the road, I guess. Thanks so much for your hospitality, Tara. I'll see you in June, if not before."

Eli is barely out the door when Kayla gushes, "Wow. He's so cute! If he looks anything like his dad, no wonder you're getting married."

"A handsome face is not the primary benchmark for a husband, Kayla."

"Really? What is?"

I think for a moment, and consign Cliff to his proper place in the not-husband-material ranks. "The ability to care for you properly, and the desire to put your needs above his own. Followed by the handsome face."

"Um . . . *is* there a guy like that?"

"I hope so." Then I amend, "I believe so."

"So how come Eli was here? Does he visit you often?"

I spend a few minutes explaining Eli's circumstances, omitting the part about his mother living in Sacramento, a coincidence that's a little too close to Kayla's front yard. "But you're not shopping for a new boyfriend, are you?"

Kayla shrugs. "Maybe."

"What about Cliff?"

"You were right. He's a loser. He dropped out of school and moved back in with his mom. Not to mention, he cheated on me."

So much for love. "Sorry."

"Don't be. Obviously, there are better guys out there."

The Eli reference is clear. I wish I knew for sure he was actually superior. I invite Mel to join me in the kitchen for a cup of coffee, hoping Kayla will decide the looming adult conversation will be much too boring.

The tactic works. "If it's okay, I'll go upstairs and relax for a while."

Relax, meaning text her friends, no doubt, and I'm pretty sure what about. "Sure. My plan is dinner out before the play. Curtain is at eight, so I'll make reservations for six. We'll need to leave here around five thirty."

Melody watches Kayla go, making certain she's out of earshot before following me into the other room. Despite her earlier cheerfulness, when I offer her a mug, she has lost any semblance of a smile.

"What's wrong?"

Mel dampens her voice. "The usual."

"Graham?"

She nods. "He's being totally unreasonable about this, Tara. It's not just a 'no way' now, it's a 'if you support this, you're not supporting me.' He even mentioned divorce."

"That's a bit radical, don't you think?"

"It's completely irrational, and that's what I told him."

I give it two beats. "Can I ask you a personal question?"

"Of course."

"Was your marriage in trouble before this? Because it almost seems to me like he's looking for an excuse to talk divorce." If so, she's never said a word.

She sits quietly for several long seconds. "We've been together twenty years. All marriages suffer after so much time. People grow apart. People's opinions change. The passion cools. Arguments last longer, become harder to forgive and forget. I don't know if that fits your definition of trouble, but I'd say that's where we are."

"What are you going to do about it?"

"Nothing."

"Nothing?"

"I don't want to tear my family apart, Tara. Divorce was easier for you, not having children."

"So, it's better for you and the kids to live unhappily?"

"The kids would be more unhappy if we split up. As for me, it doesn't matter. Happiness is overrated because it's fleeting. Happy one day, miserable the next. That wouldn't change because I got divorced."

It was a very big confession. My sister is rarely so forthright. "But Kayla's starting college in the fall. The other two will be out of the house in just a few years. You're young enough to start over, Mel."

"I've spent close to two decades building the life I've got. Why would I want another one?"

"What about love?"

"That's a word I don't often hear coming out of your mouth. You talk about sex. You talk about stability. But love? No."

"I guess it's because I've never been in love before. But now that I am, it feels important — critical, even. Marriage without love is little more than a business relationship, with or without fringe benefits, you know?"

I've stunned my sister into silence. She sits staring at me, openmouthed.

"What?"

Mel shakes her head slowly side to side. "And to think this all started with a fall at Heavenly. Weirdly ironic."

"It is, isn't it? But before we stray away from the topic at hand, what about Kayla and the Institute? I've been informed that her acceptance is definite."

"Well then, she will attend the college of her dreams. I can't thank you enough for your help with that, Tara. Whatever I can do for y—"

"I thought you weren't willing to risk divorce."

"That isn't what I said. I said I don't want to tear my family apart. If Graham is ready to go that far, I guess that's what will happen. But the truth is, he's all talk, not much action. In more ways than one."

"And that's enough for you." It's a statement, not a question.

Since it's a statement, she doesn't bother to reply.

Next door, the neighbor's dog begins a volley of barks and yips. I sigh loudly. "Not again."

"Is that a regular routine or something?"

"Lately, yes. And it's weird because I never noticed that animal existed until a few weeks ago. It has always been quiet. Polite."

"Maybe it's had some disruption in its life. It sounds like nervous barking."

Or like it's on alert.

FORTY-SEVEN

The weekend hurries by, and it's rather exceptional. Kayla's choice of shows — *Kinky Boots* — is brilliant, and right at home here in San Francisco. Cyndi Lauper's music is wonderful, and the dancing spectacular, especially considering the height of the heels in some of the numbers.

Kayla is likewise impressed. "Wow. How do they dance like that in those ridiculous heels? I can barely walk in shoes half that tall."

"Lots of practice?" is Melody's guess.

"Lots and lots," I agree.

The experience is positive enough to make Kayla want to shop for shoes, so we spend some time combing stores pre–museum visit. I choose the Haight, which isn't far from Golden Gate Park and the de Young. Parking can be tough on weekends, so we go early, arriving just as the fog begins to burn off.

"Wow, this is a cool neighborhood," observes Kayla.

"It's definitely changed since the hippie days," agrees Melody, "not that I was here to experience it then. But I've seen pictures."

"It's totally upscale now," I say. "Great boutiques. Vintage clothing. Bookstores and music. Awesome restaurants. And, yes, a high-end shoe store. You'll probably want to shop the sale racks there, unless your mom has a lot of room on her credit card."

We park on the far edge of the Whole Foods parking lot, which is supposed to be for customers only, but who's going to notice which direction we go? I'm not the only one with this idea, obviously, as we have to circle to find a spot. As we set off down Haight Street, we pass a couple of homeless guys (at least, they're making every effort to look like homeless guys), panhandling. One of them whistles at Kayla.

"Just keep walking," I urge, before addressing the scraggly dude. "Now, you wouldn't want me to tell that bicycle cop over there that you're making threatening moves toward my niece, would you?"

He smiles, revealing a jaw missing a few teeth. "Your niece? I thought you were her sister."

"Nice. But I'm fresh out of change."

Mel and Kayla are waiting up ahead. I encourage them to go at their own pace as I manage a slow cruise along the sidewalk. My leg feels strong, but after an hour, the knee is pretty sore. Hopefully there will still be a wheelchair available when we get to the museum. If not, I'll spend the afternoon on my butt, admiring the sculpture garden or something.

It's a gorgeous spring day, richly scented with early blooms — magnolia and gardenia. I walk as fast as I can manage beneath a sprinkle of sunlight, noting which stores attract Kayla. Mel, I know, couldn't care less about shoes and handbags, preferring antiques and reimagined clothing. Eventually, they reach the shoe store I mentioned. I find a planter to rest on, wait for them to reappear.

When they finally do, Kayla carries a large shopping bag and is all smiles. She hustles over. "Check 'em out." She produces a pair of floral-patterned ankle boots with a distinctive heel — not as tall as the ones in the play, but shaped curiously. "Aren't they darling?"

"Thank God they were on sale," says Mel, joining us. "You were right. That store is crazy pricey."

"Most everything in San Francisco is. But some things are worth the expense. I mean, how many people own boots like that?"

"How many people would want to?" jokes Mel. "I tried to talk her out of them, and into something a little less kitschy, but I'm not nearly as persuasive as my daughter is."

Over the course of the afternoon, Kayla convinces Melody to buy her more than a pair of overpriced shoes. She returns to the car with a new handbag, two summery skirts, a feather-trimmed lace blouse, three pairs of panties, and a felt fedora. As if that weren't enough, a visit to the museum store nets her two fabulous scarves, a couple of books, and a Monet water lilies folding umbrella. The girl is a skillful negotiator.

Though I'd never think to create an outfit like the one she comes up with on Monday morning, I have to admit she looks great in it. The peach-colored skirt is calf-length and gauzy, and goes perfectly with her boots. I'm glad she didn't go for a mini like the one she wore on Saturday — not at all the dress-to-impress mien she has accomplished here.

Larry Alexander greets us personally and shows us around the campus. The architecture is an interesting juxtaposition of Old California plus modern steel and glass, with views of the bay and Coit Tower across an expanse of city hills. The Institute's massive walls and bell tower are impossible to miss, of course, even at a distance. But it's the treasures tucked away inside that make the place special.

After our tour, Larry introduces Kayla and Mel to an undergrad admissions counselor, who escorts them inside her office to talk about goals and curriculum. Larry and I sit outside in the courtyard, discussing mutual acquaintances, including my ex-husband and his younger wife.

"I hear Hannah had her babies."

"Babies?"

"Twins. A boy and a girl."

I'm surprised, but not so much about the multiple births as the fact that he knew about them.

"You and Finn must be very good friends."

"Not really. But our daughters are more than friends. They're partners. Their paths first crossed here, but then Laurie moved to Boston to get her PhD. She and Claire ran into each other on Cape Cod a couple of years ago. They hit it off, and there we are."

"Huh. I didn't even know Claire was a lesbian. I never actually met her. I don't think she approved of me. She never once

401

came around."

"I don't think Claire approves of any of Finn's relationships, especially the current one. According to Laurie, she's livid about the twins."

Worried about her inheritance, no doubt. I carved out a chunk of that already. In fact, I'm living in it, mortgage paid. But she should blame her father, not me. "Funny, Finn never mentioned Claire's sexuality."

"Laurie was Claire's first serious girlfriend. I doubt Finn had any idea himself until they moved in together. By then he'd decided to take his company public, and a number of his major investors are Bible Belt Tea Party Republicans, who either assume themselves to be good homophobic Christians, or pretend to be. Finn would prefer not to talk about Laurie and Claire, though he is generous to the girls financially."

This new information is surprising, and I keep trying to figure out the chronology, though it really doesn't matter. The end result is the same. Perhaps a change of subject is in order before I say something I shouldn't. "I so appreciate Finn breaking the ice for Kayla. This is a huge dream, and she's worked hard to get here. Thank you, too, Larry."

He smiles in a hungry sort of way. I

haven't had to fend off a man in a while, so I'm a little out of practice. One thing I do know, however, is how to categorize flirtation, and on a scale of one to ten, ten teetering awfully close to lechery, this is no more than a three. Probably because Larry is somewhere over sixty and, if the ring on his finger is truly representative, married.

"It's the least I could do for a talented young woman and her quite beautiful aunt," he says.

"You didn't know I was beautiful when you offered to help. But thank you for that as well."

"I anticipate seeing you at some of our functions," he says hopefully.

Perfect lead-in. "Not sure how I can avoid that at this point, although I'll be living at Tahoe a good part of the year."

"Really?" Now he sounds disappointed.

"Well, yes. I'm getting married again myself. I don't plan on babies, though. Especially not two at once!"

"I understand completely."

"But just FYI, I do a lot of fund-raising, so if you ever need my help, please don't hesitate to ask."

Connections.

"I'll definitely keep that in mind."

Familiar voices on the approach interrupt

our conversation. Kayla appears, animated and chattering. Mel just tries to keep up with her. A flurry of happy comments descends.

Awesome school.

The counselor rocked.

Have to send a portfolio.

Can't wait for fall.

And then a few less expected remarks.

By the time we take our leave and make our way back to the car, I have learned a couple of expensive things. Tuition for two semesters is closer to $40K, and incoming undergrads are required to live on campus for the first year, adding another $11,000 to the price tag.

It's the Christmas gift that just keeps on giving. And speaking of giving, a thought occurs to me. I pull Larry aside. "Is there a way I can donate her tuition, get a tax write-off, and earmark the money toward a scholarship for Kayla?"

"I think that can be arranged."

Connections.

Forty-Eight

Friday morning, my brain kicks into gear predawn. I lie in bed, thinking about all I must accomplish before tonight, when thirty elite San Franciscans will make an appearance at my fund-raiser house party, each eager to make an impression by trying to write a bigger check than the other guy. Encouraging them will be a short video, highlighting the accomplishments of Lost Souls Found.

The director wanted to bring a lost soul or two along with her, but I nixed that idea. Not only would my neighbors not approve, but the fact is my guests don't want to see homeless people in the flesh. Not even if they are showered, shaved, and fed. Seeing them on a big-screen TV is close enough contact.

As it's too early to make any calls yet (caterer; florist; Charlie; Cavin, who's supposed to drive over for the event), I decide to go ahead and put in some time on the treadmill. I keep the speed at a steady 4.5 miles per hour — fast enough to raise my heart rate but slow enough so I'm still walking. Jogging would not be a good plan. On my mind this morning, repeated in the rhythm of my steps, are two words: withholding information.

When I talked with Eli about the relative merits of deceit by omission, I was rather glib about it, considering the conversation was mostly for his benefit. But the recent conversations have made me reanalyze the points I made. Yes, there may be times when omitting facts can spare feelings, or keep someone from making a decision he might come to regret. But I don't appreciate it when I discover someone has kept secrets from me, whether or not it's for my own good.

Mel was happy enough when I informed her that Kayla's tuition could, indeed, look like a scholarship from anonymous donors. Many SFAI students benefit in such a fashion. But then I asked, "Do you think Graham will be fooled?"

"Doubtful. He knows you arranged the interview, and he knows you'd offered to pay her way in. Simple logic dictates a scholarship now would have everything to do with you."

"So what will you say if he confronts you?"

"I will deny, deny, deny. He'll have no way to confirm his suspicions, and I think he'll let it drop after a while. He does want what's best for Kayla, despite the way he sometimes acts."

I believe that. There are a lot of things I don't like about Graham, but the way he cares for his kids isn't one of them. This, at least, offers him a way to save face and graciously send Kayla off to jump-start her future. Will he find some small sense of gratitude? Not that it's a requisite. Will the tension between him and Mel ease?

The fact that she has never once admitted her marriage was anything but sitcom perfect, well, that kind of bothers me. Should the relationship dissolve after twenty years, leaving her high, dry, and middle-aged, would it have been better to confide the fact that Graham had tried to sleep with me? Would it have made any difference, or would she have discounted my words completely? Would I have achieved any sense of satisfaction in hurting him if I hurt my sister, too?

Life is complicated.

Post-cooldown and shower, I make the necessary phone calls that will assure my party is a huge success. I never leave anything to chance, and always double-check with suppliers the morning of. I do not need a last-minute surprise. When my guests arrive, I want to be cool and confident, not harried or angry. And tonight, I'll have someone to show off.

I catch Cavin at lunch. "Can't wait to see you. Has it only been a week? It seems like forever."

"Aw, come on. You've been too busy to notice."

"Only during the day. At night, it's terribly lonely. My bed is looking forward to an encore performance, no hoisting me up the stairs required."

"I thought you liked the Rhett Butler approach."

"Tonight, all I want is the Cavin Lattimore approach. Maybe we'll even try something other than missionary."

"Sounds intriguing. You'd better let me go now. Don't want to be late."

"I love you." The words still sound foreign.

"I love you, too."

He hangs up and information withheld swirls around me. I haven't as yet mentioned Kayla's tuition, or the deception involved. I'm not sure I need to. Neither have I brought up Sophia and Eli. That, I must mention, but definitely not over the phone. I want to look into his eyes, where the truth lies in wait. I've got a feeling it's going to be an interesting discussion.

The afternoon is a whir of activity. Charlie arrives at four, and I leave him in charge of the flowers and food while I spend way more time than any woman should indulging my skin with expensive potions before carefully applying makeup — enough to create smoky eyes and hints of peachy blush, but not so much as to make me look like I'm trying too hard to compete with the aging supermodel who'll be in attendance tonight. She must *always* be the most beautiful woman at any gathering, at least in her own estimation.

I've finished with the cosmetics and am halfway dressed when my cell buzzes. It's Finn.

"Hello, Tara. I wanted to let you know I can't make it tonight."

"Oh, I'm sorry. Are you unwell?"

"No, but unfortunately Hannah is, so I'll have to take care of the babies."

"Babies, yes. Larry told me about the twins. Congratulations, although to tell you the truth, I'm having a hard time picturing you pushing a double stroller."

He clears his throat. "I hear congratulations are in order on your end as well. Who is the lucky fellow?"

The problem with gossip is it works two ways — for you, and against. I recite a truncated bio and add, "Too bad you're not coming tonight. You could meet Cavin. I think you'd like him."

"Larry said you'll be living at Tahoe. I was wondering if you've given any thought to selling the Russian Hill house."

"I have *not*. Why?"

"Well, um . . . uh . . . it seems like a massive waste of resources."

He means his resources. "This is my home, Finn. There are no provisions in our agreement regarding my marrying again."

"I understand that. It's just, the mortgage payment is an incredible drain, and —"

"I didn't leave *you*, Finn. I didn't chase you into Hannah's arms and make her get pregnant. Besides . . ." Insert very long pause, for maximum effect. "I'm told your company is doing very well, thanks in no small part to your evangelical investors."

I leave it there, no stated threat, just the assertion that his finances aren't so dismal after all.

He can't have missed the implication, however, and immediately withdraws. "No need to dredge up any ugliness, Tara. I wasn't insisting you list the house, only making a suggestion. You hang on to it until you're ready. But it does seem more like a tool of ego than need, to be honest. Take care of yourself."

"You, too."

But he's already gone.

Bastard! This house is irreplaceable and I will not be strong-armed into liquidating it. If I did, I might clear close to a million dollars. But then what? I could invest it, yes. However, I don't need that much investment capital, and in this real estate market, who's to say that's even a possibility? Both of Cavin's houses are gorgeous, and I'll be happy spending time in either one. But they're *his*. This one is *mine*. If we sign an honorable prenup, that won't change if for some reason we don't last.

I don't expect something bad will happen between us, but my experience insists it's possible. Maybe even probable.

I'm afraid even love can't change that.

However, when Cavin arrives, thirty minutes before the party is scheduled to start, handsome as ever in khaki pants and a flannel shirt, any thought of a future breakup dissolves in the ardor of his hello kiss. Lost in the moment, we barely notice the activity swirling around us — Charlie placing bright spring bouquets as the caterer arranges colorful trays of food and the hired bartender opens bottles. And when Cavin goes upstairs with his suitcase, his presence in my house is noticeable, even though he's not in view. He's in my bedroom. No, our bedroom, regardless of whose name is on the deed. (Or who's paying the mortgage.) Guests begin to fill the living room, spilling onto the patio, despite the evening chill, and Cavin still hasn't reappeared. When he finally does, he's traded his casual clothing for a striking silk suit. Every head turns. Cavin sweeps past them all, across the room, taking his place at my side.

"Sorry I took so long," he murmurs into my ear.

"That's okay. You made quite the entrance. Everyone seems quite impressed, including our lovely supermodel."

Cavin turns to study the woman in question. "Hey, that's Genevieve Lennon."

"Yes, I know. What do you think?"

"That's she's very tall, wears too much makeup, and quite likely has an eating disorder."

"The supermodel model."

He lowers his voice even more. "Just so you know, you are much more beautiful than she."

I pivot to face him, slide my arms up around his neck, dive into his eyes. And for the first time, real time, I promise, "I will always love you."

Always is a murky concept.

FORTY-NINE

The house party is a barn burner, as they used to say in Idaho, although this is about as far from rural America as you can get. Perhaps it's because of the news Cavin and I share, as a lead-in to introducing him. Perhaps it's strictly because of the heartwarming video Lost Souls Found has produced, with the help of a few lost souls, who have learned to script-write and edit. Perhaps it's simply because of the bottomless glasses, expertly poured for maximum benefit. (Tip that bartender well!) Whatever the reason(s), we manage to raise sixty-three thousand dollars.

That includes a most generous five-thousand-dollar gift from my fiancé. Not to be outdone, Genevieve Lennon doubles the amount. She also flirts obnoxiously with Cavin, who is keenly aware of the fact that I'm observing every move. He doesn't falter.

"Orthopedic surgeon, huh?" clucks the aggressive woman, who is totally unconcerned about my reaction. Why should she be? She just cut a major check. "Guess I'll have to go sledding or something. I don't ski."

"You know, I have yet to see a sledding injury that demanded a trip to Barton. But should you be able to manage that, we'll take very good care of you." He is careful to use the plural "we." "Of course, there's always mountain biking once the snow melts. That won't be long now."

He is completely charming, and not just to Genevieve. People keep pulling me aside to congratulate me, or joke about bedside manner, or comment about how *it must have been fate.* Three or four ask if I'll be keeping my house in the city. Each receives an enthusiastic "Of course!"

Cavin mingles, and so do I, but we don't stay apart very long, and I think it must be obvious that the key to our relationship is affection. I would say love, but most of the people here are connected to one another by need, or familiarity, or carnal attraction, and I'm not really sure the word "love" means more to any of them than it did to me just a few weeks ago.

Duty done, people start to wander off around ten. The last is gone at half past the hour, and the cleanup begins. Cavin tries to help, but I waylay him. "The crew is still on the clock. I'll leave Charlie in charge and we can go to bed. That is, if you're ready."

"A whole week without you? Dear lady, I'm way beyond ready."

That makes two of us. I hope sex with Cavin doesn't become something to get over with as quickly as possible. Considering we haven't had the chance to experiment yet, and it will still be a while before we can move all the way into the "wild" category, I think I'm happy this is how we started out.

I give envelopes to the caterer and bartender. Both contain generous tips on top of the invoiced amounts. Then I instruct Charlie to make sure everything is in order before they leave, and to lock up behind them. I pay him in cash, and he is very pleased.

"You tired?" he asks.

"Exhausted. But not quite ready to sleep."

He laughs. "Gotcha. I'll make sure no one disturbs you."

At the top of the stairs, Cavin and I go to different bathrooms. I take the master, ask him to use the one in the hall. I remove the makeup, so carefully applied just a couple of hours ago. Moisturize every inch of skin with delicately scented lotion. Brush my hair, and the appetizer crumbs from my teeth. Once all pretense is gone, the mirror reveals a fortysomething woman who, thanks to good genetics, plus a little work and a whole lot of expensive potions, appears to be a few years younger. She is healthy, her body athletic, muscles taut. Those things aren't new, but there is something different: contentment in her eyes.

By the time I finish, Cavin is already in bed, and his presence warms the room. I turn off the lamp and he lifts the covers. I slip underneath, into his arms, where his scent swallows me. This, I've missed: the cologne of hot skin; the taste of mint in the mist of his sigh; the embers of desire, awaiting the wind of touch.

He touches me now, in a rush of need. I struggle to keep up with him, but he urges me to lie still. "Don't move. I want to make you wet."

He lifts himself above me, kisses my face. My neck. My shoulders. Right. Left.

His tongue traces my lips, the circumference of each ear. Left. Right.

Licks my collarbone. Right. Left.

Down between my breasts, to my stomach. Circles my belly button, then up again.

His lips pluck at my nipples as if they're berries he's lifting from a vine. Left. Right.

I'm moaning now, and he smiles at that. "There's my lady. Now let's see how well I've done."

He throws back the blankets, moves all the way to the foot of the bed, puts his hands together in an open V, which he slides between my thighs, prying them gently apart. His fingertips keep moving inside of me, as far as they can reach.

Enter. Exit. Enter.

"Oh, yes. You're wet. But I want you dripping."

He accomplishes the deed with his mouth and tongue, teasing in less than elegant fashion, bringing me oh so close to orgasm. But I slow myself. Slow him. "Easy, big guy. Let's try something different."

I turn onto my side, coax him behind me. Completely engorged, his cock crawls up the backs of my legs, and when it thrusts between them, I am very happy to be dripping. The angle of entry brings him full stop against my favorite spot, and the pressure is divine. Push. Pull. Again. Again. Harder. Deeper. Again. Again. He's all the way inside me, and I feel him tense, then start to withdraw, as if to delay.

"Don't stop!"

I maneuver myself so I can help with the motion, urging us both to the point of no stopping now. Orgasm is mutual, extended, intense.

He rolls onto his back and, still inside me, pulls me backward so I'm lying on top of him. "Holy Christ!" It's a rough whisper. "You are one hell of a woman."

"And you are the man I love."

We lie this way until our breathing calms and our hearts slow their drumming. Then we turn sideways again, and he cradles me tightly. I close my eyes, but all hope of sleep is lost in a silent tumble of words. *The man I love. Always. Passion cools. Talk is cheap. You might want to remember that.*

Now I've got Eli on my mind. I hear his voice. *I love older women.* Smell him, wearing my soap. *Admired many.* See his eyes, the exact same gray over jade as his father's. *Sexual relationship with one.* Hear his heavy-footed approach. *You starred in one or two.* Feel his hand brush my hip. *Are you a liar?*

"Cavin?" I keep my voice quiet in case he's drifted off.

"Huh?"

"Can I ask you something?"

"Of course. Anything."

"Why didn't you tell me about Eli and Sophia?"

His arms, still cradling me, tauten. "What do you mean?"

Now my body stiffens. I extricate myself from his hold, turn so I face him. "About them having sex."

He rolls onto his back, sits up, turns on the light. "What are you talking about?"

I sit up, too. "Eli told me, Cavin."

"Told you what?"

"That Sophia seduced him, and they had an affair."

"What?"

"That your PI discovered it, informed you, and you caught them together."

"Tara, I . . ." he sputters. "None of that is true. I mean, if he was having sex with Sophia, I never even suspected it, and I certainly never witnessed it."

I did not expect denial. "But . . . why would he make something like that up?"

"To impress you? Interest you? I have no idea. Come here."

He opens his arms, and I accept the invitation, burrowing against him where it's cozy and safe. A click of a switch and the room goes dark again. Cavin strokes my hair as I listen to the march of his heart and the regular beats of his breathing. Both slow as he sinks into sleep, a place where I will not be able to join him for a while.

I revisit my conversation with Eli — the one that turned into a revelation about

Sophia and him. There was more to it than the basics I reported to Cavin just now. What did he say? Something about holding her until he finished . . . Cavin slamming the door . . . asking his father later what he would have done in that situation and Cavin calling him morally bankrupt.

That's awfully detailed for a total fabrication. If he made it up on the spot, the boy is a talented liar. I'm extremely good at catching lies, and I never read his story as fiction. And why go to all that trouble?

On the flip side, what would Cavin have to gain by denying the incident ever happened? No matter how long I linger here, just this side of slumber, I can't for the life of me figure out a good reason why. One word becomes my mantra.

Why.

Why.

Why.

WHY LOOK FOR MEANING

in little things:
the murmur of a sparrow's
wings, questions
asked of wind and seed
lost in autumn grass;

the stubborn reach
of surf, intent on whittling
beach and arranging
curls of seaweed
on driftwood statuary;

the copper scent
of rain on prairie shoulders,
bent by drought,
slivers of creation, wet
in shallow reflection.

Why look for meaning
in a lie:
the mosaic of a chameleon,
riled by passion into beauty,
exquisite, but destined
to retreat into mediocrity;

the painted face
of the dune, its inconsistent
features ever redrawn

at the whim
of temperamental wind;

the comely mask
of the monster, a disguise
deftly worn to soothe
suspicion, an open invitation
to love, quite unique.

FIFTY

Cavin returns to the lake on Sunday morning. I send two suitcases of clothes, three boxes of personal stuff — books, business files, candles, toiletries, favorite glasses, and kitchen gadgets — and five cases of wine along with him. I haven't been down to the cellar in weeks, and I take careful inventory. Everything appears to be in order, but I want to leave nothing to chance, in case my phantom visitor returns with an oenophile in tow. The wines that Cavin takes home would be hard to replace.

The Audi is stuffed — wine in the trunk, the rest on the seats, including a box riding shotgun. "It'll make a good armrest, at least," jokes Cavin. Then he turns serious. "Promise you'll only be a couple of days? I sort of despise being without you."

"Promise. But you'd better clear some wall space. I don't want to leave all my art behind."

425

"You're not really worried about a break-in, are you? Why don't you hire a security service?"

"I'll do that first thing tomorrow. But there are a few pieces I'm very fond of. I'd rather they move to the lake than I have to visit them here."

Cavin and I did discuss some pertinent questions yesterday. How many homes do we need? What are the relative merits of each? The Tahoe house is a given. But two more come into play. Do we want to maintain two near the ocean? Does Carmel trump San Francisco? If it's important to me to maintain a property that is completely mine, how important is it to keep this one? Would it be better to divorce myself completely from Finn and invest in something else? Unfortunately, but not surprisingly, we did not come to definitive conclusions in that one conversation.

The prospect of marriage, I'm discovering, is simpler when love does not interfere.

After Cavin leaves, Charlie comes over to help me crate the art. He's not particularly happy about my plans to largely relocate to the lake. "Tahoe is nice and all, lots of recreation and everything, but you're a cultured woman."

"The implication being culture is largely

lacking in the High Sierras?"

"Well, yes. I mean, what's up there? Sports betting and chili cook-offs?"

I don't say, compared to Vegas — not to mention Idaho — Tahoe is a hotbed of culture. "What's wrong with chili? Besides, there's plenty to do. Renaissance Faires. Shakespeare on the beach. Music festivals. And if I need more, Reno is only an hour drive."

"Reno is a cow town."

"Well, I can always visit San Francisco anytime I like."

"So, you're keeping this house?"

The question of the week. "That's currently under discussion. For now, yes."

"Will you still need me to check on things here?"

"From time to time, although I'm hiring a security service, so probably not as often. What I will do for you, however, is put in a good word with a few busy people I know. You're a treasure."

He grins. "That's right. Be sure to mention how *valuable* I am."

Charlie demonstrates his value with the care he puts into packaging the art, sleeving it in cardboard before bubble-wrapping it. He carries each piece down to the Escalade, so I won't have to do it on Tuesday, when I plan to leave. After his final trip, I invite him to stay for dinner.

"My friend Cassandra is coming. I'll introduce you, and tell her how valuable you've been."

"I'll help you cook."

By the time she arrives, we have concocted a fabulous minestrone and Caesar salad. Charlie makes himself useful, mixing drinks and setting the table, while Cassandra and I chat in the living room.

"Sorry I couldn't make your party on Friday," she apologizes. "Taylor was home on spring break, and I didn't want to leave him there by himself."

"Why not? He's going on eighteen, isn't he?"

"Exactly."

I think about leaving Kayla or Eli alone here in my house and understand what she means. "That's okay. You missed a great evening, though, and you could have met Cavin."

"That almost swayed me. But the truth is, Taylor's gotten into some trouble at school. He's smoking. Drinking. Who knows what else? Oh, and there have been some cyber-bullying incidents. They suspect Taylor, who denies it, of course."

"Cyberbullying? You mean like threats, or what?"

"Not overt threats. I guess someone set up a fake Facebook page on Taylor's computer at the school. Whoever that was posted on one of the younger students' timelines, saying he was a fat pig and he'd better watch out or he might end up bacon. There were other things, too, of a similar nature."

"So if the page was set up on Taylor's computer, they have good reason to believe he did it, right?"

"Yes, except other people have access to it. It's in his dorm room. That room is never locked. Anyone could go in there and do it. And if that person's real target was Taylor, well, this would be one very sneaky method to get to him. Either way, there's no proof."

"God, kids are cruel nowadays. Not only that, but devious."

"Kids have always been cruel. Think back. Our generation wasn't much nicer. The difference was, we actually had to look into the eyes of whomever we wanted to call a fat pig. Now, social networking allows a sense of anonymity. That, plus privilege, is a deadly combination."

"Literally or figuratively?"

"Either. Both."

Charlie informs us that dinner is on the table. He pours a spicy zinfandel, and I raise a toast to friends, old and new. "I'm hoping the two of you might form a mutually beneficial relationship. Or maybe you know someone who could use Charlie's help, Cassandra? He's been impressive. Not cheap, but worth every penny."

"You're really getting married again, aren't you?"

I shrug. "Looks that way."

Now she lifts her glass. "To beginnings."

Which also means to endings. Maybe I should seriously consider selling this house, excise Finn and his family from my future completely. Who needs old complications when new ones are inevitable?

As we start on our soup and salad, a question pops into my head. "Has Taylor ever told a lie so blatantly untrue that you couldn't understand why he invented it?"

"You mean like the time I smelled smoke, found him holding a lighter and a big burn hole in the curtains. He told me a burglar lit them on fire, handed him the lighter, and ran. He was about ten."

"Something like that, I guess. Only this just happened, and Eli is seventeen." I share his story about Sophia, and Cavin's absolute denial. "Why would Eli make that up?

430

What's the point?"

"Shock value?" guesses Cassandra.

But Charlie has a different theory. "Entertainment."

FIFTY-ONE

As much as I loved my time in the city, my home on Russian Hill was missing one very important thing. Cavin. The day before I returned to Tahoe, I did accomplish three important tasks. The first was to hire King Security Services to do random mobile patrols past the house several times a day. The second was to visit my accountant and discuss the financial implications of my upcoming nuptials. Finally, I talked to a high-end real estate company about possibly listing the house.

The agent was quite excited by the prospect, and why wouldn't she be, considering the possibility of a very large commission? She assured me properties like mine are rare and highly sought after. Despite the sagging market, the recession didn't dampen certain areas, and upscale San Francisco is one of them. Comps have recently sold for upward of $5 million. She urged me to sign the listing documents right then and there. But I'm still weighing the pros and cons ten days later.

The Glenbrook house wears my artwork well. It surprised me, actually, although we either need to install track lighting or find a way to let in some natural light. I talked to Cavin about removing a few evergreen branches closest to the place. There are strict rules about cutting down entire trees — something about erosion and Tahoe water clarity — and this, plus skylights, would be a decent compromise. Anything to fight the slight sense of claustrophobia living in the woods initiates.

I do love waking up in the morning and cracking the sliding glass door to let in the frosty, pine-scented air, and the cacophonous call of the Steller's jays. I'm usually up before Cavin, unless he's got an early surgery, and I'll have coffee ready when he comes stumbling into the kitchen, hair tousled and hanging, too long, over his eyes. He looks more woodsman than doctor that way, and it's sexy as hell.

Primitive.

Masculine.

Arousing.

Love crashes into me then, a megawave engulfing me until I think I just might drown in a tide of longing. It's ridiculous, really. I'm glad I've got the time and energy to invest in this experience, not to mention perspective. One thing I'm sure of. This isn't infatuation that I've indulged in before, and this is something completely different.

It hasn't, however, totally disintegrated my flirtatiousness. Cavin recommended a local gym, and I chose a personal trainer based on (1) his familiarity with rehabbing sports injuries, and (2) his rather striking physique. I have no need for "outside services" but don't have a problem admiring a little eye candy while I work out. Between physical therapy and the stationary biking I'm doing at home, I'm exercising an hour and a half every day. By June, I'll probably still limp a little, but I should be able to dance at our wedding.

I finish up at the gym around three, and by the time I get home, Cavin's car is already taking up space in the driveway. He's earlier than expected. I go on inside, but before I can call out a greeting, I hear him talking on the phone.

"A year? Goddamn it, Melissa! Can't you take him with you?"

I can't hear her reply and have no idea what this is about, but a name materializes in my brain. Eli.

"Well, do you have any ideas about another school, then? I guess he can stay here for the summer, but we have to do something with him in the fall."

Definitely Eli.

"Fine. I'll look into it. When do you leave? I'd like to reach an agreement before then."

This sounds like a problem requiring hard liquor. I go to the bar, pour a couple of sidecars, and hand one to Cavin as he hangs up the phone. "Thought maybe you could use this."

"Hope you made it strong."

"What's going on?"

"Eli got expelled."

"Oh."

"Well, technically, he's been asked to withdraw. Expulsion would make it almost impossible to enroll him in another school. Melissa and I convinced them it was to their financial benefit for him to leave 'voluntarily.' "

"I see."

"Yes, well, to complicate things further, Melissa will be heading to Dubai next week. Her husband was appointed to the embassy and they'll be gone for at least a year."

"Meaning Eli is moving in here."

"Through the summer, yes. We're looking into another boarding school, but he'll have to finish this semester at Whittell High School."

"Kind of late in the year to start a new school. Can't he finish up online or something?"

Cavin looks at me like I've lost my mind. "And have him *here* all day, every day?"

Good point. "May I ask what he got expelled — er, asked to withdraw — for?"

Cavin takes a big gulp of his drink. "Remember the thing about someone hacking the school computer and changing grades? Turns out it was a fairly lucrative business, and one of Eli's customers had a change of heart. After that, there were some incidents of cyberbullying. Do you know what that is?"

The Athenian is, indeed, a very small community. "Actually, yes. In fact, I heard about the incident from my friend Cassandra, whose son goes to school there. Eli was responsible?"

"They believe so. Can't prove it because it was someone else's computer, but the kid who was picked on the worst is the one who turned Eli in."

"None of what happened was considered criminal, though?"

"Fortunately, no, or at least not prosecutable. Apparently cyberbullying is only a crime if it involves overt threats of violence, posting sexually explicit pictures, or taking photographs of a person in a place where privacy would be expected. Whoever set up that fake Facebook page, and I have no doubt it was my son, was informed enough to not do any of those things. As for the grades, the headmaster just wanted the problem to go away."

Probably embarrassed a teenager could so easily defy their system. "So, when will Eli be moving in?"

"Anytime. He had to pack up his stuff and have it removed from the campus today. Melissa signed the paperwork on that end this morning and expects me to enroll him here. I'll contact the high school tomorrow, and if it all works out, he'll start on Monday. Unless, of course, you *want* to homeschool him."

"Uh, no thanks. Don't think that's my calling."

It's not my calling to parent, either, especially not a difficult kid like Eli, but I don't really have much of a choice. Anyway, acting the part of coldhearted stepmother is probably wiser than trying to be his friend. Maybe fairy tales got it right.

Cavin takes a deep breath. "I don't understand the kid at all. At his age, succeeding in school meant everything to me. I knew I wanted to be a doctor, and my sights were set on accomplishing that goal. What is wrong with him?"

At his age, I was all about a singular goal, too — survival. But that's a story I've yet to share with Cavin, and probably never will. "Privilege, that's my guess. He's never had to work for anything, really. I see it in my niece, too, although not to this extent."

Then again, how much do I know about Kayla and what she does in her spare time? I believe she wants to succeed as an artist, but mostly because Mel says she does. And as far as illicit activities go, I know about a couple she wholeheartedly embraces. So why couldn't she be a cyberbully, or a hacker, or a cheat?

"Work," says Cavin. "That's a thought. I think maybe a summer job is called for."

"Good luck with that. Meanwhile, let's worry about his finishing his junior year. Academically, I assume he'd be ahead of his public school peers?"

"One would think so."

"You have surgery tomorrow?" Thursdays, he generally does.

"Three. Spring skiing has been generous this year."

"So how will you find time to get hold of

the high school? Is there something I can do?"

"Lady, I love you. Do you know that? Yes, you could call and find out what paperwork they'll need." He finishes his drink, reaches for mine. "Another?" He goes to the bar and refreshes our glasses. "Funny, but this is the first time it's ever been up to me to enroll my kid in school. I have no idea how to go about it."

"It can't be that hard. What reason should I give for his leaving the Athenian?"

"Private-school burnout?"

"Fair enough."

I'll come up with something a little more creative.

Turns out, dealing with a school's administration isn't much different from dealing with any other bureaucracy — a little bullshit goes a long way. I have to work my way around not being an actual parent/guardian. "Almost stepmother" doesn't count for much, but I'm well practiced in the art of persuasion through manipulation. The school secretary doesn't stand a chance.

"I just love this kid!" I gush. "I can't believe his mom would desert him and run off to the Middle East for an unspecified amount of time. It was hurting his

439

schoolwork, so we decided to bring him up here, where he could be close to us, to finish the year. I know it's unusual, but we thought it would be for the best."

"There are only eight weeks left in the semester. Have you considered a virtual academy?"

"Well, yes, but he's just such a gregarious kid, we weren't sure it would be good for him. I believe he's well ahead academically."

"Okay. Let me see if a counselor is available to talk to you."

By the time I leave, I have an enrollment form for Cavin to fill out, and a checklist of paperwork they'll need — birth certificate, immunization record, transcript. The counselor is looking forward to speaking to Eli ASAP to help put him in the right classrooms to ensure his success. And I am invited to join the PTA.

Mission accomplished, I head to the gym, push myself especially hard. Exercise, I hear, is good for stress relief. And yes, I'm tense about the approaching hurricane. It has blown in by the time I get home.

FIFTY-TWO

Adjusting to life with Eli in the house has been difficult for everyone involved. Well, everyone other than the teachers at Whittell High School, whom Eli seems to have charmed. Of course, they don't know about the real reasons he has come to them so late in the year. One of the conditions of Melissa and Cavin's joint final "donation" to the Athenian was that certain information be kept confidential.

Eli can be charming, no doubt about that, and I allow him to think he has me fooled, too. The way to play a player is by making him believe, without a doubt, he has you played. And hey, maybe he does.

The space between him and his father is thick with friction. The two barely speak, and when they do, the tone is cool. Distant. Affectionless. Cavin has every right to be angry, but shouldn't the anger cool at some point? And why is Eli so indignant? He started this thing.

I finally get the chance to talk to him about it sans his dad's presence a couple of weeks after his arrival. Cavin is still at his office when Eli comes in after school. I'm in the kitchen, working on a seafood stew.

"Hey," he says. "What's for dinner?"

"Bouillabaisse. You like?"

"Who doesn't like bouillabaisse? Want some help?"

"Of course. You do enjoy playing chef, don't you?"

He goes to the sink, washes his hands. "Actually, yes, I do. It's creative. And relaxing."

"Have you given any thought to doing it professionally?"

"You mean, like as a career?"

"Why not? Do you have anything else in mind?" I hand him a knife and an onion. "Dice that into fairly small pieces, please. Oh, and do the same for three stalks of celery?"

He reaches for a cutting board. "Actually, other than maybe doing something techie, I have no solid plans for the future. Not sure Dad would appreciate my going the culinary route, and Mom would freak out completely."

"I don't see why, especially if you don't

have your heart set on medicine or law or something. Top chefs earn substantial salaries. Maybe you could even open your own restaurant."

"That would require school."

"There's a Le Cordon Bleu academy in Sacramento. One in San Francisco, too."

"As you know, I prefer the city by the bay." He winks. "You gonna let me stay in your house? Maybe Dad would pay you rent."

"Let's not put the cart in front of the horse."

"A return to the land of clichés, eh, or maybe the kingdom of idioms?"

This kid is a study in contrasts. "May I ask you something?" I pour olive oil into a large saucepan, put it on the stove to heat.

"Sure."

He watches me add the chopped onion and celery, plus the garlic I've sliced. It hits the hot oil with a fragrant sizzle. "Stir that, would you please?" I hand him a wooden spoon.

"That's what you wanted to ask?"

"Don't be a smart-ass." I reach around him to turn down the burner, add fish stock and white wine to the pot, along with fresh fennel, saffron, and thyme. "What I want to know is why you changed those grades."

He turns to face me. "Entertainment."

I had hoped Charlie was wrong. "What?"

"Not really. Look, the first time was just to see if I could do it. It was easier than I expected. A friend and I were drinking one night and in a drunken stupor, I mentioned I'd managed to hack in. He asked if I could 'fix' his algebra grade. I did, and then he told someone who told someone else, and pretty soon people were paying me to upgrade their GPAs. I know Dad thinks I did it for the money, but no way. I mean I took it. But I didn't need it, obviously."

"But didn't it occur to you that someone might turn you in?"

"Well, yeah, it crossed my mind, but I didn't really expect it to happen. And even after it did, I thought it would just blow over. Who knew they'd get so serious about a practical joke?"

"Well, that combined with the cyberbullying kind of indicated a pattern."

"Hey," he huffs. "I did *not* set up that Facebook page. I'm not a pussy like that. If I wanted to pick on Fat Boy, I'd do it straight up in his face."

Interesting. "So who did set it up then?"

He shrugs. "It was Andaman's computer. My guess is he did it. What else can I do to help with dinner?"

444

Subtle subject change, one I'm not quite ready to accept. But first I give him directions for making the rouille while I go about preparing the fish and seafood. I'm deveining shrimp when I mention, "Taylor's mom said they think whoever created that fake Facebook page was actually targeting Taylor."

Eli thinks about that for a minute. "You mean to make him *look* like a bad guy. Who would go to all that trouble? Taylor doesn't need any help in that department. He's a total tool all on his own. But it definitely wasn't me. Tool or no, I've got no personal problem with him."

I've only met Taylor a couple of times. He seemed nice enough, but most kids do in strange settings, especially under parental supervision. Who knows what he's like when he's off on his own? And as for Eli, I'm leaning toward believing him, although I'm determined to keep my guard up.

"Thanks for sharing KP duty with me. We'll leave the broth to simmer until Cavin gets home, then toss in the seafood to cook. Oh, I will need those tomatoes chopped, if you wouldn't mind."

"No problem."

I will now attempt small talk. "How's school?"

"Piece of cake. I'm so far ahead, it's crazy."

"Your dad's been looking for another private school. Apparently, there's a great one nearby — Squaw Valley Academy. Have you h—"

He slams the knife on the cutting board. "What? No! That's a boarding school."

"I know, but it's close, so he thought it might work out well. I guess if you maintain a decent GPA, they let you ski or ride every day in the winter, too. It seems perfect for you."

He picks up the knife again, begins to cut the tomatoes. Slowly. Methodically. Finally he says, "Why can't I just stay at Whittell next year?"

What am I supposed to say? That Cavin doesn't want to deal with his son on a daily basis, and really, neither do I? That we're both used to ordered lives and are already working overtime to establish a mutual rhythm? That we're not even officially newlyweds yet, so how could we possibly commit to full-time parenting a teen — any teen, let alone *this* one?

I'll lay it on Melissa instead. "I don't think your mom will agree to you living here. She's afraid of your dad's influence."

"Fuck Mom. She doesn't want me, either. You know what I feel like? A dog, dropped

446

off at a shelter because I'm not a cute puppy anymore." He scrapes the chopped tomatoes into a bowl, rinses the knife, turns to face me. "The thing about shelter dogs is some of them get mean."

I look at the blade in his hand.

Eli laughs and puts the knife on the counter. "Not me, of course. I'm totally placid."

That switch flipped awfully quickly, but before I can consider the implications of that little scene, Cavin comes in the door. "Honey, I'm home. Hey, what's that incredible smell?" He sweeps up the hallway, into the kitchen, kisses me on the forehead before noticing the pungent air of tension between Eli and me. "What's going on?"

Eli responds first. "What does it look like? We're making bouillabaisse and talking about dogs."

"Dogs?"

"And schools," I add.

"Ah, schools."

"Yes," says Eli. "And since that discussion has everything to do with my future, you might consider including me in it. Jesus, Dad, I'm almost eighteen. Don't you think my opinion about where to spend my senior year should count?"

Cavin throws up his hands. "Of course.

But it's not like we've made any decisions yet. We've just been looking at options." Anger shimmers in his eyes, and I believe it's directed at me.

"I'm sorry. I didn't mean to imply we'd settled on Squaw Valley. I was just excited by the prospect, and thought you would be, too, Eli."

"Oh, really?" Sarcasm infiltrates his voice. "And here I thought you were celebrating dumping the pup at the kennel."

"Ah, dogs," sighs Cavin. "Look, can we adjourn to the other room to have this conversation?"

He locks eyes with mine and adjusts his jaw, and I understand his meaning.

"You two go talk in private. I've got work to do here. Dinner's in a half hour."

Obviously, he thinks I overstepped, and maybe I did. But this is indicative of a larger problem. Exactly where does that boundary lie? And if we're getting married, should there be boundaries at all?

One thing I do know. I'm not going to dance around Eli.

After dessert, and once the men have retreated to their separate rooms, I go into the study to check my e-mail. There's a message from Mel: *Mom's in the hospital. She had a major allergic reaction and didn't know what it was until it was almost too late. Luckily, Will had the presence of mind to call 911 right away. The paramedics shot her up with antihistamines and got her to the ER in time. Guess she'll be okay. Looks like you inherited your mango allergy from her. In other news, Graham won't be coming to the wedding. His band has a gig that day. I asked him what was more important. He said fourth weddings don't count. Sorry.*

I e-mail back: *No worries about Graham. I'd just as soon he stays away. It's supposed to be a happy day. As for Mom, it couldn't have happened to a more deserving person. Just think. If they had more mangoes in Idaho, there might not have even been a Graham! Of course, we both might be married to ranchers. Or Mormons, God forbid. Can you picture me with six kids? Ha-ha. We're still on for trousseau shopping and (a mango-free) lunch, aren't we?*

FIFTY-THREE

My waltz-around-Eli moratorium proves nearly impossible. For one thing, he's home a lot. And when he is, he spends an inordinate amount of time in my vicinity. Don't all teenagers want to waste their off-hours playing video games or watching porn or something? I expected he would hang out in his room, harboring resentment, like when he was here before I moved in. Instead, he volunteers to help in the kitchen, or make lists of things to accomplish before the wedding. What I can't tell is if he's trying to be useful so we'll let him stay in public school, or just wants to irritate me.

I'm also vaguely uncomfortable about the way he so obviously ogles me. The weather is warming, so I've taken to wearing shorts or simple thigh-length shifts. Both show off the accomplishment of my regular workouts. Other than my knee, which is still slightly swollen and wears the scars of the incisions, my legs are toned and pretty. I'm hoping a little sun will help conceal the flaws, so I spend some time every day outside on a lawn chair. Too often I glance toward the house to find Eli spying.

Today when I get home from the gym, his Hummer is parked on the street, so I know he's back from school. When I go inside, however, the house is eerily quiet. Usually I can hear the bass from his stereo up here on the second floor. As I start down the hall toward the bedroom, I notice the door to Cavin's study is open. "Eli?"

"In here," he calls.

I poke my head inside the room. Eli's sitting in the big office chair, and on the desk in front of him are two things: my laptop, which appears to be on but sleeping; and an open file. With Eli here I've been using the study to work. I might have left my laptop open; I often do. But the rest of the desk was clear when I left. I'm positive about that. "What are you doing?"

"Rereading some of this stuff." He looks up at me and grins. "Your history is fascinating."

My temper flares. Cavin was supposed to dispose of that. "Really? Like what part?"

"I never would have guessed you were

451

from Hicksville. I don't see much Idaho in you."

"We moved to Vegas when I was a kid. I barely even remember Idaho."

It's a lie, and he must know it.

"No mention of your father anywhere. Do you even know who he was?"

"That's a personal question, one I'm not required to answer. But I have a question for you. Why are you doing this?"

His shoulders twitch. "I was bored, so I decided I want to get to know you better. In fact, I want to know *all* about you."

I point toward the desk. "That isn't the way to do it."

"Maybe not. But what if it's the only way to get to the truth?"

"As I told you, I prefer honesty to deception, except in certain circumstances. You can always try the direct approach first."

"Would you tell me what your net worth is, if I asked?"

"Probably not. But why would you care about that?"

"Just looking out for my own interests."

"You're safe."

"I know. In fact, I think you're the one who needs to be careful."

"What do you mean?" Again, the game ages quickly.

"I'd suggest a prenup, and a carefully worded prenup, at that."

Okay, I'll bite. "Why?"

"Did you happen to notice the date on this report?" He swings the file so it faces me, pushes it to the edge of the desk.

I have no choice but to take a look. December 31. "And?"

"If memory serves, I first met you a few days before Christmas. We shared crème brûlée after your date with my dad. The two of you had just met, right?"

"That's correct."

"So why did he put Caldwell on you then? He couldn't have been serious about you yet. Could his sudden interest have had anything to do with your money?"

"What are you talking about, Eli? Your dad doesn't need my money."

"If you say so."

He retrieves the folder. Closes it. Puts it away.

The little shit, planting seeds of doubt where none need to be sown. But now that he's done it, they've sprouted already. The timeline is, in fact, suspicious. I turn on one heel, go into the bedroom I so happily share with Cavin, lie down, and close my eyes to think.

I did not shut the door and I hear Eli

pause on the far side of the threshold.

"Whatever Dad's reasons, I'm glad you're here." Off he goes.

Whatever reasons. And what was my reason for not doing a background check on Cavin, even though I promised myself I would? Love. Yeah, that's it. How many women have been screwed over in the name of love?

Now my thoughts ping-pong.

Cavin's a surgeon, with a thriving practice.

How much is malpractice insurance again?

He's got two beautiful houses.

With dual mortgages, and hefty property taxes.

Speaking of taxes, is he current with the IRS?

According to the prenup, any tax debt belongs solely to the one of us who owes it. Ditto any other debts.

Will the prenup stand up in court?

Yes, says my attorney. Yes, says his attorney.

What about my insurance policies? Do I name him beneficiary?

Who else is there, other than Mel?

Besides, *someone's* got to bury you.

Besides, besides. After you're dead, who cares, anyway?

By the time Cavin gets home, my head is

pounding. When he comes to check on me, I do my level best to hold the anger and confusion inside. Instead of shooting off like a geyser, they leak out like steam.

"Hey, lady," he says, sitting on the edge of the bed. "You okay?"

"Headache," I manage. "How was your day?"

"Same ol'. Broken tibias. Meniscus tears. Arthritic knuckles."

"Sounds lucrative."

"People might assume so."

What does that mean? He reaches out to stroke my hair back from my forehead and I flinch without meaning to.

"What's wrong, Tara? It's something more than a headache."

Honesty. Honesty. Honesty. Why try to make this work if I can't be honest with him? I sit up and swing my legs over the side of the mattress. Cavin slides a hand along my upper leg. I don't push it away. "Okay, look. Eli pointed out something, and it's bothering me."

"Yes?"

"Dirk Caldwell's report —"

"Wait. Eli had the file?"

"He was in your study reading it when I got home."

"Goddamn it. I meant to shred it. I'm sorry."

"Doesn't matter. Apparently, he'd seen it before. He mentioned it when he stayed with me in San Francisco. Testing me, I guess."

"Get used to it."

"I am. Anyway, today he mentioned the date on the report — December thirty-first, which is before we went to Carmel."

"Right."

"But you told me you hired the PI once you decided you wanted to marry me, which had to have been after that."

"I don't believe that's what I said, although I realize the explanation was embedded in the same conversation. Sweetheart, what reason could I have possibly had, other than I didn't want any negative surprises to derail our budding relationship? I needed to know there was no ulterior motive. I couldn't be certain until after I got the report. Then, to tell you the truth, I felt like an irrational fool."

Sort of like I'm feeling now. Still, I make a mental note to conduct my own investigation, so I can be certain Cavin truly has nothing but the purest of motives himself. "Sorry. It's just, Eli can be quite convincing."

"What have I been saying? But what was he trying to convince you *of*?"

I could tell him, but for what purpose? He already knows Eli's a troublemaker. And if I do, it will paint an inelegant portrait of me.

"Doesn't matter. You have successfully dispelled my discomfort."

"Excellent. Now let's make out."

He pulls me into his lap, kisses away any residual doubt.

Well, almost.

FIFTY-FOUR

With the wedding only three weeks away, I've got some substantial decisions to make. Like what to do with my house, which has little real value to me, except it's mine. If I sell it, the proceeds minus capital gains belong to me. Should I reinvest them post-marriage, they become community property unless Cavin agrees in writing to keep the investment separate. It's a discussion I'd prefer not to have, but it's definitely on the horizon.

I also own three cars, which at this juncture seems excessive. Selling the Corvette makes the most sense. It's not really a mountain car, and it's silly to keep it garaged. Still, the idea of letting it go makes me sad. It was the best present I ever got from Jordan and reminds me of life in the fast lane. I've definitely slowed way, way down. But I'm not positive I don't want to accelerate again, especially in a very fast car.

I did hire a private investigator to dig up information on Cavin. For the most part, he's squeaky clean. Other than the mortgages, no major debt. No overdue taxes, though there was one bad audit a few years back, resolved. No alimony or child support to pay. Melissa's husband is quite well off, so the decision was made to simply split Eli's bills — tuition, insurance, college fund — down the middle. Thank God for reasonable divorces.

Some interesting facts turned up on his family. His mother's death was a suicide, something Cavin hasn't mentioned. His father, Andrew, now retired, was a pioneer researcher in antisense therapy — a gene-slicing technique that shows promise in treating conditions such as muscular dystrophy, arthritis, and certain cancers.

Cavin's brother, Paul, graduated from the Air Force Academy and currently holds the rank of major. He's married, with two children, and stationed at Edwards in California, where he's a test pilot. Their sister, Pamela, is still single at thirty-two and living the good life in Chicago.

I will meet all of them in twenty days.

Eli is out of school for summer vacation, which means he's even more underfoot than before. His getting a job sounds better and better, at least to me, and I corner him outside on the deck to advance the idea.

"Do you have any plans for the next few weeks?"

"No. Why? You inviting me along on the honeymoon?"

"Actually, I was thinking you might consider looking for work."

"Work? Like, a job?"

"Exactly like that."

"Uh, I don't think so."

Okay, that went well. He didn't even bother to think about it. "Why not? Wouldn't you like to earn some spending money?"

A grimace crinkles his face, and the overall picture reminds me of a bored cat. "Tara, I don't suppose you've noticed, but I'm not exactly short on cash. My parents give me a large allowance, and I don't have any bills. Besides, what would I do? Flip burgers?"

"There are worse things."

"Did you have a job at my age?"

"Of course. It was that or go hungry." Oops. Said too much. Caldwell's report mentions where I was born and where I went to college, but a big slice of my childhood, including my teen years, is missing. Fortunately.

"Really? Huh. Was that in Las Vegas?"

"Yes. Not a good place to be hungry."

"I thought everyone was hungry for something in Vegas."

That inspires a small laugh. "True enough. But in my case, there was rarely enough food in the house for my sister and me. My mother was not the best provider."

He turns that over for a moment or two. You can almost see his brain working through the lenses of his eyes. "So you married your first husband for money."

"Security," I correct. "Believe me, I worked for the money."

His expression morphs into a sly smile. Okay, more like a leer.

"That's not what I meant. Look, Raul put me through college. I earned my degree. I also helped him run his businesses and learned the finer points of finance through firsthand experience. I'd say trial and error, but Raul taught me quite a bit."

"And from there you just kept getting lucky."

"There's an element of luck in all success stories."

"Right. And sometimes it's someone else's *bad* luck. Like skiing into a tree."

"Sometimes."

This boy is wicked. Maybe even evil. I suspect the latter when he asks, "Did you love Raul?"

"I loved many things abou—"

"No. Were you *in* love with him?" Thrust.

Parry. "I don't think anyone that age really understands the meaning of being in love. He was in love with me. That's all that mattered."

Thrust. "Except he died."

"He died happy, which is more than a lot of people can say." Parry.

"How about you? Will you die happy?" Thrust.

Feint right. "I suppose that depends on when I die." Feint left. "But if I died today, I'd have to say yes. This truly is the happiest I've ever been."

In for the kill. "Are you in love with my dad?"

"Absolutely." Zero hesitation. Zero negative body language. Parry riposte.

"Good. Because if you can love my dad, you can love me, and it won't be so bad having me around next year." He vacates the lounge chair, comes over and gives me a hug, and his voice is a low breeze in my ear. "We'll be, like, one happy, loving family. Won't that be nice?"

His hands linger, too long, and I extricate myself from his embrace. "I wasn't aware a decision had been made about next year yet."

He smiles. "Sucks to be the last to know. You might even get me longer than that. I'm thinking about Sierra Nevada College in lieu of the Cordon Bleu. SNC is close, and they've got a great interdisciplinary studies program that combines outdoor adventures leadership with ski resort and business management."

Eli full-time was not part of the deal, and why was I not included in this conversation? "Sounds like you've done some research. And what are your chances of admission?"

"Pretty good, I'd say. It's not the easiest school to get into, but it isn't the toughest, either. I scored 2230 on my SAT. I think that qualifies me."

It probably overqualifies him for a cooking academy, but so far anyway, I haven't seen his ambition catch up to his intellect. Then again, the program he mentioned sounds like a good direction for him. Maybe we can talk him into living on campus instead of commuting. The bigger issue is what school he'll attend for his senior year.

"We can certainly look at Sierra Nevada College. But now, if you'll excuse me, I've got some calls to make."

"I'll bet you do. At least one, anyway." He glances at his watch. "With luck, Dad will be at lunch."

It actually takes me an hour plus to reach him. I should have cooled off by now. Instead, I'm livid. "Can you spare a minute?"

"Of course. What's wrong?"

"Oh, nothing. Except somehow, sometime, apparently you and your son decided he could stay here and go to Whittell next year?"

"Calm down, Tara. Who told you that?"

"Who do you think?"

"Sweetheart, I haven't given him a definitive answer, and wouldn't without consulting you first. Obviously, Eli enjoys yanking your chain. I really wish you'd quit listening to him."

My blood pressure drops, but not much. "That's hard to do with him in the house all the time. And speaking of that, are we really leaving him alone here while we're off on our honeymoon?" We had planned the Alaska cruise before Eli moved in.

"He's pretty self-sufficient, and I'm not sure what else we can do. He's a bit old for a babysitter. Unless your sister wants a nice summer vacation at Tahoe?"

"That's a thought. Except, she'd probably

want to bring the girls, which would not be the best idea." Come to think of it, Eli just might try to put the moves on Mel, or at least wheedle information out of her.

"I wouldn't worry too much. He hasn't made a whole lot of friends here yet, at least I don't think he has, so there won't be blockbuster parties. He can feed himself, and wash his own clothes. He'll be fine alone for two weeks."

Sixteen days, actually. And it doesn't take friends to party. All it takes is money, and according to Eli, he's got plenty of that. He's also got balls, plus he's a brilliant liar. Nope. Nothing to worry about.

Except when Cavin gets home, all hell kind of breaks loose. He arrives, already grumpy from a long, irritating day filled with patient complaints and a problem with an ER nurse. My earlier phone call only exacerbated his mood. The truth is, I've rarely seen him this distant.

Eli sits at the dinner table wearing headphones with music pumping loudly through them. Cavin gestures for him to remove them, which Eli does reluctantly.

"That's rather rude, don't you think?"

"Look, it's not like the conversation is so stimulating, you know?"

What happened to him? He's usually

465

happy to monopolize the small talk.

Cavin overreacts to his blunt dismissal.

"Are you just trying to cause trouble? Because I won't stand for it."

Eli brings his gaze level with his father's. "What the fuck did I do?"

"Do not talk to me like that."

"Then don't be a dick."

Cavin's face flushes, visibly red from chin to ear tips. "You have no right to call me a dick, and if you plan to continue living here, I'd better never hear that word again, at least not in reference to me. And speaking of living here, did you tell Tara we'd agreed to let you go to Whittell next year?"

"We did, Dad."

"We absolutely did *not.*"

"Dad, you said it was probably the best option."

"Which is *not* the same thing as making a concrete decision."

"Fine. If you don't want me here, I'll find somewhere else to live!"

He starts to get up, but I put a hand over his arm. "Wait. First of all, both of you need to calm down. It's obvious this is a miscommunication, and I'm sorry for the part I seemed to have played in it."

Did I just apologize? I guess it worked because Eli relaxes and Cavin's face slowly

466

returns to its normal color and we manage to finish dinner without another blowup. But why did *I* apologize?

And does this mean Eli has become a permanent fixture?

After dinner, I leave the boys to decide on dessert, which I skip in favor of checking my e-mail and escaping any chance of yet another argument. I don't care if the two can't agree, as long as I'm not inserted between them and expected to moderate. I didn't sign on for that, nor for the stress their quarrels initiate.

Not much in my inbox. There's a string of annoying advertisements. I hate when I end up on a mailing list. It's almost enough to set me off, especially when I can't figure out how it happened. It's not like I hang out on social networking sites designed to steal my private information and determine my buying habits.

I take the time to unsubscribe from each, then respond to Cassandra, who's written to ask if it's okay for her to bring her son to the wedding. *Of course. Eli will be there, and also my nieces, plus some kids from Cavin's side. And hey, go ahead and bring a date if you'd like.*

I hit the send button and am about to sign off when a *ding* announces a new e-mail.

The address is unfamiliar, and I consider writing it off without opening it, but what stops me is the subject line, which reads: *Last Warning.* And the message: *I'm not fucking around anymore. You think you hold all the cards but you're wrong. I'm not power-less. I hear you're getting married. How much does he know about you? And how safe is his car?*

Enough is enough. I'm not powerless, either, and now I'm more angry than scared. But first, I've got to identify the mysterious sender. If I involve the cops, they'll wonder why I waited till now, and Cavin will be roy-ally pissed that I didn't mention the follow-up messages. Not to mention he might want to know what some anonymous stalker has on me.

I pick up the phone and call my PI.

FIFTY-FIVE

Nine days and counting to the big day, I drive over the mountain to go shopping with Melody. Sacramento wouldn't be my first choice of cities to scour for wedding wear, but there is a giant mall in Roseville, which is this side of the city proper and boasts several decent stores. They open at ten, so I time my trip to pick up Mel at nine thirty. Obviously, she's been watching for me, because when I arrive the door opens immediately and she barrels straight to the car.

"Let's go." Her voice is calm but tinged with anger.

"What's wrong?"

"Can we please just go?"

Wordlessly, I start the engine and we are on the freeway before I insist, "Talk to me. Is this about Graham?"

She crumbles but refuses to cry. "Who else? He has decided to 'take some time to reconsider our relationship.' Apparently, he thinks a good place to do that is in Las Vegas, where he'll be vacationing for a week."

"Alone?"

"You'd have to ask him."

"I'm sorry, Mel. Do you think this is a genuine bid for a separation?"

"I wish I knew."

"Did something precipitate this? The scholarship?"

She shakes her head. "No, not that. It's been coming for a while. I just refused to believe he'd follow through, and I'm still not sure he will."

"You might consider talking to an attorney now. Also, I'd recommend moving some money into a personal bank account. Accomplish that before he does."

"Oh, I don't know. I doubt that's necessary. He still cares about us. The girls, anyway."

"Mel, trust me. If he's serious about this, he will be looking out for himself first. Be smart."

She sits quietly for a minute, processing. Finally, she tips her chin up and straightens her shoulders. "I'll tell you what. If he walks out on this family, I *will* make him pay." Rarely have I heard such resolve in her voice.

"Do you have a lawyer?"

"Just the one who wrote our wills."

"I'll give you the name of a good one. And, really, don't wait. If he decides to come crawling home, you can always let him in." My experience, however, tells me it's an unlikely outcome.

We have reached the exit for the mall, but Mel's news has put a damper on the day. "Do you still want to go shopping?" I ask, certain she'll say no.

But she surprises me. "Of course. In fact, I can't think of a better day to spend some money. Maybe even a lot of money."

So we do. I find a killer off-the-shoulder summer dress, in white, no less. I've actually never been a bride-in-white, but why not? This wedding is very different, and somehow white feels right. Mel chooses a pretty floral and buys her girls complementary dresses in solid shades of fuchsia, violet, and lime. We will look lovely in the photos.

We move on to accessories and pick sandals with short wedges. Heels wouldn't work in the location Cavin and I finally settled on — midmountain at Heavenly, where you can see clear across Tahoe to the mountain beyond. It's a fitting venue, if a bit ironic.

I convince Mel to purchase a brilliant Michael Kors handbag, plus smaller (if not much less expensive) purses for her girls. Finally, we spend almost an hour picking out pricey panties, bras, and some sexy lingerie that should please Cavin very much. Overall, I'd say my sister came very close to maxing out her credit card, and that makes me happy.

We finish the day with a late lunch at the Cheesecake Factory, and I drop her off a little past three. "Aren't you staying over?" she asks.

"I thought I might, but I'm going to beg off. See you next week."

No need to poke sticks at snakes, and Graham is a cobra. I turn up the music and head home, thinking about the impermanence of relationships. Twenty years, one wife, three kids, and two dogs, tossed aside, just like that? Yes, I've experienced the dissolution of marriage. But never a marriage rooted in love. Did Graham ever really love Mel? I know she was crazy in love with him. But how much love remains?

This turn of events could have me reconsidering the path I've recently chosen. Instead, it's got me more determined than ever to dedicate myself to keeping my marriage to Cavin intact. If love is, in fact, the difference, and I must believe it is, I will cultivate the emotion. A phrase comes to mind, as cliché as it might be: growing old together. I've never seriously contemplated the idea, mostly because I don't enjoy thinking about aging, let alone actually morphing into a senior citizen. But what's the alternative? Would it be better than solitary decay?

On that morbid note, I'll focus on beginnings rather than endings, other than the end of this trip, anyway. As I approach the driveway, I notice a strange car parked in front of the house. Friend of Eli's, perhaps? When I go inside, music rises loudly from the lower floor.

"Eli?" I call, knowing there's no way he can hear me.

I take my packages into the bedroom, hang my dress in the closet, and put my new shoes on a shelf. Then I take the lingerie down to the laundry room and start panties, bras, and teddies on a hand-wash cycle. Who knows how many strange appendages have touched them? When I pass Eli's door, I notice a female voice behind it. I consider knocking but wouldn't want to disturb a private whatever, so I go back upstairs to the kitchen for a glass of wine.

Before long, a drift of laughter precedes

the approach of footsteps — two pairs: one heavy, the other light. I go to say hello, surprising the pair with my presence.

"What are you doing here?" demands Eli.

"What is *she* doing here?" I ask.

Sophia smiles. "You must be Tara."

"I thought you were spending the night in Sac," says Eli.

"Changed my mind. But you didn't answer my question." This time I address Sophia, who is even more stunning in person, in a short yellow shift (and probably nothing beneath it), which shows off her slender body and perfect tan. "What are you doing here?"

"I bumped into Eli at Skunk Harbor. He invited me over." Skunk Harbor is a local nudie hangout. I can guess what he invited her over *for*. "Does Cavin know you're here?"

"Why would he?" asks Eli.

"I thought maybe you were trying to provoke him."

He grins. "Now why would I want to do that?"

"I don't know, and I really don't care. The thing is, this is my house, and I'm sorry, Sophia, but you are not welcome here."

"Excuse me," says Eli. "But this is *not* your house. It belongs to my dad, and I don't have to ask your permission to bring someone over."

Sparklers ignite, hot and electric, and arc inside me. But I won't completely blow it in front of this woman. "This *is* my house, Eli. Don't make me prove it. Sophia, in my opinion you coming here was in extremely bad taste. I assume you realize that Cavin and I are getting married next week?"

"I'm aware of that, yes."

"Obviously Eli is making a statement. Are you?"

She studies me intently for a second or two. I have a hard time reading her, can't tell if she's high or not, or if she's intent on playing some game. Finally, she admits, "I have nothing to say except congratulations. Forgive me, Eli, but I think it's best I go now. You know how to get ahold of me. Call if you like. We can hang out at my place next time."

"Do you really think that's advisable? Technically, sleeping with a seventeen-year-old is not statutory rape. But he's just a kid. Can you not find someone closer to your age to seduce?"

Her turn to smile. "I'm afraid you're misinformed. Eli is very much a man."

She lifts herself up on her toes, kisses him full on the mouth, then spins and leaves soundlessly.

We watch her go. Once the door closes behind her, I ask, "What did she mean you know where she lives? Did she invite you to New York?"

"Didn't Dad tell you? She's back in Reno for a while, producing a show at Harrah's."

My blood pressure fountains. I suppress it as best I can and hiss, "Where's your father?"

"I don't know. He said he had to work late, and then he was going out for a beer with some friends." Eli draws closer. "If I'd known you were coming home, I wouldn't have brought her here. I didn't mean to upset you."

The kid should be an actor. He seems completely genuine. "Eli, that was absolutely inappropriate, on every level. If you want to live here, you'd better understand that I never want to see that woman again." Regardless of where the bitch lives.

He reaches out, dares to stroke my cheek. "Jealous?"

I pull away from his touch. "Hardly." The truth, however, isn't quite so straightforward.

I start toward the kitchen and the glass of wine I left on the counter.

476

Behind me, Eli says softly, "Just so you know, I did call Dad to ask if I could bring her over. He said okay."

FIFTY-SIX

I'm driving an old Ford pickup way too fast on a rutted dirt road, headed toward the beach. Except I'm in Idaho, and the nearest beach is far, far away, unless you count river gravel. In the bed of the truck, Eli and Sophia are mostly naked and making out, and I keep looking in the rearview mirror to try to see just how much of a man Eli really is. I'm pissed that Sophia knows and I don't. There's a hill on my left, and I circle a big jutting boulder, and when I look away from the mirror, Cavin and Melody are standing in the road, on opposite sides. I can miss one, but not both, and I don't know which way to swerve and . . .

I rip myself from the dream, trying to scream, but the sound gets stuck and I swallow. And now I know where I am — in Cavin's big bed, which is my big bed, too. My bed. My bedroom. My house. I settle back against the pillows, catch my breath, and listen to my heart as its racing slows. Every nightmare returns me to Idaho.

It's dark in the room — shades drawn against the morning. I glance at the clock. A little after nine. Cavin and I are supposed to go to the beach today, try to relax a little, and remember falling in love. We had a tiff when he got home last night, fueled by Eli's passing comment. I meant to stay calm, but when he breezed through the door well past dinnertime, reeking of beer, I lost it.

"What are you doing here?" he'd asked. "I thought you were staying at your sister's."

"She and Graham are having problems so I decided to come on back."

"You should have called to let me know. I would have been home sooner."

Yeah, right, I thought. *With luck you could have had a threesome.* My voice began to rise. "If you would have come home sooner, you could have handled the situation instead of my having to do it."

"What situation, Tara?"

"Eli and Sophia."

"What?"

"They were here together. In his bedroom. Pretty sure they weren't just listening to music. Did you tell him it was okay to bring her here?"

"No!"

"He said he called and asked if it was okay and you said yes."

"Tara, I would never agree to that. He told me he ran into an old girlfriend at the beach and asked if she could come over. He never said it was Sophia."

Same story. Different details. Again. I couldn't figure out a reason for Cavin to lie. Except maybe one. "Did you know she's living in Reno again?"

His gaze, which has been fixed on me, drops toward the floor and he reluctantly admits, "Last time I saw her, which was the day we had lunch together, she mentioned it was a possibility."

"Why didn't you tell me?"

He crossed the room in two long strides, stood very close, one hand on each of my cheeks so he could tilt my eyes toward his. "Because I didn't want you to worry about it, and I knew you would. For the millionth time, I love you. You. And if it takes to the end of my lifetime, I swear I will prove it."

His kiss was tender, but then he swept me into his arms and carried me straight to bed. No soap or lotion or mouthwash. His beer met my wine, and our bodies intertwined. Tenderness dissolved into an ocean of desire. He kissed me hard and long. Then he buried his face in my hair, whispered fiercely, "I don't want Sophia. I want only you. Want to inhale you, breathe you inside me. I want you under my skin. I've never felt this way about another woman, and I'm sure I could never again."

Love welled up and pulsed through my veins, foreplay to first orgasm. Then another, and another, until he finally let himself come, too. Exhausted, ecstatic, I tumbled into sleep, then woke up with this morning midnightmare.

I slip on a robe, go in search of coffee, and find it in the kitchen, where a shirtless Eli is whirring something in the blender. I push away the recollection of how he appeared in my dream, reach for a mug. "Where's your dad?"

"He said he had early rounds and he'd pick you up for the beach around eleven."

I pour coffee, sip it as I watch his culinary efforts. Finally, I have to ask, "Do you bastardize conversations to purposely try and piss me off?"

"Not very often." All the answer I need, I guess. But then he adds, "Why? Do you have a certain conversation in mind?"

"I do. Your dad said when you asked about bringing an old girlfriend home you didn't mention it was Sophia."

He stops the blender, opens the silverware

481

drawer, extracts a spoon. "I guess I didn't mention her by name. But I figured he'd know who I meant. He's generally pretty good about reading between the lines." Eli stirs whatever he's got in the blender, takes a sip with the spoon. "Yum. Want some smoothie?"

"What's in it?" It looks enticing, and I'm starving, having skipped dinner last night.

"Fruit juice, yogurt, honey, and ice."

"Sure, I'll try some."

Eli pours two tumblers, hands one to me. "Cheers!"

I take a sip. Delicious. Take a gulp, then another, trying to discern the flavors. Banana, for sure. Something else, something sweet and . . . All of a sudden, bumps pop up on my tongue and my mouth starts to itch. My pulse quickens. Shit. I've been here before.

Everything begins to bloat — lips, tongue. Megahives swell in my throat, which closes around them. This is critical. I can barely suck in air.

Eli doesn't react. He stands there staring with those cold lead eyes. "What can I do?"

"EpiPen," I manage. "Pu-purse. Bedroom."

He strolls down the hallway.

Strolls.

Is gone too long.

Where is he?

My head grows light. The ceiling begins a slow spin. I put my hands to my face. It's double the size it should be, and my bulging cheeks make it hard to see. I concentrate on drawing breath through constricted airways. Every inhalation is a painful rasp.

Finally, Eli returns with my bag. I find the EpiPen without a problem, but my hands shake, my eyes are slits, and I can't open the packaging. "Help me."

Eli does as instructed, gives me the injector, and I slam it into my thigh. The needle is made to go through clothing, and the thin material of my robe doesn't do much to slow its entry. Bloody hell! It hurts! But the epinephrine goes to work almost immediately. The itching lessens as the hives begin to shrink. I can see again.

Breathe again.

"Are you okay?" asks Eli, quite calmly, once it's clear I'm not going to die. "What was that?"

"Food allergy. Was there mango in the smoothie?"

"Maybe in the juice. It was called Tropical Fruit Blast or something." He goes to the recycling bin, locates the plastic container and reads the label. "Oh yeah. Passion fruit.

Guava. Banana. And mango. Wow. That was awesome. Your face looked like a fucking ten-dollar balloon." Then, as an afterthought, "Do you need paramedics?"

All the literature says to call 911 or go into the ER after an episode capped with epinephrine. But I want to go to the beach and, after all, Cavin is a physician. "I think I'm okay. But can you call your dad and tell him what happened? I'm feeling nauseous."

I run to the bathroom, make it just in time to reach the toilet and empty my stomach of smoothie. Shimmering sweat, I slump onto the cool tile, heave until there's nothing left. When I think it's safe, I get to my feet and go to the sink to rinse my mouth and chance a look in the mirror. Not pretty. The swelling has subsided, but my skin is slack from being stretched so far out of shape. I wash my face. Apply tightening lotion. Hope for the best.

I stumble back to bed, crawl beneath the top sheet, and close my eyes, expecting Eli to come check on me. Instead, the base boom of too-loud music vibrates the floor.

I think he knew. But he couldn't have. I've never mentioned it to him.

Above the percussion, I hear the front door slam and the pounding of hurried feet. Cavin rushes through the door, straight to my side. "Are you all right?"

I look up into his eyes, which overflow with worry. "A little queasy, but I'll be fine."

"Oh, God. I'm so sorry. I never even thought about the mango thing when I bought that juice. I promise to be more careful in the future." He studies my face. "You look like hell."

Cavin forgot about my allergy.

Eli didn't know about the allergy.

It was just an accident.

Wasn't it?

SO-CALLED EXPERTS

Swear I'm incapable of love,
that my limbic system is turned off
to such powerful connection.

Why do specialists settle for easy
explanations? Till a little deeper,
the facts are fascinating.

The truth is, I do love, with
unparalleled intensity, and it's a wildfire
burning, uncontrollable. Uncontainable.

It is both a thing of beauty, and one
that must be feared. To stand
in the way is to beg incineration.

My love is like a child's — all
encompassing. Possessive. Egocentric.
It's my toy. Only I can play with it.

And no one — no one — better take
my toy away. I'd just as soon destroy
it. Smash it flat against the ground.

Fifty-Seven

I chalk the mango up to an immense mistake, make a mental note to check every label from now on, and obtain another EpiPen ASAP. This episode was bad — worse than the last, and I have no doubt another could result in dire consequences. I won't be so careless in the future. I've got every reason to live.

The week is busy. My brush with eternity encouraged some decisions I otherwise might not have made. Every one revolves around Cavin and my determination to be his ideal mate. If I'm going to do this thing with him, I'm damn sure going to do it right. People like me aren't meant to fall in love. That I have is a miracle, and those are once in a lifetime.

Trust.

I'm working on it.

I call the Realtor in San Francisco, tell her to go ahead and list the house on Russian Hill. Half of whatever I clear will go into my portfolio; I'll invest the rest in another house, in Colorado, maybe. Aspen or Vail. Someplace new to ski. Cavin can help me decide. The deed will be joint tenancy. As long as he agrees to put this house, at least, half in my name and make Eli damn well understand that it is, in fact, mine.

Trust.

Is best achieved when it's mutual.

That reminds me to tweak my living trust. I keep Mel as executor. I know she'll honor my wishes, and it gives me a small sense of control of my hereafter. She's already slated to receive a large share of my investments, with the understanding that Graham gets nothing from me, and anything left to the girls must go into a trust until they reach the age of thirty. I name Cavin as beneficiary to my insurance policies and bank accounts. Should I predecease him, he'll be able to retire early.

Trust.

It's easier when the details are in writing.

At some point, I'll establish a foundation and feed some of my posthumous earnings toward funding it in perpetuity. Not so much because any one cause is truly close to my heart, but rather to keep my name alive forever. The Tara Lattimore Foundation. I like the sound of that.

Trust.

Either built or destroyed by love.

The paperwork is tedious, but I comfort myself in knowing it will all be accomplished before the honeymoon. I go into the study to use the fax, decide to check e-mail while I wait for the pages to send. When I log in to my home page, news headlines pop up in my feed. I scroll through them, and one catches my eye: JORDAN LONDON PLEADS GUILTY IN PLEA BARGAIN DEAL.

I skim the story. Apparently, he'll serve less than two years in a federal penitentiary. The evidence was overwhelming. Good. Glad I won't have to testify. But I would have, even if it meant he'd find out it was me who turned him in. Payback's a bitch sometimes, and a deal isn't really a deal if it's forged in lies.

When I get to my e-mail, there's one from Melody. *Don't mean to put a damper on your excitement, but you need to know that Mom is very ill. Apparently the tests they ran when she went in for the anaphylaxis revealed a growth. Stage-three lung cancer. Inoperable. They'll start radiation treatment, but the prognosis isn't good. I tried to call, but your phone seems to be off.*

I take a deep breath, notice a slight tremor in my hands. Why am I shaking? It's just another small reminder that none of us is immortal. And in Mom's case, death is nothing more than the ultimate desertion. Stage-three lung cancer. Guess she should have given up those cigarettes after all. Wonder how much black magic her secondhand crap worked on Mel and me. I suppose I should consider a checkup. I'm the kind of person who only goes to the doctor when I feel like I'm croaking.

I locate my phone, which I did, in fact, turn off while it charged, and call Melody. "I got your cheerful e-mail."

"Sorry. The timing is bad, I know."

"It would be a lot worse if I cared."

"You really don't, huh?"

"I really don't. But it's weird. When did I see Mom last? Five months ago? She didn't look sick, did she?"

"Not at all. Well, other than that little cough." She is quiet for a moment. "Do you think she suspected it? I mean, with all that stuff about connection."

"Mel, you know as well as I do that all she wanted that day was money. Besides, I'm pretty sure Mom thought herself invincible." I get that from her, too, I suppose. If not for an ER visit for something unrelated, she'd probably still feel that way. How sick do you have to get before you consider the idea that you might die?

"At some point, I'll have to go down to visit her," says Mel. "I don't suppose you'd consent to going along?"

"You don't suppose correctly."

"She needs some help, putting her affairs in order. You have more experience with that than I do."

"How hard could it be? She's never owned a thing except for a dog and a beat-up Ford truck."

"How do you know that?"

That stops me. I've worked very hard not to know anything about her, or let her know anything about me. "I guess I don't."

"Can't you find a shred of forgiveness in your heart?"

"Forgiveness" is not a word in my vocabulary, especially not when it comes to my mother. "I . . . uh . . ."

"She forgives you. She wants you to know that."

"Forgives me for *what*?" The words explode in a froth of rage.

"For not forgiving her." The anger subsides for a moment. But then she adds, "And for not inviting her to any of your weddings."

Bam. "Does she know I'm getting married?"

"Afraid so."

"Who told her?"

"Calm down, Tara. Kayla mentioned we were coming up for your wedding. She didn't realize Mom didn't know. Besides, she's excited. All the girls are. And in the long run, what does it really matter?"

She has a point. "Totally changing the subject . . ." Because this conversation has grown stale. "What's up with Graham? Did he go to Vegas?"

"Yes."

"That's it? And?"

"Apparently whatever remained in Vegas excised the wanderlust from his system. He's decided to stay with his family."

Right. For now. "He didn't change his mind about the wedding, though?"

"And miss a gig?"

Of course. "I'd still talk to that lawyer and start squirreling some money away. Can't hurt to be cautious."

"I know."

We sign off with a promise to see each other on Friday. Before I close up my laptop, I cycle through old e-mail to make sure I've responded to everything important and trash anything unnecessary to keep. I happen across the last e-mail from Melody — the one that mentions Mom's allergic reaction to mango. That makes me flash back to the day Eli was reexamining Dirk Caldwell's information. My laptop was here, asleep but not completely shut down. Eli could have been in my e-mail. He might have known, after all.

Another flare of temper sends me on a fevered quest for an answer. I find Eli on the deck, reading and listening to music. My body language is screaming. He puts down the book, slips the headphones around his neck. "What now?"

"Do you peruse my e-mail?"

"Peruse? You mean read? Why would I want to do that?"

"Don't answer my questions with questions! Do you?"

"Not regularly. I mean, I've seen some of it up on your screen before, but I don't actively go looking for it."

"Did you know about my mango allergy?"

"What? No, of course not." He stands. Inches closer. Unsettlingly close. "You don't think I'd purposely try to hurt you?"

I stand my ground. "I don't know."

"I don't want to hurt you, Tara." He brushes a strand of hair from my face. Gently. "I want to love you." His voice is genuine, but there's something more — a hint of vulnerability. My instinct is to reach for him. I sway, take a step backward, and he amends, "Like a mother, of course."

"Stepmother?"

"Wicked or regular?"

"Which would you prefer?"

"I think you know."

Stop the ridiculous repartee.

He's a kid.

Cavin's kid.

I'm afraid you're misinformed. Eli is very much a man.

To silence her, not to mention the scolding of my inner voice, I go over to the chaise where Eli was sitting, look at the book he was reading. "*Confessions of a Sociopath?* Research?"

He laughs. "Self-help, maybe."

As usual, his meaning is unclear. I'll have to gnaw on it. Right now, I need to talk to Cavin. I find him toweling off after a shower.

"Are you okay?" he asks immediately. "You look a little shaky."

"I just got an e-mail from my sister. It seems my mom has lung cancer. Stage three."

"Oh no. I'm sorry, honey."

"Don't be. She's had more years than she deserves."

"You don't mean that."

"I wish I didn't."

"Do you want to talk about it?"

I haven't given him many details about my childhood, but he knows it wasn't the best. I shake my head. "But can I ask you something?"

"Anything."

"Were you close to your mother?"

He goes to the sink, finds a comb, and runs it through his hair. Then he steps into a clean pair of boxers. Finally, he answers, "My mom lived on her own planet. Bipolar disorder is vicious. In her manic phases, she was the mother every kid wants — fun, loving, full of life. But when the switch flipped, she barely spoke to any of us, just hid out in her room, watching TV. She didn't bathe. Didn't eat. She refused her meds, preferring alcohol. No one, least of all Dad, could convince her otherwise. And then one day, she was gone."

"You mean dead."

"Yes." He shimmies into a pair of jeans.

"Why didn't you tell me she committed suicide?"

He doesn't even ask how I know, though he must suspect. "It's not something I talk about, Tara, any more than you talk about your mother. But I suppose I should have.

Secrets are counterproductive to relationship building."

Secrets. I need to hold on to a few. But this doesn't have to be one of them. I go over, slide my hands up his chest, wrap my arms around his neck, and look into his eyes. "What do you want to know about my mother?"

He can ask. If I don't like the question, I'll manufacture the answer.

FIFTY-EIGHT

Friday, wedding day, I can barely drag myself out from beneath the blankets. I'm not sick, unless you count an overwhelming sense of apprehension as an illness. I haven't had second thoughts until this morning. Suddenly, everything seems wrong. Am I making a huge mistake?

I lie in bed until Cavin brings coffee — strong and black and steaming. That's right. Usual. Routine. Except by this time of day, I'm always out of bed. Cavin sets the mug on the nightstand. "You okay?"

I sit up, lean back against the pillows. "I'm not sure."

"What's wrong?"

"Nerves," I admit.

"You're not backing out now, are you?" He takes my hand, kisses my fingertips. The gesture is so sweet that I can't help but smile.

It's really much too late to call it off. I've

signed away a good chunk of my independence. Not all, of course. Never all. "Not backing out. Mostly, I'm nervous about meeting your family. What if they hate me?"

"Not possible. You are nothing less than an angel."

"And you are a liar."

He puts the back of his hand to his forehead, feigns hurt. "You wound me, madam."

"Open the blinds, will you, please?" I need to yank myself into the morning, shake off drowsiness and anxiety.

Cavin goes to the window and with the pull of a cord, sunshine filters into the room, lifting my mood slightly. It looks to be a spectacular day. "Breakfast?" he asks.

"I'm not sure I can keep it down, but I'll give it a try."

What I need is a workout, and after managing to swallow a couple of bites of eggs and toast, I spend forty-five minutes on the stationary bike, then lift and do one hundred crunches. Afterward, I shower and take a long, relaxing bath before heading out to get my hair and nails done. By three o'clock, when I'm slated to meet up with Mel and the girls, eighty percent of my earlier trepidation has melted away. I can deal with the other twenty.

They're staying at the Timber Lodge, so we can walk to the gondola for the ride up to the observation deck. From there, the wedding party will hike a short distance into the trees for a small, private ceremony. Cavin and I chose the simplest option, mostly because the more formal possibilities were already booked by the time we finally settled on Heavenly as our venue.

By the time I arrive at the suite, the girls are already dressed, with the fresh flowers I had delivered earlier pinned in their hair. "Wow. You ladies look amazing," I tell them, even though I think their makeup is a tad heavy. Kayla must have done it.

I change in one of the bedrooms and Mel comes in with my small bouquet of roses and lilies. "How are you feeling?"

"Determined."

"Does that mean scared?"

I repeat one of my favorite phrases, or at least a bastardization of it. "Nothing scares me." It doesn't sound very brave.

"If you say so. You ready?"

I twirl once. "How do I look?"

"Scared. And gorgeous."

"Then I guess I'm ready."

It truly is a picture-perfect afternoon, with a sky so blue it's almost purple, and a baby-soft breeze puffing at a few white clouds. The ceremony is scheduled for four, and we're to meet everyone up top, which allows me the opportunity to make a grand entrance. It's a short ride. The girls chatter the entire time. Mel and I sit silently, wading through personal reveries. Bet Graham is on her mind.

The officiant, who is short and round and wearing an awful hairpiece, greets us at the platform, escorts us to where the wedding party awaits. It's a small but eclectic group. Cassandra has come with Taylor, and it pleases me to see that Charlie has accompanied them. He seems attached at the hip to Cassandra. Romance? Lust, at the very least. Well, that answers the question about his sexual preference, at least for today.

Those three, plus Mel and crew, are all who are here for me. On the groom's side, I recognize Cavin's family members from photos. His father stands talking with two of Cavin's colleagues. His sister is huddled up with his brother, whose wife and kids look vaguely uncomfortable. Also in attendance is Rebecca. Interesting that his receptionist has made an appearance, but I guess if my boy Friday showed up, why not?

Cavin and Eli lean against the railing,

checking out the view. Even in profile, the resemblance is uncanny. The two wear matching charcoal tuxes, and I really couldn't say which one is the more hand-some. Eli has the youth thing going on, but his father has matured into a striking man. As soon as the girls notice Eli and Taylor, the whispers fire up.

Who's that?

Cavin's son, Eli.

O-M-G! He's so cute!

I know, right?

Who's the other one?

I have no idea.

Would you two shut up? People are staring.

Eli spots us first and, despite the girls vy-ing for his attention, is drawn to me im-mediately. Even from here, I can see him assess me approvingly. Our eyes meet and there is meaning in the smiles we exchange.

But now Cavin's head swivels in my direc-tion, and my heart harbors no doubt that he's why I'm here. He excuses himself from his clan, strides across the deck, straight to me. He takes my hands in his. "Oh my God. You are so incredibly beautiful! I am, sincerely, the luckiest man alive." He leans forward, kisses me just this side of R-rated, then whispers into my ear, "I have never been quite this turned on."

502

"Obviously, the white dress hasn't fooled you. Wait till you see what I've got on underneath."

"What?"

"That's for me to know and you to find out. Oh. The minister is looking at his watch. I think we're boring him."

"Shall we?"

He guides me over to the group. After some quick introductions, we all follow the officiant's flapping toupee off the deck and into the woods. The man, who does similar services throughout the Tahoe basin, delivers a standard wedding-chapel liturgy — quick, simple, and lacking both homilies and Bible verses. I barely have time to double think.

There is one surprise. Cavin and I had picked out simple gold wedding bands, but when it comes time for the "with this ring, I thee wed" part of the ceremony, the ring Cavin slips on my finger is ornate pewter, studded with diamonds. "My mother's," he whispers. "Hope that's okay."

I study the ring, which is easily the most beautiful I've worn, though likely not the most expensive. It looks like a custom design, however. Unique. And that feels right. This relationship is unique. This wedding is unique. This surging love is unique.

Cavin is given permission to kiss the bride, which means it's official, or will be once our witnesses sign the marriage license. Bliss and terror wage battle inside me. Can love survive the seasons? What if I don't love him at all? Either way, a celebration awaits us, and I'm always up for a good party.

Chef Christopher has given us his entire dining room for three hours. Well, okay, we're actually paying him very well, and it's worth every penny. The food, as always, is exceptional. Alcohol flows freely, and most everyone is imbibing, including, I can't help but notice, Eli. No one says a word.

At some point, he, Kayla, and Taylor disappear outside. My hunch is they're smoking weed, a fact that's confirmed when they return, red-eyed and moving like tortoises. No one says anything about that, either, too caught up in the merriment to chance a scene. Or maybe no one really cares.

Except I do.

I find an opportunity to tap Eli on the shoulder. "May I have a word with you, please?"

"Guess so."

We move into a quiet corner. "I can guess what you were doing with Kayla. Kind of inappropriate, don't you think?"

"Hey, it was her idea. I only went along to

keep her safe from Andaman. He's a legendary perv, and I know she means a lot to you."

I choose to believe him.

After we've eaten, the music begins. The trio we hired does covers of pop and rock standards, plus three or four songs I have on my own playlist. Happily, I am able to dance. And when we start tossing around toasts, I propose, "To orthopedic surgeons, without whom I would definitely not be here tonight."

When the band launches into Gin Blossoms' "As Long as It Matters," Cavin pulls me into his arms and we slow dance, something I've done very few times in my life, and never this filled with an emotion I truly supposed had been denied me. It's a defining moment.

One I'll never forget.

FIFTY-NINE

The problem with leaving Eli alone at home while we honeymoon has solved itself. Cavin's dad volunteered to hang out for a couple of weeks and enjoy the mountains. Andrew is an interesting man, though cool. Apparently, it's a family trait. Still, I've enjoyed spending a little time with him. He's brilliant, so conversation is easy.

Cavin's brother is okay in a military sort of way. Which means, rather patriarchal, but seemingly quite devoted to his wife and kids. His sister is the life of the party. Only problem that night was no one to party *with,* at least not if that meant someone to sleep with. Best she could manage was sidling up to Chef Christopher, who appreciated it, I'm sure. I'm just as sure his wife would feel differently. Pam's an awful flirt, worse than I am. I like her.

Cassandra and I didn't have much time to talk, but I did corner her long enough to ask about Charlie. "It's a fling," she said. "And a fun one." Taylor, however, doesn't think it's so funny. Of course, Charlie is only four years older than Taylor, not to mention "hired help."

After the wedding, Mel and the girls stayed for a couple of extra days. "Giving Graham some space" was her explanation, but I think she's giving herself a little room. Hopefully she's contemplating going it alone. They'll leave tomorrow, about the time Cavin and I drive down to Reno to catch our flight to Vancouver, so this afternoon we're at the beach and not Skunk Harbor.

The girls have rented a paddleboat and are on the lake, scoping out guys.

Mel and I kick back on short lounge chairs in the shade. The UV at Tahoe is killer, especially midday and near the water. "You ever think about getting some work done?" I ask.

"What are you talking about? I work all the time."

"No. I mean, like, plastic surgery."

"Are you trying to tell me something?"

"Not at all. But sometimes I think about having a little more than fillers done."

"You can't fight age with technology. Anyway, why would you want to fight it?

You look absolutely amaz—"

"For my age." That's obviously what she means. "You *can* fight age with technology, by the way. And exercise. And water. And diet. And a whole lot of things. But to regain a more youthful face, why not resort to technology?"

"Expense?"

She's got me there.

"Anyway, what's the point? I'm approaching middle age, the mother of three teenage girls. I've got an okay career, but I'm sure not well off. Even if I looked like Miley Cyrus, what guy would be interested in me?"

"Alan Thicke?"

"Ha-ha."

"Is that why you're so intent on hanging on to Graham?"

Growing old together.

"You know what? If Graham decides to walk, I won't be looking for a replacement. I don't mind being alone."

Easy to say when you're not alone, and in a few years her girls will all be out of the house. Which reminds me, "When does Kayla leave for San Francisco?"

"Middle of August. There's an orientation week before her classes begin."

"Sorry I couldn't make it over for her graduation."

"Not a problem. She knew you were crazy busy. She ended up graduating seventh in her class, by the way. Not that it matters. She's in at the Art Institute regardless, thanks to you."

"Hey, what are rich sisters for?"

Wonder how many stoners end up valedictorian. Conversely, wonder how many valedictorians end up stoners. Or just plain losers. Or dead before their time.

"Hey, Mel?"

"Hmm?"

"How do you feel about Mom?"

"Sad. But then, I've always felt a little sad about her."

I think about that. Have I ever felt sad about Mom? Maybe when I was really little?

"Why? I mean, why not angry?"

"Oh, don't get me wrong. There's plenty of anger. But she's one of those people who can't accept love. She should never have had children."

Stating the obvious.

"When you go down to see her? I won't go along. But if you need help with her will or whatever, let me know."

It's the best I can do.

I still have some last-minute packing, so I part ways with Mel in the late afternoon, promise to keep her updated on the honeymoon by e-mail. When I get home, I'm greeted by the sound of raised voices coming from the study.

"Don't you think she has the right to know?" Eli.

"What business is it of yours?" Cavin.

I creep closer.

"Maybe none, except it was my college fund you spent."

"Look, son. I just borrowed a little. I'll pay it back, no problem."

"How? Extra surgeries?" Sarcasm infuses Eli's voice.

"Yes, in fact. I've managed to secure more OR time, finally. Once I get back —"

"Bullshit! God, Dad. You need help."

"I'm already getting it."

"I wish I could believe that."

"I promise I am. Don't you understand? Everything changed when she came along."

"Then you need to be honest. You can't keep something like that from your wife. I really like her, Dad. I want her to stick around."

"So do I. But you need to let me handle this in my own way."

The doorbell rings. I back away, hastily retreat toward the kitchen, and as Cavin exits his office I call, "I've got it."

On the far side of the door is Andrew, carrying a large suitcase in one hand and a briefcase in the other. "Ready for me?"

"Absolutely. Come on in."

Cavin has appeared by my side. "Let me help you with that, Dad." He shoots me a quizzical look. "I didn't know you were here."

"Got home just now. In fact, if you'll excuse me, I need to use the bathroom. The restroom at Zephyr Cove was disgusting."

The men start toward the stairs and I head in the other direction. Eli stands in the hallway, watching. "Do you really need to pee?" he asks as I pass.

I stop. "I can hold it."

We are very close, and I am hyperaware of his body heat and shallow inhale-exhale. "Did you happen to overhear any of that conversation?"

I could lie. "Some of it. Is there more to tell?"

He searches my eyes. Looking for what, I've no clue. Finally, he shakes his head. "That's up to Dad. I hope he tells you the truth. I'd hate to see you get hurt."

"By your dad?"

"By anyone."

He shuffles off, leaves me treading confusion. What the hell hasn't Cavin told me?

And when did Eli transform from foil to ally?

I'm not sure how to approach the subject and can't even try until bedtime. I'm brushing my teeth when Cavin comes in after saying good night to his father. He lifts my hair, kisses my neck. "All packed?"

"Mm-hm," I manage, mouth foaming. I remedy that situation. Spit. Rinse. "You?"

"Just about. Should I bring my camera, or should we just use our pho—"

"Cavin, is there something you want to tell me?"

Our eyes meet in the mirror. "Like what?"

Go for it. "Like what you and Eli were arguing about when I got home."

He sighs weightily but doesn't hesitate, so I know he's considered his answer. "I should have already mentioned it, but didn't think it was something you needed to worry about. I had an issue with the IRS four or five years ago. I had a large gambling win and neglected to claim it on my taxes. They audited me and came up with a rather large bill, with penalties and interest. Rather than make payments, I tapped Eli's college fund. He happened to open a letter that came from the investment firm, saw the amount left in the account, and freaked out."

"I see. Well, if he's serious about college . . ."

"No, I'll pay it back, of course." His arms enfold me. "Don't worry your beautiful head about anything. I've got it all under control."

Just like that, I'm worried about everything.

This is not the way love should feel.

SIXTY

I'm reclining on the upper deck of a
magnificent ship, basking in tepid Alaska
summer air, observing the spectacular
scenery of the Inside Passage. It's the fifth
day of our cruise and I don't think I'm
drunk enough. I signal to the cute waiter to
bring me another sidecar.

Cavin is enjoying the shipboard casino. I
guess he's enjoying it, considering he's
down over two grand. He says not to worry,
he'll earn it back. And you know, maybe he
will. I am starting to think, however, that he
might have a tiny — or larger — gambling
problem. It has even occurred to me that
Eli's college fund might have gone to pay
more than the IRS. And then there's that
second mortgage on the Carmel house. Not
to mention late arrivals back to the room,
no real explanation. Paranoia is a bitch.
However, intuition is a good friend.

Cavin promised Eli he was getting help. Is

he really? If so, it's not working. This is not something you should keep from your spouse. You can't disguise an addiction forever. And the deceit involved with the attempt will continue to crack the foundation of your relationship. Love is not a strong enough mortar.

I keep returning to Eli warning me that words are cheap.

Eli pointing out the date of Caldwell's report.

Eli saying he doesn't want me to get hurt.

Eli asking for my love.

Eli. Eli. Eli.

It was you who hacked your way into my house. Taylor came clean and admitted the two of you did it together for kicks, and the chance to sample my cellar. But other than that and helping yourself to my larder, you never really disturbed anything there, and that was before we had the chance to connect in a more personal way.

Was I wrong to have doubted you?

Was I wrong to place my absolute trust in your father?

Because here's the thing. If I discover that I was no more than a means to an end, I will liberate the part of me I work very hard to keep detained. My knee will have healed by next ski season and there are a lot of trees at Heavenly. Cavin is probably a better skier than Raul, but I've secured a stash of opioid painkillers. Two or three in a cup of prerun cocoa could deteriorate one's skill. It only took one for Raul.

If "regret" was in my vocabulary, I might feel guilty about what happened. I didn't mean to kill Raul, only to cause a small accident, something to keep him off the mountain. His ski instructor that trip was an attractive girl, a bit younger than I was, and his flirting, innocent or not, became way too obvious. He took lessons in the morning and after lunch we skied together. As always, stepping off the cornice brought a sharp rush of pleasure, but when Raul hit that tree, what I experienced was very close to orgasmic.

His death was unintentional, but its immediate benefits — an immense trust fund, coupled with the freedom to be and do anything I wished at age twenty-three — were immediate, and that it was so easy intrigued me. I might have succumbed to the temptation to extract similar revenge on Jordan and Finn, whose infidelities were much more concrete. But Raul's demise was, in fact, an accident. Law enforcement conducted only a cursory investigation. Had the next two husbands died, however, it might have raised a little suspicion. Tapping into their power meant more than taking a chance on death row. I didn't love them. Better to toss them aside, make them pay with what they valued most.

I almost regretted that decision when the private investigator finally discovered it was Jordan behind the text and e-mail threats after all. But he was already serving his sentence, and the plea bargain eliminated the need for continued harassment. I'm not sure what he thought he could blackmail me with, other than my mental health issues, which he only got glimpses of. I may have inherited brain abnormalities from my mother, but unlike her, I mostly maintain self-control.

I could lose it completely if I discover Cavin has done nothing but play me. But until such deception is a proven fact, I'll continue to love him with everything I'm capable of. If he gets back to our cabin early enough, I've got lingerie he still hasn't seen, and I think my knee can accommodate doggie style tonight.

I pick up the book Eli loaned me as the waiter delivers my sidecar. He looks at the cover. "*Confessions of a Sociopath*? Doing some research?"

I smile at the echo. "Self-help, maybe."
The honeymoon, I'm afraid, is over.

LULL

The woods are lovely, dark and deep,
But I have promises to keep,
And miles to go . . .

                — Robert Frost

A shrug of dawn
slips beneath the window blind, shimmies
impatiently through cracks
between eyelashes, tugs you
toward another morning.

You resist,
reluctant to leave the deep, pacific
woodland, haven
from the burgeoning storm —
the year's darkest day.

You want to stay
and watch the forest fill with dreams'
gentle snowfall, listen to wind
and downy flake
sweep against your pillow.

So you pull your blanket
over your face, tuck it under your skull,
weight it with a stir of unease, questions
prowling your brain,
sneak thieves.

Can that watery light
mean daybreak? What promises
are left to keep? How many miles
must you go before retreating
again to the woods of sleep?

ACKNOWLEDGMENTS

A huge shout-out to my publishing family at Simon & Schuster, especially my Atria clan, who never lost faith in me. Here's to new journeys, in whatever formats. Also, a giant thank-you to my immediate family, which has grown, bringing challenges, successes, disappointments, and obstacles overcome, not to mention more love than most will ever experience.

ABOUT THE AUTHOR

Ellen Hopkins is the #1 *New York Times* bestselling author of eleven young adult novels, as well as the adult novels *Triangles* and *Collateral.* She lives with her family in Carson City, Nevada, where she has founded Ventana Sierra, a nonprofit youth housing and resource initiative. Visit her at EllenHopkins.com and on Facebook, and follow her on Twitter @EllenHopkinsLit. For more information on Ventana Sierra, go to VentanaSierra.org.

The employees of Thorndike Press hope you have enjoyed this Large Print book. All our Thorndike, Wheeler, and Kennebec Large Print titles are designed for easy reading, and all our books are made to last. Other Thorndike Press Large Print books are available at your library, through selected bookstores, or directly from us.

For information about titles, please call:
(800) 223-1244

or visit our Web site at:
http://gale.cengage.com/thorndike

To share your comments, please write:
Publisher
Thorndike Press
10 Water St., Suite 310
Waterville, ME 04901